She was so ignorant – so innocent and naive that she thought just wanting to work on a ship was enough. Joe realized he had cruelly raised her hopes even telling her about the stewardesses who worked on the liners. When she persisted, he had to tell her the truth—

'Look at yerself! Yer an Irish emigrant, norra penny ter yer name. Yer can't speak properly. The only life yer've known is the slums. Yer've no education, an' I don't mean just bein' able to read an' write. Yer've gorra 'ave real education, know 'ow ter dress, talk proper, deal with people. Forgerrit! Everything's against yer. Yer'll soon find out 'ow 'ard life is without fillin' yer 'ead with dreams that can't ever come true.'

But Cat couldn't forget, however hard the odds were against her. She was determined to get the qualifications somehow – make that first step towards her private dream.

Also by Lyn Andrews

Liverpool Lou
The Sisters O'Donnell
Ellan Vannin
and published by Corgi Books

THE WHITE EMPRESS

Lyn Andrews

CORGI BOOKS

THE WHITE EMPRESS
A CORGI BOOK 0 552 13482 1

First publication in Great Britain

PRINTING HISTORY
Corgi edition published 1989
Corgi edition reprinted 1992

This book is set in Baskerville 10/12pt by
Chippendale Type, Otley, West Yorkshire.

Corgi Books are published by Transworld Publishers
Ltd., 61–63 Uxbridge Road, Ealing, London W5 5SA,
in Australia by Transworld Publishers (Australia) Pty.
Ltd., 15–23 Helles Avenue, Moorebank, NSW 2170,
and in New Zealand by Transworld Publishers (N.Z.)
Ltd., 3 William Pickering Drive, Albany,
Auckland.

Printed and bound in Great Britain by
Cox & Wyman Ltd., Reading

AUTHOR'S NOTE

I was once told that 'scouse' is a spoken, not a written, dialect and on commencing writing this book I found this to be profoundly true. Therefore, I have used it only in the first chapter to ease the burden not only for myself, but for those readers not fully acquainted with the dialect of my native city. I have, however, kept the conversations of the O'Dwyer family in 'scouse' to help lend 'flavour' to the background.

I would like to express my thanks to everyone who has helped me in researching this book. Mr George Musk, Archivist for Candian Pacific Steamships. Nancy Williatte-Battet, Archivist of Canadian Pacific Railways. My Aunt, Mrs Eileen Sabell, a former Chief Stewardess on the *Empresses* for her invaluable memoirs of life at sea and of conditions appertaining to work in the munitions factories. My Father, Mr Frank Moore, for his recollections of the City and Port of Liverpool up to and including World War II and his own experiences in the Royal Navy during that conflict. My Mother, Mrs Monica Moore, for her advice on fashion and its cost and many household details. My many 'Gorry' cousins, especially Marie Hazel Winter (nee Gorry). Number 18 Yew Tree Road, the home of my late Great-Aunt, still stands despite the ravages of war and I spent many happy hours there during my childhood. The Eldon Street of both the pre- and post-war years has now gone, for what the Luftwaffe started the City Planners have continued to this day, to the detriment of Liverpool and its citizens. But the residents of Eldon Street, forming themselves into a housing co-operative, have rebuilt their homes on the sites they lived and worked on – an example of the dogged determination of the native Liverpudlian to overcome all obstacles. A determination so characteristic throughout the dark days of World War II.

In memory of the men who fought – and died – to save the s.s. *Malakand*, No.2 Husskison Dock was renamed the Malakand Dock. Captain Kinley and Mr Lappin both survived the May Blitz, but thousands of men, women and children – on both sides of the Mersey – did not. All the movements of shipping and losses are as accurate as I have been able to make them; also the timing of the raids during November and December 1940 and May 1941. HMS *Firefly* is a figment of my imagination. However, I have tried to reconstruct her demise with what I hope is some degree of accuracy.

And finally, I would like to dedicate this book to my husband, Robert, whose patience, understanding, tolerance and interest have sustained me not only over the ten years of my writing career, but through twenty years of marriage.

(L.A.)

No ship ever fitted her name more than the *Empress of Britain*. She was, indeed, an empress, with pride and grace and dignity in every inch of her. She had millions of devoted subjects, in many countries, for she was primarily a cruise ship, and she had been seen and admired in more out-of-the-way harbors than any other liner. Her white paint was a coat of ermine that set her apart from the throng. It was always a thrill to see her come in the blue Mediterranean or in more distant ports of call; it was always an event in our own harbor when the great white Empress came in.

She now lies blackened and twisted on the ocean bottom, the largest of all ships that have gone down in this war; but she lived up to the traditions of her flag and to the very end for the Admiralty has praised 'the resolution and efficient handling' of her anti-aircraft guns in her death struggle.

The memory of this fine ship will survive until a new Empress of Britain inherits her name.

NEW YORK TIMES 29 October 1940

Part One

1931

CHAPTER ONE

She hadn't meant to climb so far down. In fact she hadn't meant to climb down at all and fascination now turned to fear. The sea, which from the deck above had appeared in her young, inexperienced eyes to resemble a green meadow – its surface as calm and viridiscent as dew on summer grass – had now turned grey and menacing. Its depths as dark and unfathomable as the peat bogs she had left behind in the Old Country. Its voice, the sonorous lapping of the waves against the hull, now just a few feet below her, was murmuring a warning.

It had been easy to clamber down. There had been all kinds of niches and projections to assist her descent. But they had apparently vanished. Panic swept over her and she pressed her back against the cold steel, her fingers scrabbling desperately for something to cling to, to stop her from falling.

'I won't look at it! I won't look down!' She forced herself to utter the words aloud, but there was no escape. The sea surrounded her. Everywhere her petrified gaze rested presented the same vista. She closed her eyes but that only made her feel dizzy. 'Oh, Sweet Jesus, help me!' she gabbled. One lurch of the ship, one wave a little larger than the others and . . .

'What the bloody 'ell are yer doin' down there!'

11

The voice came from above her and she opened her eyes. Squinting up into the sunlight she could see no one. She could see nothing but that sheer slope of black steel.

'Keep still! Don't try ter move!'

The voice sounded very faint as if coming from far away.

''Ang on a bit, just wait til I think! Can yer sit down on that ledge?'

She looked down at the ledge on which her feet rested. It was barely wide enough for standing.

'Ease yerself down! Slide yer back down against the 'ull an' then gerrold of the ledge!'

Every muscle was frozen. She couldn't move an inch. She tried to cry out but it was as though a huge hand gripped her throat.

'If yer can't manage it then just keep still! Stay as still as yer can, I'll be back!'

He was going away! The only person who stood between her and . . . A tremor ran through her as a wave washed over her feet. She was going to die! Something heavy hit her shoulder and despite the blind panic she twisted her head. It was some sort of ladder made of rope.

'Grab it!' The voice from above yelled.

She needed no second telling. Her fingers locked around the rough hemp and she clung to it. Her cheek, wet with tears and salt spray, pressed close to the thin wooden rung.

'That's it, girl! Now, put yer foot on the first rung! Go on! Yer won't fall!'

Everything was swaying. The ship. The sea. Her lifeline. 'I . . . I can't!'

'Gerron it! Yer've got to! Yer can't 'ang there forever!'

12

Slowly she inched one foot upwards and the thin cardboard sole of her battered shoe felt the wooden slat beneath it. But it was still moving!'

'Now, move yer right 'and up the rope an' get yer other foot on the rung! Go on!'

In a moment of desperate courage she released her grip and then grabbed frantically for the ladder again.

'Keep goin' an' don't look down! When yer gerra bit further up I'll climb over an' 'elp yer, but yer too far down yet!'

Inch by inch she clawed her way from rung to rung, her eyes tightly closed, fighting down the sobs. Then a hand with a grip like an iron vice caught her wrist and she was hauled bodily upwards in one swift movement. She felt the broad width of the deck beneath her feet and slumped down in an exhausted, quaking heap, her back pressed against the superstructure. She could hear the buzz of voices around her.

'What the 'ell were yer tryin' ter do, kill yerself or did yer think yer could walk on water?'

She opened her eyes. Her saviour stood towering over her. A black-haired, dark-eyed young deck hand.

He wiped away the beads of sweat from his brow with the back of a large, tanned hand and then pushed up the sleeves of the black jersey across the front of which was emblazoned 'The B & I Steam Packet Co' in large white letters. Despite his remark he watched her intently as he effortlessly pulled the rope ladder up on to the deck and began to coil it.

The faces of the crowd were pressing forward.

'Come on, move back, give 'er some air! She's

alright now! Come on, shift yerselves, it's not a bloody peep show!'

As they drew back, drifting away now the brief spectacle was over, she rubbed the sleeve of her blouse across her face. At least she had stopped trembling.

'Well, yer deaf or somethin'?'

'No,' she managed to stammer, trying to remember why she had done such a desperately foolish thing in the first place. Why had she been such an eejit?

'What's yer name?' He asked, hauling her to her feet. The grip on her arm was strong. His hand felt warm on her clammy skin.

'Cat. Cat Cleary.'

'What kind of a name is that?'

A little colour crept back into her cheeks and she tossed back the tangled, unruly chestnut curls. 'It's short for Catherine!'

'Then why aren't yer called Kate or Cathy? Why Cat? Bloody daft name tharris!'

Her fear was rapidly subsiding, being replaced by smarting resentment. The warmth of the sun adding resolution to put on a brave face. 'Sure, didn't me sister Shelagh give me the nickname when I was five years old!' She grimaced. 'Nasty, sneaking little cat! Isn't that just the name for you Catherine Cleary, for that's what you are! A cat! Cat Cleary!' she mimicked. 'So everyone's called me that ever since!'

The crowd had completely disappeared. He had finished coiling the ladder and they both lapsed into silence, staring at each other. She wasn't bad looking, he thought. She was skinny and pale and the faded, cheap cotton blouse and creased linen

14

skirt looked as though they had been intended for someone of much more ample proportions. He noticed that the skirt was held up by a large safety pin. Her shoes, sodden with salt water, were worn down at the heel and one was laced up with string. She was too pale and thin and looked as though a gust of wind would knock her over, but her small oval face, with its pointed chin, wide mouth and high cheekbones, was one that in a few years' time men would look at twice. Her eyes were her most attractive feature. They were wide and almost the same shade – of pale green flecked with grey – as the sea which had so nearly claimed her. Her finely drawn, dark brows arched upwards and the thick mass of curling red-brown hair gave the piquant features an elfin look. Aye, with some flesh on her bones and filled out in all the right places, in a few years she'd be what his mates would term 'a good lookin' judy'.

Beneath his pentrating gaze Cat turned her head away. She should be grateful to him. She *was* grateful to him, but the way he stood looking at her – barely disguising the fact that he considered her a brainless eejit – irritated her. He was tall. Much taller than her Pa, his stature enhanced by his powerful build. His shoulders were broad and his chest, beneath the regulation jersey, was deep and expansive. His hair was thick and dark. So dark it looked like the sooty embers of a kitchen fire. It was blown back from a broad brow by the breeze. His skin radiated raw good health for a life spent in the open had darkened its colour to nut brown. He had a wide mouth and when he spoke he revealed strong, white teeth. It was a face full of vitality, mobility and, she suspected, a sharp wit.

There was nothing in his manner of the weary, down-trodden, despair that grinding poverty and hard drink had stamped on her Pa and most of the other men she had known in her life. He seemed not to have a care in the world and obviously feared nothing. He was about eighteen or nineteen she judged shrewdly, and she caught the hint of a smile in the depths of his dark eyes and she felt annoyed and stupid.

'What's your name? I suppose I've to thank you for . . . for saving me?'

'Joe. Joe Calligan an' yer could sound a bit more appreciative, like!'

'I'm sorry, that I am!' She did try to sound more grateful but failed.

He leaned on the rail beside her. 'Yer sorry I dragged yer back on board?

'No! No, it's sorry I am that I snapped at you!'

He grinned, showing a flash of white teeth. 'I still don't known why yer did such a daft thing as to climb down on to that ridge? Yer must 'ave finger-nails like magnets, there's nothin' to gerrold of!'

Cat turned her head away. Golden sunlight sparkled on the calm green water below and her panic had completely evaporated. 'I've never been on a boat before, not ever. I'd never even seen the sea until we set out from Dublin Bay. It just looked so . . . big and . . . it sparkled . . .' She faltered, unable to find the words to tell him how that vast expanse of shining water had fascinated her so. How lulled into a sense of security she had become as she had been borne across it so effortlessly by the sturdy, little steam packet, the *Leinster*. He remained silent and preoccupied and she sensed that somehow he understood. Perhaps he, too, felt the fascination that for her had become almost fatal. She had only wanted to get closer to it, to smell its strange odour, to let it trickle through her fingers and wash over her hot feet. Well, it had done that alright! And now she felt acutely idiotic.

She turned her back on it and gazed upwards at the black and green funnel with its narrow band of white, from which belched a cloud of dirty grey smoke that rose in a column, sullying the clear blue sky. Her eyes moved across the deck to where a white flag with its green and red cross fluttered from the stern rigging, alongside the red ensign.

'It's a ship, norra boat. If yer goin' ter live in Liverpool yer'd berra get that right ter start with! Are yer stayin' in Liverpool or are yer goin' on?'

'We're staying. Pa's heard that there's work to be had.'

There was such hope in the green eyes that looked up to him that he couldn't bring himself to tell her that one man in four was out of work. That men tramped the city streets from morning to night, looking for work – any kind of work. He was lucky. He had been a deck hand for the British and Irish Steam Packet Company for a year now. 'What kind of work did 'e do in Dublin?'

She shrugged. 'Anything he could get. Labouring mostly, but he hasn't had anything for nearly two years now.'

'So yer've packed up an' come to try yer luck?'

'There wasn't much to pack!' she answered bitterly, her gaze flitting over his strong, muscular frame. He'd never gone to bed hungry night after night. He'd never had to go begging along O'Connell Street, dressed in rags and with not a shoe to his foot in the freezing depths of winter. Getting

17

precious little in the way of money but plenty of cuffs and curses. No, he'd never had to go back to the one stinking room they all shared in a crumbling, damp old house in a dark court off the mean, dirty streets that bordered the quays beside the River Liffey. No, nothing could be worse than the life they'd left in Dublin. 'One of Pa's friends told him there was work here, that they are digging a great tunnel right underneath the river so that trains and trams and cars can go right from one side to the other. Is that the truth of it?'

'Yes,' he answered, laconically.

'It is the truth, isn't it? Sure, haven't I wondered myself if it wasn't some joke they'd made up! Won't it burst open and flood the whole place?'

'Geroff, do yer think they'd dig it if they thought that would 'appen?'

It was obvious that he considered her an ignorant Irish slummy. Two bright spots of colour appeared on her cheeks and her dark brows rushed together. 'Well, if that's the case, he'll soon find work, won't he?'

'Don't bet on it, 'alf the men of Liverpool are lookin' fer work, too. An' they've been diggin' fer ages now.'

'Well, aren't the Irish famous for navvying? Didn't they build all the railways over here!' she flung back at him.

'An' where are yer goin' ter live when yer get there? 'As yer Pa's friend found yer all a 'ouse as well?'

By his tone she knew he was goading her again. 'Well now, just for your information he has that! Almost.'

'Believe tharran' yer'll believe anything. 'As he or 'asn't he?'

18

'We've got the address of a relation of Pa's friend and he's got a house. A proper house, not just a room like we had in Dublin!'

Joe looked down at her animated face. God help her! God help them all! Every trip he made he saw them, hundreds of them, just like her. Their heads filled with tales of work, decent houses, money in their pockets. And he'd also seen what happened to most of them. They usually finished up living in the same squalor and poverty they had left behind. They lived in the cramped, narrow streets along the Dock Road or those between Vauxhall Road and Scotland Road that comprised the Catholic–Irish ghetto and were often worse off than when they had sailed from Ireland.

'How many of yer are there?' He tried to sound interested.

'Me, Ma and Pa, our Shelagh – she's older than me – and me brother Eamon.'

'Eamon?' he repeated.

'Didn't me Pa name him after the President!' she shot back. Why was it this Joe Calligan had the knack of increasing her irritation with every word he uttered? Then a fleeting smile crossed her face as she thought of her young brother. Didn't he have her poor mother banjaxed with his antics and any similarity between him and Eamon de Valera ended with the name. Young Eamon Cleary hardly ever went to school so there was little chance he'd end up as president of anything!

'An' what grand plans 'ave yer got fer yer new life?'

'I'm sixteen! I can get a job! I can read and write and add up in me head!'

He laughed. She was a pert one. She'd already

forgotten her narrow escape from drowning. All his questions had been intended to divert her mind and the ploy had worked.

She rounded on him. 'Aren't you the quick one to be poking fun and laughing at the likes of me! I'll get a job, you wait and see and so will Pa and our Shelagh!'

'Yer name suits yer alright! Proper little cat, aren't yer! All sharp claws an' spittin' temper! Come on, I'll take yer up to the bow, yer might as well gerra look at the place yer all goin' ter get so rich in!'

He was treating her like a six-year-old child and she was about to tell him she didn't want him to show her anything. Then her instinctive curiosity got the better of her. Besides, he was smiling without mockery now and had taken her arm and placed it protectively in his and no one had ever done that before. In fact no one had ever shown anything but a cursory interest in her. She was sixteen and had never had a boy to 'walk out' with.

The deck of the *Leinster* was crowded with people, mainly emigrants like herself, huddled in family groups. But here and there were groups of well-dressed people. She caught sight of her sister leaning against the rail, simpering up at an uncouth-looking man in the shabby clothes of a labourer. Cat grinned to herself as she saw Shelagh's eyes widen and her mouth gape as she caught sight of her younger sister, arm in arm with a 'company employee' and a young, handsome one at that! Cat looked up at Joe and, for the first time since her ordeal, smiled. He was handsome and, despite her initial belligerence, she realised that she quite liked him.

The crowd parted as the young seaman shouldered his way through. He cleared a space for her at the bow end and with the breeze bringing a blush of colour to her cheeks, the sun picking out the coppery tints in her hair and her eyes sparkling, he felt a stirring of affection towards her. They had long since passed the bar light, where they had taken on the bowler-hatted pilot, who would guide them through the treacherous shoals that were forever shifting, and into the deep water of the Crosby Channel, between the line of restless buoys. On the starboard bow he pointed out a low sandbar that ran four miles parallel with the Wirral coastline.

'That's Mockbeggar Wharf an' the seabirds come from miles to rest up an' feed on the spits. In the owld days ships were wrecked there by men who purrout the light on Perch Rock. There's an owld sayin':

> 'Wallasey for wreckers
> Poulton for leaves
> Leasowe for honest folk
> Seacombe for thieves.'

He turned and pointed over the port bow. 'That's Crosby, yer can just see the big, owld 'ouses. 'An just down there is the new dock, the Gladstone Dock. The docks start there an' run for miles along the coast to Dingle an' there's a railway that runs overhead all the way.'

She was not sure if he was joking. 'Go on! Is it a fool you take me for, Joe Calligan?'

'It's the truth, it's the longest in the world!'

'Will you take me for a ride on it, then?' she teased, still not fully believing him.

'I might, one day.'

She shaded her eyes from the strong sunlight as the outline of the buildings in the hazy distance became clearer. It was a grand sight to be sure. Surely in such a fine city there would be plenty of work for everyone? She tried to count the docks but lost count after eight, her attention drawn to the number of ships that were either in dock or standing out in the river. She watched, mesmerised, as with alarming accuracy the dredgers, barges and the ferry boats criss-crossed between cargo ships at anchor and the towering double-and triple-funnelled liners.

'I've never seen so many bo—ships! Where do they all come from and don't they ever bump into the little ones?'

He laughed at her childlike questions. 'The little ones don't run on clockwork, they 'ave captains as well! They're the ferries, takin' people an' cargo backwards an' forwards to Seacombe, Wallasey, Birkenhead an' New Brighton. The big ones, the liners . . . '

Cat waited for him to continue but he just stared ahead of him, lost in some private dream. She tugged at his sleeve. 'Where do they come from?'

'All over the world. America. Australia, China, an' one day I'm goin't to gerra job on one! That's a "real" job. A safe job fer life an' yer get paid for seein' all the places yer've only dreamed of. Yer 'ave a proper uniform, norra second-'and jersey!'

She looked at him with renewed interest. 'How are you going to get a job like that?'

His dark eyes clouded and he shrugged. 'Yer gerra job like that if yer lucky or if yer 'ave the right qualifications an' know the "right" people!'

'What are quali . . . quali . . . ?'

'Qualifications. Yer take examinations, a lorra writin' an' things like that, then yer get qualifications.'

She thought she understood. She had once met a boy who had gone to a proper school and worked at his books day and night and had passed what he had called an examination and was going on to be a priest. She supposed it was something like that. 'Well, how do you know who the "right" people are?'

'Yer've gorra lot t' learn, Cat Cleary, especially when it comes ter people!'

'You're laughing at me again!'

'No, I'm not! I bet yer already know a lorrabout people. Girl like you must be used ter livin' off yer wits an' that's what I mean about "knowing" people! If yer nothin' else, Cat, yer streetwise!'

She completely misunderstood him. A scarlet flush arose from the base of her throat as anger swept over her and raising her arm she struck him hard across the cheek. 'Don't you be calling me names like that! I'm no street girl! I'd starve before . . . I'd do anything like that, so I would!' She stood facing him, her thin body shaking with indigna-tion, her eyes flashing green fire.

'If yer wasn't a girl I'd belt yer for that! I didn't mean anythin' like that, what d' yer take me for? I only meant that yer can probably look after yer-self!' He rubbed his cheek ruefully. 'Bloody little wildcat! Good job yer norra lad!'

Vituperative words sprang to her tongue but he silenced her by grabbing her by the shoulders and turning her to face port. 'Now there's a sight yer'll never 'ave seen before an' probably won't see again!'

As quickly as it had risen her anger died. 'What?'

'There, tied up at the landing stage!'

'I can only see those big buildings with those birds on top. Are they real birds, won't they fly away?'

He became exasperated. 'Don't yer know nothin' Cat Cleary? Those are the Liver Birds! 'Aven't yer 'eard of them, even?'

Her eyes narrowed. Of course she'd heard of them. Everyone had. They were not real birds, she'd heard them called 'mythical' but what that meant only the good Lord knew, she didn't. But she wasn't about to let him know that. 'Sure, I have! They're my—mythical.'

'Sailors all over the world know the Liver Birds, an' Liverpool is the biggest port in the world!'

She cast him a sceptical glance. He was certainly prone to boasting. First he had boasted that he was going to get a job on a liner, now he obviously thought his native city was the biggest port in the world. And that she knew to be untrue. Hadn't her mother's brother gone to New York and hadn't he written that that was the biggest port in the world?

'My Uncle Pat says New York is the biggest port in the world!'

'Aye, I 'ear it's big, but I'll see it fer meself when I gerra job on the *Mauretania* or the *Aquitania*. They 'ave ballrooms an' swimmin' pools an' restaurants an' whole suites of rooms fer first class. You see, I'll gerroff these "cattle boats" someday!'

She scowled. She resented being referred to as 'cattle'. 'They'd need hundreds of people to work on them if they're all that big!' The note of disbelief was obvious.

'They do 'ave 'undreds, from the captain down

ter the deck 'ands. 'An they are that big, an' yer 'ave ter 'ave 'undreds of pounds to go luxury class!'

An idea took hold of her. If he could boast, then so could she. 'One day I'm going to be rich! Very rich!'

He threw back his head and laughed. 'Yer'll never be rich enough fer that! It's only the likes of millionaires an' royalty that are *that* rich! Yer might get ter be a stewardess, though,' he joked as an afterthought.

'What's a stewardess?'

'A girl who looks after the women passengers.'

'Doing what?'

'Usually makin' beds, cleanin' cabins an' bathrooms an' generally 'elpin out.'

'Is that all?'

'That's what most of them do. Only the chief stewardess an' the first-class stewardesses look after the "real" ladies, an' yer don't stand a cat in 'ell's chance of ever doin' that!'

'Not even if I get "qualifications" and get to know the "right" people?'

His demeanour changed. All the laughter had gone from his eyes for he had been quick to perceive the ray of hope that lit up her face. Talk like this could only hurt her. 'Look, Cat, forget I ever said anythin' about stewardesses. It's not fer the likes of you! Bloody 'ell, I'm sorry I even mentioned it, it was a joke!'

'Why?' she demanded, stubbornly. If all you had to do was clean cabins, she could surely manage that.

'Just look at yerself! Yer an Irish emigrant, norra penny ter yer name. Yer can't speak properly. The only life yer've known is the slums. Yer've no

25

education, an' I don't mean just bein' able ter read an' write an' add up in yer 'ead! Yer've gorra 'ave *real* education, know 'ow ter dress, talk proper, deal with people. Oh, forgerrit! Gerra job in a factory, the pays good, yer'll be 'appier there, amongst . . .

'Amongst me own kind, is that it? I can't help how I dress and speak but I'm no fool, Joe Calligan! I can learn and I can learn quickly!'

'Cat, forgerrit! Everythin's against yer! Yer'll soon find out 'ow 'ard life is without fillin' yer 'ead with dreams that can't ever come true!'

'I can't see that it would be so hard if all they do is make beds and clean? You don't need an "education" for that!'

He began to lose patience with her and guilt stirred in him. 'I said forgerrit! It's not fer the likes of you!'

'But you think its alright for you? Just what makes you so different from me? You don't speak "properly", you haven't got any better education than I have or else you wouldn't be working on this "cattle boat"! You'd be working on one of those fancy liners now, not just dreaming about it! You're no better than me and if you can dream, then so can I!'

He drew away from her and stood scowling at her. She had touched his Achilles heel. She had made him face the reality. His, too, was a dream. A dream nurtured by hours of watching the stately liners, fully laden with passengers and crew, pull away from the Princes Landing Stage, nudged and guided by their accompanying tugs. To sail majestically down the Mersey to the Bar, the Irish Sea and the Atlantic beyond. Hours of watching and listening to the captain and mate on the Dublin to Liverpool ferry and dreaming that one day he would rise to the dizzy heights of captain of a liner such as the *Aquitania*. Now this sharp-featured, sharp-tongued, little Irish slummy had forced him to see that it was just a dream and he was furious. Furious with her and for allowing himself to become so vulnerable.

'We'll be dockin' soon. I'd berra get ter me station! Yer'd berra go an' find yer family. It's everyone fer 'imself down the gangway!'

She brushed back a tendril of hair. 'I don't suppose I'll see you again?'

He thrust his hands deep into his pockets. 'Reckon not.'

She turned away, feeling strangely lonely and slighted. 'Oh, thanks for pulling me up!' she called over her shoulder.

He watched her push her way through the crowd that was gathering on the port side and shrugged his broad shoulders. Soon she'd disappear into the warren of slums and he probably wouldn't see her again. But she wasn't a girl who would easily be forgotten, he mused darkly.

CHAPTER TWO

Shelagh Cleary was struggling with a battered suitcase, made of thick cardboard, tied up with string, and a bundle of assorted clothes, tied in an old blanket. Both items contained all her worldly goods and entire wardrobe. She resembled Cat closely except that her hair was less curly and had been cut short and she was possessed of a more ample figure, of which she was extremely proud.

'Where've you been and who was he?' she snapped.

'Mind your own business! Here, Ma, give me that sack and that big bundle, they're too heavy for you!' She took the objects that were weighing down Ellen Cleary's thin, rounded shoulders. Cat forgot Joe Calligan and her sister as she watched her mother wrap the old black shawl around her gaunt body. She was shivering even though the sun was warm. Her face was ashen. 'Aren't you feeling well, Ma?'

'I'm fine, Cat, 'tis only this boat swayin' under me.'

'Where's Pa and our Eamon?'

Ellen Cleary shrugged helplessly, biting her lower lip from habit.

'I'll give you two guesses!' Shelagh fulminated.

Cat's heart sank. 'But the Bar's shut and anyway Pa's got no money for drink!'

'And when has that ever stopped him?' Shelagh

retorted. 'He could wheedle a drink from a temperance society, that he could!'

'Don't talk like that about your Pa, he tries . . .' Ellen Cleary half-heartedly defended her husband but her tone lacked any conviction. Years watching the strong young lad she had married turn into a desperate, drink-sodden man had drained the colour from her cheeks, the laughter from her eyes and the hope from her heart.

'Well, where's Eamon? We'll be docking soon?'

'God knows! Probably trying to pick a pocket or beg a copper or two, little sod!'

'Shelagh, that's enough!'

Shelagh ignored her mother's warning. 'He'll turn out a right bad one!'

'You're no angel yourself!'

Shelagh glared at her sister. 'What's that supposed to mean?'

Before Cat could reply a grubby, ten-year-old lad tugged at her skirt. He had a shock of unruly brown hair and was clad in a pair of cut-down trousers and an old shirt. On his feet were a pair of patched boots, a size too big for him.

'Where've you been? I hope you've not had your hand in anyone's pocket or Pa will take his belt to you!' Shelagh scolded.

He stuck out his tongue then dodged behind Cat to avoid the swipe his elder sister aimed at his head.

'Have you seen Pa?' Cat questioned him.

'Sure, he's sittin' over there, drunk as a fiddler's bitch!'

This time it was Cat's hand that shot out and boxed his ears. Anger, disappointment and disillusionment adding strength to her action. He'd promised! He'd sworn on everything he held sacred that he was finished with the drink for good! Oh, he'd promised them all a better life and it had been such a rosy future he'd enthralled them all with! He'd get a job and stick at it. He'd bring his wages home and they'd have good food on the table, decent clothes and a real home with a fire in the hearth all winter long! Oh, she should have known! How could she have been such a fool to have trusted him, believed him . . . But they all had because they desperately wanted to. And now the reality had been forced on her. She was stuck on this crowded ship with a sick mother, a petulant, selfish sister, a young tearaway and a drunken father. And he had probably spent every last halfpenny they had all struggled to hoard to start this wonderful new life! Tears of anger pricked her eyes and her mouth felt dry. Dropping the things she held, she snatched the suitcase and bundle from the hands of her startled sister and thrust them at the lad.

'Here, you'll have to carry these!' She turned to Shelagh. 'And you'll have to go and get Pa and you'll have to manage him as best you can! Ma can't and you've always been his favorite!'

Shelagh uttered a yell. 'Give me back me things! He'll lose them and they're all me clothes!'

Cat ignored her protests and gave her a sharp push. 'Shut up and go and get him! I'll watch your things! Go on or we'll never get off!'

Disconsolately she watched her sister push her way through the throng. How they were going to manage she didn't know. She only hoped Pa hadn't lost the scrap of paper with the precious address on it, if he had . . . she couldn't think of that now. They had to get off the ferry first.

She was too preoccupied with their dilemma to take much notice of what was going on around her until there was a thump and the ship shuddered, causing people to lose their balance. They had docked alongside the half-mile long Princes Landing Stage that floated on the River Mersey itself. Already figures on the dockside below were dragging the heavy hausers cast down from the *Leinster* and were winding them around the bollards to hold the ship fast. Then there was the grating rattle of the chains that held the gangway, accumulating in a clanking crash as the gangway hit the cobbles of the landing stage.

Immediately the crowd surged forward. Cat tried to turn to see if there was any sign of her sister and father, but movement was impossible as she was caught up in the press of bodies.

'Try to hang on to my skirt but if you can't then just wait at the bottom for me!' she yelled to Eamon who had been behind her before the crowd closed in. She herself kept her eyes fixed on her mother's black-clad form, surrounded and crushed by the solid, moving mass. There was no way on earth that she could get to her and she prayed she wouldn't stumble and fall.

At the top of the gangway the jostling crowd was halted by three burly deck-hands who had linked arms and were forceably holding the passengers back while an officer in shirt sleeves was shouting 'Only a dozen at a time, if you please! Then no one will get hurt! You'll all get off if you'll just be patient!'

She felt herself being dragged to one side and out of the crowd. Looking up she saw, with a flood of relief, the figure of Joe Calligan towering above the heads of the crowd.

'Where's the rest of them? Your Ma and Pa?' he yelled.

'Ma's just over there, is our Eamon behind me?'

'If you mean the little lad with the bundle and the case, I've got him! It's always the same every trip, like a bloody stampede! No wonder they're called the "cattle" boats! Where's your Pa?'

'I don't know and I don't much care! Shelagh went to find him, he's drunk!'

'So are half the men aboard, its nothing new!'

'But he promised! He promised . . .'

'He probably meant it at the time, they all do, until they have the next drink!'

'But we all believed him! And now . . .'

He could see she was near to tears and he remembered their conversation not an hour since. Poor little sod. For her the dream had ended abruptly. It hadn't slowly disintegrated, it had been instantly shattered. 'Cheer up. It'll all come out in the wash, as our Mam says! Here, lad, give me those things and get hold of your sister's skirt, I'll get you off safe and sound.'

She felt Eamon's hand grasp her skirt tightly as Joe hoisted both the case and the bundle on to one shoulder and with the other arm gripped her securely round the waist. Some of her trepidation fell away as she was pressed against his broad shoulder and she began to relax within the circle of his arm. Then he was guiding them towards the steep, wooden gangway that rose and fell gently as the waters of the Mersey ebbed against the landing stage, buoying it up on the tide. He shouted cheerfully back to his mates who yelled ribald comments and then they were ashore.

The crowd still milled around but was thinning rapidly as people moved off in groups, some towards the Riverside Station but most trudging towards the floating roadway that led to the city itself. Cat gazed around her, her eyes wide, her fear and anxiety forgotten temporarily. There were people everywhere and carts drawn by huge horses. There were some cars and vans and she could just glimpse, at the top of the floating roadway, the outline of the green and cream tramcars. Joe's arm was still around her and he was guiding her towards the northern end of the stage.

'Wait! Where's Ma?'

He stopped and released her and twisting round she caught sight of her mother's forlorn figure, the expression on her face vague and confused.

'She's there! Oh, Joe, she is terrified, please go and get her!'

She watched as he tapped her mother gently on the shoulder, spoke a few words to her and pointed in their direction. Relief replaced confusion in her mother's eyes.

'It's alright, Ma! We're safe! Eamon's with me. This is Joe. Joe Calligan, he helped us get off.'

Mrs Cleary nodded her thanks to the tall young lad. 'Have you seen your Pa, Cat?'

'No and I don't want to! I hope he falls in the dock and takes our Shelagh with him!'

'That's a bit hard, ain't it! He is your Pa,' Joe admonished. 'Do you want me to see if I can find them, Mrs Cleary?'

Ellen Cleary nodded wearily. She had already

realised that life was not going to be much different but she was too tired and too ill to care very deeply about it. If this pleasant lad could just get them all together it would be a small blessing.

With strict instructions to them all to 'stay put' he was off and before long was back, grinning widely as he supported her staggering father and followed by a glowering Shelagh.

'Here he is, safe and sound and at least he's not paralytic drunk!'

'He's not far off it! I've had the divil's own job with him, that I have! Trust you, Cat, to go dashing off and leaving me with him!' Shelagh was perspiring and her thin dress was sticking to her body. Cat noticed that Joe's eyes strayed to the thrusting breasts, outlined by the damp cotton, and she felt embarrassed and annoyed. He was her friend and he had no right to look at her sister like that!

'Well, now what are we going to do? Have you still got that address Paddy O'Dwyer gave you, Pa?'

'It's no use asking him, you'll get no sense out of him! I'll look in his pockets.' Shelagh made a thorough search of the pockets of the greasy old jacket. They revealed nothing but a torn rag that sufficed as a handkerchief. And a few pennies. At the sight of the coins Cat's heart sank further. Obviously this was all that was left of the money he had had when they sailed.

'Nothing there, you hold him still while I try his trouser pockets,' Shelagh instructed Joe.

Apart from a few obscure articles, the first pocket revealed no piece of paper, but with a small cry of triumph Shelagh drew out of the second pocket a creased, dirty scrap of paper on which handwriting was just visible. She scrutinised it closely then shoved it towards Cat in disgust.

'I can't read it, the paper's too creased and dirty. You try!'

Cat took it from her. Her sister's protest was just an excuse. Shelagh couldn't read. She screwed up her eyes for the writing was very small and almost obliterated by greasy fingermarks.

'Here, give it to me! At least I know the names of the streets round here!' Unceremoniously Joe dumped the sagging figure of Mick Cleary down on the cobbles. He studied the scrap of paper. 'It looks like Eldon Street.'

'Where's that? How far is it?' Cat questioned.

'Just off Vauxhall Road, but it's a fair walk up Chapel Street, Tithebarn Street and past Exchange Station. It's almost opposite Tate and Lyles Sugar Refinery.'

Her gaze rested on the sprawling figure of her father. Joe read her thoughts.

'You won't get far with him in that state, the scuffers will chuck him in the battle-taxi – drunk and incapable!'

The look she returned him was confused and he laughed. 'It's 'scouse' for the police and the prison van. You'll have to get the tram, if they'll let him on!'

'And what are we going to use for tram fare?'

'Its only tuppence, how much did he have in his pockets?' The question was directed at Shelagh.

She looked at the coins in her hand. 'Fourpence ha'penny.'

'That will pay for Ma and Pa.' Cat said resolutely.

'How's Ma going to manage him? If he starts

yelling they'll both get thrown off.' Shelagh retorted hotly.

Cat glared at her, she knew her sister of old. She would never walk anywhere if she could help it. 'Well, Ma's not walking, she's not well enough!'

'Hell! This is turning into Fred Carno's circus! Here, take this!' Joe held out a silver shilling. 'You'll have enough left over to get your Ma a cup of tea, she looks as though she could do with one! Go on, take it!'

Before Cat had a chance to tell him that she wanted none of his charity, Shelagh had grabbed the shilling. Cat could cheerfully have slapped her face.

'Now go up the floating roadway, there's a tea stall up there, get your Ma a cup and take meladdo here with you, I can't keep my eye on you all!' He pushed young Eamon gently in Shelagh's direction, then turned to Mrs Cleary. 'You sit yourself down here, Ma, on this box, and rest. He'll be alright.' He nodded in the direction of her husband who was now snoring loudly through flacid lips, his back against a lamp-post. 'There's something I want to show Cat.'

Cat dragged her eyes from the disappearing backs of her sister and brother. It had been her intention to take him to task over his familiarity with her mother, not knowing it was the usual and polite address given by Liverpudlians to any woman over the age of forty, but curiosity again got the better of her and she let him take her arm.

'Where are we going now?'

'You'll see. Didn't I tell you on board I'd show you a grand sight?'

'I've seen the Liver Birds!'

'I didn't mean them.'

They walked along the landing stage to where crowds were gathering. Amongst them scarlet-capped porters could be seen struggling from the Riverside Station with piles of baggage. She caught sight of dark-green uniforms frogged with gold braid and the sounds of music drifted to her ears. Two burly policemen or 'scuffers' as Joe had called them, were supervising the crowds. Their faces beneath the conical helmets, that bore a silver-crested Liver Bird, were red from the sun and the heat of their high-buttoned tunics, but both were smiling broadly. The music played by the City Band grew louder and the atmosphere reminded her of the St Patrick's Day Parade down O'Connell Street in Dublin.

She tugged at Joe's sleeve. 'What's going on? Is it a parade?'

'Something like that! Look, I promised you a sight and there she is!'

Cat stopped dead in her tracks, her eyes widened and she gasped. In her entire life she had never seen anything to compare with the vision that now confronted her. Tied up at the Landing Stage was the biggest, most majestic ship she had ever seen. Bright sunlight reflected off the towering, white-painted hull and to Cat it looked like a snow-covered mountain, rising up and up, reaching almost to the sky. She craned her neck and saw the three, dark yellow funnels, each bearing the emblem of a red-and-white-chequered flag. Flags and pennants of all colours fluttered from the rigging and whisps of pale-grey smoke spiralled upwards from the funnels into the clear blue heavens.

All around her people were laughing, shouting and cheering, while those high above on deck were shouting back and throwing down brightly coloured paper streamers. She felt a bubble of excitement rise in her. A bubble that grew and grew until it reached her throat and she found she was cheering too, caught up in the waves of emotion and ebullience that had engulfed everyone.

'Oh, Joe! Joe! Isn't it grand! Isn't it wonderful, isn't it . . . huge! It's like . . . a huge white mountain!'

He squeezed her arm. 'It's not an "it", it's a "she", ships are always called "she".'

'Oh, what's she called?'

'Look up there, it's painted on her bow!'

Her excited gaze followed the line of his outstretched hand. The bold black letters sprang out at her, contrasting sharply against the white hull. She read them aloud. *'Empress of Japan'*.

'An Empress is even grander than a Queen. She's the flagship of the Canadian Pacific Line. The White Empress and this is her maiden voyage!' There was pride in his voice and his face was so animated that she hardly recognised him. She noticed, too, that the corded muscles in his throat were working, but she understood how he felt for she felt it too. Pride, longing, a core of exhilaration that made her whole body tremble. The White Empress evoked all these emotions in both of them.

'Oh, Joe, I wish I was sailing with her!'

Again he squeezed her hand and laughed. 'There's an even bigger one being built at the John Brown yard on the Clyde.'

She gasped. 'Bigger! Bigger than her?'

'She's 26,000 tons, but the *Empress of Britain* will be 42,000 tons!'

The figures meant nothing to her but she could not envisage anything bigger than this magnificent white liner. With a surge of emotion she wished with all her heart that she could change places with one of those elegantly dressed women high above her, laughing and shouting, about to take the trip of a lifetime.

'Where's she going, Joe?'

'To Quebec in Canada.'

Even the very name 'Quebec' sounded exotic.

'And after that she'll sail the Pacific Ocean, to Japan and China, Australia and New Zealand and all the islands.'

Her estimation of him rose higher as he reeled off the names of places she had never heard of. 'Oh, Joe! I'd give anything, anything to sail on her!'

'You'll not see her in Liverpool again. After this voyage her home port will be Southampton.'

Her face fell. 'Never?'

'Cheer up, Cat, there will be other Empresses.'

'But not like this one. Never like this one!' Now she understood his hopes and dreams, for sights like this were the stuff that dreams are made of. She remembered their conversation and one word rang in her head with the clarity of a bell. 'Steward-ess'. The tide of excitement surged again. 'Joe, they carry stewardesses, don't they?'

'Of course they do, who do you think looks after all those rich women and . . .' He broke off, sud-denly remembering that it was he who had planted that word in her innocent mind. 'I told you, Cat, forget it! Its not for the likes of you, nor me either if it comes to that! It's a dream, nothing more! I wouldn't have brought you to see her if I'd have realised that—'

'It's not a dream, Joe! It's not! I won't let it be just a dream!'

He took her by the shoulders and shook her hard. 'Stop it! Stop it! It's a dream beyond your reach! Settle for what you have!'

She had learnt early in life that tears seldom solved anything so none stung her eyes, but they scalded her heart for he had forced her to face the truth. 'What have I got, Joe? I've got nothing! My Pa's a drunk, Ma's ill, we've got no money, no home, nothing! You can't settle for nothing, Joe Calligan! I won't! I won't let it be just a dream, I'll make it happen! I'll find a way! One day I'm going to sail on a White Empress and not just as a stewardess, I'm going to be a chief stewardess!'

He cursed himself aloud. This was all his fault. He'd filled her head with dreams, dreams of a life she would never know. Places she would never see. A position in life that was totally unattainable for a poor, ignorant Irish slummy. He looked steadily into the green eyes fringed with dark lashes. A hard light shone in them. A light he recognised with a deadly clarity. It was raw, unquenchable, inexorable ambition and determination. Her face was implacable, her features as though carved from granite, and he shivered. The light in her eyes frightened him. He'd seen it in the eyes of ruthless men. Hard, embittered men who pitted their existence daily against the elements. But he had never seen it in the eyes of a woman, let alone

41

this slip of a girl who barely came up to his shoulder. He shivered again. Her name suited her. It was very apt, she reminded him of a cat. Those feral eyes, the feline grace with which she moved, the thick mane of tangled curls.

'Then God help you, Cat Cleary, and I mean that!'

CHAPTER THREE

Eldon Street resembled the streets that ran off O'Connell Street in Dublin. Rows of small, narrow houses the back yards of which contained the privy and the midden, only separated from the back yards of the houses that backed on to them by a narrow alley. An alley filled with decaying rubbish through which mangy dogs and cats rooted for anything edible.

When they had been built they had been of red brick but a thick, continuous rain of soot, emitted from the three tall chimneys of the Clarence Dock Power Station – known as the Ugly Sisters – had long since turned them black. The belching smoke, like filthy tresses of hair blowing in the wind, showered deposits of soot on every windowsill, doorstep, roof and chimney for miles around. The lines of washing that were hung out every Monday morning in the back yards were permanently grey with it, despite the valiant efforts of the women in the public washhouse or in small, dark sculleries where the wash boilers steamed.

The whole area was depressing: factories, their small, grimy windows staring like dull eyes over the river, lined the south side of Vauxhall Road. Along Great Howard Street and Waterloo Road – commonly known as the Dock Road – bonded warehouses towered above houses and pubs crowded in their shadows. All day long and late into the night, too, the carts, wagons, vans and trams rumbled over the cobbles.

Cat had stood and watched the dockers. Watched them waiting, often fighting, just to be taken on for a day's work to provide a few shillings to feed their families and keep a roof over their heads. She had watched the teams of carthorses that were kept in reserve to help pull the heavily laden carts up the floating roadway. When the tide was at the ebb, the road was an almost vertical slope up which the horses sweated and strained, their owners cursing, swearing and sweating, too. She had soon become accustomed to the quick, cutting, humorous Liverpool wit and the 'scouse' dialect, full of colloquialisms and malapropisms. It was a city where everyone was addressed as 'luv'. Where every female from the age of five to forty was addressed as 'girl', the older women being afforded the more respectful 'Ma'. Where boys and men were called 'lad' or its diminutive 'La'. A city that boasted great architectural beauty and wealth, beside poverty and squalid slums. A city in which one man in four was out of work. Where children ran barefoot in the streets and old women, clad in the voluminous black skirts and shawls and known as 'shawlies', stood gossiping on their doorsteps or in small corner shops. Where men congregated on street corners and alleys, playing an illegal game known as Pitch and Toss. The object of this was to guess which side two pennies or halfpennies would land after being tossed in the air. It was a place where on almost every street corner there was a public house. A city that boasted a fine library and museum, yet was so desperate to find work for its populace that the project of the tunnel under the Mersey had been conceived in part to ease this situation. No, Liverpool had not proved to be the Promised Land. Not for Cat Cleary. It was not much better than Dublin.

They shared the rooms in the small house in Eldon Street with the O'Dwyers, who were already overcrowded. But at least it was better than sharing just one room and there was cold running water and an outside privy, all of which were improvements. Mrs O'Dwyer had taken one look at the dejected group who had landed on her doorstep and had instantly taken them in. Shooing out a brood of small, grubby children, she had instructed Cat to put their things in the back yard 'just fer now'. Drawn her tired mother into the cluttered kitchen and pushed her gently down on to the old, battered chair and had fixed Mr O'Dwyer with a piercing stare and told him sharply to 'Ger 'im out an' sober 'im up!'

Their arrival had generated a certain amount of friendly curiosity on the part of the neighbours who had all called, one after the other, to inspect the new arrivals and ask about the 'Old Country' for many still had relatives there. Cat had soon found that doors were never locked or bolted. Hard times were endured with grim fortitude, interspersed with outbreaks of witty humour; and good times, too, were shared, as was good fortune.

Her new neighbours and friends had helped to dispel some of the depression that had settled over her when she had gazed for the last time on the White Empress and had fled back to where her family was waiting for her.

The good weather had evaporated and now she

sat on the doorstep of number eight Eldon Street with the O'Dwyer baby on her knee, watching leaden clouds, that threatened rain, roll in from the river. Both her father and sister had set off early that morning to look for work. At least Pa has stayed sober, she thought, but this she put down to the two obvious facts: that they were broke and that he was undisguisedly afraid of Maisey O'Dwyer's sharp tongue. But he was trying to find work and she supposed that this was a small point in his favour. Her mother was being well cared for as Maisey insisted they all share her rations, until such time as Pa was bringing in some money, and so they hadn't gone hungry.

It had been Maisey who had prodded Shelagh into tidying herself up and going down to Tate and Lyle's factory at the bottom of the street to see if there was any work to be had. In fact that redoubtable lady's sharp tongue had prodded her husband and Cat's Pa out every morning at six o'clock to look for work, telling them not to 'cum back 'ere before tea time, either, if yer ain't found none!'

Cat sighed and jiggled the baby on her lap, wondering what today would bring. It would be her turn next. It wasn't that she was averse to work, she had always done more than her share in the home, but since the day she had landed she had refused to let go of her dream. She blocked out the memory of Joe Calligan's warning. One day . . . one day . . . but meantime she wasn't going to work in a factory, of that she was determined. There must be other kinds of work – in a shop maybe.

Two large, heavy drops of rain splashed on to her face and she rose to her feet. Now she would have to go back into the kitchen that smelled of boiled cabbage, wet washing and stale sweat. As she turned she heard the sound of running feet and looked up. Shelagh was tottering up the street in a pair of high-heeled shoes, lent her by Bessie Abbot, one of the girls next door.

'Cat! Cat! Hold on a minute! I've got a job! I've got a job!'

Shelagh fell against the peeling lintel, trying to catch her breath and wincing. Then she bent down and pulled off the shoes. 'I'm fair crippled, that I am! I know it was good of Bessie to lend them to me, but they pinch like 'ell!'

'Come inside, you're getting soaked. What sort of a job? When do you start? How much will you get?'

Shelagh closed the door behind her and they stood in the gloomy, miniscule lobby. 'Sewing sugar sacks, I start tomorrow and I was lucky to get it! Five shillings a week, Monday to Saturday! Five whole shillings, I've never had so much money before!'

'You haven't got it yet and don't forget you'll have to give some to Ma and some to Maisey, we must owe her a small fortune by now!'

'I thought Ma pawned her wedding ring and gave Maisey the money? Anyway, I'll still have a lot over. Now I'll be able to buy some decent clothes and go out on the town!'

'Don't you ever think of anything else?'

Shelagh looked at her scornfully. 'What else is there to think about? You've hardly been over the doorstep and we've been here a week and more. Miss Scaredy Cat!'

'I'm not scared! I just don't see any point in traipsing round the shops looking at things you can't buy!'

'Well, I'm not going to Paddy's Market to buy any

47

more clothes either! I'm having new ones, not flea-bitten old cast-offs!'

She disappeared into the kitchen to be greeted with cries of delight at her good fortune, while Cat remained in the lobby. She'd always had cast-offs, usually Shelagh's old hand-me-downs. In fact, now that for the first time she really gave it some serious thought she realised that she'd never had a single new garment in her entire life. The thought made her disgruntled, something she'd never felt before. She'd always accepted the fact that there was never enough money for new clothes for everyone. But it would have made her feel better if she had had something, anything!

She had accompanied her mother and their bene-factress to St Martin's Market – known to all as Paddy's Market. Here great piles of old clothes, linen and blankets were sold for a couple of pence. The market did sell other things as well, but it was the clothes that drew the crowds, among them sailors from all the foreign ships. They had all been 'rigged out' as Maisey put it, for a couple of shillings. But everything was second-hand. She pulled herself out of her reverie. If she wanted new clothes then she would have to get out and work for them, like Shelagh.

Evening brought more good news: when her Pa and Mr O'Dwyer returned home it was to tell everyone, and that included most of Eldon Street too, that they had both been taken on as navvies, working on the Mersey Tunnel. They were both covered in dust, their faces streaked where sweat had run down in rivulets, for they had started work at noon that very day, but no one commented on the fact that their Sunday shirts were filthy.

Maisey produced some coins from her battered purse, stuffed down the back of the sagging sofa, and gave them to Shelagh with the instructions to 'nip down ter the "Glass 'Ouse" an' gerra bottle of somethin' ter celebrate' while she went up to Rooney's corner shop for some boiled ham for a 'nice' tea for the 'workers'. Whereupon Mr O'Dwyer, with a rare show of spirit, informed her 'We don't want no boiled 'am, luv, its norra wake! We'll 'ave steak an' kidney pie, so gerrup ter the chippy!'

'Don't you swear at me, Hughie O'Dwyer, or yer'll get no pie!' his wife rejoined, beaming, as donning her shawl, she departed.

Cat crouched on the floor beside her mother while her father went into the scullery to wash. 'Things are looking better, Ma. You'll be able to get your wedding ring back from Stanley's now. And if Pa and Shelagh get kept on, we might be able to get a house of our own soon. Wouldn't that be grand, Ma?'

'Aye, it would that. I've never had a place of me own. Not in all the years I've been married.'

'And if I get a job, too . . .'

Her mother's hand closed over hers. 'I'll need you, Cat, to help me in the house. I'm not as strong as I should be and you need eyes in the back of your head to watch Eamon!'

'I'll get something, Ma, just to help at first and don't worry about our Eamon, I'll sort him out! He can go to school! I'll go round to see the Priest at Our Lady's, they have a school. He can go to that even if I have to drag him there kicking and screaming every day! He's run wild for long enough!'

* * *

At first it looked as though their luck had really changed. Every morning both Shelagh and Pa went cheerfully to work while she dragged a sullen, resentful Eamon round the corner to the primary school supported by the Catholic Church of Our Lady, and handed him over to the parish priest, of whom he was mortally afraid, though he would sooner have died than admit this fact. Her days were spent cleaning, washing, ironing, shopping and cooking – chores that seemed to have no end and left precious little time for dreaming. Whenever Shelagh complained about her not getting out and finding a job, both her mother and Maisey would rush to her defence, saying they just didn't know how they would ever manage without Cat. But for Cat life became a round of endless drudgery, her world confined to the immediate neighbourhood, while every Saturday night her sister would dress herself up in her new finery and go out with the girls she worked with. Her 'pals' as she called them.

Cat was usually asleep when she finally stumbled into the bed they shared with two of the O'Dwyer girls. Shelagh would wake late and bad-tempered on Sunday mornings, complaining that she had a throbbing headache or felt too ill to go to Mass. Excuses which fooled no one and drew vitriolic condemnation from their landlady, for they were now paying rent and board. The O'Dwyers, like all their neighbours, were devout Catholics and even her Pa always managed to get up for Mass, no matter what state he had been in the previous night. She had noticed that his predilection for the bottle had returned now that he had money in his pocket. She had heard one of the neighbours telling another that Mick Cleary was to be seen in the ale house at dinner time these days and, in fact, seemed to spend more time in there than at work.

'An' yer know wot that means?'

'Aye, 'e'll gerris card marked soon,' the other had added.

Her stomach had turned over as she had quietly closed the door. Just when they all seemed to be getting on!

The following day had seen the first real blazing row when Shelagh had arrived home and announced that she couldn't pay more than a shilling towards the rent because she owed one of her 'pals' most of her wages. It was the first time for years that Cat had seen her mother's cheeks burn with anger. Good food and a steady wage, less grinding drudgery and a security of sorts had all served to strengthen Ellen Cleary and bring back some of her old spirit. She had demanded to know why Shelagh had owed money and what she had spent all her wages on. Her sister had replied coolly that she'd borrowed some money from Maggie Abbot for the new dress she'd bought at C & A Modes last week, and with what they'd spent in Ma Boyle's Oyster Saloon, a shilling was all she had to last her until next pay day. Cat had jumped physically at the sound of the slap and Shelagh's startled yell, for her mother had actually slapped Shelagh's face! Shelagh had thrown the shilling down on the table and had stormed out of the house, pushing past her, thrusting her face close and mouthing insults. And she hadn't come home all night. Cat resolved to go and meet her from work next pay day, for that incident had upset her mother so much that she had taken to her bed.

* * *

The following Saturday, late in the afternoon, Mick Cleary staggered up Eldon Street, weaving his way from lamppost to lamppost. It was Cat who first saw him as she raised her head after just finishing the task of whitening the front step with donkey-stone. It was the last chore of the day and she was hot and tired. She sat back on her heels and pressed her hands into the small of her aching back, admiring her handiwork but thinking that by Monday morning it would be as dirty as the cobbles in the road. Then she looked down the street and saw him.

From the condition he was in she knew what had happened. It was all too obvious. He'd been sent packing. Sacked. And he'd already spent what money he'd been paid off with, for in the first flush of merriment he was always over-generous. He'd probably bought drinks for the entire crowd in the pub. Now there would be all hell let loose. Now the only money would be whatever Shelagh had left over when she came home – if any! She got to her feet and stood, hands on hips, as she watched him stagger on and when he was within reach, she grabbed him by his shirt front and shoved him inside the house. A drunken father was nothing new in the neighbourhood and no one would mock or pity her, but that fact didn't help much.

She slammed the door and rounded on him. 'Why, Pa? Why did you keep on drinking? You knew you'd lose your job and you know you won't get another one! There's a hundred more waiting in line!'

He muttered something unintelligible and she turned her head away as the smell of whisky and tobacco assailed her nostrils. The voices in the kitchen grew louder. Well, she wasn't going to stand and watch her mother's face cloud with worry and despair, or listen to the tart remarks of Maisey O'Dwyer. She squared her shoulders. This was one night when Shelagh was going to come straight home from work with her week's wage intact!

She ran down the street, the faded blue cotton skirt flapping round her bare legs, the grubby plimsoles she wore on her feet making no sound on the cobbles. Already she could see the workers streaming out through the gates of the sugar refinery and the air was rent with the 'knocking-off' whistles of all the factories. Vauxhall Road was crowded with workers finished for the week, their wages in their pockets.

She dodged between bicycles, carts and trams. Pushing and shoving her way through the crowds, trying to see the familiar face beneath the white cotton turban all the girls wore covering their hair. She spotted Bessie Abbot and called out to her. Bessie waved cheerfully.

'Where's our Shelagh? Bessie, have you seen her?'

'Last time I saw her she was off with our Maggie and the others.'

'Off where?'

'Ma Boyle's, I think they said. She'd brought her clothes with her, said she wasn't goin' home to get bawled out for spending her own money. Said she was going to enjoy it.'

'Oh, did she now! Where's Ma Boyle's?'

'Old Hall Street, next to The Albany. Ask anyone, you can't miss it!'

It took her nearly fifteen minutes to reach the junction of Vauxhall Road and Tithebarn Street, so congested was the traffic. By the time the imposing façade of Exchange Station came into sight she was breathless. She leaned against the corner of the building that flanked Bixteth Street, her heart hammering against her ribs. She didn't care how much of a scene she made, Shelagh was coming home with her! She walked on and turned up Old Hall Street. There were plenty of pubs and all of them full. The bowler-hatted, stiff-collared brigade of office workers only frequented these pubs and saloons at lunchtimes Monday to Friday and most of them finished at noon on Saturday, so the clientèle on Saturday nights was not of the usual, more refined sort.

She'd never been inside a public house before and with some trepidation she pushed open the door of the first one she came to. Its name 'The Coffee House' was emblazoned above the door though she suspected that that beverage was seldom drunk on the premises. The heat, the smoke and the smell of beer hit her full in the face and she began to cough.

'That's it, girl, ger it off yer chest!' Someone slapped her hard on the back. A group of men and girls were leaning against the wall, glasses in their hands.

'Where's Ma Boyle's Oyster Saloon?'

'Gerroff, luv, yer too young to go there!' came the good-natured reply.

'I'm looking for my sister, where is it, please?'

A girl with very brassy blonde hair and a bright red-and-green-flowered dress smiled at her. 'A bit further up, luv, you can't miss it.'

Nodding her thanks she pushed her way out into the street again. The air was fresh and clean and she could smell the river on the breeze. How anyone could choose to be stuck in places like that, choked with tobacco and beer fumes and packed like sardines in a tin, was beyond her understanding.

The girl had been right. The Oyster Saloon was unmistakable. It was very old and unique. Its door stood open giving a glimpse of low ceilings and plush upholstery. Like the Coffee House it was packed but gritting her teeth she elbowed her way in, blinking in the dim light. She knew she looked out of place. A skinny girl with untidy hair and smudges on her face. Bare legs and old plimsoles. The grubby, faded skirt and the old calico blouse that was split under the arms and damp with sweat. But she wasn't going to let all that deter her.

She ignored the amused and scornful glances, the heads jerked in her direction, the smirks on the faces of the women and girls in their crisp print dresses and high-heeled sandals.

'Can I help you, luv?'

She looked up to find a middle-aged man beside her. 'I'm looking for my sister. I think she's here. Shelagh Cleary.' Her voice shook a little.

'Is there anyone called Shelagh Cleary 'ere?' he bawled over the din.

'Who wants 'er?' a man's voice replied.

'Over there, in that corner by the window. Go on and then get off home with you or we'll get our licence taken off us!'

Cat pushed her way through and saw her sister with Maggie and two other girls sitting at a table near the small window. They were surrounded by a group of young men who already seemed to have had enough to drink. The smile instantly vanished from Shelagh's face as she caught sight of Cat.

55

'What the 'ell do you want? You've come spying on me, haven't you, you little sneak!' She stood up and grabbing Cat's arm, shoved her into the corner, placing herself between Cat and her friends. 'Just look at the cut of you, you dirty little slut! You followed me, just to show me up in front of them, didn't you?'

Her nails were biting into the flesh of Cat's arm and she yelped and struggled. 'No, I didn't! I went to meet you from work and Bessie told me you'd come here! You've got to come home now!'

'What for?'

'Pa's lost his job. He came home drunk and broke!'

Shelagh laughed in her face. 'Is that all! Jesus! I thought Maisey had had a heart attack!'

Cat was furious, not only because Shelagh was laughing at her and taking the catastrophe so lightly, but because she had never heard her sister blaspheme and was shocked. She could also hear the titters of laughter behind her.

Shelagh turned to her friends. 'She's run all the way here just to tell me me Pa's drunk again!'

Their laughter battered against Cat's ears and grated on her raw nerves, but she tried again. 'You've got to come home before you waste all your wages! You know how we'll need that money! You've got to come home and I'm staying until you do!' she finished defiantly.

'Oh, no, you're not! It's my money, I worked for it and I'm not keeping the whole lot of you! That drunken sod can go and find another job, I'm not keeping him in booze and you can get out and find a job, too, and so can Eamon! He's old enough. In fact he's too bloody old to be at school when he could be out earning a few bob! You get out of here, you whinging little bitch and leave me alone!'

Cat stood her ground. 'No! I'm not leaving without you!'

'Then I'll have you thrown out, you're too young to be in here anyway! I'll call the barman, Kate Boyle don't stand no nonsense and if you make a scene the scuffers will come and we'll all end up in the nick! Now get out!'

Cat's resolve broke under these threats and she darted towards the door.

'Scruffy bloody brat, shouldn't even be allowed in here!' Shelagh called after her.

She didn't stop running until she reached the corner of Prussia Square and then she sank down in the doorway of an office building and began to cry. She had failed and she couldn't face going back. Everything had gone wrong and she couldn't understand why Shelagh couldn't see that. But her sister had changed. She'd always been prone to selfishness, but now it seemed that she didn't care about anyone, not even Ma. That thought and the humiliation she had suffered brought on a bout of fresh sobbing.

'What's up with yer?'

She rubbed her arm across her eyes and looked up. The figure of a man was outlined against the darkening sky. 'Nothing,' she muttered, sniffing.

'What are yer whinging for then? I 'ate to see a girl cryin'.' His voice was slightly slurred and she got to her feet.

'I wasn't crying!'

'Liar!'

She could see him more clearly now and she didn't like what she saw. He was stocky and bull-necked. His

57

hair was plastered down with a sickly smelling oil and glistened, as though it were wet, in the dim light cast by the street lamp further down. His eyes were small and close-set and she could smell the beer on his breath.

'I'm waiting for my Pa, he'll be along in a minute, so will my brother.' She hoped she sounded convincing for a pang of fear gnawed at her stomach.

'Are they now? Which pub are they in?'

'The Coffee House. I think I can hear them coming now.'

He turned his head slightly and then smirked at her. 'Not unless they're two drunken swabbies!'

The two sailors passed by, holding each other upright, a bottle clasped in both their hands. She'd get no help from them. The fear was growing. She'd heard about girls who had been caught alone in the dark back streets.

'Yer not a bad lookin' judy, a bit skinny like, but not bad.' He leaned closer and she backed further into the doorway, frantically wondering if she could make a dash for freedom for she guessed he wouldn't be very quick on his feet.

'Not thinking of runnin' out on me are yer?'

'I'll scream! I'll scream so loud that the scuffers will hear me!'

'What about yer Pa and yer brother?' He moved closer and reached out, his stubby fingers touching her small breast.

She seized his hand and sank her teeth into the flesh as hard as she could.

'Yer bleedin' little bitch! Just fer that I'll teach yer what happens to girls like you!'

She felt his hands tearing at the calico of her blouse and she began to scream and struggle. He pushed her back against the wooden door, banging her head hard. A pain shot through her head and her vision clouded, but she still fought on, trying to claw at his face with her nails.

She wasn't fully aware of what was happening until she heard him swear again, then scream in agony before crumpling in a heap at her feet, clutching his groin.

'My God, is that you, Cat Cleary? Are you alright, has he hurt you?'

She had never heard anything so sweet as her name on the lips of Joe Calligan who had knocked down her attacker with one swift, well-aimed kick. She fell against his broad chest, giving way to the hysteria that had swept over her.

He held her thin, trembling body tightly. He hadn't known it was she. He had only known that some poor girl was being molested and he had instinctively gone to her aid. He hadn't seen her since the day she had landed but it was obvious that things hadn't got any better.

When her sobs began to subside he lifted her face gently with his hand. 'Did he hurt you, Cat? What are you doing here by yourself at this time? Come on, I'll take you home.'

She drew away from him. 'No! No, I can't go back there! I won't go back there!'

'Are things that bad?'

She leaned her head against his chest again. Oh, if only he knew.

'How long is it since you've eaten, Cat?'

'I . . . I can't remember.'

'Then first of all let's get some food inside you and then you can tell me what's the matter.'

'I don't feel hungry, I feel sick.'

59

'You will if you haven't eaten and you've had a shock.' He prodded the still-writhing figure contemptuously with the toe of his boot. 'Come on, there's a clean, cheap little cafe down past the station.'

Suddenly she did feel hungry. She also felt a little calmer and with his arm supporting her she felt safe.

Over a cup of steaming hot tea and a plate of fish and chips she related to Joe most of the events of that night and also those of the previous weeks.

'So, nothing much has changed then?'

She pushed the empty plate away and rested her chin on her elbows. 'Nothing.'

'You could take up Shelagh's suggestion and get a job yourself. Is there something wrong with you that you can't work?'

'No! I told you, I've been looking after Ma and the house and seeing that our Eamon goes to school.'

'From what I hear your Mam's well looked after and it is Maisey's house and she's got enough kids of her own to clean it and as for "meladdo", well if things are so bad, why shouldn't he leave school and get a job? Oh, I know fourteen is the official leaving age, but the School Board don't pay much attention to it when it comes to the likes of him – not when things are so bad.'

She stuck out her chin stubbornly. 'I want him to finish school and get a decent job.'

'The only job he'll get is a gofer.'

'What's that?'

'You know, running errands. 'Go fer this, go fer that!'

'Well, I'm not going to work in one of those stinking factories!'

'Why?'

'Because . . . because I can do better than that!' Seeing the quirk of amusement twist his lips, her colour heightened. 'I can! I know I can!'

'Oh, aye, you can read and write and add up in your head! So can most people and it hasn't got them anywhere!'

'I could get a job in a shop!'

He was not cruel enough to mention her burning ambition, not even in jest. 'You could go into service.'

'That's just the same as being at home.'

'Except that you get paid for it.'

She wanted to change the subject, the food had made her feel sleepy and she was in no mood to argue with him. 'Are you still working on the cattle boats? Shouldn't you be halfway across the Irish Sea by now?'

He ran one finger up and down the trellis design on the oilcloth tablecloth. 'I got laid off. Last in – first out. That's the company rule and I was last to join.'

'What about the Cunard ships?'

His handsome face clouded and he rose abruptly, the legs of the chair grating on the wooden floor. 'Come on, I'll see you home!'

She was sorry she had brought the subject up. He had obviously tried and failed to get any other kind of ship. And he had been kindness itself. In fact he seemed to have the knack of turning up when she needed him most. 'I'm sorry, Joe. I didn't mean . . . thanks for the supper.'

He ushered her out and they began to walk down Tithebarn Street.

'I have got a job. A shore job.'

'Doing what?'

'A sort of handyman, cum gardiner, cum every-thing, at one of the big old houses on Everton Valley. I could ask Ma Travis if she would take you on, that's what I meant about going into service. She's a widow. Her husband was a captain but he was lost at sea years ago. She's very houseproud and particular, especially about all the stuff the captain brought home. That's how come Rosie up and left her.'

'Rosie?'

'The housemaid she had. She dropped a vase and there was a right bust-up over it. The upshot was that Rosie packed up and left. The old lady's been doing it all herself and she won't let me help.' He laughed. 'I don't suit an apron!'

She laughed with him.

'But it's getting too much for her now and I reckon, the way things are, that she'd take some-one on recommendation, without experience.'

'What would I have to do?'

'What you've been doing at home, except that she'd pay you and she'd probably want you to live in.'

It was this last piece of information that made her really take interest. No more having to share everything. Being woken up constantly by Dora who had a habit of jabbing her knees into her, or Ethel who often talked in her sleep. No more waiting – jumping up and down in the yard – until whoever it was, finished in the privy. No more having to wait to see if you could have a whole slice of bread instead of half when Maisey had finished cutting up the remains of yesterday's loaf for breakfast. But best of all, no having to listen to the constant bickering and rows. She wouldn't have to see the dejection and despair on her mother's face either when Pa rolled in from the pub drunk. 'Won't I ever have to go back to Eldon Street?'

'She'll probably let you go home one afternoon in the week and most Sundays.'

The first initial rush of excitement at the thought of these undreamed of luxuries faded, to be replaced by guilt at leaving her mother. But if she could go back and see her, just for a day or so . . .

'Well, do you want me to ask her or not?'

'Would you, Joe? Would you really? But what if she says no?'

'If you don't ask, you don't get! Besides, she likes me.'

He was boasting again, she thought, but this time she hoped it wasn't just an idle boast. It was with reluctance that she realised that they had reached the corner of the street. 'How will I know if she will take me on?'

'I'll let you know. I only live in Silvester Street.'

Her eyebrows shot up in amazement. He only lived a few streets away and yet she'd never seen him, until tonight. 'Have you always lived there?'

'All my life, with our Mam, me Dad and two brothers, but I've been away at sea, in case you've forgotten.'

They stood under the street lamp on the corner as Cat was still reluctant to go home.

'Cheer up! I've got to go up Everton Valley tomorrow, I'll ask her then. I'll come round and tell you what she says.'

'Promise?'

'Cross my heart and hope to die! And if she says yes we'll go out and celebrate. I'll take you on the overhead railway.'

Her face lit up with a rare smile and in the pale light he thought how transformed her features became when she smiled. Impulsively he bent down and kissed her gently on the cheek, then straightened up, feeling embarrassed. He hadn't meant to do that. 'I'll see you tomorrow, Cat!' he called as he walked quickly away.

She watched him go, her hand going to her cheek which his lips had brushed. She'd never had a boy kiss her before. Not that it had been much of a kiss, more a peck. She'd never considered herself to be attractive enough for anyone to want to kiss. She sighed. Oh, she owed him so much. She watched his tall, broad figure disappearing down the road, his hands in his pockets. She could hear him whistling. She stood watching until he was out of sight, then she turned and ran up the street, her feet skimming lightly over the cobbles.

CHAPTER FOUR

They had only gone as far as the Sandon Dock on the Overhead Railway for Joe had appeared at eleven o'clock on Sunday morning to tell her that Mrs Travis wanted to see her at two o'clock sharp and that he was to take her there. This news had thrown her into a panic because she had told no one about the events of the night before.

Upon his arrival, Joe had been ushered into the house and his mother's health enquired about solicitously by Maisey, who seemed to know the entire population of Vauxhall on a personal basis. It had been Maisey who had told Cat to 'liven yerself up, girl!' as she had stood staring at Joe blankly. Her father had just stared at her through blood-shot eyes, her mother had looked confused and bewildered.

'Shelagh, luv, go an' borrow Maggie's best skirt an' blouse an' ask their Bessie fer those shoes of 'er's. They'll all be back from Mass now an' as it's Sunday it will all be out of 'ock an' won't need ter go back until termorrer!'

Cat did not feel uncomfortable. It was the usual practice for best clothes and indeed everything of any value in the house, to be pawned on Monday and redeemed on Saturday night. And the custom of borrowing and lending for special occasions was also an old one.

'I'd best go and wash my face . . . ' she stammered, as Shelagh with a face like thunder slammed out.

'Yer'd better do somethin' with that 'air, too, Cat! It looks like the Liver Birds 'ave nested in it! Purrit up or somethin', like Bessie next door does.'

Her cheeks burning with embarrassment, her stomach churning with apprehension, she ran upstairs to the bedroom she shared with half the household. As she struggled with her unruly locks, Shelagh entered and dumped a navy-blue rayon skirt, a white blouse covered with small sprigs of blue flowers, and a pair of black shoes with high heels, on the bed.

'Maggie said to be careful not to spill anything on them and Bessie said to mind you don't get the heels stuck in the tramlines!'

'I won't.'

Shelagh leaned against the wall and watched her as she tried to wind her thick mass of curls into a small bun. 'He's the lad you met on the boat, isn't he?'

Cat nodded, her mouth full of hairpins.

'Proper little sneak, aren't you? How long has this been going on?'

'Mind your own business!'

Shelagh curled her lip. 'Doesn't look as though he's got much in the way of prospects.'

'He's a damn sight better than the lot you were with last night! He's got me a job – nearly!'

'Some job, skivvying for some daft old bat!'

'At least I won't have to put up with you all week, and I won't have to share a room or a bed or a privy with a dozen other people!'

Shelagh sniffed and left her, still struggling with her hair.

The navy skirt and neat little blouse fitted her well but the shoes were tight and she wobbled on the unaccustomedly high heels, but when at last she went downstairs, even her sister grudgingly admitted she looked neat and tidy. Her mother said she looked so grown-up she hardly recognised her and from the look on Joe's face she knew all the compliments were true. She did feel different. She felt clean and smart for the first time in her life and as she stepped into the street she smiled shyly at Joe as he offered her his arm.

In place of the old trousers and jersey he wore grey-flannel trousers without the customary braces, and a clean white shirt with the collar attached and covering his dark hair he wore a jaunty cap, for no man was seen without some sort of hat on his head. She herself had Shelagh's red felt beret clipped over her smoothed-down curls.

She was conscious of the stares and nudges of the neighbours as they walked down the street, but it only made her feel more confident. She could hear them whispering to each other. 'Cat Cleary's finally got herself a feller. Walkin' out, now she is, an' he ain't bad-lookin' either!' It was a good feeling and even Joe's remark of 'Mind you don't fall off those heels and break your neck!' failed to arouse any annoyance in her.

They had taken the tram to the Pierhead and then boarded the Overhead Railway that ran in a straight line along the docks to Seaforth. Joe had pointed out all the ships and all the docks. The Princes Half Tide, Waterloo, Victoria and the Trafalgar that also encompassed the Clarence Dock Power Station. The Collingwood and Salisbury Docks, the Nelson, Bramley Moor, the Sandon Half

Tide, the Wellington and finally the Sandon Dock itself.

He had pointed out the ships of so many lines that her head buzzed. The Blue Star, Black Star, White Star. The Port Line, Shaw Saville & Albion, the Henderson, City and Ellerman Lines. Brocklebank, Booker and Booth Lines. The Houlder, Harrison and Blue Funnel, the latter known as the 'Blue Flue' Line. He seemed to know so much about ships and shipping, while she knew nothing at all.

The sensation of being hurtled along above the roadway, looking down on the houses and up the rows of narrow streets, was exhilarating. It must be like flying, she thought. The carriage windows gave a good view of all the shipping and she could see figures moving across the decks. But none of these ships was as big or as beautiful as the White Empress. In her mind she called it 'her ship', her 'White Empress' and despite everything she had not forgotten the words she had spoken with such determination to Joe. One day she would sail on that ship. She didn't know how she would do it, but she would find a way! Somehow!

They got the train going in the opposite direction and got off at the Bramley Moor Dock, walked up Blackstone Street and caught the tram up Boundary Street to the junction of the Rotunda Lyric Music Hall and Kirkdale Road. Then they changed trams and got halfway up the steep decline called Everton Valley before they got off. Big three-storeyed houses, all soot-grimed but with small, neat, walled gardens, clean paintwork, whitened steps and lace curtains flanked both sides of the road and the pavement was flagged. At its junction with Saint Domingo Road was the obligatory public house, aptly named 'The Valley' and beyond, on the left-hand side loomed the soot-stained bulk of the Methodist Church. On the right-hand side a four-storeyed, square edifice jutted obliquely forward, narrowing the roadway.

'What's that, it looks like a workhouse?' she asked, twisting her head to take in all the sights of this new district of Liverpool, for it was the furthest she'd ventured beyond Scotland Road.

'A convent and there's a private school for girls there as well. Notre Dame, it's called. Some of the girls board there but most of them go home each day. I often see them at four o'clock. They wear straw hats in the summer and black ones, shaped like po's in the winter. They don't half look daft!'

Cat lost interest in the convent and the description of its pupils as they stopped outside a large house with a brown-painted front door, which boasted a highly-polished, brass letterbox and knocker. It looked daunting and some of her ebullience faded. 'Is this it?'

He nodded and pushed her up the three steps, rapping sharply on the brass knocker. Cat stood fidling with the top button of her blouse until, after what seemed like hours, slow, shuffling footsteps were heard beyond the door.

'It's me, Mrs Travis! Joe! Joe Calligan and I've brought the girl I was telling you about.'

The door opened and a small woman with white hair, pulled tightly back from her face into a bun, stood peering at them through a lorgnette. She wore an ankle-length black dress with a high collar and leg-o'-mutton sleeves.

'Bring her in then, don't stand cluttering up the doorstep!'

Cat noticed that her voice bore only the faintest trace of the Liverpool accent. She followed Joe and Mrs Travis down a wide hallway, painted in brown and cream, the walls covered with prints of old sailing ships. The floor was of highly polished wood and a runner of brown and cream carpet ran along the middle of it. Mrs Travis had disappeared through a door on the left and Joe stepped aside, motioning her to follow.

She'd never seen a room quite like it. It reminded her of the parlour in the priest's house, but it was much bigger. It was also very dark for beside the lace curtains that covered the windows, heavy maroon-coloured drapes were half drawn. The furniture was old-fashioned and large but highly polished, in fact the whole room held a faint fragrance of beeswax. There were tables and lamps that had obviously come from foreign parts. Strange pictures of even stranger looking places covered the walls and stuffed animals and birds, queer little ornaments and jugs covered the mahogany side-board, the cane tables and corner cabinets, one of which held a collection of vividly coloured butter-flies of all sizes. A piano, draped with a dark-red chenille cloth stood in one corner of the room and on the top of this, too, was a collection of exotic bric-à-brac. Mrs Travis had seated herself in a button-backed chair and motioned Cat towards the shiny hide sofa with its array of brightly coloured cushions.

She sat cautiously on the edge, finding it hard and slippery. Joe stood behind her, his cap deferentially in his hand.

'So, you're looking for work? Have you been in service before?'

'No, but I've kept house for as long as I can

70

remember and I can cook, too, simple things. M'am' she added.

'By your accent I assume you are Irish.'

'That I am, from Dublin.'

'I have always found that the Irish can be divided into two categories. Those who are honest, hard-working, devout and make excellent servants, and those who are lazy, sluttish, with a fondness for liquor that usually leads them to theft, and who don't make good workers of any kind! Which are you?'

'I've never taken a drink in my life! I work hard and I've never touched anything that doesn't belong to me and I go to Mass every Sunday and sometimes in the week as well!' It all came out in one long sentence which left her short of breath and wondering if her predecessor had been guilty of any of the crimes mentioned.

'What's your name, girl?'

'Cat. Cat Cleary.'

The sharp, birdlike eyes flitted over her then were raised to the ceiling in impatience. 'I mean your real name! No one is ever christened with a name like that!'

'Catherine.'

'Well, Catherine Cleary, I will give you the chance to prove that you are all you say you are. I'll give you a month, starting tomorrow. You will live-in, there are plenty of rooms in this house, most of them shut off since my husband, God rest him, was taken by the sea. You'll clean, wash and iron, cook and do the shopping. You will have Sundays off and Wednesday afternoons and I'll pay you five shillings a week and I'll feed you. I can't say fairer than that!'

*　　*　　*

From that day on Cat's world changed radically. She quickly found that Mrs Travis had a sharp tongue but a kind heart and generous nature. She also suspected that the old lady was lonely for there did not appear to be any relatives or friends and the only callers to the house were tradesman. She worked hard but she found it far less like drudgery because, for one thing, there was no hoard of children and adults to be constantly undoing everything she had just done. She polished and dusted the curiosities with loving care, trying to imagine where they had come from, trying to picture in her mind the exotic, foreign places where they had been made. It was with real pleasure that she ironed the crisp, white linen, most of it embroidered or edged with lace.

She had her own room at the top of the house with a single, narrow bed with a brass bedstead, clean sheets and warm blankets, these in themselves luxuries never before experienced. There was a small wardrobe for her few clothes, a washstand with a marble top and a jug and bowl of real china, decorated with huge pink roses. She took her meals in the kitchen with Joe most of the time, but on Saturdays – pay day – both she and Joe sat with their employer at the table in the parlour when any outstanding jobs were discussed and the menus and shopping for the next week were all worked out.

She frequently found excuses not to go home on Wednesday afternoons, although on Sundays she returned to Eldon Street to give her mother three of her five shillings wages. But she was always glad when it was time to leave the cramped, cluttered house which now appeared so small and dirty. She would sit up in her bed on these nights, her knees drawn up under her chin and indulge herself in daydreams. When she got that job on 'her' White Empress, she would find a small house in a nice area, just for herself and her Ma. It would have a scullery with shelves covered in clean, chequered oilcloth. A food press and a meat safe. A white earthenware sink and a proper wooden draining-board, scrubbed white. A small, cheerful kitchen with a range for cooking. Rag rugs on the floor, a comfortable rocker with a patchwork cushion for her Ma. A big table and a dresser with fancy dishes. There would be a parlour where Ma could entertain Maisey and her other friends from the Union of Catholic Mothers. A bedroom each and good fires in all the rooms in winter. And she'd bring all kinds of treasures like Captain Travis had, for the house – when she was a stewardess.

She had no definite plans, for life had taught her to take one day at a time, and that the hold on material possessions was perilous. But she could dream. 'Dreams cost nothing' she'd always said to herself, but her dream was becoming consolidated. It was becoming, even if she didn't fully realise it, the foundation of what she expected from the future; what she would, in time, demand of life – demand and expect realisation.

Between herself and Joe there had developed a close friendship. He had never tried to kiss her again, but she often caught him watching her with a strange look in his dark eyes and sometimes she wondered if he did consider her to be more than just a friend. She had filled out and even in the plain, dark working dresses Mrs Travis had given her, she knew she had a good figure. Her waist was small, as were her hips, and her legs beneath the

73

calf-length skirt, were slender and well-formed. Her breasts had developed and were firm. Her cheeks had filled out and gone was the pinched, half-starved, little waif with the mane of unruly hair. She had followed Shelagh's example and had had it cut to just below her ears. She had no need to waste money on a Marcel Wave for it curled naturally.

After completing her second month, Mrs Travis had two dresses 'made over' for her by a local dressmaker. One was of cornflower-blue linen. The hemline had been shortened, the full skirt had been tapered in, with two inverted pleats set into the front and back. The collar was cut into reveres and edged with white piping, as were the sleeves that had been shortened to just above the elbow. The other dress was of a heavy, navy blue crêpe, embossed with a fretwork pattern. The skirt of this had been left full but recut in a semi-circle. The sleeves were puffed at the shoulder but narrowed into a cuff, again at elbow length. The stiff, high collar was fashioned into a soft, round one and a belt – made from the cut-off material – was tied in a sash around the waist. A row of shiny navy buttons added detail to the front.

She was ecstatic as she tried on the completed garments, twisting and turning in front of the long peer-glass that Mrs Travis had had Joe bring downstairs. The words tumbled from her lips as she gabbled her thanks at such generosity. At last she had some 'new' things of her own. There was her brush and comb set, the little china trinket box, bought at Great Homer Street Market and as yet empty of trinkets. They were all hers, and now these two beautiful dresses. Although the material wasn't new they had been especially made for her. No one else. And she had never known anyone who had their clothes made for them.

'Now you need a hat and a decent pair of shoes.' The dressmaker remarked, well pleased with her handiwork for which she had been amply rewarded.

'And a pair of gloves,' Mrs Travis added.

'Gloves? Sure, whatever will I need gloves for, it's not winter?'

'All respectable girls wear gloves and a hat!' Came the tart reply. 'That is what makes them instantly recognisable as respectable and ladylike. I know you turn up most of your wages to your mother, to use a colloquialism. So I have put some-thing extra in your wages this week.' The old lady nodded thoughtfully. 'I think we'll suit each other very well, Catherine Cleary. You work hard, you don't chatter idly all day long and you seem to appreciate all the things my Dear Departed col-lected over the years and that's something I'm impressed with. Take yourself off into town and get a hat and a pair of gloves and then tomorrow you can go home and look down your nose at that slut of a sister of yours!'

Cat knew that Joe had told her mistress all about Shelagh, for she had heard the old lady quizzing him one day when they thought she was still out. Impulsively she bent down and kissed the withered cheek.

'God bless you! No one has ever been this good to me!'

'Oh, get off with you, girl! I can't stand being fussed and kissed, not at my age! You'd better keep

75

one of the dresses on or they'll not let you in any of the shops!'

The hat, which she bought in Lewis's department store on the corner of Ranleigh Street and Renshaw Street, was a small white pillbox that had cost her 2s 6d. She kept it on, but accepted the cardboard hatbox the sales assistant had offered to pack it in. At the glove counter she tried on at least half a dozen pairs of gloves in assorted colours and fabrics, luxuriating in smoothing the soft cottons over her work-worn hands, then holding them out to admire the effect, as if she bought gloves every day of her life. She settled for a pair of short white cotton ones, the backs of which were decorated with a cut-out design in the shape of a daisy. She glanced fleetingly at the leather and kid gloves, knowing they were far too expensive for her rapidly dwindling hoard of coins. She had managed to save a small amount and with the extra Mrs Travis had given her, she felt like a millionairess. She kept the gloves on, too.

As she walked past Central Station and the Lyceum Club on the corner of Bold Street, she felt as though she were walking on air. That every head was turning in her direction with glances of admiration. Once in Church Street she stopped and gazed into the windows of the Bon Marché at the expensive, well-cut clothes and displays of perfumes and cosmetics. In George Henry Lees, just around the corner, similar displays of clothes, hats, jackets and bright scarves held her interest. She wandered into Woolworths – and after much deliberating she purchased some Evening in Paris perfume, its dark-blue glass bottle and silver-coloured top quite the most elegant things she had ever seen. Next she went into Timpson's shoe shop. As white seemed the obvious colour to suit both her new dresses, she picked a pair of white, low-heeled leather pumps with a single strap across the instep, but not before she had indulged herself in trying on black, navy, cream, brown and other assorted coloured shoes. When she had paid the 2s 6d. for them she had just enough left for her tram fares and the 3s still untouched for her mother.

She was loathe to leave this newly found treasure trove and so she started at the end of Church Street, wandering into Coopers where the aroma of dozens of different types of fresh coffee beans was heady and strong. Every edible commodity could be purchased here with produce from all over the world and she stood, mouth watering, gazing at the pyramid-displays of exotic fruit and vegetables. Then she meandered through the departments of C & A Modes which sold cheap but cheerful clothes for men, ladies and children. Across the congested roadway she stopped outside Henderson's, but one look at the liveried doorman changed her mind about entering its exclusive portals. She did venture into Marks & Spencer where sales girls methodically tidied their counters on which were set out a range of mass-produced garments.

She caused something of a sensation as she walked up Eldon Street early on Sunday morning. Children scattered before her, diving into houses only to dart out again, followed by avidly curious adults.

'Cor! If it ain't little Cat Cleary!' Maggie Abbot

exclaimed, leaning against the open door of their house with her hair still screwed up in curling papers. 'Eh, our Mam! Bessie! Cum an' look at 'er! Dead posh she is an' all! Gorrup like a dog's dinner!'

Faces crowded behind her as she pushed open the front door of number eight, to be greeted by a wide-eyed Eamon. Shelagh's face was a picture as she took in the hat, gloves and dress.

'Have you been paradin' up and down Lime Street then? You didn't get those from Paddy's Market!' she questioned venemously.

Cat ignored her. Lime Street was the haunt of prostitutes.

'Cat, is it really you? Where did you get those grand things?'

'It's really me, Ma! Mrs Travis had the dress made over and I've got another one, too, and she gave me an extra week's pay to buy the hat and shoes and gloves!' She stretched out a small, white-gloved hand.

Her mother touched it with reverence.

'But don't worry, I've not touched a penny of what I give you. Here!' She pressed the coins into her mother's hand.

'God bless you, you're a fine girl, Cat, and you deserve to be treated well, that you do!'

'Not like some as what we could mention!' Maisey jibed, casting a contemptuous look at Shelagh. 'Stoppin' out 'alf the night, wastin' money an gerrin' to bed at all hours an' gerrin' up to God knows what!'

'What I do is me own affair, Maisey, and I work for it don't I?' came the quarrelsome reply.

'An' so does she!'

Cat drew off her gloves. *Nothing ever changes here*, she thought.

'We'll be dead proud of yer this mornin' at Mass, won't we, Ellen? Will yer be stoppin' for tea? It's not what yer used to but . . .'

'Just because I've got a few new things doesn't mean I'm a snob, Maisey. I'm still a working girl. But I'm sorry I won't be here for tea. Joe is taking me to New Brighton on the ferry and we're going to have tea over there.'

This statement caused Shelagh to snatch up a gaudy print dress from over the back of the chair and slam out of the room.

'Take no notice of 'er, Cat. She's as jealous as 'ell cos yer've got some sense an' are goin' up in the world an' she's not!' Maisey advised.

'I've never taken any notice of our Shelagh and I don't intend to start now,' she replied laconically.

'She'll cum to a bad end will that one, sure as I've gor eyes in me 'ead!' Maisey muttered ominously, amidst the fevered preparations to get herself and her brood ready for Mass on time.

The *Royal Daffodil* ploughed its way into the Mersey under a clear azure sky, while a fresh breeze blew the smoke from her single funnel back towards the Liverpool waterfront. Joe had helped Cat climb up onto the top deck and they stood with the other day-trippers watching the two-mile-wide strip of murky grey water and the distant verdigris-green dome of the church of Saints Peter and Paul set high on its hilltop looking down on the seaside resort of New Brighton.

Joe placed his arm around her slender waist and

she smiled up at him. The day promised to be a wonderful one, with a trip to the seaside, a tour around the fairground and maybe one up the tower and a fish supper before their return trip home. The wind tugged at her hat and she wished she had anchored it more firmly, instead she held on to it with one hand.

'It suits you, makes you look older!'

'Not too old, I hope!' she laughed.

'You're not worrying about wrinkles already are you?'

She laughed again and leaned against him. He wore the grey flannel trousers and white shirt that were his Sunday Best, but the shirt was covered by a new tweed sports jacket and his cap was set at a jaunty angle over one eye. They made a handsome couple, she thought.

'A penny for them?'

She came back to reality and blushed. 'I was just thinking that we . . . well, we look grand together!'

'Do we?'

'I think so.'

To her confusion he bent and kissed her. Not on the cheek this time, but full on the lips. At first she was so surprised that she made no protest, but then when she tried to pull away, his arm had moved from her waist to her shoulders and his embrace had become stronger. The mocking cry of the seagulls faded away overhead, as she closed her eyes and responded to his lips, feeling a warm glow spread through her while her heart fluttered in a strange way.

At last he drew away from her and she felt a little dizzy and leaned her head against his broad chest.

'Can't we be more than friends, Cat? You've . . .

you've never been out of my mind since the first time I saw you on the *Leinster*.'

'I'm not sure what you mean,' she stammered, not knowing how to cope with the situation. She liked him, she more than liked him, but she didn't want him to think of her as 'fast' or 'bold' as her Ma would have said.

'I mean, can't we . . . can't I take you out?'

She misunderstood him. 'You are taking me out, to New Brighton.'

'I think your Ma would call it "walking out".'

'Oh!' No one had ever seriously asked her this before and so she had never seriously considered it. She became flustered. 'You won't . . . you won't . . .?'

'Take advantage of you? You know me better than that, Cat!'

Her smile was shy and the blush crept back into her cheeks as he kissed the tip of her nose.

'Can I kiss you again or would that be asking too much?'

'Everyone is looking at us!'

'So, let them look, I don't care, do you?'

'No, I don't—' Her words were cut off as his lips sought hers again, and again that dizzy feeling crept over her, making her knees go weak and trembly. But she had never felt so happy in her whole life and when he drew away from her she noticed that his breathing seemed to be laboured. She straightened her hat and settled into the crook of his arm, leaning comfortably against his shoulder, feeling the muscles ripple beneath his jacket. She rubbed her cheek against the rough tweed of his jacket and for a few minutes they were both silent. She soon found the silence a little oppressive, not knowing what he was thinking. Not yet completely resigned or comfortable with this new situation, or these disturbing feelings.

'Is that the *Aquitania*?' she asked him, more to break the silence than out of real interest, pointing to where the Cunarder was standing out in the river while she took aboard the hausers of the two tugs that had gone alongside her.

'No, its the *Scythia*.

He sounded slightly annoyed and this disturbed her. She looked up at him and saw a look she had never seen before in his eyes. She wasn't to know that he was trying to suppress an overwhelming feeling of longing that had risen when he had first kissed her and held her, feeling the firm young breasts pressing against his chest.

'I'm sorry, I didn't mean to remind you about . . .'

'About wanting to go back to sea? You've no need to apologise for that, the sea is in my blood, it always will be!'

'Always?'

He nodded emphatically.

'So you still want to sail on one of those?' She gestured with her head in the direction of the liner.

'Of course I do! I don't want to stay with Ma Travis forever. I want a job at sea!'

She was hurt. He'd just asked her to walk out with him and now he was saying he wanted to leave her. She didn't understand him. Her green eyes became mutinous. He wasn't the only one who had a dream. Even though fortune had smiled so benevolently on her, she still lay awake at night, staring at the ceiling. The majestic outline of the White Empress was imprinted on her mind, still as vivid as the day she had first seen her.

'Well, I haven't given up my dream either! One day I'm going to sea, too!'

He turned on her, his dark eyes flashing, his face thunderous. 'Aren't you satisfied with what you've got? Have you forgotten that not two months ago you were half-starved, homeless and penniless? I thought you were happy?'

'I am! I am! And I'm grateful to both you and Mrs Travis!'

'Then why don't you stop dreaming about that damned ship! You haven't got a hope of ever getting a job like that and you know it!'

'But you can go sailing off whenever it suits you!'

'That's different!'

'Why?'

'Because . . . because men can and do! Women don't, not girls like you anyway!'

His argument only increased her stubbornness and perversity. 'Well, I'm going to prove you wrong, Joe Calligan!'

He turned away and pushed through the crowd of laughing people all pointing out the ferris wheel and the tower, now clearly visible. He left her to stare after him, the tears pricking her eyes. The day was ruined and she only had herself to blame. Why had she ever mentioned that damned Cunarder!

CHAPTER FIVE

The day hadn't been totally ruined by their first quarrel for she had put her pride in her pocket and had gone looking for him, just before they tied up. Looking back, it hadn't really been a bad day after all. His good humour had returned as he had watched her hitch up the skirt of her dress, slip off her shoes then run down the beach to paddle her feet in the cold water.

He had watched her splashing about among children and young people who were braving the chilly sea. She was just like a child herself, he had thought, as she had run back to him her eyes sparkling, her feet caked in sand and the skirt of her dress soaking wet. She'd never been to the seaside before she confided. The first time she had even seen sand was when they had entered the mouth of the Mersey on the *Leinster* and that had only been at a distance.

He had given her his handkerchief to wipe off the sand before she replaced her shoes and then, arm in arm, they had toured the fairground. They had indulged in one daring ride on the ferris wheel which had her in paroxysms of laughter one minute and screams the next, when she had clung to him like a limpet. Then they had sat on the promenade while he pointed out the sights of local interest and explained the history of the Tuscan-style fort on

Perch Rock that had once had a battery of six cannons to protect the entrance to the river, but which was now the site of the lighthouse.

They had had their fish supper and had boarded the *Royal Daffodil* tired, broke, but happy and she had snuggled against his shoulder and fallen asleep as the ferry headed for home. It had been then that he had felt the longing rise up again and with it a fiercely protective instinct. She was so young and naive, yet at the same time she had experienced the harshness of life. She was intelligent and she had guts. She also had a temper and a stubborn streak, he admitted ruefully to himself. But as he looked down at her he knew she was the girl he wanted for the rest of his life.

There had been other trips after that first one. To Southport on the electric railway, although she said she hadn't enjoyed Southport as much as New Brighton. It was much bigger and far more sedate and affluent with its grand hotels, esplanade, botanical gardens, golf courses and the expensive and exclusive shops along Lord Street and down the Cambridge and Wayfarer's arcades.

On the last day of the summer season they had taken a trip to the north Wales seaside town of Llandudno, three hours sail from the Pierhead. Cat had said it reminded her of Southport except that the people spoke with what she called 'funny' accents.

'No more funny than yours or mine, come to that!' He had laughed.

'But you can't read the names, they're all foreign.' She had exclaimed.

'So is your language.'

'My language?'

'The Irish Language, Gaelic, or haven't you heard of that either?'

'Oh, that. Only the people in the far West, in the sad lands, speak it now. Everyone else speaks English.'

'Aye, but not the King's English!'

She had poked him in the ribs, knowing he was trying to rile her – or have a go at her, as he would say.

His restlessness came to the fore again after that trip, mainfesting itself in long, brooding silences. She knew he was bored with his work and as winter approached she noticed he found more excuses to go into Liverpool. She asked him directly where he'd been and what for, one evening when he returned late and soaked to the skin by the rain that had poured from gunmetal skies since noon.

'Ask no questions and you'll get no lies!'

'You've got your best overcoat on and it's soaked! Here, give it to me while I put it over the rack to dry!' She helped him shrug out of the black melton coat, then undid the cords that held a clothes rack suspended across the ceiling. She draped the coat over it and then hoisted it up again, securing the ends round a nail in the wall. 'It's dripping all over the floor. You're saturated! Here, dry your hair and get those wet boots off!' She handed him a towel with which he vigorously rubbed his thick, dark hair until it was tousled. He looked like an older version of Eamon, she thought as she watched him.

He bent and began to unlace his boots.

'You've been down to the shipping offices again, haven't you? You wouldn't go all that way in weather like this in your good clothes, just to get some things for the Missus! You wouldn't be so late coming back either!'

'What if I have?'

She sighed. Obviously he had had no luck or he wouldn't be so bad-tempered, but she had to ask. 'No luck?'

'Not at the moment. They said to keep coming in each week, that I haven't had much experience.'

'How many did you go to?'

'About a dozen.' He flung the boots down on the hearth.

She knew what it was like to go cap in hand, begging, and it hurt her to think of him going from one place to another and having the door slammed in his face. 'What about The Pool?' she asked quietly, referring to the office at the Pierhead, at Mann Island, where crews were taken on and signed off. It was a collective marketplace where men offered their services. A pool of labour, which was how it got its name.

'You know I go down there every week.'

'I'll get you something to eat.'

She clattered the dishes as he sat staring darkly into the leaping flames. She hated to see him like this, yet she knew she couldn't hold him ashore forever but she didn't want him to leave her.

'Wouldn't the Missus know someone? Someone important I mean. Mr Travis was a captain, wasn't he?'

'Aye, on the old tea clippers, he's been dead for years and so have his cronies, probably. Besides, I can't go asking her she'll show me the door and then I'll have no job at all!'

She passed him a cup of steaming hot tea. 'I could hint to her that although you like working here, you're not really settled, having the sea in your blood, wasn't that what you said? She'd understand that.'

'Don't you say a word to her, Cat! Do you hear me! Mind your own business!'

'I thought it was my business.'

She crossed the kitchen and knelt beside him, resting her head on his knee. 'I won't lie and say I want you to go, but I hate to see you like this, Joe. You're changing, right before my eyes and there's nothing I can do about it!'

He stroked her hair. 'I'm sorry, Cat. I didn't mean to yell at you. But I can't stay here for much longer. It's not bad in summer but in winter, I feel like I'm in prison, cooped up . . . '

She thought of the cramped quarters all crews of merchant ships shared and his words took on an obtuse meaning, but she kept her thoughts to herself. 'I'll miss you when you do get a ship.'

He bent down and gathered her into his arms. 'Oh, Cat, don't you think I'll miss you too! You won't find someone else will you, like Johnny Todd's girl?'

She nuzzled his ear and began to sing softly.

> 'Johnny Todd came home from sailing,
> sailing on the ocean wide,
> And he found his fair and false one
> was another sailor's bride.'

'Now how will I find anyone else cooped up here and with the Missus watching me like a hawk?' she chided.

He continued his search in the weeks that followed and as the weather grew worse so did his moods. There were times when he refused to utter more than a few words to her and times when he would shout at her, taking out his increasing frustration and restlessness on her. And then she, too, would lose her temper and shout back, flinging her own hopes and ambitions in his face, telling him he didn't own her and that she'd live her own life.

In the middle of November on a dark night when the screaming wind stripped the few remaining leaves from the trees in the Convent Garden, and howled around the chimney and rattled the loose window sills, Cat opened the front door in response to the hammering that had echoed through the house. Ready to give the caller the sharp side of her tongue. On the step, huddled in a dirty, threadbare old jacket, stood Eamon.

'What do you want? It's nearly nine o'clock! You've hammered on that door loud enough to wake the dead in Anfield Cemetery!'

'Maisey sent me, our Shelagh wouldn't come!'

She pulled him inside and forced the door shut against the gale. 'What's the matter? Quick, tell me?'

Mrs Travis appeared from the parlour, a shawl of fine cashmere over her merino dress, a piece of embroidery still in her hands.

'It's my brother. Mrs O'Dwyer has sent him,' she explained. 'What's wrong, Eamon?'

'It's me Mam!' he stammered, his astonished gaze taking in all the pictures, ornaments and carpet.

'What's the matter with your mother, boy? Is she ill?'

Eamon could only nod as he viewed Mrs Travis from the comparative safety of his sister's sheltering arm.

'What's wrong with her?' Cat shook him. Her mother hadn't been well for a long time, but she had seemed well enough on the previous Sunday.

'He's frozen. Take him in the kitchen and give him something to warm him up! Then perhaps we'll get some sense out of him.'

Cat propelled the boy into the kitchen where he stood as close to the fire in the range as he could, without setting himself alight, while Cat boiled some milk.

Mrs Travis sat down in the old rocker in front of the boy. 'I'm not going to eat you. Now, tell me what is the matter with your mother?'

'She's got a cough. It weren't very bad an' Mais . . . Mrs O'Dwyer was rubbin' her chest with grease or somethin', but this mornin' she weren't no better an' this afternoon she could 'ardly breathe an' had cum over all 'ot. Fever, Mrs O'Dwyer said it were. Can she cum 'ome with me, Missus?'

Cat handed him a mug of hot milk, her eyes fixed on her mistress, the fear for her mother plain in their pleading eloquence.

'Get your coat and hat, Catherine, while he finishes his drink. I'll give you some medicine and flannel binding and if you think she's really bad, then you must call the doctor in. Where's Joe? I can't let you both go back there at this time of night alone.'

'He went up to The Valley for a bottle of Green Ginger Wine. He said it was good for keeping out the cold.'

'It is, as long as that's all he's gone for!'

'You know he hardly touches a drop, except the odd pint of beer. He'll be back any minute now, I'm sure.'

As if to reinforce her statement they heard the back-yard door slam shut.

'Go and get your coat on, girl!'

When she returned to the kitchen Mrs Travis was handing Joe a small black leather Gladstone bag and a piece of writing paper folded in half. 'He's got the flannel and the medicine. Wrap the flannel in a hot brick first to warm it, and I've given him a note for a doctor I know who lives not too far away, in case you should need him.'

Cat could only stammer her thanks as Joe shepherded them towards the door.

All the way on the tram she plied Eamon with questions, the answers to which were mostly very vague.

'It may only be a cold that has gone to her chest, or influenza. With care she'll probably be fine, Cat,' Joe tried to calm her fears.

'She's never been strong! What if . . . Oh, Holy Mary, Mother of God! What if she's . . .'

'If she was that bad, Maisey would have come herself or sent your Pa! Stop working yourself into such a state, Cat!'

Eamon was not paying any attention to the conversation. It was not often he got to ride on a tram and he was enjoying it. Like most of the lads in their neighbourhood, he usually only managed to hitch a ride for a few yards by running and clinging on to the back, until the conductor caught him.

They all crowded into the clammy bedroom with its faded wallpaper where the figure of Ellen Cleary lay huddled beneath a pile of coats. Cat sank down on the bare floor beside the bed and groped for the thin hand. It was burning hot. Her mother's face was thin and drawn, her sunken eyes too bright, her face flushed and a veil of perspiration covered her skin.

'Maisey, how long has she been like this?'

'Since about four o'clock. She weren't too bad until then. Just the cough.'

'It's not the cough wot carries 'em off, it's the coffin they carry 'em off in!' Eamon chanted, trying to ward off his own fears by attempting to joke about the situation. The street rhyme fell flat.

'Get that 'eartless little sod out of 'ere!' Maisey yelled.

Joe complied, boxing Eamon's ears hard, while Eamon yelled in protest.

'Joe, you'd better go for the doctor?' Cat pleaded.

'Doctor! We ain't got no money fer no doctor! Didn't she give yer anythin' to bring with yer?'

Cat ignored the protest but continued to gaze imploringly at Joe who nodded and left the room.

'Where's he goin'?'

'For the doctor and I've got money to pay him. Pass me that bag!'

Eyeing her suspiciously, Maisey handed her the bag. She'd never had a doctor over her doorstep, not even when old Ma O'Dwyer had been dying.

'Let's try and get some of this down her, you hold her up!' Cat instructed, pulling out the dark-green pharmaceutical bottle.

'What is it?'

'Some medicine Mrs Travis gave me. There's some strips of flannel in there, too, but they have to be warmed up first. Where's our Shelagh?'

Maisey went to the door and bellowed for Shelagh to 'Gerrup 'ere right now!'

Between them they managed to get some of the medicine down Ellen and a sullen Shelagh was sent to heat up the bricks in the range. When she

93

returned with the strips of red flannel wrapped around them, her demeanour had changed to one of concern.

'Eamon said Joe Calligan has gone for a doctor. I didn't think she was that bad!'

'Yer wouldn't! Yer never think of anyone but yerself! 'Ere, 'elp me with the flannel while Cat 'olds her up!'

When they had finished she looked a little less fevered but Cat insisted on pulling her own grey wool coat up around her mother's chin. She chaffed her arms. The room was damp and cold.

When the doctor arrived Cat cleared everyone out of the room although Maisey objected strongly. But with Joe's help she got her own way. She stood watching while Dr Devlin examined her mother.

'I've given her some of this, Doctor. What's the matter with her, is it bad?'

He took the bottle from her and examined the label, then nodded.

'I'd say it is pleurisy and she should be in hospital.'

Cat crossed herself. Hospital! Most people died in hospital! 'Oh, does she have to go? Can't she stay here? I'll look after her and Mrs Travis is so good I know she'll help me, lend me blankets and coal! I'll nurse her! Oh, don't take her away, please?'

Dr Devlin was of the old-fashioned school who, while admitting that hospitals had changed greatly, still preferred his patients to be nursed at home wherever possible. 'This room is damp, is there another she could be moved to?'

Cat clutched at this straw. 'Yes! Yes, I'll find one! Just tell me what she needs, what to do . . . !'

'I'll write everything down for you but if she

94

loses consciousness then you will have to call me straight away!'

Thankfully passing a hand over her own damp forehead, she nodded as, taking out a black pocket-book, he began to write.

Joe, with the help of Mr O'Dwyer and her Pa, but hindered by Eamon who in his anxiety insisted on helping, moved the bed downstairs. They had cleared out some of the old furniture and rubbish from the front room. Joe went back to the house in Everton Valley to inform Mrs Travis of the events and to ask for her help. He returned with sheets, blankets, two flannel nightdresses, half a sack of coal and the promise that more would be delivered first thing in the morning by Mrs Travis' own coal merchant, and a message that Cat was to stay for as long as she was needed and that all bills must be sent to her.

For the next five days and nights, Cat nursed her mother, washing her, changing her nightdress, changing the soiled linen, coaxing her to take the medicine Dr Devlin had left. The doctor called every day and Cat was grateful for these visits, knowing they were prompted by her benefactress who had continued to give her support in every way, sending Joe down each day to report on the patient's condition and to ask if there was anything else she needed.

On the third night Joe insisted that Maisey sit up with Mrs Cleary as Cat was grey from exhaustion and worry and could barely keep her eyes open. He had cradled her in his arms until she had fallen into a deep sleep, then he laid her gently on the sofa and covered her with his own overcoat and left after giving instructions that if any of them woke her he'd personally beat them black and blue! And it was on that night, while Cat slept, that her mother pulled around. The fever left her and the pains in her chest subsided, leaving her weak and exhausted but breathing more calmly, her eyes clear.

They woke Cat who ran in and threw herself on the bed to be clasped in the thin arms, while she sobbed with sheer relief.

'Hush. Hush now, Cat, you'll make yourself ill and then where would we be?'

'Oh, Ma! Ma! I thought I was going to lose you!'

'Hush, the good Lord won't take me until it's my turn and only He knows when that will be. But I thank Him with all my heart for giving me such a daughter as you, Cat.' The words were barely more than a whisper.

'An' don't ferget 'er Ladyship up there in Everton Valley! I never thought I'd see the day when one of them would 'elp the likes of us, but she's a saint, that's what she is! Supplied everythin', paid fer everythin'. God bless 'er!' Maisey added.

Cat sat up. 'She's right, Ma. Without Mrs Travis I don't know what I'd have done. The doctor wanted to put you in hospital.'

Like most of the poverty-striken, Irish labouring classes, the word hospital was synonymous with workhouse and Mrs Cleary shuddered.

''Ed 'ave 'ad to get past me first! I don't 'old with them hospitals! Once they get yer inside, yer don't gerrout again, norr in one piece anyway!' Maisey muttered darkly.

'The most important thing is that you're on the mend now, Ma, but you'll have to look after yourself! You'll have to eat!' She turned to Maisey. 'Has he got a job yet?'

'No, an' not likely to', sittin' on his arse all day!'

'Then he'll have to get off it and find something! What about Shelagh?'

'She's gone to work at the B & A now, better money.'

'And free fags, no doubt!' Cat retorted. The British and American Tobacco Company was situated further down Vauxhall Road. 'Then she can turn up more. I know Ma, what I give her she gives to you and Pa. Well, I'm not working to keep him! If I give it to you will you see he doesn't get his hands on it? Just make sure Ma and Eamon get decent food. Our Shelagh can look after herself and if she spends all her money on clothes and drink, then let her starve, Maisey!'

'I'll do just that, luv! Yer money will be in safe 'ands with me, I'll see to yer Ma and meladdo there! Mick Cleary can starve, too, or gerroff 'is backside an' if either one of them complains, then out the door they'll go, I'm sick of the pair of them!'

At the end of November Joe signed on a small freighter for a short trip to Hamburg. He broke the news to Cat and Mrs Travis simultaneously, preferring to face the hurt of one and the wrath of the other at the same time.

'So when do you sail?' Mrs Travis did not appear to be too angry; in fact she seemed to be taking the matter complacently.

'Day after tomorrow.'

'And how much are they going to pay you and what prospects are there for the future?'

'The wage is a bit more than you pay me and as

97

for prospects, well . . . they did say if I suited they may sign me on again.'

'So it's for one trip only? A trial period? No firm promise?'

'No. But that's not unusual.'

'Not for small-time tramp steamers. It would be different for a reputable line such as Ellermans or the City Line.'

He flushed, knowing what she meant.

Cat had remained silent, her eyes downcast.

'And if they don't keep you on, what then?'

He shrugged. 'I don't know.' He couldn't maintain his composure any longer. 'I'm sorry, but I can't help it! There's a passion for the sea that was born in me – me Dad and brothers are merchant seamen! I just can't help it!'

The old lady's eyes strayed to the framed photograph that hung above the mantelpiece. A portrait of a stern-looking man with a full beard and moustache, in the old-fashioned uniform of a merchant captain. She sighed. 'Someone else once told me the same thing. We'll miss you, Joe. Now, I have some letters to write.' And with a wave of her hand she dismissed them both, but as he reached the door she spoke again. 'Will you be back in time for Christmas?'

'Yes. A week before, I hope.'

'Then we'll see you then and if they don't keep you on, I'll keep your job open until the New Year.'

'Why couldn't you have told me first!' Cat demanded when they reached the seclusion of the kitchen.

'Because . . . because, well, I didn't want to upset you!'

'You mean because you were afraid to! You know I don't want you to go!'

'I'm not afraid of any woman and you knew sooner or later I'd go! You know how I've tried and tried to get a ship!'

She turned away but he placed his hands on her shoulders. 'She understands, why can't you?'

'Because I'm not like her, that's why! I . . . I've only got my Ma and you . . . that I care about anyway, and now . . .'

'It's only for a couple of weeks, Cat! I'll be back before Christmas and I'll bring you something really nice and we'll go out on the town, and—'

'I don't want your presents! I won't be fobbed off with presents and promises!'

'I thought you cared for me, Cat?'

'I do!'

'Then stop yelling at me! Can't you be happy for me?'

Her face crumpled and he gathered her into his arms. 'It's only a couple of weeks, I'll be back before you know it!'

She hadn't gone to see him off and the day he sailed Mrs Travis called her into the parlour.

'So, he's gone?'

Cat nodded and picked at the edge of the duster she was holding.

'Put that away and sit down.'

She stuffed the cloth into the pocket of her pinafore and sat on the edge of the Chesterfield.

'How old are you, Catherine?'

'Seventeen. I'll be eighteen next June.'

'With your whole life ahead of you. Oh, how I envy you, Catherine.'

Cat fidgeted, wondering where this conversation was leading. It was obvious she hadn't been called in for just a chat.

'You're fond of Joe, aren't you?'

She nodded miserably. She missed him already.

'And how is your mother?'

The change of subject startled her; she was expecting a homily on etiquette. 'She's coming along very nicely now, thank you.'

'Good.' The old lady fingered the brooch at the neck of her dress. A brooch in the shape of a ship's wheel. A brooch she was particularly fond of. 'Take my advice, my dear, don't marry a sailor!'

'Oh, Joe hasn't . . . I mean . . .'

Mrs Travis held up her hand. 'I didn't for a minute think he had. But believe me, it's a lonely life for a woman. Months of waiting, wondering, worrying . . .' She fingered the brooch again. 'No matter how good a man is, it's still no consolation and so often they don't stick to their principles.' She paused. 'You have to be mother and father to your children, except that in my case I never had any. It was God's will and I became resigned to it. But there are many women who would have changed places with me. Women left alone to bring up families on a pittance or nothing at all. Often deserted . . .'

'Joe's not like that—' she burst out, unable to stop herself.

'I'm not suggesting he is, but he'll never rise any higher than a deck steward.' Again she silenced Cat's protests with an uplifted hand. 'Think about your mother, Catherine. I expect she started married life in good health and spirits, and look at what life has left her with! You're a good girl, you're not without intelligence and you work hard. I wouldn't like to think that you would end up like your poor mother. You can do better, much better, for I think you have sense beyond your years. Think about it.

Think long and hard. Have you any ambitions? Any plans for the future?'

Cat shook her head. She couldn't tell Mrs Travis about her aspirations, she wouldn't understand. She lived in another age.

'Then you should start to think about some. Joe Calligan isn't the only man in the world. It's not more than five months since you came here and look how you've changed. I saw potential in you. You've grown up into a pleasant, presentable young woman. A long way from the scrawny child who sat there not so long ago. Given another year . . . I think you understand me. Don't fall into the trap, Catherine!'

'There is something . . .'

'I knew there was. I sensed it. You would have disappointed me if there hadn't been "something."'

'I want to be . . . I want something I've never had! I want to be respected, admired.'

'Very commendable. Is that all?'

She faltered for an instant beneath the penetrating gaze. 'I want . . . I want to become a stewardess, but not just any stewardess on any liner!'

'Ah, so you, too, have salt water in your veins. Go on!'

'I want to be a chief stewardess on a White Empress!'

To her suprise the old lady smiled wistfully. 'Nothing is impossible, my dear. Highly improbable but not impossible. There is nothing I can do to help you either, apart from a good reference, for the few men in the Canadian Pacific Line that I was acquainted with through my husband are all dead. But work and don't let go of your dreams! Let nothing and no one stand in the way of your ambitions! Oh, I know I'm an old woman, brought up in a different age, but women today have more choice. More freedom to shape their own destiny. Don't fall into the poverty trap, keep your goal clearly in sight and don't be swayed by arguments or promises! I wish I had the chances you have. The freedom and the rest of my life ahead of me instead of behind me. Fight for your dream, Catherine, and don't give up!'

Cat smiled at her, wondering what circumstances had driven her to speak so forcefully about freedom and choice. She had also given her the encouragement she needed and a few harsh facts to think about. She rose. 'I won't! I won't ever give up! I'll make it one day and you'll be proud of me!' Suddenly it became so important that this frail old lady should respect her.

'Unfortunately, I doubt that I'll live long enough to see that day, but I have great faith in you!'

Cat drew out the duster. There was work to be done and she wasn't going to sit around moping for the likes of Joe Calligan.

'Remember what I said. Don't marry a sailor!' The gentle voice with overtones of humorous remorse floated after her as she left the room.

CHAPTER SIX

The following week it snowed and the roads and pavements quickly became treacherous as a heavy frost set in. It was Mrs Travis's custom to take tea with Mother Superior at the Convent of Notre Dame every Wednesday afternoon. For many years she had been a benefactress to both the nuns and the church of Our Lady Immaculate in Saint Domingo Road. Cat, who on the Wednesday after Joe's departure had no desire to go to Eldon Street, offered to escort her, seeing how slippery it had become underfoot.

'I'll come back here and keep the fires banked up, finish the mending and then nip back for you. You usually leave about five o'clock don't you?'

'That's very kind of you, Catherine, it is difficult to cross that road even at the best of times.'

So, wrapped in heavy coats, scarves and golloshes, they walked slowly and carefully the few hundred yards to the convent gates. Cat helped her mistress up the steep flight of steps but as a black-robed figure opened the door, she turned and left. As she stepped out on to the icy pavement she collided with another girl and they both slipped and landed on their buttocks. Cat was about to launch into a tirade of accusations when she noticed that the girl was wearing the regulation uniform of the convent school and that she was laughing.

'What a cut we must look!' she gasped. 'Here, give me your hand and I'll pull you up or we'll both have wet drawers!'

Cat took the proffered hand and they stumbled to their feet. Cat's own eyes were full of laughter at the black velour hat with the wide brim, that Joe had described as looking like a po, for the fall had knocked it over one of the girl's eyes. It also amused her to hear this convent-bred girl talking of 'drawers'. Whenever she had seen the girls from the convent, walking in single file and flanked by the nuns, they had all looked so prim and proper. This one certainly didn't fit into either category.

The girl smiled at her. 'We've just been let loose for the holidays!'

She presented a comic figure in the long navy-blue coat, black wellington boots, navy-blue woollen gloves and that awful hat on which was pinned a badge depicting a sprig of Lily of the Valley and some gold lettering. Cat smiled again.

'What's so funny?' The girl demanded.

'That hat!'

She straightened it but it didn't look much better for it seemed to rest on her ears. A fringe of sandy-blonde hair protruded from beneath the brim and hung in loose curls over her shoulders. 'It's bloody awful, isn't it, but we have to wear them otherwise there's hell to pay! What's your name? Mine's Marie Hazel Gorry.'

Cat was shocked. Only men and sluts like her sister used words like that. 'Cat Cleary, it's short for Catherine,' she stammered, forstalling the usual question.

'Do you live round here?'

'Sort of. I'm in service with Mrs Travis.'

'Oh, her! She's the one who comes to tea with Mother Exterior every week!'

'Don't you mean "Superior"?'

'No. All those sweet smiles and pious looks are "exterior", underneath she's a holy terror! Where are you going?'

'Back to Mrs Travis's house, I'm collecting her at five.'

'Oh.' She sounded disappointed.

'Aren't you going home? Do you live round here?'

'No, I have to get the tram to Walton.' She brightened. 'Walk down Royal Street with me, there's a park at the bottom – Lester Gardens – we can talk!'

'It's freezing!' Cat protested.

'It's not that bad!'

Cat warmed to her. She had experienced little company of girls of her own age, although this one looked a bit younger. Cat surmised that if your parents could afford to pay for you to go to an expensive school, then you obviously stayed there a lot longer than if you went to an ordinary school. She nodded and so hanging on to each other for support they made their way precariously across the road, presenting an incongruous and rather comical sight.

Her new-found friend chattered on while Cat listened, mesmerised, of tales of life at a convent school as seen through the eyes of Marie Hazel Gorry. When she could get a word in edgewise, she asked her about her rather unusual name.

Well, our Mam – only I'm not supposed to call her that, I have to say "Mother" or "Mummy",' she grimaced, 'wanted to call me something different,

105

a bit unusual and she'd read this novel where the heroine's name was Hazel. But when they took me to be baptised they had to have a good Catholic name as well, so I got both.' She jerked her head back in the direction of the convent and the hat slipped down again. She pushed it up. 'They call me Marie, 'cos when I started there – when I was six – Mother Exterior said Hazel was the name of a nut and that there was nothing remotely saintly about a nut, so everyone must call me just Marie. Everyone at home calls me Marie, too, except our Mam.'

'Have you been at the convent since you were six? How old are you now?'

'Nearly sixteen. I'm leaving soon, once I've matriculated.'

'What's that?'

'Passed my exams.' She indicated the satchel slung over one shoulder.

'What will you do then?'

'Oh, they've already sorted that out – not that I had much say in the matter! I'm going to Machin & Harper's Commercial College in Colquitt Street, off Bold Street. To learn shorthand and typing and "Office Procedures". I'm to be a secretary when they get finished with me.' Again she jerked her head in the direction of the convent. 'They wanted me to go on and be a teacher, but I've had enough of kids and schools to last a lifetime!'

They had reached the bottom of Royal Streeet and crossed the road, trudging through the grey slush churned up by the trams, carts and lorries, for Walton Road was a main road and always busy with traffic. As they entered Lester Gardens a group of urchins who had been pelting each other with snowballs, stopped and stared at them. Then one lad, bolder than the rest chanted mockingly:

> 'Catty, catty go to Mass
> Riding on the Devil's ass!'

Marie Hazel glared at him.

> 'Proddy, proddy on the wall
> A penny bun to feed yez all!'

she yelled back.

It was obvious she was well used to dealing with the insults frequently hurled at known Catholics in this mainly Protestant area. The religious divisions were deep and cut across all sections of society, but among the poorer classes were more virulent. Cat herself had been the object of this kind of abuse on more than one occasion. On St Patrick's Day and Orangeman's Day there were always fights between the rival factions which had been known to degenerate into full-scale riots.

The lad came closer, thinking he was dealing with one of the quieter, more refined girls from the convent. 'Eh, girl, lend us yer 'at, we're 'avin' soup!' he mocked and the others doubled up with laughter.

Marie Hazel was nonplussed. 'You should be on the stage, lad! The landing stage, feedin' bread to gummy pigeons!'

This time the laugh was on him and he bent down and picked up a handful of snow. Marie Hazel was too quick for him. With a well-aimed swipe she caught him across the head with her satchel. He roared with pain and the others fled.

'You wait, girl! I'll get me Da onter youse, 'e'll sort yer out! Bleedin' Papist!' he bawled.

'Oh, aye, him and whose army? I'll get my Da and my six brothers to sort you lot out! Now sod off!'

Cat fell on to the park bench, convulsed with laughter. She'd never met anyone quite like this girl.

Marie Hazel had snatched off the offending headgear and sat down beside her. 'Our Mam doesn't know what I have to put up with from this lot round here! It's the same every day!'

'Have you really got six brothers?'

'Don't be daft!'

'How many of you are there?'

'Me, my elder sisters Doreen and Marlene, my eldest brother Tom, but he's married, and Mam and Dad, of course.'

It was still a big family, Cat thought, and they couldn't be short of money either. 'What does your Dad do?'

'He's in business. Coal. We've got four lorries. He owns some houses, too, and rents them out.'

She had deduced correctly.

'He inherited the business from my grandfather. He started with one horse and cart. A right rum old thing he was, too. Married my grandmother when he was sixty and she was only in her twenties. She came from Ireland. You're Irish, aren't you?'

'Yes, from Dublin.'

'She came from Tipperary. We went there on holiday once. It rained every day!'

Cat digested all this. It had never occurred to her that an Irish immigrant could end up a wealthy man, owning a thriving business to pass on to his son. If he could do it, so could she and she remembered her conversation with Mrs Travis. At the thought of her mistress she also remembered her promise. She stood up. 'I'll have to go now. I was supposed to bank up the fires and do some mending before I collected her at five. What time is it, do you know?'

Marie Hazel had a watch and she pushed up the sleeve of her coat. 'Nearly quarter to five. I'd better go myself or our Mam will have the police out looking for me!' She seemed reluctant to go, even though it was dark and they were both shivering.

Cat guessed that with no sisters at home close to her own age, and because quite obviously she wasn't the usual type of pupil at the convent, she was looking for a kindred spirit. 'Well, it's been grand talking to you. I'll have to run back now.'

'You won't get into trouble will you for not doing the chores?'

Cat smiled, she seemed genuinely concerned. 'No, she's as good as gold to me and it really is my afternoon off.'

'Do you get other days off?'

'Sundays, but I usually go to see my Ma, she lives in Eldon Street.'

'Oh.' There was a note of disappointment in her voice.

'But I don't stay all day, not every week,' she replied, thinking of Joe.

'Come to tea on Sunday afternoon then?'

'Oh, I couldn't do that!'

'Why not? We're not snobs, everyone's welcome in our house! I'll tell them you're coming, they're always asking me why I don't bring friends home like the others do!'

Cat was perturbed. She liked Marie Hazel Gorry but she doubted that Mrs Gorry would be very impressed with her daughter's choice of friend. Probably the friends of her other children came from the same background they did and that was still very different from hers.

'Come at three o'clock. It's number eighteen Yew Tree Road, it's at the top of Rice Lane, past Walton Hospital! Get the number 22 or 30 tram – it stops on the corner. Tell you what, I'll meet you! Oh, here's my tram! See you on Sunday!'

Cat watched her running along the pavement, slipping in her haste. She caught the tram and stood on the platform, waving her school hat. 'I haven't got much choice!' she said aloud. She'd just have to go and endure it. She shrugged. She'd usually had enough of her family and the O'Dwyers by lunchtime anyway and with Joe away ... Oh, why not, she thought, it would be an experience. Even if she was politely shown the door after one quick cup of tea. At least she could go and see for herself the proof that an Irish immigrant could become rich and respected.

She alighted from the number 22 tram on the corner of Yew Tree Road at 2.55 to find Marie waiting for her. She was dressed in a bright red coat with black velvet collar and cuffs, her long, strawberry blonde hair covered by a red Tam-o-Shanter edged with black velvet. Cat's apprehension deepened as she pulled her bottle-green plain, tweed coat closer to her. A small green beret was pinned to her hair and she felt plain and dowdy.

'I wasn't sure if you'd come. You didn't sound very enthusiastic.'

'You didn't give me much choice. What did your mother say when you told her?'

'She said, "Good, it's about time you had a friend of your own age." '

'Didn't you tell her that I don't go to your school, that I'm in service?'

'Of course I did! I told you she's not a snob!'

Cat looked around at the houses as they walked up the quiet street. They were large and well-built but not grandiose. The road was wide and tree-lined and quietly affluent. Some of the houses even had cars parked outside. Even Mrs Travis didn't own a car.

Marie pushed open the wrought-iron gate that led into a well-kept garden and Cat followed, slowing her steps as her new friend opened the front door. The hallway was wide and a staircase swept up one side of it. On her right was a door with stained-glass windows which proved to be a cloakroom.

'She's here!' Marie called. 'Give me your coat and hat!'

Cat complied and the garments were duly hung up while she smoothed down her dark-grey skirt and pulled down the grey jumper to which she had added a small lace collar. Both had been bought from Marks & Spencer for the occasion. Marie wore a paisley-patterned wool dress that was obviously expensive.

'Come on in and meet everyone, they won't bite!'

With mounting apprehension Cat slowly followed her into a large room furnished with good, solid

111

furniture. Heavy curtains reached from the ceiling to the floor and flanked french windows that opened out on to the walled back garden. A roaring fire burned in the modern fireplace.

'Come on in and warm yourself, you look half-starved!'

Encouraged by the unexpectedly friendly greeting she ventured further into the room. Mrs Gorry was a buxom woman with fair hair and blue eyes that crinkled when she smiled. Mr Gorry was a tall, thin man with greying hair and a pair of spectacles perched on the end of his nose. He smiled and she began to relax. Of the two older Gorry girls there was no sign.

'I said to you, Bernard, didn't I, that it was about time our Hazel had a nice friend. Come and sit down here, it's warmer. Hazel, go and see if those two have finished doing the tea, will you?'

Mr Gorry lowered his newspaper. 'Don't fuss, Leila.'

Mrs Gorry tutted. 'It's Polly's day off, so our Doreen and Marlene are making the tea. It will probably be stone cold, the cake will be burnt and the sandwiches curled up at the edges!'

Cat was taken aback afresh. They had a servant, too, yet they seemed so . . . ordinary. There were no airs and graces about them.

'Do what your mother tells you, Marie, or we'll get no peace!'

It seemed strange to Cat that only Mrs Gorry called her daughter Hazel.

'So you work for Mrs Travis, Cat?' Mrs Gorry continued. There was no questioning about her name, but before she could answer Mrs Gorry carried on. 'Some of my relations are called Travis, but I don't think she's one of us.'

Feeling obliged to make conversation Cat said, 'Marie . . . I mean Hazel, tells me that you have a coal business and that your parents came from Ireland.'

Mr Gorry nodded. But it was his wife who answered. 'His mother came from Ireland. The old man was Manx. Came from the Isle of Man originally. Oh, but she was a lovely woman was Mary O'Donnell. A saint. Went to Mass every day of her life, even when she was dying of consumption. But he was a cantankerous old so-and-so! I never met him, he died before I met Mr Gorry. Eighty he was when he died!'

Before she could embark on the family history any further the door opened and two older replicas of Marie appeared. Smartly dressed and laden with trays of sandwiches, cakes and a china tea service.

'You must be Cat, Marie's friend. I'm Doreen and this is Marlene.'

Cat liked them both instantly. All her fears vanished and she basked in the warmth of the fire and the friendship extened to her by this rather unique family, who although they were obviously well off, did not look down their noses at her or patronise her, but who seemed to accept her as an old and valued friend.

Mrs Gorry ushered them all to the table and began to fuss over the milk that Marlene had slopped from the jug.

'She's always like this, she's a real scatterbrain at times,' Marie whispered, handing Cat a delicate bone-china cup.

After tea Cat insisted on helping to wash up, despite protests from Mrs Gorry that she was a guest and that either 'the girls' could do the dishes later, or Polly would do them in the morning. After that Marie took her on a tour of the house while her sisters got ready to go out dancing. It was a far more modern and well-designed house than Mrs Travis's. There were no small pokey rooms or narrow passages. It was tastefully decorated and furnished and had an upstairs bathroom and toilet. It also had a narrow staircase that led from the kitchen to the upstairs landing and was obviously meant for Polly's use, for a servant would be expected to use the back-stairs. But it appeared that everyone else used it as well.

In the parlour with its fine furniture and orna-ments and rich Persian carpet stood Marie's particular pride and joy. A pianola. An instrument that looked like a piano and sounded like a piano but produced the music from rolls of paper, per-forated with holes, which were fitted over a metal cylinder. It was worked by pressing up and down on two pedals at the base. Cat was mesmerised at the way the keys moved by themselves.

'You can use it as a proper piano as well, but Dad bought it because he got so fed up with listening to us all practice. We all learned to play but none of us is any good at it. Go on, have a go!'

For the next half hour the sounds of Strauss, Schubert and Gershwin filled the room while Cat and Marie took it in turns, with great flourishes and peals of laughter, to pretend that they were both actually pressing the keys and playing the music.

All too soon it was six o'clock. Cat was reluctant

to leave but she was always back with Mrs Travis by seven on Sunday nights. Marie wanted to walk with her to the tram but Mrs Gorry insisted that her husband drive Cat back, telling Marie that she could go too. It was the first time Cat had ever been in a car and, she found the journey quiet, luxurious and warm. She was loath to step out of the car when it stopped for it was like stepping out of a dream. She felt she had found a new world and Mrs Travis's words came back to her again. She *did* have more choice, there *were* better things in life and success was not unattainable. The Gorrys had proved all that. She thanked Mr Gorry profusely, wishing she had some small gift to give him, wishing she had a father like him.

Marie poked her head out of the window. 'Will you come again next week, Cat?'

'Can I?'

'You're welcome any time, Cat', Mr Gorry said, patting her hand.

'See you next week!' Marie called as the car pulled away.

Cat hugged herself. At last she'd found a friend, a real friend and how she envied Marie. Not for the material things she possessed, but for the warmth, affection and security of a closely knit, loving family. A family into which she had been welcomed. She hoped it would last, this new friendship, but instinct warned her that nothing lasted forever. That people change and circumstances change. But as she watched the car disappear little did she know that she had just forged the links of a friendship that was to last for the whole of her life.

CHAPTER SEVEN

The *Marguerita* docked in Liverpool on 22 December and Joe was signed off. There was to be no second trip, so with his pay in his pocket and the gifts he had bought for Cat and Mrs Travis, he made his way, with mixed feelings, back towards the home of his old employer. Although he had missed Cat, he had felt the blood pound in his veins as the deck had rolled under his feet, the salt spray had stung his face and the cold North wind had cut through his duffle coat. Not that he had spent much time up on deck. The engine room, cramped, smelly and ankle-deep in bilge water had been his domain. One of the crew had failed to turn up and he had been promoted to Stoker and for this he had been paid the princely sum of £1 12s.

Cat was up to her elbows in flour, making (under supervision) the mince pies, when the knocker echoed through the house. 'Oh drat!' she exclaimed.

'You stay and finish that pastry, I'll go!' Mrs Travis instructed.

Joe's expression changed when he saw the frail figure that opened the door to him. He had been expecting Cat.

'Home is the sailor, home from the sea! Come in, Joe!'

'Thanks. May I see Cat?'

Mrs Travis nodded as she ushered him down the hallway and into the kitchen.

Cat gave a little cry of surprise, dropped the rolling pin and wiping her hands on her apron, rushed to him.

He held her at arm's length, laughing. 'You've got flour on your nose but you look wonderful!'

'When did you get in?'

'This morning.'

Cat looked uncertainly at her mistress but the old lady gestured her to sit down.

'The pies will wait. I think a little drop of Madeira is called for.' She opened the cupboard and took out three glasses and poured a small amount into each glass. She handed one to Joe who held it as though it would snap between his fingers.

'To your safe return and to the festive season!'

Cat took the glass from her, having washed her hands, and sipped the sweet wine. There was a tenseness in the air and she knew Joe felt it, too, as he slowly twisted his empty glass between his fingers.

'Did you have a good trip?' she asked, to break the silence.

'Not bad.'

'Well . . . ?'

He delved into his kit bag and pulled out two parcels. 'I bought you this, I was going to save it for Christmas but you might as well have it now.'

She took the parcel from him and began to carefully unwrap it. Inside was a box. She lifted the lid and a brooch, shaped like a butterfly, nestled on a bed of cotton wool. Brightly coloured stones formed its wings and gold wire its body and antennae. She knew the stones weren't real gems but she had never owned a single piece of jewellery. 'Oh, it's beautiful! Look how all the colours glow in the light! Oh, Joe, thank you!'

'Aren't you going to put it on?'

'No, I'm keeping it to wear with my best clothes. I'll pin it to my coat. Oh, it's lovely!' She wanted to fling her arms around him and tell him how she had missed him, but the presence of the old lady stopped her.

Joe stood up and placed a second parcel into Mrs Travis's hands. She was surprised.

'You shouldn't have wasted your money on me, Joe!'

'I wanted to.'

She pulled off the wrapping paper to reveal an elephant carved in ebony with long tusks of ivory and two smaller elephants completed the set. 'You must have searched hard for something like this, they're not the sort of thing you can pick up easily.'

'I bought them from an old Chinese cook, I thought you'd like them.'

'I do, I like them a great deal but are they a form of bribe?'

He looked abashed.

Cat looked from one to the other. They had obviously cost him more than the butterfly brooch. Obviously they were not keeping him on and he had come back for his old job. The little frown disappeared when she saw that Mrs Travis was smiling.

'So, you've come back to us then? Well, I did promise to hold your job open, didn't I? Do you still want it?'

He nodded, twisting his cap between his hands. He was grateful to her but it hurt his masculine pride to have to come, tail between his legs, to get his

119

job back. His hopes had been so high. He had promised himself he was never going to take a shore job again. But it was a hard winter and there was little work for, although the Port was thriving, the country was not and Liverpool was not the only city in the grip of unemployment, economic and social depression. 'Take what you can, lad, until things pick up!' the captain of the *Marguerita* had advised. But it still galled him that he had to settle for second best. One day he'd get a steady job at sea. One day he'd make it. He realised that Cat was speaking to him.

'At least I'll have someone to help me get the tree home from the market and put up the holly!'

He smiled at her. 'I come in handy for some things then?'

'Aye, that you do!'

That Christmas was the one Cat swore she would always remember, no matter how long she lived. It was the first 'real' Christmas she'd ever had, she told Joe as they struggled home on the tram on Christmas Eve. He with the tree and boughs of holly and she with the goose, vegetables and the fruit. Everyone was in festive mood. The market stallholders, shop-keepers, policemen and the crowds of shoppers who thronged Church Street, congregating around the huge Christmas tree while the Salvation Army band played carols. Even the conductor of the packed tramcar sported a sprig of holly in his buttonhole and one of mistletoe in his cap and demanded a kiss from all the women who crushed aboard. There were many ribald remarks from some of the older ones, too. To his jocular 'Move along there, Ma, there's hundreds waiting behind yer!' came the reply, 'If I move up any more I'll be drivin' the tram meself an' we'll all end up in Church Street!' Which caused more ribald remarks as to who would look best, dressed up as the Christmas Fairy, the old shawlie or the driver!

They had decorated the tree and then Joe had sat by the warmth of the kitchen fire and watched as she had plucked and cleaned the bird and prepared it for roasting. Then he had helped her prepare the vegetables.

Mrs Travis had asked her if she wanted to spend the holiday with her family, but comparing the comfort and warmth of her surroundings with those of the little house in Eldon Street, she declined the offer, although she was to go home early Christmas morning and stay until just before lunch.

'Why don't you bring your mother and Eamon here for dinner?' Mrs Travis had generously offered.

'She wouldn't come. She'd feel uncomfortable and as for our Eamon, his table manners would disgrace a pig, so they would! But thank you, you're very kind.'

So she had gone home with her brown-paper carrier-bag of gifts and was surprised to find everyone up and the little house decked out with paper chains and holly. The big table, which took up most of the kitchen, was laid with a red cloth and was already set for the meal. On the old dresser stood bottles of ale and a bottle of cheap sherry.

'I see someone's been busy or has Santa come early?' she laughed as she kissed her mother's cheek.

'Oh, Ellen and me went down the market late last night. They're practically givin' stuff away by ten o'clock! Perked 'er up no end, too! Now youse lot, sit still while I get me 'at and youse can gerra cloth an' wipe our Ethel's fingers an' that toffee from round 'er mouth. It's a good job she's too young for Communion!' Maisey instructed the eldest of her brood. ' 'Ave you been eatin', our Dora?'

'No, Mam!'

'Yer'd berra be tellin' the truth! Father Maguire can sniff out food like a blood 'ound an yer'll disgrace us all if yer get turned away from the altar rail!'

Cat delved into the brown-paper bag. 'Is there time for me to give them their presents, Maisey?'

Maisey paused, still poking whisps of hair under a dark-blue felt hat that had seen better days. 'Aye, luv, go on, but hurry up!'

She felt like Lady Bountiful as she handed out the presents. She had bought something for everyone. Packets of toffees and Everton Mints for all the O'Dwyer children. A pair of silk stockings for Maisey who declared she had never had anything so fine for years and quickly moved her ample bulk into the scullery to put them on. There was a tie for Mr O'Dwyer and another for her father, although she had begrudged spending anything on him and it was only at Joe's prompting that she had done so. For Eamon there was *The Boys Own Annual* with which he was not very impressed and a big bag of coloured glass marbles, with which he was, taking each one and holding it up to the light. For Shelagh she had bought a colourful headscarf in shades of pink, purple and lilac. She had deliberately left it in the 'Owen Owen's' bag, as this was one of the better-class shops that Shelagh did not frequent. She received a cold peck on the cheek and a muttered 'Thanks, it's lovely' in return.

All her savings had gone towards her mother's present. She had discussed with both Mrs Travis and Marie just what she could buy but it had been Marie who had come up with the most inspired and touching suggestion.

'If you buy her anything like jewellery it will spend most of its time in pawn.'

'Anything I buy will!' she had retorted.

'So write off to the Cenacle Convent.'

'What for?'

'If you send them five shillings, they will say a Mass for her every day for a year and will send a nice Mass card and a lovely rosary. He can't pawn them, can he?'

Cat thought about it. It was rather a strange gift, but her mother was a devoutly Catholic woman who would appreciate the prayers offered up at Mass on her behalf by the nuns. She would also appreciate and treasure the rosary beads and neither would be pawned. So she had done as Marie had suggested and had received in return a Mass card bearing a coloured picture of the Nativity inscribed,

> A Mass will be said for Ellen Cleary
> every day for a year at this Convent.
> This is the gift of her daughter,
> Catherine Cleary.

Accompanying it was a rosary of imitation pearls in its own little white-leather purse, engraved with a gold cross. Feeling that this was not enough, Cat bought a pair of warm knitted gloves, around the wrists of which was threaded bright ribbon, decorated with two tassels.

The glow she felt from being able to distribute

such largesse, to bring such gasps of delight and such obvious happiness, grew as her mother first tried on the gloves, exclaiming over the tassels. But it was with eyes full of tears that she reverently opened the card and read the inscription. There were tears in Cat's eyes as Ellen drew out the rosary and spread it across her thin, chapped hand.

'Oh, Cat . . . Cat . . . !' Ellen Cleary's words became choked as a sob caught in her throat.

'I wanted to get you something very special, Ma, something more than just a brooch or gloves!'

'You couldn't have given me anything more . . . more beautiful . . .' She choked again, then held up the card to Maisey.

'What's all the fuss about a card?' Shelagh grumbled, craning her neck to peer over Maisey's shoulder. Trust Cat to go one better than her! And she'd spent 1s 6d on a bottle of lavender water and her mother had only kissed her, put it to one side and said 'You shouldn't have spent so much on me, Shelagh.'

Maisey read out the inscription in a strangely strangled tone, then blew her nose loudly on her clean handkerchief. 'Yer've got one to be proud of 'ere, Ellen!' She struggled to find the right word. 'One who thinks! She's . . . sensitive!'

'What's sen . . . sen . . . that word mean, our Mam?' Dora enquired, for a strange atmosphere had suddenly descended on the room.

'It means she really understands 'er Mam an' what she *really* likes, an' 'as got 'er somethin' special – that can't end up in Stanley's pawnshop every Monday mornin'! Eh, yer've gorra proper little treasure there, Ellen!'

The warm glow had continued as Cat, the butter-fly brooch pinned to the lapel of her coat, tucked her mother's gloved hand through her arm as in bright, crisp sunlight they all trouped around the corner to Our Lady's to morning Mass.

The festive atmosphere had disappeared without trace two weeks later when, in driving rain that stung her cheeks, Cat paid her weekly visit home. Blowing off the Mersey was a 'lazy' wind, as people called it, for it cut through you instead of going around you. She knew there was something seriously wrong as soon as she opened the kitchen door. The room was silent. Her mother sat huddled close to the pitiful fire that was struggling against the down-draught from the chimney. Maisey was peeling potatoes in a bowl at the table and of Shelagh, her Pa, Eamon and the entire O'Dwyer brood there was no sign.

'What's the matter? Where is everyone?'

'Out!' Maisey's lips snapped closed into a thin line.

As this was unheard of Cat crossed and placed a hand on her mother's shoulder. 'Ma . . . ?' Her question died as her mother turned towards her. The right side of her face was badly swollen, her lip cut and her eye half-closed and surrounded by purplish-blue bruising.

'Oh, my God!' Cat whirled around and faced Maisey. 'Where is he? Where's that swine, I'll kill him! I'll kill him with my own two hands!'

'Cat, he didn't mean to . . .' The words came thickly from her mother's swollen lips.

Maisey thumped the bowl down hard on the table. 'It was all 'er fault, that little slut!'

'Shelagh?'

125

'Right! Cum 'ome drunk an' with 'er blouse all undone an' her skirt all torn! Yer Da, who'd 'ad one too many 'imself, laid into 'er, yellin' at 'er, callin' 'er a whore, a common little tart. An' he's right! She's the talk of the street, carryin' on . . .'

'What's that got to do with . . .'

' 'E took 'is belt off and laid into 'er. Give 'er a good thrashin! Holy Mother of God! Yer could 'ear the screams all the way t' the Pierhead! Yer Mam tried t' stop 'im an' he caught 'er with the buckle end.'

Cat's eyes blazed with a ferocious green light. 'Where is she, Maisey?'

'All the neighbours was out, someone went fer Father Maguire, but the scuffers arrived first!'

'So she's in jail?'

'No. I told 'em t' clear off, that we sort out ourselves an' hadn't a father the right to give 'is own daughter a good hidin' for the way she'd been carryin' on, disgracin' us all! They went off, saying, "Alright, Ma, seeing as it's a domestic we won't interfere, as long as it doesn't get out of hand." Then Father Maguire arrived. 'E calmed yer Pa down, talked ter yer Mam an' carted that slut off with 'im!'

'So where are they now?'

'Yer Pa was collared by Himself after Mass. I 'ope Himself gives 'im a good talkin' to, an' as fer 'er . . . I won't 'ave 'er over me doorstep again! Norreven if the Pope 'imself were ter ask me!'

'So where is she?'

'Sent packin' ter some 'ome fer wayward girls.'

Cat sank down on the floor and took her mother's hand. She was still seething. If only she could get her mother out of this house. To the little home she dreamed of providing – one day. Frustration was added to fury. She was no nearer to the White Empress than she had been the day she landed. Mrs Travis had been kindness itself but she couldn't ask her to take her mother in. 'Are you sure you're alright, Ma?'

'A bit shaken . . .'

She clasped the trembling hand in her own, wishing vehemently she could get her hands on both her sister and her father. 'I'll stay as long as I can, Maisey. He won't be in a very good mood when he gets back!'

Maisey grunted. She was a God-fearing woman, a hard worker and she was respected by her neighbours and if it hadn't been for Ellen she would quite cheerfully have thrown the lot of them out on the streets.

They had all crept back, one by one. Mid-afternoon saw her father enter the house in the company of Mr O'Dwyer and the parish priest. He was somewhat shaken for Father Maguire had far more influence and was held in far more esteem than a station full of 'scuffers'. After ascertaining that Mrs Cleary was alright and informing them all that from now on he expected no more trouble at all, he turned to leave.

'Father, where is my sister?'

The stern features relaxed a little as he looked at Cat. 'Ah, Catherine. Don't you be worrying over that one, she's with the Sisters of Charity.'

She nodded. Despite their name she knew Shelagh would find little charity with them. It served her right.

The atmosphere had livened up a little after the priest's exit. The younger children resorted to their usual noisy horseplay, Maisey to her boisterous denunciation of them all and Mr O'Dwyer to his newspaper.

Her father remained white-faced and silent. She had never held a very high opinion of him. She had hoped he would change, but since they had arrived he had been content to shove the burden of his wife and family on to someone else. She despised him even more now. The only thing that could be said in his defence was that at last he had shown some parental responsiblity, although it had taken a bellyful of ale to bring that about. And to the detriment of her poor mother.

She was reluctant to leave but as seven o'clock drew nearer she picked up her hat and coat. Maisey followed her to the door and Cat pressed the coins into her hand.

'If anything else like that ever happens, or . . . or if she comes back, send one of the kids straight up for me, Maisey.'

'It won't 'appen again, cos she's not cumin' back 'ere, an' as fer 'im, 'e gets 'is courage out of a bottle an' if 'e starts, I'll be straight round fer the priest!'

'Oh, I wish I could take her with me!'

'Well, yer can't, luv, an' that's that! Yer doin' everythin' yer can for 'er, God knows! Now, ger-roff with yer, yer'll be late!'

CHAPTER EIGHT

As she lay in bed that night listening to the rain lashing against the small attic windows, she tossed and turned, thinking of her mother in the cold, cheerless bedroom at Eldon Street. She must do something! The dreaming *had* to become reality. She pulled the quilt up to her chin, her feet curled around the stone jar with its tight rubber stopper, filled with hot water. Such comforts were denied her poor Ma. She made her decision. On Wednesday afternoon she would go to The Pool and if she got no satisfaction, she'd go to the offices of Canadian Pacific. She had to do something positive, she couldn't just wait and dream. Even if, like Joe, she had to go to every shipping line and beg, she'd do it. Joe had got the job on the *Marguerita* in the end!

She wore her best coat and hat, her only coat and hat, and had polished her shoes until they gleamed, but gazing at her reflection she realised she didn't present a very smart picture. She felt drab and plain.

As she got off the tram it started to rain and her shoes became dull and splashed. The wind blew her hair across her face in damp, untidy whisps. The walk to Mann Island across the dirty cobbles added to the dejection that was already setting in, but she pushed open the door of The Pool and went straight to the counter. A middle-aged man in a rather shabby suit looked up from his paperwork.

'Yes, luv?'

'I've come to see if there are any vacancies for stewardesses?'

He looked her up and down quickly. 'Had any experience? Have you got your Discharge Book?'

'What's that?'

He sighed. '*Seaman's Record Book and Certificate of Discharge*. It's like a passport.'

'No. I didn't know I needed one.'

'Never been to sea before. Thought not!'

'Well, where can I get one?'

'You can't, unless you've got a job – a ship.'

'That's what I came here for!' She was getting impatient.

He leaned forward across the counter. 'Look, luv, we get dozens of girls in here, all looking for work on the liners. We don't take you on here. You have to go to the company and they decide if you're, well . . . suitable!'

'And you don't think I am?'

He sighed again. 'I'll be honest, no good building up your hopes. No. You're probably a good worker, honest, decent, but that's not enough for them and the competition is tough!'

'Isn't there a form or something I can fill in?' she pleaded.

'I can register you, that's all. You go up to the Liver Buildings and see them, you may be lucky! Tell them Arthur Hanson sent you, it may help.'

She nodded her thanks and turned away.

She crossed the windswept pierhead, the rain soaking into her cheap coat. She felt cold and dejected. She had known it wouldn't be easy. As she entered the Royal Liver Buildings a porter stopped her and asked her her business. He directed her to the offices she asked for. Canadian Pacific, Cunard and the Booth Line. Her confidence waned with each step she took up the flight of wide stairs. She was so nervous by the time a haughty-looking clerk in a stiff, winged collar asked in clipped tones what she wanted, she could only stammer, 'I . . . I want to go to sea!'

'Any experience?'

She shook her head.

'Sorry, we've no vacancies! Try Cunard, White Star.'

Her hand was shaking as she pulled open the door. She had forgotten how it felt to have to beg. Her thoughts flew back to those cold, winter days in Dublin when, as a child, she had accosted the wealthier citizens begging for 'a halfpenny please, sir? Tis starved I am!' She couldn't go on! She leaned against the wall. She *had* to! Joe had!

She received the same treatment in the Cunard office but resolutely pressed on, her self-confidence in tatters. The polished wooden counters, carpeted floors and tastefully framed prints of their ships, the offices of the Booth Steam Ship Company exuded quiet, old-fashioned gentility. The clerk was a middle-aged man in a dark suit and stiff white collar. It appeared to be a uniform among shipping clerks.

'May I be of assistance, miss?'

She took courage from his tone and manner. It was neither openly hostile nor arrogantly patronising. 'I've come to see if . . . well, if you might be having any vacancies for a stewardess?'

'Have you been to The Pool?'

'I have that, sir. Arthur Hanson told me to try . . . here.'

'He often does tell them that.'

'Even . . . even if you don't have anything right now, could I put my name on a list or something?'

'We are an old-established company, miss?'

'Cleary.' She supplied eagerly. At least he was treating her as a person of some account.

'Well, Miss Cleary, our ships are away for nine months of the year, we sail up the River Amazon – that's Brazil – and we don't carry too many lady passengers so therefore we don't employ many stewardesses. The ones we have have been with us for years and are likely to remain until they retire. Have you tried Cunard, White Star or Canadian Pacific?'

The tiny ray of hope that had flickered at his pleasant treatment of her, died. 'Both.'

'I'm sorry. There are others.'

She turned away and then turned back to him. 'Sir, I was told that to be a stewardess I would need to have qualifications, to talk properly and be able to get on with people. Is that the truth of it? Is that why they won't take me on?'

He placed the pen he was holding neatly down in front of him in a precise, definite movement. Then he clasped his hands. 'Yes, most of that is true, sadly.'

She turned and ran. Everything Joe had said was true! How could she have ever believed she could turn that dream into reality! Because she had risen, with Joe's help and Mrs Travis's, a step higher than the slum girl she had been, she had thought she could just walk in and expect to be handed her dream. It was patently obvious that she was still little

132

more than that Dublin slummy who had stepped off the cattle boat! And it hurt. It hurt so much that her chest felt tight, her throat was dry and her eyes burned with unshed tears! She had no chance. No chance at all!

'Settle for what you have,' Joe had said, but she had refused to listen to him. Now it was a fact she could no longer refute. 'Never give up your dream! Fight for your ambitions, Catherine!' Mrs Travis's words. But there was no fight left in her now. There was nothing she could do except go back to Everton Valley and try to come to terms with defeat.

There was no one she could tell about the disastrous attempt. She couldn't go to Mrs Travis and tell her she was looking for an alternative job, not when she had been so kind. She was afraid Joe would sympathise and pity her, but would also say 'I told you so' and even her severely lacerated pride wouldn't tolerate that. She was tempted to tell Marie, but she felt she hadn't known her long enough; that their friendship wasn't yet so close. She knew it was pride that kept her tongue silent. What little she had left of it. So she was miserable and silent and not even her visits to Marie's could dispel her utter dejection that was increased when Joe again got a month's work on the *Marguerita*.

He and Mrs Travis had a very long talk in the parlour and he had told her later that they had come to an agreement. The old lady understood his restlessness and agreed that, whenever the opportunity arose, he should take it. She would manage, he did his work well enough to be absent for the odd month or two whenever he managed to get a ship.

Despite Maisey's threats Shelagh had returned home and whenever Cat paid her Sunday visit there was an argument between them. Shelagh resented the security and luxury she lived in. She was jealous of the few clothes Cat had, for they were of a superior quality to her own and made Cat appear older, smarter and more attractive than herself. All she wanted out of life was a bit of fun, surely that wasn't too bad, but Cat always seemed to be looking down her nose at her, disapproving. Cat blamed Shelagh for the decline in her mother's health. She caused nothing but worry and trouble. She wasn't stupid – she could get a better position if she worked harder and took things more seriously. She could be more considerate, she should help more in the house instead of complaining. But Shelagh had always been lazy and selfish and Cat knew that it was only her mother's pleadings that had swayed Maisey to take her back.

One spring morning she was walking up the street on her way home. She walked slowly, not really wanting to go at all. She was more dejected than usual for Joe had sailed the previous day. This time he would be away for nearly three months and had been promoted to donkey man, keeping the donkey boiler going at all times. The *Marguerita* was tramping around the ports of Europe and was even venturing as far as the Mediterranean, hopefully, he had said. Marie was working hard for examinations and on the previous Sunday immediately after afternoon tea, she had taken a reluctant farewell as Mr Gorry led his daughter, with all her books and writing materials, into the parlour to 'study'. She had wished desperately that she could have joined them. She wanted to learn. Her experiences at the shipping offices had made her realise the truth about herself and she was trying to improve. In the evenings and when there was time to spare, she would borrow a book from the bookcase in the parlour and pore over it. They were mainly books on navigation and the like, which were totally beyond her, but there were a few on foreign countries and these she did find interesting. But there were so many words she couldn't pronounce and many whose meaning was lost to her.

Her attention was diverted by the clanking and clattering of cans, the high-pitched yowling of a cat and the sniggering laughter of young boys, followed by the sound of running feet. At the junction of the alley-way between the houses – known as 'the jigger' – and the street, she was knocked sideways by three lads who charged blindly into the street. She grabbed two of them by their collars. One was Eamon.

'What do you think you're doing? What have you been up to at this time on a Sunday morning?'

He glared at her from under the thick fringe of hair. 'Nothin'!'

She shook him hard. 'Don't give me that, Eamon Cleary!'

He refused to answer. She was making him look stupid in front of 'the gang'.

'We was only playin' kick the can.' The other lad muttered sullenly.

She knew him. He lived at the top end of the street. 'Kick the can on a Sunday, Vinny O'Brien! You should be home getting ready for Mass! And what was all the yowling, it sounded like a cat?'

The third member of the group had sauntered

135

back, courage restored, seeing it was only a girl who had caught the others. She didn't recollect having seen him before. 'Where do you live? Round here?'

'What's it ter you?'

'Hard-faced little sod, I'll box your ears!'

He ignored her. 'We was only 'avin' a birrof a laugh! Tied a can to the tail of a jigger rabbit. What's wrong with that?'

'It says a lot about you! No more sense in your head than to be persecuting a poor cat!'

'Dinny's got a job, he don't go ter school no more!' Eamon piped up, emboldened by his friends obvious lack of fear. 'He's a delivery boy!'

'I didn't think they let you out of school until you'd grown up and had some sense in your thick heads!' She replied sarcastically.

'Who're yer callin' thick?'

She had released Eamon and Vinny O'Brien and her hand shot out and Dinny Lacey received a stinging slap across the side of his head that made his ears ring. 'Now you can get home and tell your Da that Cat Cleary boxed your ears for your cheek, then you can get to Mass and if I don't see you there I'll tell Father Maguire about these shenanigans! Clear off!'

He turned and ran with Vinny close on his heels. Eamon was about to follow but she grabbed him by his ear and he squealed like a stuck pig.

'Hasn't Ma got enough to worry about without you playing the eejit with the likes of them! Get home!'

He rubbed his tingling ear as she pushed him into the house. Her father had just come downstairs, looking grey and needing a shave. Cat pushed her brother at him.

'Can't you do anything with him? Don't you care about him at all?'

'What's he done now?' he muttered.

'Only woken half the street and tormented the daylights out of a poor cat, and he's hanging around with back-crack lads! Don't you care what happens to him? Don't you care what happens to any of us? For the love of Heaven, Pa, can't you do something – anything to help Ma? You know she's ill, you know she's worn out and worried to death about this boyo and . . . Shelagh!'

His bleary eyes rested on her for a second then he looked away. 'What can I do about anything? We should have stayed in Dublin.'

'So, you've given up again! You just don't care, do you?'

'I do . . . in me way.'

'And what way is that Pa? Getting drunk as often as you can so you won't have to face up to things?'

'You've got too much to say for yourself, that you have! Isn't a man entitled to some respect from his own daughter?'

'Respect! Respect!' she yelled, not caring if the whole street heard her. 'You have to earn respect and you've never done anything to make me respect you! And I don't want to hear about "honouring Thy Father and Thy Mother". I honour, love and respect Ma but I'll never be able to say the same about you! I despise you!'

With the attention diverted from himself, Eamon had slipped into the kitchen, leaving his father and sister in the lobby.

'Eamon, is that Cat shouting at your Pa?' his mother asked.

'Yes, I think she's tellin' him ter gerra job,' he replied, the picture of innocence.

'Well, she'll have no luck there, it's like talkin' ter the wall an' I know!' Maisey answered tartly.

The hot, sticky days of summer dragged on. Four postcards had arrived from Joe and with the arrival of each, she missed him more and more. She was looking up Algiers on the big globe of the world, mounted on its polished wooden stand, when Mrs Travis quietly entered the room.

'It's in North Africa, Catherine, and from what I remember of Captain Travis's description, it's not a very nice place at all. Hot, dirty, swarming with flies, wretched beggars and thieves.'

She turned, her cheeks flushed.

'You look feverish, have you a headache?'

'Just a bit of one, it's probably the heat.'

'I know you miss him – I do myself – but I did warn you. The sea is in his blood and you'll never keep him ashore for long!'

'I know, but it makes it harder when . . . when I get these.' She held out the postcard that depicted an Arab bazaar.

'What's the matter, Catherine? For months you've been quiet and withdrawn. Is it entirely to do with Joe, or is something wrong at home?'

The parlour was cool for the heavy drapes kept out the glare, but she did feel feverish. Suddenly, it all gushed out. A verbal torrent that couldn't be stopped. Shelagh, Eamon, her father, her mother's declining health, Marie's commitment to her exams and the feelings of exclusion this caused. The pain, despair and humiliation of her visit to the shipping offices. When she was finished she looked down. Unconsciously she had torn the postcard to shreds.

Mrs Travis sighed. 'You can't take the worry of them all on your shoulders, child. You're too young! Obviously your father is beyond all help and your sister, I'm afraid, will go her own way regardless of any attempts to correct her. Your brother is your father's responsibility – not yours! If he can't control him and he gets into trouble, it will be your father and not you, that the authorities will blame.' She held out her hand and Cat dropped the torn fragments of Joe's card into it. Without being told to, she sank down on to the sofa.

'What about Ma?'

The old lady neatly stacked the mutilated card, piece by piece, in her lap before she spoke. 'All my life I have tried in my small way, to help alleviate the sufferings of the poor familes in this parish, but it's a drop in the ocean. Your mother was ill when you first came to Liverpool, wasn't she?'

Cat nodded.

'This city, indeed this area, is not healthy. The air is damp and contaminated by the filth that pours into it from all the factories. For someone with your mother's constitution, it is not good, not good at all! But until there is full employment, good housing and something done about the air we breathe, nothing will change. Nothing can change, for poor souls like her. It's hard to accept, very hard, but there is very little any of us can do.'

'That's why I went . . . I wanted to try to change things for her, help her! I . . . I was desperate!'

'And do you really believe that she would have left your father, her husband of many years, her son

139

and daughter to live most of the time alone? Even with all the things you want to provide for her?'

'Yes! Yes, I know she would!'

'Then you have a lot to learn about people, Catherine. Especially about the vows of marriage.'

'I have a lot to learn about everything!' she answered bitterly for the old lady had planted the seeds of doubt in her mind. She had never stopped to think what her mother's reaction would be to the dream home she had visualised. In fact she had never really thought about her mother's feelings at all.

'What can't be changed must be endured, without bitterness!'

She wanted to cry out that she couldn't accept that! That life was unfair! Instead she pushed a loose strand of hair behind her ear and bit her lip.

'I notice that you've been reading.' Seeing Cat's quick, guilty glance, she smiled. 'I can't think that any of these old books on navigation could make interesting reading. Why didn't you ask for one of the books I keep in my room?'

'I . . . I didn't want you to think I was being forward or—'

'Dickens, Jane Austen and the Brontë sisters would appeal to you more.'

'I . . . I don't understand so many of the words!'

'Then I'll teach you to use a dictionary. Go upstairs and bring me *Jane Eyre* and the Oxford Dictionary. We might as well start now, it's the least I can do and I think you'll find inspiration and an escape from the worries of everyday life. I know I do.'

After that she read voraciously. She read anything and everything and Mrs Travis had been right, she could escape from life through the pages of books, into the lives of the heroines. And, without realising it, she was learning, too. Her vocabulary increased, she began to grasp the social changes that had taken place, to realise that life was better in so many ways.

Marie had passed her exams with flying colours and called one day bursting with excitement.

'Oh, it's such a relief! I never want to see another book!'

'Oh, I'm so pleased for you! I really am! But how can you say that? I love books! Mrs Travis has lent me so many and helped me so much.'

'I'm sorry, Cat, I haven't been much company have I, lately?'

'Your exams were far more important, you know I realise that!'

'I was terrified when the envelope came. I thought Mam was going to faint. You see, the other two did so well, but it was so hard for me and I didn't want to let her down, or Dad either. Not after all the money they spent on me.'

'You didn't.'

'No, I didn't and now Dad has promised to take us on holiday! He asked where I wanted to go, it was my choice, as a reward! I know Mam didn't want to go back to Ireland, she's always gone on and on about Bournemouth, so that's where we're going. To stay in an hotel for two weeks!'

Even though she was so very pleased for Marie, she couldn't help the stab of envy. She had hoped to have seen more of her only friend now she had finished at school.

'Is Joe still away?'

'Yes. But he is on his way back now. He said he hopes to be home some time in September.'

141

'That's not far off.'

'When will you get back?'

'A week before I start commercial college.' She pulled a wry face. 'Mam had one of her "serious" talks with me. I've got to grow up now, she said. "Got to act more ladylike and not romp around like a tomboy any more." I've got this horrible feeling that everything is going to change! That everything will be different.'

The thing Cat had dreaded since the day she had returned from her first visit to Yew Tree Road seemed about to happen. She had thought then that things changed, people changed. Her face reflected these fears.

'Oh, cheer up, Cat, I won't change that much! You can't make a silk purse out of a sow's ear, as the saying goes! I'll always be the same underneath, you'll see! You've grown up. You're quieter, more thoughtful, well . . . just older, if you know what I mean!'

'Am I?' She had never thought about it before, but she supposed that she, too, had changed. It must have been gradual, something that had crept up on her, without her noticing it.

'We'll always be friends, Cat! Even when we're old ladies like Mrs Travis. I'll write to you and send you some funny postcards; on second thoughts, I'd better send the ones with 'Greetings from Bourne-mouth' and pretty scenes. Mrs Travis might take offence at the 'naughty ones'.'

'I'll keep them with the ones Joe sent me.' Then she remembered the one she had destroyed. Still, he would be home soon and that was better than any postcard.

* * *

The first week in October saw the *Marguerita* back in the Mersey but to Joe's disappointment, he was paid off. The trip hadn't been so much of a success as her captain had thought. He'd only just broken even, so he would have to lay up; besides, the old girl needed a rest, repairs, a coat of paint, he explained as he counted the notes out into Joe's hand. So he came back to work and both women were glad to see him.

At first Cat felt strange with him. The way she had felt when she first knew him, not as close as they had been before he had left. Sometimes she hestitated before she spoke, something she had never done before.

She had mentioned it casually to Mrs Travis with the words 'It seems strange to have him home again.'

Her employer laughed. 'It's all part of the charm, like getting to know him all over again.' And Cat knew she was speaking about her husband and not Joe. She had noticed lately that the old lady was living more and more in the past. She kept referring to things that had happened years ago as though they had only happened yesterday.

The days lengthened into weeks and November came with its thick, choking fogs when it was almost impossible to see your hand in front of you, when the clanging of the trams as they crawled through the eerie streets like giant beetles, was the only sound on those streets. When for days and nights the mournful sound of the foghorns of ships trying to negotiate the river, carried across the shrouded city.

The fog frightened her. Whenever she ventured out to the shops, with a scarf tied around her face leaving only her eyes exposed, she felt as though she were walking in a nightmare world where there were no familiar landmarks. No familiar sounds, shapes, colours. Shapes would suddenly loom into view, taking on human form. There were no shadows to warn of their approach. No lights.

Mrs Travis, peering through the lace curtains into the cavernous gloom, summed up her feelings in a little rhyme:

> No sun, no moon,
> No night, no noon – November.

At the end of the week it finally lifted, blown away by a howling gale that swept in from the Irish Sea. On Sunday she went to see her mother. She looked a little better and for this she was thankful. Maisey had forbidden her to leave the house. 'Them fogs is murder on the tubes!' she had warned. Wasn't half the street bad with their chests? She wasn't going to Marie's that day for Doreen Gorry had just become engaged and her prospective 'outlaws', as Marie called them, were coming to tea. She had been invited but she had declined, sensing that the occasion would be tense for Marie had made no secret of the fact that Mr and Mrs Gorry did not really like their eldest daughter's choice of future husband. A situation that was viewed in the same light by Doreen's fiancé's parents!

She turned her collar up against the wind as she alighted from the tram. The rain had stopped but it was a raw night. Her head had begun to ache. All day confined in the overcrowded kitchen in Eldon Street was enough to give anyone a headache, she thought, as she turned her key in the lock. The house was silent – obviously Joe was not back yet.

Usually he was a bit later than her for he always bought the twopenny bundles of wood 'chips' used to kindle the fires, on his way in.

She stirred up the fire and held out her hands to the warmth. She'd better get the kettle on. Joe would be cold and no doubt Mrs Travis would be waiting for her cup of tea and digestive biscuits. She hadn't answered her call and Cat surmised that she was dozing before the parlour fire. She took a lot of little naps lately, she thought. She set the tray and as there was no sign of Joe, she carried it into the parlour.

'I couldn't wait any longer for Joe, he'll have to make his own.' She set the tray down on the polished buffet. Mrs Travis sat in her usual chair, her eyes closed, her embroidery in her lap. Cat smiled. After the day she'd had, the sight of such tranquility was balm to her soul. *This is how everyone should live*, she thought. *Surrounded by peace, security, warmth and luxury*. She bent down and gently shook Mrs Travis's arm. 'I've brought your tea and biscuits.'

There was no reply. No response. Usually she stirred at the sound of her voice. She shook her again and then snatched her hand away as though she had been burnt! She started to tremble all over. The old lady's skin was cold! 'Oh, God! Oh, Holy Mother! She's . . . she's dead!' She stuffed her fist into her mouth to stop herself from screaming and her wild eyes darted around the room. She was dead! Dead!

Somewhere a door slammed but she still stood frozen with shock. It wasn't until she felt the hands on her shoulders that the paralysis left her.

'Oh, Joe! Joe! She's . . . she's . . .'

'I know, Cat.' He gathered her into his arms as she gave way to hysterical sobs, clinging to him.

'Come on, let's get you into the kitchen! There's nothing we can do now and she . . . she went peaceful enough.'

'But . . . she went . . . alone!'

Gently he drew her from the room and back into the kitchen where he eased her into a chair. 'You need a drink. We both need a drink!' He went to the sideboard and opened the door, taking out a small, squat bottle and two glasses which he filled. He held one to her lips. 'Drink it!'

The brandy burned her throat and made her cough but he forced her to finish it. Then he tossed off his own glass.

She felt a little calmer, although she was still shaking.

'How do you feel now?'

'Better. It . . . it was . . . the shock.'

He held her tightly in his arms and some warmth and strength flowed back into her.

'Joe, what will we do?'

'Call the police, I suppose.'

CHAPTER NINE

It wasn't until after the funeral that she opened the envelope that had been addressed to her. While looking for names and addresses of relatives Joe and the police sergeant had come across the envelopes. One addressed to Cat, the other to Joe.

The Gorrys had been kindness itself in those bleak days that followed Mrs Travis's death. She had refused to go back to Eldon Street. Joe had argued with her, pleaded with her, telling her that she couldn't stay for the nuns from the convent had taken the old lady to be laid out. It had been then that the realisation had come that not only had she lost a dear friend, the house she looked on as her home, but also her job. In the end, in response to her half-hysterical pleas, he had taken her to Marie's.

Word had been sent to Eldon Street. Mr Gorry had dealt with all enquiries and formalities and Mrs Gorry had had a black dress and coat speedily altered for her in time for the funeral. The interment had taken place in Anfield Cemetery and afterwards she had politely declined the invitation, extended by Sister Superior, to attend the quiet 'tea' they had laid on. She also declined Marie's offer of a trip into town to 'take her mind off things' and explained as best she could, the desire to be alone.

She crossed the road intent on walking for a while in Stanley Park and found Joe waiting for her.

'I thought you'd gone.'

He shook his head and tucked her arm through his. 'I've hardly seen you since . . . well . . .'

'I know. It's only been a couple of days but it seems like weeks. They've been very good to me.'

They wandered for a while along the deserted pathway. Everything was still covered by heavy frost, although a watery sun had broken through the clouds and was slowly melting it. The bare, gaunt branches of the trees and shrubs, the empty flower beds, suited her mood. They skirted the frozen lake on which a few ducks huddled together.

'You can't stay with Marie forever, Cat.'

She sighed deeply and pulling her coat closer to her, sat down on the wooden bench beside the lake, staring out over its glassy surface.

'I know. I know I'll have to go back sometime.'

'Is it that bad?'

'It will seem so now. I . . . I'd come to look on her house as . . . home.'

'So, what will you do?'

'Look for another job, I suppose.'

'Not many people still have servants, Cat, and I don't think there is anyone who . . . Well, Mam says "God broke the mould when he made her." I reckon that sums her up very well.'

He was forcing her to face reality and it depressed her further. 'Then I'll have to try for shop work, won't I?' she snapped.

He put his arm around her. 'We could get married.'

She stared up at him, her eyes widening. 'What?'

'We could get married. I could look after you! You know how I feel about you!'

She leaned her head against his shoulder. She knew he cared and she cared for him, too. But she had never thought about marriage. 'What would we live on and where would we live? With your Mam or mine? You've got no job either, Joe.' The practicalities sprang to her mind as a defence. She needed time to think. He had thrust it upon her so suddenly and at a time when she was already so confused.

'We could have our own house.'

She twisted her head to see if he was teasing. He wasn't. 'And where will we get the money for that? A decent house costs 12s. 6d. a week rent!'

'Haven't you looked in the envelope she left you?'

'No.'

'Well, look! Have you got it with you?'

She opened her bag and took out the envelope. She had forgotten about it. She ripped it open. She drew out a single piece of paper and a bundle of crisp, white five pound notes. At first she looked at them as if she didn't know what they were, then she slowly began to count them. Fifty pounds! There was fifty pounds right here in her hand! A lump rose in her throat. 'Oh, Joe! Joe!'

'She left me the same. A small fortune! With a note telling me to spend it wisely and hold fast to my principles. You see, Cat, we can get married, we can have a fine house, and . . .'

She wasn't listening, she was reading the lines of neat copperplate handwriting.

My dear Catherine,

I want you to have this small sum in return for the hours of companionship you willingly gave a lonely old woman. It may seem like a large amount of money but it won't buy you all the things you desire. You will have to work for them and work hard, but it will help you. If it gives you a start in achieving your ambition, then it will have served its purpose and I will be content.

You once said I would have cause to be proud of you and I know you won't go back on that. Don't lose faith and don't let go of your dream, Catherine. Dreams can become reality – with a little help. God bless you.

Yours,

Evelyn Mary Travis.

She could hear Joe's voice, she could feel his arm around her shoulder, his body shielding her from the wind, but the words of the letter stirred up a memory that had lain dormant for a long time. Instead of the dreary, barren park with its grey, frozen lake, the flag-bedecked rigging, the three yellow funnels and the towering white hull rose before her eyes. Her heart began to beat more quickly and she clutched the note tightly in her hand. 'Dreams can become reality!' she heard the gentle voice whisper before it was drowned out by the familiar sound of a ship's siren as a captain called the last of his crew aboard from The Stile House pub, far away in the distance. The vision danced before her and her lips formed the words, unknowingly spoken aloud. 'The White Empress!'

'Damn you, Cat Cleary, you're not even listening to me!'

She was back in the park and Joe was glaring at her. 'What . . .?'

'I said, when shall I go and see Father Maguire?'

'You won't!'

The green eyes were clear and in them burned the light that had shocked him once before and he knew he had lost her.

'Don't be a fool, Cat! I love you, you've always known that! We can get married, we've got one hundred pounds between us!'

'No! No!'

He drew her to him and crushed her lips beneath his and for a second she faltered. Then she drew away.

'I'm sorry, Joe! Oh, I'm sorry!'

His eyes darkened. 'No you're not! You're still set on making a fool of yourself over that damned ship! We're rich, Cat, don't you understand?'

'But it's not everything, Joe, is it?'

He sprang to his feet. 'For God's sake what do you want? You won't ever get more money than that and you won't have men running around offering to marry you! Oh, they'll flock around you, but it won't be marriage they'll be offering, and if they do it will only be to get their hands on the money!'

She got to her feet. 'I'm not interested in other men and I want to be more than just rich, as you put it. I want to be respected, admired! I want to be able to look at myself in the mirror and know that what I've got I've earned. That I've achieved something, made something out of my life! She understood, why can't you?' The still painful memory of her rejection and her inadequacies, so patiently

151

explained by the clerk in the Booth Line offices, now added strength to her desire to gain respect and with it a measure of revenge for all the slights suffered.

He just stared at her, his eyes like pieces of hard, glittering coal. He had offered her himself, his love and protection for the rest of her life and she had flung it all in his face and for what? So she could chase a dream!

'You're a fool, Cat! And a greedy fool at that! You can't see when you're well off! You'll go on wanting more and more, you'll never be satisfied!'

She grasped his arm. 'Joe! I don't want to hurt you, really I don't! You should know how I feel, you have your own dream! Can't you understand it's not greed, it's ambition!'

He threw off her hand. 'Then take your ambition, Cat, and I wish you well of it! But don't come crawling to me when the money's gone and you're worn out working like a skivvy, because that's all you'll be! A skivvy at the beck and call of people who are no better than you and who have even less money than you have! It's not all millionaires, those ships carry emigrants to Canada, too!' He turned on his heel and walked away, his boots crunching on the gravel path and the sound cut through her.

She didn't go after him. She just sank back on the bench, the note and the money still tightly clasped in her hand. Was she a fool? For an instant she thought about running after him. Telling him she hadn't meant it and that she would go with him to see Father Maguire and post the Banns. She fought down the impulse. She wanted to try! She hadn't lied to him. She hadn't wanted to hurt him. She'd held on to her dream, although as she

watched his disappearing figure, she wondered
how much that dream would cost her.

She discussed the whole matter with Marie. It was
the first time she had really opened her heart to
her friend and asked for advice. There was no one
else she could ask.

Marie looked serious. 'Cat, it wouldn't be right of
me to tell you what to do. Only you know how you
feel, about Joe and about . . . this ambition. But if it
were me, well . . . marriage is something for life,
isn't it? And it would be a different life. Totally
different to anything you've known. Only you can
say you would be happy. Only you know how you
feel. Only you really know Joe.'

'I . . . I am very fond of him and I know he
would be good to me . . .'

'But? It's the *but* that worries me, Cat. It shouldn't
be there at all.'

'But am I throwing everything away for a dream?
What if I don't make it, or hate it?'

'Is it what you really want to do?'

'I want to try, Marie! Ever since I saw the *Empress
of Japan* at the landing stage, the day I arrived, I've
dreamed of sailing on a White Empress!'

'Then all I can say, Cat, is try it. You won't know
until you try it!'

Some of the depression lifted. She had given the
money to Mr Gorry for safe-keeping for there was
no place to hide it in Eldon Street. Reluctantly she
had returned to the little house, to suffer all the
overcrowding and the jibes of Shelagh. 'I feel better
now. I'll give it a try – if they'll have me.'

Marie laughed. 'I've always wanted to take a trip

153

on a liner. Swim in those fantastic pools, have cocktails and dinner with the captain.'

'It won't be like that for me. It will be hard work. At least that's what Joe said.'

'What else did he say about it?'

'That I'd need to speak properly, dress well, have qualifications and know the right people.'

'You can learn to speak correctly and you can buy some really nice clothes, but I don't know about the "right" people. Dad might though.'

'What about the qualifications?'

'You're not stupid, Cat, you could easily learn. They have evening classes you know, where you can go and learn and take exams.

'Where?'

Marie stood up. 'There will be a list in the library. Come on, let's find out and our Mam knows a lady who teaches elocution. She's always threatening to send me!'

The elocution lessons were duly arranged by Mrs Gorry who added that it wouldn't do 'Hazel' any harm either to spend an hour or two with Mrs Grindley. Cat was enrolled for evening classes at Warbreck Moor School. To study English, arithmetic and – as the sea was her intended career – geography.

On the following Saturday she followed Marie and Mrs Gorry through the lofty portals of George Henry Lee & Company in Basnett Street. If the doorman had any doubts about her inferior attire they were not noticeable as he held the door open for Mrs Gorry, bedecked in a camel-hair coat and large-brimmed hat, a fox fur draped around her shoulders. After her forays into C & A Modes,

154

Frost's on County Road, where Miss Kay superintended the 'rigging out' of those customers who had paid into a savings scheme called a 'cheque', and the slightly more competitive Marks & Spencer, this emporium reminded Cat of a church.

It sold furniture and toys, dress materials and household linens, but it was to the model dress department that Mrs Gorry steered them first. Here Cat selected – helped by a very deferential sales assistant – one wool day dress. In the outerwear department she bought a smart herringbone tweed coat with a shawl collar, fastened down the front with large red buttons. In the shoe department she bought good quality leather court shoes in black and a matching handbag and kid gloves that were as soft as satin. She also bought three pair of silk stockings. They spent nearly an hour in the millinery department as, despite Marie's protests, she insisted that she could only afford one good hat which would have to match everything. She settled in the end for a stiffened, black velvet picture hat, decorated with a single red feather that curled around the base of the crown, forming a bandeau. To her horror she realised that she had spent twelve pounds of her precious fifty and was determined to spend no more.

'I feel so guilty and extravagant!'

'Don't be daft! You'll have to be smartly turned out for interviews!' Marie advised.

'But I haven't got an interview yet, I've not even started evening classes!'

'Stop worrying, Cat, it won't be hard.' She turned to her mother. 'Can Cat leave these things in our house, our—' she stopped herself. 'Mother?'

Mrs Gorry nodded, pouring herself another cup of tea for they had gone to the Kardomah tea rooms to await the arrival of Mr Gorry with the car to transport them home.

Cat said nothing to anyone in Eldon Street about her new wardrobe, elocution lessons – which she found very frustrating at times – or her intended disappearance on three evenings a week. The excuse she had ready for any unusual absence was that she was visiting the Gorrys.

'We're not good enough for her now! Miss High and Mighty, now she is! Used to better things!' Shelagh sneered.

Cat ignored her.

'And what I want to know is, when is she going to get another job? How long is she going to hang around the house while others have to go out and work?' Shelagh was still employed by the British and American Tobacco Company and had quietened down a little. At least on the surface.

'I've told you, I'm looking for something else and I help Mrs Rooney out in the corner shop over the busy times and while I'm still paying for my keep, I don't see that it's got anything to do with you, so shut up and mind your own business!'

'Oh, just listen to her! She even talks like them now. "Looking for something else!"' Shelagh mimicked, emphasising the 'g' on the end of the words.

'Shut up!' Cat snapped, gathering up the books she had bought from Phillips, Son & Nephew in Whitechapel and the pen and pencil she had purchased in Woolworths.

Warbreck Moor Secondary School was situated at the bottom of the incline of the same name. It was a red-brick building and quite modern and therefore bright and spacious. The school and the adjoining yards were segregated. Half for boys and half for girls, but in the evenings it was mixed classes. Cat, after some initial enquiries, found the large classroom. Other girls and young men were chatting to each other and taking their seats in the rather small desks and benches. She stared around her in some confusion.

'Are you Miss Cleary?'

She turned and looked at a young man whom she judged to be in his late twenties. He had fair hair and moustache and looked sympathetic.

'Yes, it's the first time I've been, where do I sit?'

'There.' He pointed to an empty place almost directly in front of the dais on which stood a large desk and chair, behind which was a blackboard. 'I'm Stephen Hartley, your teacher.'

She eyed the proximity of the empty desk to the dais and her heart sank. She would have preferred to have sat further back where her struggles wouldn't be so obvious to him or the rest of the students. Instead she nodded and sat down. After exchanging a few words with two young men, he came over to her.

'Don't be afraid to ask questions, Miss Cleary. No one will think any the worse of you, they are all here because they want to learn and haven't had the time or inclination before and my job is to help you.' He studied the list he carried attached to a clipboard. 'I see you're here for English grammar, arithmetic and geography?'

'Yes.'

His blue eyes looked amused and instantly she felt defensive.

157

'Geography is rather an unusual choice of subject?'

'I intend to make a career at sea.'

He nodded and then called his class to order.

She hated every minute of it. She had struggled to keep up with everyone else, but she felt so foolish, so slow and so utterly confused by all the verbs, adverbs and nouns! She had managed the arithmetic quite well as she had a natural aptitude for figures, and she even found the geography quite interesting, but it was with a sigh of relief and a thudding headache, that she left the building and started walking towards the tram stop. Her head bent against a wind that was still cold, although it was the middle of March.

'Miss Cleary! I walk home this way, I'll walk with you, that's if you don't object?'

She smiled shyly at Stephen Hartley. 'Of course not. I didn't do too well, did I? To be honest, I don't think I'll ever grasp the difference between nouns and verbs, let alone pronouns, adjectives and conjunctions!'

He smiled. 'It's not that hard. Don't forget you are only just starting out.'

'Oh, I don't know whether this is going to work!'

'Why not? You have an agile mind and a natural intelligence.'

'You're flattering me, do they pay you on the number of pupils you teach?'

He laughed and brushed back a strand of blonde hair. 'You're very direct!'

'I'm sorry, I didn't mean to be, it was meant to be a joke!'

'I know and I didn't mean to make you feel uncomfortable. But, yes, I'm paid that way so I hope you'll stick at it, if only for my sake!' he joked.

Cat found herself liking him more and more. He was easy to talk to, once she was away from the rest of her fellow students. 'Do you really think I'll ever be able to pass any kind of examination? I know just how ignorant I am!'

They had reached the tram stop.

'Yes, I do think you'll pass, Miss Cleary. Especially if you work hard, as most of my students do, having become mature enough to realise that education will open many doors for them and they work harder to make up for lost time. The only ignorance I abhor is wilful, culpable ignorance!'

She made a mental note to look up the word 'culpable' in her new dictionary.

'If you like, I will help you in any way I can?'

'That's very good of you.'

He was about to speak when the tramcar rumbled up and clanked to a halt.

'I'll see you tomorrow evening, Miss Cleary.'

'That you will! Good night, Mr Hartley!'

A friendship soon sprang up between them for he seemed genuinely concerned and impressed by her efforts to catch up on the years of schooling she had missed. Often she would stay behind for half an hour or so while he patiently went over the intricacies of English grammar, fractions and decimal points and the climates and rainfall of the various European countries she was studying.

At times she would become so despairing she would throw down the pen, her fingers stained with ink, her cheeks flushed, her head throbbing. Declaring she would never, never understand it all. He would pick up the pen and put it back in her hand and they would begin again. Each night he walked her to the tram and only then would the proprieties be dropped. During lessons she was 'Miss Cleary' and he 'Mr Hartley', beyond the doors it was Cat and Stephen.

In him she confided her ambition and determination, fuelled by regular Saturday afternoon strolls along the landing stage, regardless of the weather, to watch the arrival and departure of the liners. Hoping against hope that one Saturday she would see, far out in the river, that gleaming white hull above which the three yellow funnels towered. But each week when her eyes scanned the river, she was disappointed. The White Empress's home port was Southampton and she had to make do with the black hulls and red funnels of the Cunarders which, by comparison, were dull and ordinary.

It was Mr O'Dwyer, who like herself was an avid reader of anything he could get his hands on, who read out from the *Journal of Commerce* that the Cunard's *Scythia* was due to sail from Liverpool to New York the following day.

'Isn't that the one that Joe Calligan 'as gorra job on?' Maisey asked innocently, while eyeing Cat sideways. She sensed there was a serious rift between them and he hadn't been round to the house since just after Mrs Travis had died.

'Aye, I don't know how many palms 'e greased ter gerrit, but it must 'ave been quite a few! Yer don't gerra job in the engine room on one of them without givin' out a few back 'anders, these days. Especially if yer've only done a few trips as deck 'and with B & I an' a few trips on an owld tub!'

Cat kept her eyes on the page of the book she was reading, but the words became a jumbled mass. So Joe had finally made it. At least he had a foot on the ladder. It must have cost him something, too.

'What time does she sail, then?' Maisey asked.

'On the four o'clock tide, termorrer.'

'Are yer goin' ter see 'im off, Cat?'

She finally looked up. 'Why?'

'Ter wish 'im luck, like.'

'I might.'

Maisey and her mother exchanged glances.

'Do you not think you should, Cat? He was good to you.' Her mother chided.

She closed the book. 'Yes. Yes, I suppose I should. I owe him that much.'

She didn't see Maisey mouth the words 'Lovers' tiff' behind her back as she watched her mother's head move in agreement.

The *Scythia* was not a very large ship, but she looked well enough Cat thought as she walked down the floating roadway to the landing stage the following afternoon. There was the usual hustle and bustle that accompanied a departing ship. A young man in uniform stood at the bottom of the gangway and she pushed her way towards him.

'Is Joe Calligan aboard?'

He scanned the list he carried. 'Sorry, miss, no one by that name here.'

'I'm sorry, he's not a passenger, he's crew, Engine room, I think. This is his first trip with you.'

He grinned, then glanced at his watch. 'In that case you'll probably find him in the Stile House being inaugurated. Just make sure he arrives before we sail and can walk up the gangway on his own!' he called after her as she turned away.

She crossed the cobbled expanse known as Mann

Island, which indeed it was, separated by a floating roadway from the pierhead itself. The Stile House was the pub frequented by the crews of all the ships docking and leaving the landing stage and it was crowded. There were a few women inside but it was obviously a very male domain.

'Looking for someone, luv?'

'Yes. Joe Calligan, he's due on board the *Scythia*.'

'Aren't we all, luv! Girl here looking for Joe Calligan!' Her informant bellowed above the din.

She saw him shouldering his way towards her, through the crowd around the bar, and she smiled. She'd never seen him in uniform before, except the old black jersey on the ferry, and he looked older and even more handsome.

'I came to see you off. Mr O'Dwyer told me you'd got this job.'

He took her arm and propelled her outside. It was the first time they had seen each other since that day in the park and she felt awkward, unable to look him directly in the face.

'I wondered if you would come, Cat.'

'Did you, Joe? Did you really?'

He took her hand. 'Really, I did, and . . . and I'm glad.'

She looked up at him. 'You look grand in that uniform.'

'I won't get to wear it very often. It'll be a boiler suit and up to my armpits in grease and oil most of the time.'

'Isn't it what you wanted?'

'Of course! It's better than being a steward or galley boy!'

She remembered his bitter words about steward-esses and looked away.

'Oh, you know what I mean, Cat! They're going to train me, it's sort of an apprenticeship. I'm a bit older than the others, but . . . ' he shrugged.

'How much did it cost you, Joe?'

'Don't ask!'

'But it is what you want?'

He looked closely into her face, then nodded. 'Next to you, Cat.'

'So we're still . . . friends?'

'If that's the way you want it, Cat.' He replied cautiously, hoping he sounded indifferent. He had vowed he would never speak to her again for she had hurt him. But when he had sat and thought about it he realised that the thing that hurt most was his pride. Seeing her again had made him realise that he still cared about her. But he was wary. He would never give her the opportunity to turn him down flat again.

'I'm glad, Joe. I didn't want you to go away and us still be . . . enemies!'

'We'll never be that! Come here!' He lifted her chin in his hand and bent and kissed her.

She clasped her arms around his neck and clung to him. She did care about him and now she realised how much she had missed him. It was just like the first time he had gone away and somehow she knew it would always be like this.

'It's a lonely life for a woman. Waiting, wondering, worrying!' An echo sounded in her mind. 'Oh, you dear soul, you were right!' she whispered into his shoulder.

He kissed her again as the deafening blast of the *Scythia*'s siren sounded, warning her crew that she would cast off in ten minutes.

Men started to push past them, buttoning up jackets, straightening ties and caps.

He kissed her again and she clung to his lips.

'I've got to go now, Cat!'

'Take care, Joe! Take care!' She hugged him quickly then released him. He quickened his steps to a run to catch up to the others, pulling on his uniform cap.

'God speed!' she called after him. 'And come home safe,' she finished quietly to herself.

CHAPTER TEN

She struggled on at her evening classes, helped and encouraged by Stephen, but there were nights when she walked from the tram stop back to the house, when hearing the ships on the river, she felt lonely and miserable.

Early in spring she had started to go to the city library in William Brown Street and once or twice Stephen had accompanied her. It was on one of these visits that he suggested they pay a visit to the Walker Art Gallery with its fluted Corinthian portico and statues of Raphael and Michelangelo which flanked the doors. It was situated next door to the library, facing the Wellington Monument. She stood in awe, gazing up at the full-length portrait of King Henry VIII in the entrance hall and remained silent and attentive as he pointed out such treasures as Stubbs' *Molly Longlegs*, Martini's *Finding of Christ in the Temple* and de Roberti's *Pieta*. She followed him, in rapt silence, through the quiet halls, totally enthralled by such beauty and splendour.

When they left, he suggested they take a trip to Otterspool promenade and park at the south end of the docks. It was a fine day and, loathe to return to the clamour and clutter at home, she had readily agreed. It was so refreshing to walk close to the river and feel the breeze in your hair, smell the salt in the air and watch the grey surface undergo a transformation as the sunlight broke through the slowly moving cumulus.

They sat on the grass in the park while she studied the catalogue they had bought in the art gallery.

'Do you still want to go to sea, Cat?' he asked.

'Of course! Why do you think I'm working myself to death, slaving over a hot pen and exercise book? Did people really have pictures like this hanging in their houses?'

'Yes, but then they were very wealthy and had big houses.'

'One day I'm going to have a fine house and fill it with objects d'art – is that what you call them? And all the luxuries I can afford!'

'Money doesn't always bring happiness, Cat.'

'I know that, but it helps to make life sweeter and besides, if used wisely, it can.'

'But why choose the sea? It's not an easy life and it can be dangerous?'

'I've already told you, a hundred times or more!'

'Of course, the White Empress! It's difficult to fight a ship, Cat.'

She looked up from the catalogue. 'What do you mean "fight"?'

'I think most men could cope with a male rival, but a ship—!'

'You're laughing at me!'

'I'm not!'

'Then . . .?'

He pulled her gently down on the grass beside him, leaning over her. 'It's so hard to fight something inanimate, but I'll try anyway. I love you!'

She hadn't been prepared for any of this and she lay staring up at him.

He traced the outline of her nose with his index finger until it reached her lips. 'Don't speak, Cat, don't spoil it!'

Before she realised it, his lips were pressing against hers. Gently at first, then harder and more demanding. One hand slid under her back, the other supported her head. The sky began to grow paler, the sunlight less bright as she responded to him. Her hands locked around his neck and through half-closed eyes, the sun began to spin slowly. Something was stirring in her that she had never felt before. These were not the feelings Joe's lips had evoked. These were the stirrings of emotions she had never felt before. She felt his hand touch the soft mound of her breast and a longing arose within her. His lips, his gently caressing fingers, were causing tremors to course through her body.

'Cat! Cat! I've wanted you since the day I first saw you!' His words were muttered with a passion he couldn't conceal.

A gull screeched overhead and the raucous cry mingled with the laughter of children and these sounds served to drag her back to reality. She pulled away from him, her hands trembling. 'Stephen, no! I . . . I can't.' Sitting up she smoothed out the creases in her skirt. He still lay on his back beside her as a young family passed them. She watched them until they were further away.

His hand sought hers.

'Stephen, I can't . . .' She couldn't trust herself. If he were to kiss her again like that, she would be lost.

'Is it because of Joe?'

'No. Well, Joe is part of it!'

'He doesn't love you, Cat, he doesn't own you!'

'No one owns me!'

'You know what I mean. Do you love me, Cat?'

She stared out over the river. 'I . . . I don't know! I don't think I even know what love is.'

He reached out for her but she jumped up and ran to the edge of the roadway that bounded the river wall, her emotions in turmoil. She stood gripping the rail. Of one thing she was certain. Whatever it was she felt for him, it was far stronger, far sweeter than anything she had ever felt before and she knew if he were to ask her to marry him now, she wouldn't be as resolutely opposed to the idea as she had been with Joe.

She gripped the rail harder, staring out down river. The sun was strong and she narrowed her eyes against the glare. Then her heart lurched, seemed to stop dead, then raced on again. Surely, surely it wasn't! At this distance and in the strong light shapes were distorted, colours faded. Her heart lurched again. It was! She wasn't just imagining it! She turned to where Stephen still sat on the grass verge.

'It's her! It's her, Stephen! It's the White Empress! She's come home!'

By the time they had reached the landing stage, via the tram and overhead railway, the *Empress* was well up-river and had taken on the massive hausers of the tugs needed to manoeuvre her alongside. Stephen and his advances were forgotten as she pushed her way through the crowd of people at the landing stage. Again she shielded her eyes from the sun. It was just as though the years had rolled back. The gleaming white hull rose like a cliff from the murky waters of the Mersey, but somehow to Cat she seemed bigger and there was something unfamiliar about her shape. Then she saw the black letters on her bow. It wasn't 'her' ship. It wasn't 'her' *Empress*, for the name *'Empress of Britain'* could be clearly read.

'So that's the shape of my rival! I've got to admit that she's certainly a formidable sight.' Stephen was beside her.

'It's the *Empress of Britain*.'

'You sound disappointed?'

'Perhaps I am, a little.'

'Then there's hope for me yet?'

She smiled. 'I'm sorry. I've dragged you all the way here for, well . . .' she shrugged.

'Not for nothing. She's a wonderful sight and besides, if we stay here longer I may see an old school friend. I heard he was sailing on this particular *Empress*.'

She clutched his arm so tightly her fingers dug into the flesh. He knew someone on board! He had never mentioned this fact.

'You're joking! You never mentioned it before!'

'I didn't want to mention it, I was trying to block these great white whales out of your mind, Captain Ahab, or don't you remember?'

She was too excited to admonish him for his derogatory remarks. 'Oh, Stephen! Can you introduce him to me? What's his name? What does he do?' She failed to notice the downward quirk of his lips.

'His name is David Barratt and he's a junior officer, but I don't think we'll be able to see him. He'll be busy and won't disembark until they tie up properly in Gladstone Dock.'

Her face fell and she suspected him of conceal-
ing something from her. She turned back to look at
the ship, now being nosed alongside the landing
stage, unaware of the hard gleam in his blue eyes.

'Do you want to wait?'

She sighed. It was too much to ask of him, he
obviously thought she was using him to further her
own ends. 'No. Let's go.'

'I'll see you to the tram, then.'

Reluctant though she was to drag herself away
from the scene, she followed him. Later she would
try to sort out all the conflicting emotions she felt
now. Later she could lie in bed, when Shelagh,
Dora and Ethel were asleep, and try to sort out in
her mind the events that had brought about such
an extraordinary day.

The *Empress of Britain*'s stay in Liverpool had been
brief. A twenty-four hour turn-round before she
sailed from the Mersey to her home port of Southampton. And she had sailed on the early tide so
Cat had not seen her go.

She had decided not to mention the matter again
to Stephen as she would not have him accuse her of
'using' him. She had also spent long hours turning
over her feelings for him in her mind. At length
she had admitted to herself that what she felt for
him was nothing like the affection she felt for Joe.
Joe had always been . . . just Joe. A friend, a close
and dear friend she knew she could rely on. A
haven and a refuge. But when he had kissed her
she had felt nothing of the flood of passionate
longing she felt for Stephen. She and Joe were,
well, just like childhood sweethearts. She'd only

been a child when she had first met him and he had been the first and only boy to take an interest in her.

With Stephen the feeling was deeper, stronger and yet, when she searched her heart, she knew that if he asked to marry her she would have to think about it. She couldn't rush into it. She wouldn't rush into it and it was this realisation that made her wonder if she really did love him. She was nearly nineteen now and often she wished for the uncomplicated, naivety of the life she had known at sixteen. When all that had mattered was money in her pocket and a roof over her head.

Thanks to Mrs Grindley's training her Dublin accent had become less pronounced and she was finding evening classes easier. She still saw Marie often, but usually only at weekends for Marie was now at commercial college and destined to be a fully fledged shorthand typist when she finished in another year's time. Stephen took her out on two more occasions, once to the pictures and once to the museum. He had kissed her goodnight on both occasions in the sheltering doorway of the shops, before she boarded her tram. She had felt that same longing, that yearning fill her each time. And the last time she had nearly missed the tram, staying within the circle of his arms, held in the thrall of his embrace until the voice of the conductor broke the spell and she had been hauled bodily on to the platform. It had been the last tram going her way that night and as she had tried to hide her embarrassment, the conductor had laughed and said, 'There's always tomorrow, luv!'

* * *

There had been quite a few 'tomorrows' until Joe had returned home. With a wallet full of pound notes, decked out in his uniform, he had called for her. Only to find out from Shelagh, who eyed him in a new light and attempted to become coy and flirtatious, that she had gone to one of her evening classes.

'I don't know why she wants to fill her head with all that stuff, it's not going to be any use to her, not when she's married and bringing up kids! I thought you and she were 'walking out'? Now if it was me, I'd be waiting on the landing stage for my bloke. One of these days I just might go and take a look myself at these evening classes. I don't know what she finds so interesting, or maybe it's *who* she finds interesting.'

He inquired where the evening classes were held and what time they finished and after giving his regards to both Maisey and Mrs Cleary, he left to catch the tram to Warbreck Moor. He tried to ignore Shelagh's innuendoes, – she was a born troublemaker.

He stood opposite in the doorway of a shop and watched while the students filed out, but he saw no sign of her. The last man he had watched leave crossed the road.

'Any more in there, pal?' he asked.

'Only Mr Hartley, the teacher, and Miss Cleary. She sometimes helps him to tidy up. You a friend of hers?'

'Sort of.'

'Sometimes he walks her to the tram, too.'

'Oh, aye, what's that supposed to mean?'

'Nothing, pal! Got a light?'

Joe delved into his pocket and brought out a box

of matches. He lit one and held it out. The man lit his cigarette, nodded and went on his way. He tried to push away the doubt Shelagh had planted in his mind. He looked at the new watch he had bought in New York. Nearly a quarter past nine. He pushed both his hands into his trouser pockets. He'd wait.

A few minutes later they came out, *laughing and joking, and he scowled as he watched Stephen take Cat's arm and guide her across the road. Then he stepped out, directly into their path.*

'Hello, Cat!'

She gave a cry of surprise that was quickly followed by one of delight. 'Joe! When did you get in? Why didn't you get word to me?'

'Late this afternoon.' He was looking past her.

She caught his arm and pulled him forward. 'Joe, this is Stephen. Stephen Hartley, my teacher and friend.'

He made an effort to smile and shake the man's hand, but he had taken an instant dislike to him. Something he did very rarely for he was gregarious by nature. There was something about him, about the way he looked at Cat. He'd seen that look before. He pushed the thought aside for Cat was linking arms with them both and chattering on as they all walked in the direction of the tram stop.

She had been utterly surprised by his appearance. Then she remembered Mr O'Dwyer saying something about the Scythia but she had been in too much of a rush to take much notice. But she hadn't failed to notice the tension that crackled like lightning between Joe and Stephen. She bade a very hurried goodbye to Stephen as Joe pulled her forward in time to catch the number 22 tram.

'I hear he often walks to the tram with you. Is that all part of the service?' he asked, unable to keep the note of sarcasm out of his voice.

She stared out of the window. 'No, it's not! I told you, you don't own me!'

'Oh, it's like that, is it?'

'Like what?'

'Has he taken you out then, are you doing a Johnny Todd?'

Her mind went back to the night in Mrs Travis's kitchen and the old sea shanty. 'I didn't say I'd stay at home and wait for you. I've got my life to live and he's been very helpful . . .'

'I'll bet he has!'

'Stop it, Joe!' She hissed. 'Don't let's quarrel, you've only just got home!'

He grunted and they sat in silence for the next two stops.

'Did you enjoy your trip?'

'It was alright.' He paused. 'Well, no I didn't, it was bloody awful, if you must know!'

'Why?'

It's a hellhole down there with those turbines going day and night. Far worse than the *Marguerita* and all the damned rules and regulations! It's stinking hot, smelly and dirty. It's a gaping cavern full of pipes, dials, stop-cocks, boilers and eternal bloody noise!'

'I thought it was what you wanted?'

'It is! I'm getting used to it. The chief says I'll make a good engineer one day!'

'Then it's better than being a steward, isn't it?'

He looked at her, knowing she was trying to goad him. 'You bet it is. I wouldn't have their job for the clock off the Liver Buildings!'

'So stop complaining!' she laughed.

As they walked down Boundary Street he slipped her arm through his. 'I've brought you something.'

'What? Oh, Joe, you shouldn't be wasting your money on me.'

He stopped and drew out a box from his pocket and handed it to her. She hesitated and he noticed. 'It's nothing nasty!'

Still she hesitated, fearing it would be a ring and wondering what she would say if it were. Slowly she opened it and her heart sank. Inside was a ring set with a small yellowish stone.

'It's what the Americans call a friendship ring. The stone is a tigers eye. I thought it very suitable seeing as how you can be a right little cat at times!'

She breathed a sigh of relief. The last thing she had wanted to do was to hurt him. She slipped it on the middle finger of her right hand. 'It's lovely! I've never had a ring before and I'll ignore your remarks about me – for now!' She reached up and kissed him on the cheek. 'When do you sail again?'

'I've only just got back! Why?'

'No reason.'

'How is it going?' He indicated the pile of books under her arm.

'Hard. It's damned hard work, but I'm finding it a little easier now.'

'I might have to go back to school myself, one of these days. That's if I want to get on and try and work for my National Diploma. I'll have to go to the Mechanics Institute.'

She was surprised. She had thought that now he had obtained a steady job he would be satisfied. 'Is that what you want? What will that mean?'

'More pay and more chances of promotion. The

175

chief said it's been known for lads like me to get as far as second officer. Only a few do though.'

She stopped and stared into his face. 'You should try, Joe, you really should! Wouldn't it be really something if you were to make second officer and I were to make chief stewardess?'

'It would be a bloody miracle! I see you've still not given up on that one?'

'No. And you know I won't!'

'And what about him? That Stephen Hartley?'

'I've been out with him a couple of times, that's all! Don't let's quarrel again!'

They had reached Maisey's front door. 'Come on in, everyone will want to hear about your voyage?'

'No thanks, I've already spoken to your Mam and Maisey and I couldn't take any more of your Shelagh's simpering and eyelash fluttering! I'll see you tomorrow. Do you go to classes again?'

'No. The night after.'

'Fine. See you tomorrow.' He bent and kissed her, then turned and walked away.

She fingered the small gold ring, feeling a dart of jealousy, remembering his words about Shelagh. She fought it down. She wasn't being fair. She was forever telling him that he didn't own her; it worked both ways after all.

The more Joe thought about Stephen Hartley the less he liked him. The look he had seen in his eyes as he watched Cat was the same as that some of his friends had in their eyes when they first went ashore. It didn't have anything to do with affection or love. It was lust. He made up his mind to find out more about Stephen Hartley.

It wasn't hard. He just enquired at the school

and found out that he didn't teach there during the day. He also found out where he did teach, waited until Hartley left and then followed him home, at a distance.

He stood on the corner of Arnot Street and watched him walk down the street. He himself was dressed in his old shabby clothes, his old cap pulled low down over his forehead, a copy of the *Liverpool Daily Post* in front of him. Hartley wouldn't recognise the smart, young merchant seaman he had met last night. He lowered the paper as Hartley stopped in front of a house. A young woman with a baby in her arms and a toddler clinging to her skirts opened the door. Joe turned away, grim-faced, as Hartley picked up the child. He'd sensed it all along. He was only using Cat! The cheating, lying sod was married!

He hammered loudly on the door of number eight and it was pulled open by a startled Cat, an apron around her waist, her arms wet and covered in soapsuds.

'Joe! I didn't expect you yet!'

'Dry your hands and get your coat on, we're going for a walk!'

Noting the dark anger in his eyes and the low, tense note in his voice she went back inside and without giving an explanation to anyone, did as he bade her.

Neither of them spoke until they had reached the bottom of the street, away from prying eyes and sharp ears.

'He's taken you for a fool, Cat! What's he promised you? What's he done to you?' He had grabbed her roughly by her shoulders and was shaking her.

'Who? What? Let go of me, Joe, you're hurting

me!' She struggled free of him, but she had never seen him so angry before.

'Stephen Hartley! What's he done to you, Cat?'

'Nothing! What's got into you, you're going too far this time, Joe, I told you . . .'

'He's married! Did he tell you that, Cat? I'll bet he didn't!'

Her mouth fell open and her eyes widened and she felt as though she had been dealt a physical blow. It wasn't true! His jealousy had driven him to make this accusation! 'Liar! You're a jealous liar, Joe Calligan!'

'Call me what you like, it's the truth and if you don't believe me then ask him!'

She was too stunned to do anything but stare at him in disbelief.

'I followed him home from the school where he teaches during the day. Arnot Street. I saw him and his wife and his two kids! He's been leading you on, Cat, and you've been fool enough to believe him! Did he promise to marry you? Did he?' He began to shake her again.

Pain fuelled by hurt and anger began to well up in her. 'No, he didn't!' She yelled at him.

'He couldn't very well could he, not seeing as how he's got a wife already! And they talk about sailors!' He released her and she stood staring at him for a second, white-faced. Then she whirled around and fled, back up the street and into the house. She leaned against the door, her breath coming in painful gasps. It wasn't true! It couldn't be true!

'Cat, is that you, luv?' Maisey's voice filtered through her wild thoughts.

She dashed upstairs and fiercely brushed her

178

tangled hair. Then she changed her skirt and slipped on a woollen cardigan. She caught a glimpse of herself in the cracked mirror on the wall. Her face was paper-white and her eyes blazed, resembling the small stone in the ring she wore. She glanced down at it. A tiger's eye. Oh, she'd claw his eyes out if this were true and she'd claw Joe's out if it wasn't!

She remembered the name, Arnot Street, and now she stood staring at the row of neat houses, wondering which one he lived in. She walked past the school on the corner and halfway down she stopped and knocked on the door of a house. Inside she was trembling but outwardly she was ice-cold. A middle-aged woman opened it.

'Excuse me, could you tell me which house Mr and Mrs Hartley live in, please?'

'Who wants them?' Came the suspicious reply.

'I was at school with Mrs Hartley, only she wasn't called that then. I haven't seen her since she got married, I've been away, working. In London.'

'We've lived round here for years and I don't remember Jenny Taylor ever mentioning anyone like you?'

'Well, Jenny and I are old friends, even though I haven't seen her for years and she never mentioned you to me, either!' she lied.

'As long as you're not from the authorities! It's number 16!'

The door was slammed and with a sickly feeling in her stomach Cat walked away. She couldn't turn back now, the woman was watching her. She'd seen the curtains move as she walked away.

With each step she took she wished she hadn't come at all. She knocked on the door of number 16 and a young woman answered it, a chubby baby on her hip.

'I'm sorry to trouble you, but are you Jenny?'

'Yes. What do you want? Do I know you?'

'Jenny Hartley?'

She nodded, shifting the baby into the crook of her arm. From inside the house Cat heard the fretful howl of a young child.

Cat cast frantically about in her mind for something to say.

'If it's Stephen, my husband, you want, he's out. Have you come about the private tuition he advertised?'

Cat felt so ill all she could do was nod. Jenny Hartley had answered all her questions without knowing it.

'Will you come in?'

'No! No, I'm sorry, I haven't much time.'

'He charges a shilling an hour and he can take students two nights a week, here in the parlour. Mondays, Wednesdays and Fridays he takes evening classes. Teachers' pay isn't all that good, not when you first start and we're trying to save up for a house of our own. Will you leave your name?'

'No. I was just inquiring, that's all. I'm sorry to have bothered you.'

It was as much as she could do to stop herself from taking flight. Her legs felt unsteady and it was an effort to place one foot in front of the other, but somehow she reached the top of the street. She was about to cross the road, heading for Marie's when she remembered that Marie would be at college. Instead she found herself walking towards St Mary's, the old parish church of Walton-on-the-Hill. Once through the lychgate she sat down on a bench among the old gravestones. He'd used her! He'd only wanted one thing from her . . . she felt physically sick and covered her face with her hands. She felt cheap as she remembered their passionate embraces, their hot, lingering kisses, the feelings his hands had evoked as they had caressed her breasts. He hadn't been interested in her education or her feelings, he'd only been interested in one thing. Her body! Disgust chased guilt to be followed by anger. Anger that consumed her. He'd pay for this! She'd make him pay for the way she felt now! She'd never be able to look Joe in the face again!

At last she rose. Wiping her eyes and running her hand through her hair. The price of her silence would come high! She'd make him squirm and feel as she felt now! She'd see to that!

CHAPTER ELEVEN

It was almost a quarter to three when she entered the foyer of the Imperial Hotel that faced Lime Street Station. She was wearing her best herring-bone tweed costume, the white lawn blouse with its lace collar, the black leather shoes and the black velvet hat. Her hands were encased in the black kid gloves and over her arm was her best handbag and Mrs Gorry's treasured fox fur which Marie had cajoled from her mother for the occasion. She glanced at the clock on the wall as a uniformed porter came forward to meet her.

'May I help you, madam?'

'It's miss. Miss Catherine Cleary. I have an appointment at three with Mr Barratt. Mr David Barratt, he is expecting me.'

'If you would follow me, Miss Cleary, I'll just check if Mr Barratt is in the hotel.' His manner was a little patronising and she stared hard at him as he motioned her to a circular padded velvet seat in the centre of the palm-filled foyer. She watched him as he went to the desk, checked some papers and then returned, smiling obsequiously.

'Mr Barratt has left a message that he may be a little late and that I am to offer you his apologies and a drink. What would you like, Miss Cleary?'

She didn't drink but she knew this would only

add to his mistrust. 'I'll have a small, sweet sherry, thank you.'

He disappeared and she glanced around her. It was a very smart hotel, she thought. Not as smart as the Adelphi, but very elegant just the same. Still, a junior officer must earn a decent wage. A waiter in a short white jacket, black bow-tie and narrow black trousers appeared, bearing a tray on which was a small glass of sherry. She took it from him and sipped it slowly. It tasted like the Madeira wine Mrs Travis had once given her. Her eyes narrowed as she thought of her old benefactress. She'd not given up her dream. She'd never give it up and she'd never trust another man again! Her gaze hardened as she thought of the scene with Stephen. At first he had tried to protest, to deny that he had a wife and children. Then he had grown angry and abusive, calling her a cheap little slut, no better than she should be! She had rounded on him then like a small fury. Threatening to tell his wife, the entire street and his headmaster just what he got up to after his evening classes. She'd seen the anger drain from his face and it was then that she had first felt the sensation of power. It was a feeling she enjoyed and she had revelled in it, watching him back away from her, nervously fiddling with his moustache. She had felt nothing but scorn for him then. The price of her silence was the reason why she was sitting in the Imperial Hotel. He had promised to obtain a meeting for her with his old friend, David Barratt, and she had insisted that he tell his friend why she wanted to meet him.

She had stood over him as he wrote the letter and she had made sure he posted it, too. Then she had waited for the reply, and, because she didn't trust him, she had made him suggest that David Barratt write directly to herself at Marie's address.

She sipped the sweet drink again and looked around, taking satisfaction from the fact that she was equally as well dressed as the women who wandered through the foyer and up the wide staircase. The waiting had been the worst part. She hadn't gone back to evening classes, she couldn't bring herself to face him again, she despised him so much, and she hated herself. Over and over she had railed silently at the naive, gullible fool she had been. She hadn't seen Joe either, until the day he sailed, when he had come round to Eldon Street to say goodbye. She had apologised to him and it had been accepted without any recriminations. Just the usual peck on the cheek and the warning to 'Take care of yourself, Cat!' She hadn't gone to see him off.

She had waited nearly ten days before she received the reply. The *Empress of Britain* was due in Southampton on 4 September but he was travelling up to see his mother and he would be glad to meet her for afternoon tea in the Imperial Hotel. It had been signed 'Yours Sincerely, D. Barratt'.

She looked at the clock again. It was a minute to three. She placed the empty glass on the table and smoothed down her skirt. She had to make the most of this opportunity. She would never get another one to meet anyone who held such a position with the Canadian Pacific Line. He was one of those 'right' people Joe had talked about. He was her ticket into the world she desperately wanted to enter. She remembered the shabby,

185

uneducated, desperate girl who had gone begging for a job – not even knowing how to go about it or even what to say. She stroked the fox fur. She was older now and wiser. Joe had once called her 'street-wise', now she hoped she was more worldly-wise. This was the first step on the ladder and she would use anyone she could to secure that first, vital step. She had learnt a hard lesson at the hands of Stephen Hartley and it was a lesson her pride would not let her forget!

'Miss Cleary?'

Her deliberations were forgotten and she looked up. David Barratt was in his early twenties, of medium height and build, with hair not unlike the colour of her own. But he had the bluest eyes she had ever seen in a man. His face was tanned and self-assurance oozed from him. Under his arm he had carelessly tucked the white-topped, stiff-peaked cap with its gold braid and corporate symbol. She stiffened, all her instincts sharpened by experience.

'Yes. You are Mr Barratt?' She extended her hand and he took it warmly.

'I'm sorry I had to keep you waiting. Shall we go through?'

With easy confidence he offered her his arm while nodding in the direction of the reception desk. The porter came over instantly.

'Would you follow me, sir. The table is ready!'

She forced herself not to gaze around her as they were ushered into a quiet lounge, tastefully furnished, where a few other couples were taking tea.

He pulled out the chair for her, waving aside the porter's efforts, slipping a coin into the man's hand, unobtrusively. She placed her bag on the table, then, with as much nonchalance as she hoped would be convincing, draped Mrs Gorry's fox fur over the back of her chair, aware he was noting every movement.

A waiter appeared beside them.

'Tea and scones, please. Unless there is something else you prefer?'

She didn't feel in the least bit hungry. 'No, that will be fine.' She left him to undertake the ritual of pouring the tea from the silver service.

'What did Stephen say in his letter?' she asked, knowing full well what that letter had contained. Even to utter his name without venom was difficult.

'That you were a remarkable young lady.'

She raised her eyebrows.

'You're not at all what I expected.'

'Indeed' She wondered if he was goading her. 'What did you expect?'

He leaned back in his chair and pretended to scrutinise her closely. 'For a start, someone a little older.'

'I'm older than I look. My mother tells me it is a fact I will learn to appreciate as I get older.'

'Your mother is a wise woman. Tell me, what does she think about this career of yours?'

She hadn't expected that. 'Not a great deal, at least she hasn't said much.' It was true. Her mother knew nothing at all about it.

'You are also independent. I like that. Why do you want to go to sea?'

She was feeling more confident and had anticipated this one. 'Because I'm bored ashore and I hear it is a good way to travel and be paid for it.'

187

'It's also damned hard work.'

'I know. I'm not afraid of work!'

'It's not very pleasant, not until you rise to the status of a first-class stewardess and you do look to be, how shall I say, a little more refined than the usual type.'

She was still unsure of him. Not really knowing if he was mocking her or just trying to find out how she would cope. She also wondered if she hadn't put on too good an act.

'Everyone has to start somewhere, usually at the bottom, and I have always worked hard and not always under conditions that could be called satisfactory let alone good.'

'You're not afraid to speak your mind, are you, Miss Cleary?'

'No. I speak as I find, Mr Barratt.'

'Can we drop the formalities? I get enough of that aboard, as you'll find out. It's David.'

It was a real effort to replace the cup on the saucer without spilling the contents. 'My name is Catherine, but I was nicknamed Cat by my elder sister years ago.'

He smiled and she noticed that there were tiny white lines around his eyes where the sun had not turned the skin brown. He appeared to have relaxed a little, but she kept her guard up.

'Stephen asked me as a favour, and God knows I owe him a few, if there was anything I could do to help you. Get a start, I mean.'

She had dictated every line of that letter but she held her gaze steady. Wondering what price she would have to pay for his help.

'I did mention to him – well to Jenny really –

that I wanted to go to sea, that I wanted to make a career of it.'

'Then you have no intention of getting married?'

'None!'

'Ever?'

She shrugged. 'Who knows. What about you?' She deftly turned the questions away from herself.

'I've been working too hard and I've not met anyone . . .' He left the sentence unfinished.

'I was once warned never to marry a sailor.'

'Oh, I thought "All the nice girls love a sailor" as the song goes.'

'This one did and lived to regret it. He was a captain on the old tea clippers and was lost at sea. She died a sad, lonely old woman.'

'I think it's time we changed the subject.'

She felt calm enough to lift the cup again.

'I'll do what I can for you, Catherine, I do have a little influence, but then so do quite a lot of people. But if you give me your number I'll phone you.'

She panicked. Everything was moving too fast and she certainly hadn't anticipated this. 'Aintree 613.' Marie's telephone number tumbled from her lips before she had realised it. She hoped Marie wouldn't mind too much.

He had written it down. 'Fine. I'll phone when I know something definite. You'll have to be prepared to go for an interview at short notice.'

'That will present no problem. I am out quite a lot so if you phone, perhaps you could leave a number and I could phone you back, or leave a message, with my sister.'

'I'll leave a message. I don't have a permanent base in Southampton, except the ship, of course.'

189

He didn't appear to have a permanent base anywhere, she thought. She felt the muscles in her stomach knot. Now it would come. Now she would find out what price she would have to pay for this favour.

'More tea?'

'Yes, please.'

'I'm terribly sorry but I'm going to have to leave you, I'm expected at home in half an hour and if I'm late again . . .'

'Oh!' The exclamation came out as a weak gasp.

'Usually I wouldn't take much notice but my aunt is home, too. Miss Eileen Sabell. Take note of that name, you'll soon hear it a great deal – if all goes well.'

'Why?'

'She's the chief stewardess on the *Britain*.' He stood up and took her hand. 'No doubt I'll be seeing you again – soon – but you'll hear from me. One way or the other. Sorry to rush off!'

He had released her hand and had left some silver coins on the table. 'Goodbye, Cat.'

She smiled. 'I hope it will only be *au revoir*, David.'

She made no attempt to steady her hand as she refilled her cup. She was still dazed. It had all been so simple. Everything Joe had said was true. If you spoke correctly, dressed well, had a modicum of education and self-confidence, knew the right people, it was all so easy. And the money Mrs Travis had left her had provided the means to this end. But she was puzzled by David Barratt's behaviour. She had fully expected him to have asked her out, at least to have made some sort of innuendo. But he had gone.

190

Pull yourself together, Cat Cleary! Maybe not everyone in life is the same and he did say that . . . that he owed that despicable toad a few favours. But she was left feeling uneasy and confused. Surely it couldn't be that easy? After months of dreaming, hoping, praying, the object of her dreams had been placed before her without any arguments, any begging, any bartering. The thing she dreamed of, the dream she had clung to, putting it before everything and everyone else, looked as though it was about to take on a definite form. Both the improbability and impossibility were things of the past – nearly.

You've not got it yet, don't start building up your hopes, a voice inside her head warned. Perhaps he had been just stringing her along. Perhaps that toad Hartley had written another letter, telling David Barratt God knows what? She hadn't thought of that before. Maybe it was only curiosity that had brought him here today, to see what kind of a girl it was who dallied with married men! She wanted to get up and run. Instead she slowly picked up her bag and the fur and walked from the room, nodding to the waiter.

She sat on Marie's bed with her feet tucked underneath her while Marie, who had acquired a lot more self-confidence and a certain amount of polish along with her mastery of business studies, sat on the stool before the kidney-shaped dressing table with its pink and white flounced draperies.

'So, when he phones I tell him you're not available and that I'm your sister and can he leave a message? You did tell him you've got a sister?'

She nodded.

'And you told him you were older than you looked? How old?'

'I didn't say.'

'What we'll have to do is write everything down so you can learn it, otherwise you're going to get in a terrible mess when you fill in the application form.'

'I haven't got any kind of form yet and maybe I never will!'

'Now stop that! You've got to think positive as I'm always being told.' She took her shorthand pad and sat with pencil poised. 'I'll write down your name and address, this address and phone number, Dad won't mind taking any calls. Now, your date of birth. How old would you like to be?'

'Marie, it's not a game!'

'I know and we'll both go straight to hell if we drop down dead, so shut up!'

They decided that twenty-one would be the best age, as it was the official age of consent and not too many years ahead for them to get confused. Marie wrote everything down, giving her a fictitious set of qualifications from a not very well-known, but very respectable convent in Dublin. All the rest of the details belonged to Marie and appertained to her life, but she was very generous with them, entering into the spirit with more enthusiasm than Cat. When they had finished she passed over the list.

'I'll never remember all this! Oh, God forgive the pair of us for all these lies!'

'If you are going to be a good liar then you need a good memory – that's one of our Doreen's favourite sayings. She's always quoting it to our Marlene when she keeps getting her boyfriends

192

mixed up! Just learn them until you can reel them off and, anyway, they're not such awful lies! I've just transferred some things of mine to you. It's sort of a gift, really!'

'It's a pack of lies and we both know it!'

'Do you want this job or not?'

'Of course I do!'

'Then shurrup an' learn them!' Marie lapsed into broad scouse.

She had learned them so well that the answers tripped from her tongue easily and her hand didn't shake when she filled in the official application form. The officious clerk she had spoken to on her first visit was nowhere in sight and she had been ushered politely into an inner office by a pleasantly mannered secretary, and given the form to complete. When she had finished and answered a few, brief questions, she was ushered out with the encouraging words, 'We'll be in touch in a few days' time, Miss Cleary.'

She had agonised over her predicament for three days until Marie, unable to wait even a few hours and heedless of the cost, had sent her a telegram.

Interview on Tuesday. 4 p.m. C.P. Office. Royal Liver Buildings.

The arrival of the telegram had been enough to cause an outcry at number eight. Telegrams were always harbingers of bad news and Maisey had flatly refused to take it from the boy and had called Cat. The entire household was mystified by Cat's piercing shriek of joy.

'Jesus, Mary and Joseph! She's gone off 'er 'ead!' Maisey cried, crossing herself.

193

'No! No! It's good news! Wonderful news!' She kissed the telegram and then hugged it to her. 'I've got an interview with Canadian Pacific on Tuesday!'

A sea of blank faces stared back at her, uncomprehending.

'If I get through it I'll get the job of stewardess on a White Empress!'

Mouths dropped open and heads shook in amazement.

'God luv 'er, but she's a dark 'orse! 'Ow did yer manage that, Cat, yer 'ave ter 'ave a letter from the 'Oly Ghost 'imself ter gerra job like that!' Mr O'Dwyer, who had worked on the docks for most of his life – when not unemployed – had summed up the situation astutely.

'I got to know the right people, as Joe calls them.'

'What's Joe goin' to say about this then? I thought you two were as thick as thieves!' Shelagh did not attempt to hide her jealousy.

'Nothing. He's known all along that this was what I dreamed of, what I really wanted to do!'

'So who did you give a backhander to, or did you pay for it in kind?' Shelagh's tone was vitriolic.

'Shelagh! What a despicable thing to say!' Her mother rebuked her.

Maisey was not so genteel. 'Nor everyone drops their drawers for a shillin' or 'angs around the dock gates waitin' to be picked up by anyone with money in 'is pockets an—'

'Maisey! Tharral do!' Mr O'Dwyer cut short the rest of the remark but not before a tinge of colour had crept into Ellen Cleary's cheeks and fury contorted Shelagh's face. He intervened again. 'Don't spoil it fer Cat by causin' a bust up! It's good on yer, girl, I say! Make the most of it!'

194

'I intend to Mr O'Dwyer, you can bet on that. I've worked hard for this chance, that's what all the evening classes and trips to Mrs Grindley's were for.'

'Well, just don't expect to see her back here when she sails off into the sunset! She'll be too toffee-nosed for the likes of us now! Probably wouldn't even spit on us if we were on fire!' Came Shelagh's venemous comment.

'One of these days, Shelagh, you'll want a favour from me!'

'Like hell I will!'

'And I'll take great pleasure in sending you packing! You've always been down on me! Always jeering, mocking and humiliating, but you'll regret it, just you wait!'

Shelagh snorted contemptuously. 'The day I come whinging to you, Cat Cleary, will be the day the Liver Birds fly off!'

Before Cat could reply Maisey launched into a series of questions, damping down the sparks of what threatened to be a full conflagration.

She had come through the interview with flying colours and had even surpassed herself by her outward show of confidence. As she left the offices, she was handed a list by the secretary. It detailed all the uniform and commodities she would require. To be bought from Greenberg's in Park Lane, out of her own pocket.

She walked down to the landing stage and leaned on the railings. The Seacombe ferry was nosing its way across the choppy waters, while a dredger moved ponderously down river, the ferry cutting across its wake. She felt like throwing her hat in the air and yelling and hugging every passer-by. She wanted to scream out and let the whole world know that she'd done it! She'd done it! Instead she looked down at the boarding pass she'd been given. A stiff white card with the words 'Canadian Pacific Steamship Company' in black type, beneath which were the crossed red-and-white-chequered flags. She ran a shaky finger across the printed lettering and the handwritten words.

Name Miss Catherine Cleary
Rating Stewardess (2nd Class)
Ship S.S. Empress of Britain
Port of Embarcation Southampton
Date of Embarcation Sunday, 14th November
Time 13.00 hours G.M.T.

Her hands began to shake and the letters became blurred as the tears slid down her cheeks. She thought of the day she had stood, petrified on the ledge of the *Leinster* so close to the sea.

It had drawn her then and it drew her now. It wasn't just ambition that drove her, otherwise she would have found another way, perhaps an easier way, to achieve status and wealth. It was the same restlessness as the ever-shifting sands, the constant motion of the waves. It was in her blood. Salt water, Mrs Travis had called it. She couldn't explain it, not even to herself. Perhaps it was the blood of the old Viking warriors mingled with the ancient Gaels, passed down over many centuries. A strange love affair begun hundreds of years ago, whose echoes had filtered down and touched her heart, stirred her blood. It was all that and more. A siren's song that had nearly lured her to her death. A song she heard again as the glaucous water lapped the stones below. A song that would send her to the four corners of the Earth, ensnared by its spell.

CHAPTER TWELVE

The small family group stood just beyond the barrier to platform 5, under the arched, glass-domed roof of Lime Street Station, Ellen Cleary holding tightly to Eamon's jacket, Maisey with her arm through that of her husband while a little way away stood Mick Cleary. His shoulders were hunched, his bloodshot eyes darting around the station as though for some means of escape. Marie stood beside Cat and they were both set apart from the others by their appearance, Marie in a lichen green, wool coat and hat and Cat proudly wearing the navy-blue bridge coat with its double rows of brass buttons and the navy-blue beret with the CP badge.

'Now yer mind what yer Mam told yer, Cat, work 'ard an' don't give no lip ter anyone an' watch out fer the men!' Maisey advised.

They weren't the words her mother had used but the meaning was the same. Cat smiled. 'Don't worry, I can take care of myself!'

'Just the same, I wish she was goin' with yer!' Maisey jerked her head in Marie's direction.

'So do I!' Marie echoed rather glumly.

'This is becoming more like a wake than a send-off! I'll write to you and you can save the stamps, Eamon, they'll be foreign.'

He stopped scowling and looked interested.

Foreign stamps were valuable currency among his gang of cronies.

A piercing, deafening whistle, followed by a rush of steam, announced that the train was due to leave and Cat picked up the heavy case.

'I'll get a porter, that's too heavy for you!' Marie pushed her way through the crowd but not before Cat had noticed the catch in her voice. She hugged both Maisey and Mr O'Dwyer then turned to where her father stood shuffling his feet.

'Bye, Pa, take care of yourself.'

He muttered but she made no attempt even to take his hand, instead she turned back to her mother.

'Bye, Ma, I'll be fine. I'll be back before you know it.' There were tears in her eyes as she hugged the thin form to her and kissed the sallow cheek.

'God protect you, Cat, and be a good girl!'

'I will! You'll be proud of me, Ma!' she whispered.

'We all are! Didn't 'alf the street want ter come ter see yer off!'

There was no mention of Shelagh.

Her case was whisked away by the porter whom Marie had found and the two girls hugged each other.

'Good luck, Cat! Take care!' Marie said hoarsely.

She couldn't speak. The excitement that had buoyed her up over the last few days had evaporated and she was afraid. Afraid of what faced her and whether, now that her desire was within reach, she would be able to cope with this new life that had beckoned so tantalisingly for so long.

'If you don't hurry up you'll miss the train!' her mother urged. So with a last kiss, she walked through the barrier, then turned to wave before she began to hurry down the platform. She was leaving behind her the old life. Ahead of her stretched a new one. A terrible emptiness filled her, as though she were suspended in a void and loneliness and apprehension dogged her steps as she wondered what faced her.

She reached Southampton tired and cold. It had been a long journey and a tedious one and the loneliness had increased. It was the first time she had ever undertaken such a long journey alone. As she stood in line at the ticket barrier she noticed that there were other uniforms in the crowd and after passing through she was struggling with her case when a girl with bright, coppery hair, dressed in an identical bridge coat and beret, called to her.

'Bring your case over here, I've got a porter!'

With relief she dumped the case on the trolley. 'Thanks, I feel as though my arm is now a few inches longer than when I started out.'

'I'm Anne. Anne Selby. You're new, aren't you?'

'How did you guess?'

'By the little-girl-lost expression on your face. Come on, we'll get a taxi and share the fare between us. It's better than fighting your way on and off trams with all that gear.'

Cat was so grateful she could have hugged her.

It wasn't far to the docks and during the journey she learned that Anne had been a stewardess for a year. She also learned something of what faced her, facts of which she had been forewarned. And then they had arrived.

She stepped out of the taxi and turned around.

Her heart began to race for there, tied up in dock, was the White Empress, even more gigantic at such close quarters. So colossal and majestic that had it not been for Anne Selby, she would have been tempted to turn and run. She stood gazing upwards, transfixed by the sight. Forty-two thousand tons of gleaming white steel, bigger even than the *Mauretania*. Rows and rows of portholes and a gangway that looked like a stairway up to the sky. The great White Empress, her white paint a coat of ermine, her three yellow funnels like gigantic points of a crown, setting her apart from the drab, commonplace hulls of all the other liners in the world. To Cat she had become not merely a symbol of wealth, power and security – she had become a friend, a vital, living thing. Stephen Hartley had called the Empress a rival and she wondered if there wasn't some truth in the description. This ship meant more to her than just a job. She had dreamt about her, longed for the sight of her; was it possible to love a ship, she wondered?

Anne tugged at her sleeve, bringing her back to reality. 'You'd better report to The Dragon right away.' Then, seeing the consternation in Cat's eyes she continued, 'Oh, she's not that bad really. She's a stickler for rules and regulations, but if you've got a problem or are in trouble, then she's a tower of strength!'

'Miss Sabell?'

Anne nodded. 'Come on.' She looked around and spotted a group of men walking in the same direction. 'Here, Bill, be a good bloke and carry these, will you, or we'll be exhausted by the time we get up that gangway!'

Two of them detached themselves and took one case each.

'A new face, eh?'

'Another lamb to the slaughter!' Anne joked. 'What's your name? I didn't even ask you! God, you must think I'm awful!'

'Cat Cleary. Short for Catherine.' She wondered if it wouldn't have been better to have introduced herself by her full Christian name. Cat sounded childish and had already caused her enough trouble.

She parted company with the others at the top of the gangway as the man who had carried her case offered to take her to report to Miss Sabell. The feeling of sheer panic intensified as she followed him down a warren of passageways, known as companionways, her heels tapping loudly on metal decks. She'd never find her way around, she thought, it was so vast! Down three steep flights of stairs they went, passing numerous doors. They descended yet another staircase.

'Here we are, D deck. Fluff Alley!'

Being totally unfamiliar with the jargon she just stared back at him.

'Miss Sabell's is the third cabin along.' He laughed. 'It's called Fluff Alley because the hair-dressers and stenographers have their cabins here. Go on and good luck!'

She paused before the door with the words that proclaimed 'Chief Stewardess', then taking a deep breath, knocked gently. On being told to come in she entered. It was a small room, low-ceilinged. A bunk, neatly made up, was set against the bulk-head. There was a narrow wardrobe, a wash basin with a cupboard beneath it and a desk facing the opposite bulkhead. The desk was littered with papers and the woman at the desk turned to face her. She was older than Cat had expected, but with a trim figure. Her short, light brown hair was tucked neatly under a small, starched cap. Her blue eyes took in every detail of the girl who stood before her.

'I was told to report to you, Miss Sabell.'

The chief stewardess picked up a list from her desk and studied it. Then she looked up.

'Miss Catherine Cleary?'

Cat nodded.

'Welcome aboard the *Empress of Britain*, Miss Cleary. I presume you have your uniforms and the booklet of company regulations, so I won't waste time on all that. As long as you stick to the regulations you can't go far wrong. In a moment I will show you your cabin. But first things first. You will work a seven-day week, while at sea. You will be on duty ten hours of each day but there will be periods for meals and rest, although you will still be expected to answer bells during those times. You will be expected to stand watch, everyone on board does. It will all be explained to you. I myself will supervise you at first, then you will be under the direction of your section head. You will be expected to do your own laundry, your meals will be drawn from the galley. Lights out at 20.00 hours and I must emphasise this fact, no men are allowed in cabins — ever! In fact no men are allowed near the stewardess' quarters except to call for you if you are going ashore in port. You will work in port, but Saturday afternoon, Sunday and Monday mornings you will have free.' She paused. 'You have, I presume, been informed of your wages?'

'Yes, M'am. £10 per month.'

'Have you made any arrangements for an allotment?'

'I have. Fifteen shillings a week to be paid to my mother.'

The allotment was a set sum of money deducted from wages and was paid to the person to whom it was allotted. This guaranteed that families had a weekly income while the earner was at sea.

'You will be given your section, a cabin – or what used to be called steerage class section. You will look after people who are emigrants and who often have very little money.' Again she paused. 'Quite often they have less than you earn a week but they have paid for their passage and are entitled to be treated with respect, even though at times they can be difficult!'

Cat's gaze didn't waiver although her mind went back to the day she had arrived in Liverpool as just such an emigrant.

'Have you ever been to sea before, Miss Cleary?'

'No, M'am. Well, not for long periods that is.'

'Then as it is November and the weather will be rough, you will probably be sea-sick. Nearly everyone is at first. You'll get over it. You will have to for there is no one to take your place, do your work, should you succumb. You will be expected to carry on – regardless! There will be a daily inspection by either the captain or the purser and woe betide you if there is even a hair out of place! Which brings me to the subject of your hair. You will have to have it cut, it's too long. Regulations state it must be no longer than collar-length. I'm strict but I hope I'm fair and I expect my girls to be smartly turned out at all times! You have had your vaccinations?'

Her arm still ached. 'I have indeed.'

Miss Sabell smiled. 'It's a necessary evil carried out every three years!' She rose. 'Are there any questions, Miss Cleary?'

'Not that I can think of, M'am.'

'Good.' Her face softened a little. 'If you have any problems, I will expect you to come straight to me.'

Cat nodded and picked up her case. The cabin was becoming hot and stuffy and the thick coat added to her discomfort.

'Just one more thing,' Miss Sabell reached over and picked up a bunch of keys from the desk.

Cat looked at her steadily.

'You will soon find that you will be knocking on cabin doors with a smile on your face and hate in your heart, but it is something we all endure, I can assure you!'

As the day wore on Cat's heart grew heavier and her head ached. She had been assigned a cabin in the bowels of the ship. A tiny room to be shared with Anne Selby. She had been issued with so many instructions from Miss Sabell and advice from Anne that her brain was like a sodden sponge. She had been taken through miles and miles of companionways, all of which looked identical, shown the galley and the pantry where her meals would be taken, standing up, as there was no crew mess. She learned that the stewardesses were lucky, they only shared with one other. The men shared with six or seven others.

She had been given tantalisingly brief glimpses of the first-class A & B decks and the dining rooms and ballrooms. Both bigger than anything she had ever imagined. Then given her *Empress* vessels emergency life-boat number and final boat station and the instruction to learn it by heart and at last had been taken back to her cabin to unpack and get some tea.

She sat down on the edge of the narrow bunk. 'I never imagined it would be like this!'

'No one ever does. All they see is the luxury, the glamour, the chance to travel and be paid for it. Well, it's not like that. It's work, work and more bloody work. Just wait until the passengers come aboard! Did she say anything about them?'

'Yes, something about the emigrants being entitled to service and respect, although most of them don't have what we earn in a week.'

Anne had hung her uniform dress on a hanger and was smoothing out the creases. It was dark-blue with a white collar and cuffs and with the same double row of brass buttons as the bridge coats. 'If they don't fall out I'll have to iron the damn thing again!' she muttered. Then she turned back to Cat. 'What she didn't tell you is that they think they are entitled to have us running back and forward all day at their every whim and bloody rude and ignorant most of them are too! It's always the same, those with nowt do the most shouting and complaining. Those who have always had money are a dream to work for! The first-class girls are damned lucky! You'll soon find out. Now, you'd better get unpacked, then I'll take you along for something to eat. We usually see one of the chefs alright, if you know what I mean, that way we get decent meals, although half the time we don't get time to finish them because of those damned bells!'

'Anne, have you got any aspirins, my head is thumping?'

Anne grinned. 'We'll go and see Mavis in the shop and get you a supply, you'll need them – at first!'

There had been no carnival send-off. No bands. No crowds. No coloured paper streamers. In fact she hadn't realised they were even moving until the ship was in the Channel where the rough sea buffeted her and the deck sloped under Cat's feet and she slid with a bump against the wall of the companionway. The tray in her hands crashed to the deck. She picked up the broken crockery and mopped up the mess with a tea towel, gritted her teeth and headed back to the galley. All the romantic dreams she had thrived on turned to dust on that first trip.

As Miss Sabell had predicted she was sea-sick, unable to keep even water down, wishing only to be left alone to die. Anne had bodily dragged her to her feet and forced her to get dressed.

'There's no one to cover for you, luv, no matter how bad you feel, you've got to carry on!'

'Oh, just leave me alone! Let me die!'

'Get that out of your head now! No one ever died from sea-sickness! Now get out and get on with it!'

She never knew how she got through those three days. It was a living nightmare. There was no let up in the weather and the ship rolled and pitched, the motion made worse by the ceaseless noise of the great turbines that drove the screws in the engine room below. All her passengers were sea-sick and despite her own nausea she had to look after them as best she could. Cleaning up vomit as she forced down the bile in her own throat. Changing linen as her stomach heaved. Bringing them food and drinks which were often late arriving as she had to stop so often. All this while still parading for inspection and carrying out her normal duties. When she fell into her bunk at night she wished that she had never, ever set eyes on the White Empress.

On the day she began to recover, at Anne's suggestion, she put on her bridge coat and went up on deck.

'You should have gone up top days ago, it helps! It's something to do with the balance!'

So she stood huddled on the promenade deck while the wind threatened to tear away her beret. She stared at the sea, cold, grey and merciless. It seemed to take a delight in tossing the ship up and down, as if in the palm of its hand. As if saying 'No matter how big or how grand you think you are, I am bigger, stronger, mightier!'

'It has many moods, Miss Cleary. You'll learn that. You'll also learn that it is dangerous, cruel and forever hungry. You will learn to respect it and those who say they don't fear it are either fools or liars – or both.'

Miss Sabell was standing beside her.

"How are you feeling now?'

'A lot better. Oh, how I've wished I were dead!'

Miss Sabell laughed. 'Everyone does! David told me you were a girl of spirit?'

Cat wondered what else David had said about her.

'You've come through your baptism of fire well,

Miss Cleary, I think you'll suit!' She glanced at her watch. 'You'd better go below now, we don't want you catching cold.'

She had reached her own section and she paused beside a cabin door. Over the noise of the turbines she thought she could make out a scream. She knocked loudly but there was no sound; then as she turned to leave she heard the agonising scream again. She opened the door. On one of the four bunks in the tiny cabin a girl was lying on her side, her knees drawn up to her chest, moaning softly.

Cat shook her. 'What's the matter?'

The girl's large, dark eyes were filled with pain and fear. Sweat stood out on her forehead and her dark hair was lank. 'Oh, Miss! Miss! Help me, I think it's the baby!'

'What baby? I wasn't informed that anyone in here was pregnant!'

'I didn't tell anyone! It was my Mam and Dad, see!' Her features contorted and she writhed again in agony.

From her accent Cat judged her to be Welsh. 'I'll go for the doctor!'

'No, Miss! Don't go! Don't leave me!'

'You've got to have a doctor if . . . if the baby is coming!' Her gaze fell on the bell push and she pressed it hard. 'Why didn't you tell anyone, you should have done you know!'

'Where I come from, Miss, the disgrace would have killed my Mam and Dad.'

Anne appeared.

'Get the doctor, quick, I think she's having a miscarriage!'

'Oh, my God!'

The girl screamed again and Cat grabbed her

and held her close as Anne disappeared. Trying to distract her, Cat questioned her. 'Where do you come from and what's your name?'

'Megan. Megan Roberts. I come from a small village outside Denbigh.' She began to writhe and scream and Cat prayed that Anne would hurry.

'But surely you could have told someone?'

'You don't know what it's like! Mam wouldn't have minded too much, but they're Chapel and very strict and I couldn't stand hurting them, see. The shame ... so I told them I was going to find work, I've got a sister in Canada.'

'Is she meeting you? Do you know where she lives?'

She nodded, biting her lip to stop the screams. Then her whole body convulsed and her screams bounced off the walls of the tiny cabin, making the room reverberate. Cat clung to her.

The doctor, a nurse and Miss Sabell all arrived at the same time.

'How long has she been like this?' The ship's doctor asked.

'I don't honestly know, sir. I've been with her for about ten minutes, but she's pretty bad.' She tried to disentangle herself but the girl clung like a limpet.

'Oh, don't leave me, miss!' she pleaded.

'The doctor has to examine you, he's here to help you, Megan! Try to relax.' She soothed.

'It's too late to move her, just yet. Nurse, bring my bag over! Miss Sabell, would you help to hold her?'

Cat gazed into the face of her superior and found courage there as they both held and comforted young Megan Roberts and while she cried

211

in agony and the doctor drew away from her the pathetic little embryo that had already lost its fight to live.

When it was all over and the patient had been sedated and removed to the hospital, Cat started to strip off the soiled bedding. Miss Sabell rolled up her sleeves and helped her.

'You coped very well, Miss Cleary. You were calm and reassuring. Many a girl would have panicked or become hysterical faced with such an emergency. Take the linen to the laundry and go and change your uniform. I will clear up here.'

Passing a hand across her forehead Cat straightened up. Her legs felt weak and she was exhausted, but she nodded and the hint of a smile played around her lips.

'May I go and see her later? She's alone.'

'Of course, but make sure it's alright with the doctor first.'

Megan was lying exhausted and still drowsy in the hospital bunk as Cat crept in. She was very pale.

'How are you feeling now?'

The girl opened her eyes. 'Not too bad, they've given me something.'

'Are you sorry?'

'That I've lost it? Yes, in a way, I'd got used to the idea.'

'Will you go back now?'

'No. There's no reason to. He wouldn't marry me anyway.'

'Did you love him, Megan?'

'I thought I did. It doesn't matter now.'

'No, it doesn't. You've got a new future ahead of you. You didn't get round to telling me if your sister is going to meet you?'

'She is. She and her husband. I'd been worried about what I was going to tell her and what she'd say, but now . . .'

Cat took her hand and squeezed it. 'Now you've no need to worry.'

'You've been good to me, you have. But . . .?'

'What? Don't be afraid to ask, Megan.'

'Well, if ever you go to Denbigh, would you call and see my Mam and tell her . . . tell her you met me. She didn't want me to go, see.'

'I will.'

'Promise?'

'Of course. Where does she live?'

'Bryn-y-Garn Farm, Henllan, about five miles outside Denbigh.'

Cat wrote it down, then tucking the address into her belt, she rose and squeezed Megan's hand. 'You get well, now! Your sister wants to see a young girl full of good health, fresh from the farm!'

They had docked in Quebec where some of the passengers disembarked, but where the crew did not go ashore. Cat stood on deck with a freezing wind blowing in from the Gulf of St. Lawrence, cutting through her, watching the activity on the dock below. High above the city rose the turreted, Chateau Fontaine, the luxury hotel belonging to the Canadian Pacific Railways but looking just like a French chateau. Everything about the city appeared fascinating and she felt excitement stirring in her.

Canada. Never in her life had she dreamt about going this far from home. The voices on the dockside were different, too – half English, half French – and she longed to follow the passengers down the gangway. But there was work to be done for they would sail again for Montreal in a few hours' time. She spotted Megan Roberts waiting at the top of the gangway and called out to her.

'Oh, Miss Cleary, I wanted to see you before I went! My sister's down there, I can see her! Look, she's waving.'

'Good. I hope you'll be happy, Megan. Put the past behind you! Good luck!'

'I will! I can't thank you enough, Miss Cleary, and you will remember your promise, won't you? They'll be so glad to see you. Make you feel right at home, they will!'

Cat smiled and gave the girl's hand a tight squeeze. 'Go on, they're waiting for you!'

She watched her go, wondering when she would ever find time to carry out her promise.

CHAPTER THIRTEEN

With a baby in her arms and two toddlers clinging to her skirt, Cat first saw the city of Montreal. The sky was cobalt blue and the sun shone brilliantly although the temperature was only a little above freezing. There had been the first heavy fall of snow in this city of northern Canada and beyond the docks the scene reminded her of a Christmas card. It appeared to be a city of churches and cathedrals, their spires and domes glistening like frosted icing.

The hours before they docked had been hectic and full of turmoil as passengers collected their belongings and the respective members of their families. All the stewardesses were busy helping mothers with their younger children and babies, collecting items that had been mislaid or unwittingly abandoned.

Cat began to shiver as she helped a young woman, who was travelling alone, to get herself and her children down the gangway to where her husband eagerly awaited them.

Anne took over from her halfway down. 'Where's your coat? You'll catch your death of cold! Get below before the dragon sees you and puts you on report for being improperly dressed – to say nothing of frostbite, and I'm not joking!'

Her teeth had stopped chattering and warmth

was seeping back as she reached her cabin, but she was exhausted. The Nolan family had been the last of her charges. Was there time for a quick cup of tea before starting the stripping down and cleaning of the cabins on her section? There was a knock on the door and she sighed. No tea. Probably Miss Sabell to read the Riot Act.

David Barratt stood outside. Her surprise must have been acutely obvious. She hadn't seen him since their meeting in Liverpool.

'Sorry to barge in, but I've not much time. Most of them are ashore now so I have to stand watch.'

He was smiling down at her with those blue eyes that had such a magnetic effect on her. She smiled back, a little shyly. He had placed her in a dilemma. The rule of 'No men' was very rigidly adhered to, yet not to ask him to step inside she felt was churlish.

'I've no time to come in and chat — even if it was allowed — I just came to ask you if you would like to see the sights of Montreal tomorrow? I've felt rather guilty about not inquiring how you were getting on, but . . . you know how it is.'

'I know how it is — now!'

He smiled again. 'I did warn you.'

'I know and I've no regrets.'

'Was it that bad?'

'It was, and your aunt was right, I was seasick.' She laughed. 'I thought I was going to die.'

He laughed with her and she noticed how different he looked when he laughed.

'So you got the pep talk?'

She nodded.

He leaned closer. 'I'll tell you a secret. On my first trip I wished I was dead! I wished I was

216

anywhere but on this ship, I even longed for a desk job like my father's! Later I changed my mind. How are you getting on with the other girls?'

'Oh, fine! Everyone's been so helpful, especially Anne. I don't know how I would ever have survived without her.' She leaned her cheek against the edge of the door, wishing she could ask him in. His manner was so different from their first meeting. Then he had been polite and friendly, in a stiff sort of way. Now he seemed more at ease and as though he were really interested in her.

'Shall I pick you up at, say, two o'clock? I am allowed down here for that.'

'Thanks, I'll be ready.'

'Two o'clock then.'

She shut the door. All she had wanted to do was to lie down on her bunk and sleep for three days, but the prospect of going ashore in this, her first foreign country, quickly dispelled her exhaustion. And the prospect of going ashore with him added an extra touch of excitement. He was so charming and he had said he felt quite guilty about not seeing her before this, and that must mean he had more than a passing interest in her. *Stop day-dreaming, Cat Cleary!* she scolded herself. There were so many things to be done now.

She decided on a cup of tea before starting her work. Then there was her own laundry to be done. Her hair needed washing. Her dress needed pressing. She had no suitable footwear for snow. Mentally she ticked off things which a little while ago she would have thought were very trivial.

Anne had said 'Lucky you!' when she had told her,

and Cat wondered if she were envious. If she was she didn't show it, generously offering to lend Cat her second best boots. An offer she gratefully accepted.

At two o'clock sharp came the knock on the door. She had been ready for a quarter of an hour. Twice she had readjusted the small fur hat – lent by another stewardess – over her neatly brushed curls. She wore her best wool dress under the tweed coat with the large red buttons. Fortunately Anne's leather boots were black and so toned in with her gloves and bag. David's black, uniform great coat covered the rest of his uniform and she began to feel strangely nervous. In a few minutes she would set foot in Canada, and with him.

'You look very smart,' he complimented her, smiling.

'So do you.'

'I find it helps, the uniform I mean, in getting reservations and service. We'll take a cab. It's too cold to walk far, it's sunny but it's below freezing.'

'Have you planned the whole day?'

'Not rigidly. If there is anything particular you want to see, any place you really want to go to, then it's up to you. I thought we'd have lunch at a little restaurant near the hospital, then go and have a look downtown. See Windsor Street Station, which is worth a visit, then we'll do some shopping along St Catherine's Street. Shopping is always obligatory, I've found, and then have dinner at the Indian Rooms at the Bellevue Casino?'

They had reached the top of the gangway and Cat paused.

'What's the matter?'

'Nothing really. This is a new experience for me.

My first time abroad.' She dismissed her arrival in Liverpool from Dublin. That didn't count.

'You're not going to kneel and kiss the ground when we reach the bottom, are you?' he joked.

She laughed, thinking of her arrival in Liverpool. 'No, I don't suppose this is the Promised Land either.'

'Here, give me your hand, we don't want you slipping, do we?'

His grip was firm and she did feel more secure as she descended. His manners were impeccable, she thought, as he went first down the steep gangway, leading her as though she were a fragile doll.

It proved to be something of an anti-climax as they were whisked away in a cab along St Lawrence Main, away from the docks which appeared to be not dissimilar to those in Liverpool and Southampton. He must have seen the fleeting look of disappointment, for he leaned closer.

'They all look the same, don't they? It's the same the world over. Warehouses, handling sheds, cranes and dock workers! But cheer up, in a while you'll see the real Canada – or at least a small part of it. It's such a vast country, it's bigger than America.'

'Is it really?' She was surprised, and surprised at his knowledge, but then he had obviously had the benefits of an education far superior to her own.

When they reached St Catherine's Street she began to realise that he was right and how different the city was. The shops were bigger, glossier and already full of Christmas gifts. The main streets were wider and there were far more cars and lorries and fewer horse-drawn vehicles. The buildings were cleaner and taller, some of them over twenty storeys high. There was a mixture of architectural styles. Old French-Canadian beside modern, oblique Canadian.

The meal in Le Jardin l'eau was her first experience of French cuisine. She let David order for her, trying to hide her embarrassment at being unable to read the menu, by searching her bag for her compact. She felt as though every pair of eyes in the room were watching her. She had no intention of using the compact – that would be the height of bad taste – but the subterfuge worked. Despite the fact that she watched David surreptitiously, but closely, in the matter of the cutlery, she enjoyed the meal.

'Now I feel much better and ready for our foray to sample the delights of shopping!' He pulled a wry face and then smiled. 'I have a wicked sense of humour but you'll get used to it, I hope!'

She laughed as he held out her coat, glad that he couldn't see the faint blush that had crept into her cheeks.

They spent two hours browsing through the shops and department stores along St Catherine's Street and she purchased a fur hat and a small, leather-bound missal for her mother; a leather wallet for Joe and a maple leaf brooch in red and white enamel for Maisey. At a craft shop she bought a real tomahawk, complete with beads and feathers, for Eamon and promptly wondered if it was such a wise choice after all, thinking of the havoc he could cause with it. At Simpson's department store she bought a sealskin muff for Marie and a walrus, carved from soapstone by the Inuits, for Mrs Gorry.

'You've got nothing for yourself!' David protested.

'What do I need?' she laughed, still thrifty and

mindful of the small amount of money she had left while trying to work out the rate of exchange.

He picked out a very chic red and black silk scarf and handed it to the assistant with the appropriate dollar bills. After it had been wrapped he placed the slim package in her hand.

'Oh, David! I couldn't! Really, I couldn't accept it!'

'You must have something to commemorate your first trip abroad. You can look at it in years to come and think "This reminds me of the very first time I went to Canada." '

With some embarrassment she accepted it. It was the most expensive accessory she had ever owned and it matched her coat and suit. Obviously he had very good taste. The thought disturbed her. It reminded her of her own inadequacies.

The Indian Rooms at the Bellevue Casino were a revelation. She had expected something eastern and exotic. They were exotic, but not in the way she had anticipated. The walls were covered in hessian which formed a natural background for the spears, tomahawks, bows and arrows, brightly woven blankets and rugs and paintings of the indigenous tribes of North American Indians. In the centre of the dining room was a full-size totem pole, flanked by two smaller ones. On the polished wood floor were rugs made from the skins of bear, moose and bison, and the pelts of wolf and beaver. At the far end of the room one whole wall was filled with the trophy heads of these animals, fascinating and frightening. But the whole effect was tasteful and dignified, the culture of a noble civilisation captured for posterity.

'I'm not really very keen on it, but I thought you would be interested to see it.'

Her gaze moved slowly round the room. It was primitive, even barbaric to her modern eyes, yet she was sensitive to its raw expressions. The figures in the paintings drew her attention: there was a wild beauty about them.

'It's so . . . so extraordinary . . . so captivating!'

'The Legend of the Noble Savage, Hiawatha, and all that. Shall we order? At least the food doesn't comprise buffalo steaks or beaver stew!'

She laughed at the face he pulled, yet she wondered just what such dishes would really have tasted like? She wanted to discover and assimilate every new sight, sound and taste.

With their meal he ordered a bottle of champagne.

'Oh, David, that's much too extravagant!'

'No, it's not! This is going to be a day you will always remember, if I have my way, that is! Today, it's nothing but the best!'

This statement had the effect of putting her instantly on her guard. She touched the silk scarf at her neck. He had been charming and pleasant and witty, but she wondered if all this were not a means to an end?

'The first time we met we didn't have much chance to get to know each other, Cat, so tell me about your life, your family?'

Her smile belied the inner panic that swamped her. The thought of telling him about her Pa, Shelagh and the O'Dwyers caused a knot to twist in her stomach. She knew she shouldn't be afraid to tell him of her family background, but she was afraid that if she did, he would scorn her, pity her or become angry that she had presented herself, by inference, as a girl from a much better class of home than number 8 Eldon Street. Besides, she had already embarked on a course of deception when she had first met him. She smiled and then told him about number 18 Yew Tree Road. When she had finished, she asked him about himself.

He was an only child. His father was a bank manager. Miss Sabell was his mother's sister and the family home was in Great Crosby. He'd been educated at the Liverpool Institute and there his friendship with Stephen Hartley had developed. He'd had to battle with both his parents in his choice of career, his father being disappointed he was not following him into banking and his over-protective mother had been horrified at the thought of all the dangers, both real and imaginary, that he would face. At this juncture his aunt had proved to be a staunch ally and he was now working hard for his ticket and would one day be master of his own ship, he finished confidently.

'So that's a short précis of my life, so far.'

She leaned back in her chair, replete. She had never met anyone like him before. With a background like that she felt she had made the right decision. Had he been aware that she was nothing more than a 'jumped-up Irish slummy' (as Shelagh had viciously described her before she left) she was certain now that the smile on his face would have been replaced by shock and horror.

He refilled her glass.

'David, do you mind if I ask you a very direct question?'

'What?'

'I really don't know how to put this, I don't want to offend you, but . . .'

'But you are wondering what I want as, shall we say, payment for all my assistance and today's

223

entertainment? I hope you didn't take offence earlier when I said something about having my way? It wasn't meant as innuendo, Cat, really it wasn't.'

Thankful that she hadn't had to voice the question herself, she nodded and took another sip of champagne.

He leaned across the table. 'You have a very suspicious and devious mind, Miss Catherine Cleary!'

She blushed. 'I have a very good reason for that.'

'Would you like to tell me about it?'

'No. I'm sorry, David, I don't want to talk about it.'

'Obviously someone, and obviously a man, has hurt you in the past. Hurt you deeply, am I right?'

She must think carefully, she was walking on thin ice. What if he had been in contact with Stephen Hartley? She didn't answer.

'And you swore you'd never trust another man?'

'Yes, something like that.' She was feeling very tense, wishing she had never brought the subject up.

'Then set your mind at rest. I have absolutely nothing devious in mind. I want nothing except the pleasure of your company. No strings attached. That kind of thing is little more than moral blackmail and I don't stoop to blackmail of any kind!'

She breathed out very slowly and began to relax. She should have known. He was too much of a gentleman, but then she'd never experienced the attentions of a real gentleman before.

He opened a cigarette case and offered her one. She shook her head. 'I don't smoke, thank you.'

'Do you mind if I do?'

'No, I'm sorry, David. I know it was wrong of me

to judge every man by . . . It's just that this job meant so much to me! Drudgery, sea-sickness, exhaustion – everything!' She gave a mirthless little laugh.

He reached out and covered her hand with his. 'There's no need to apologise, Cat. Let's just enjoy ourselves. After all isn't that what time ashore is for? Damn it, we work hard enough at sea!'

She wanted to believe him, but experience wouldn't allow her to drop her guard entirely. But she did smile as they finished the last of the champagne.

Despite the sub-zero temperatures they walked to the top of St Lawrence Main and both were in a happier mood than when they had left the ship. She felt elated, partly due to the wine and partly due to the fact that she had won ten dollars in the Casino, where David had cajoled her into playing roulette. She had never gambled in her life, she had never had money to throw away, but she felt a little reckless, although caution tempered her delight and he could not persuade her to risk another chance. She'd never come by so much money quite so easily. But as they walked briskly in the crisp air, she admitted that most of her elation stemmed from the fact that she felt more at ease with David Barratt.

They called in for a late supper at Joe the Greek's.

'Oh, someone's slumming it!' came the cheerful greeting as they sat down in the small, spotlessly clean restaurant with its chequered tablecloths and Ionic bric-à-brac. It was Anne and two other girls accompanied by three of the stewards.

'I've had the most wonderful day and I've won ten dollars!' she laughingly called back.

'At first she looked on the casino as the Pit of Satan. In the end I had to drag her away!' David teased, laughing at her indignant protests.

He bought drinks for everyone, which endeared him to all concerned, and after that supper was a very convivial affair. At the end of it, David agreed to accompany all the girls back to the ship for the men were going on to the Liverpool House Tavern and etiquette was strict. No women were allowed in any tavern.

When they reached the top of the gangway Anne and the others quickly disappeared, leaving them alone. David pulled the collar of her coat high up around her ears.

'Has it been a day to remember, Cat?'

'Oh, you know it has! It's been wonderful, I love Montreal!'

'What will you do tomorrow?'

'Oh, after inspection I'll go to Mass, then write some letters. I promised faithfully to write home.'

'I'm afraid I'm on watch tomorrow afternoon.'

'I have lots of things to catch up on. Things I didn't get time to do while we were at sea, or rather I was too tired to do.' She knew she was just passing the minutes in small talk, wondering if he would attempt to kiss her, in spite of all his reassurances. 'I have to stand watch tomorrow night.'

'And then on Monday, it's back to work. Back on the merry-go-round.'

'At least I won't be sea-sick!'

'We don't get much time off do we? At least not at the same time.'

Now apprehension was building. She had had a wonderful day and he'd been so generous and such pleasant company. She didn't want anything to ruin it.

He bent forward and kissed her gently on the cheek. 'Never mind, things should improve next trip. The St Lawrence will be frozen over so we're cruising. Then I'll be able to show you some really sensational places!'

She hadn't even thought about next trip. 'Cruising?'

'Yes. New York, the Bahamas, Jamaica, Cuba, Barbados, Haiti, Curacau, the Virgin Islands and back to New York.'

She was stunned. She had only just got used to the fact that she was really in Canada. 'But . . . but they won't be taking emigrants surely?'

'No. You'll be promoted, temporarily, to first class. All the girls are.'

Her eyes widened. 'You're joking?'

'No. Ask my aunt!'

'Oh, David! It's a dream come true! This isn't happening to me, it can't be!'

'It is and you won't consider it much of a dream when you're sweltering and exhausted.'

'I don't think I'll care!'

'Don't bet on it.'

'I'd better be getting below.' She wanted time to digest this piece of news, to ask Anne if it were really true.

'I can't come with you.' He sounded a little resentful.

'I know, but thank you! Oh, thank you, David, for a wonderful day!'

'We'll do it again, in New York, that's a promise! Good night, Cat.' He kissed her cheek.

227

Impulsively she hugged him quickly. 'Good night, David.'

They were due to sail into Liverpool for a refit and when Cat found this out her excitement knew no bounds. At last she had realised part of her dream. She would sail up river to see the familiar landmarks from the deck of the White Empress. At last she would be looking down on the Princes landing stage, instead of looking up as she had done that day that now seemed part of another age. Another life.

There were few passengers on the return trip but the work went on as usual, following the tradition of never taking a dirty ship into port. They had all been mustered by Miss Sabell and given their instructions. She listened intently, but with her heart racing as the quiet, precise tones of the chief stewardess carried clearly in the huge, empty dining room. All tourist-class girls were to be promoted, temporarily, to first-class for the duration of the cruises. Of which there would be four. They would be away from home for over four months. She read out all the regulations appertaining to the working procedures and informed them that tropical white uniform would be worn two days after leaving New York, and that those of them to whom it applied should have their vaccinations before they sailed.

Cat stood on the boat deck as they entered the Mersey. A cold wind tore at her hair and her hands were thrust deep inside the pockets of her coat. The landmarks slipped slowly by and she remembered how Joe had pointed them out to her from the deck of the *Leinster*. On this cold December day, through a mist of needle-fine drizzle, the buildings of the Liverpool waterfront looked grim and dirty, but she didn't notice their drabness. She was coming home. Already the tugs were coming alongside, fussily tooting their sirens, a sound taken up by the dredgers, the ferries, a Blue Star ship and the *City of Adelaide* standing out in the river. At the landing stage the black hull and red funnels of the *Mauretania* were becoming clearer and she thought, detachedly, that the Cunarder didn't seem much bigger than the *City of Adelaide*.

The deep-throated blast of the *Mauretania* added to the cacophany. The White Empress was coming home and Cat hugged herself. Everywhere this magnificent Empress went, her entry was greeted by a reception such as this. She was different. She was special. And she was coming into her home port. She wished that Mrs Travis could have been among the crowds waiting and a tinge of sadness momentarily marred her exhilaration.

She went below to finish her packing, keeping the gifts she had bought in a separate bag. The few passengers had disembarked and in an hour's time they would berth in Gladstone Dock and the crew would be signed off. She counted the notes before tucking them safely into her purse. There would be more next trip for they were to be paid a ten-pound bonus for sailing out of New York. A few trips and she would be able to find a nice little house she could rent and furnish for her mother. For them all, if necessary. At least Eamon and her Ma and Pa, if her mother wouldn't leave them. Shelagh could fend for herself. Maybe in a decent house, perhaps with a garden, Pa might find something to interest him, she thought. He'd liked gardens. When she had been very small he had often taken her to Phoenix Park and she remembered that he wasn't a Dubliner by birth. He'd come from County Waterford as a young man, looking for work and the excitement offered by a big city. Maybe a garden of his own could wean him away from the bottle.

She could provide all the little luxuries they had never had. She would open a bank account and save hard. This was the advice she had been given by Miss Sabell, with whom she had discussed the matter of her earnings. Her needs were small. She was clothed and fed, she needed only a little spending money for trips ashore, so most of her wages could be saved. Miss Sabell had even given her advice on what kind of account she should open and at which bank. She had worked out that after the four months' cruising she could move her mother to a comfortable house and she could increase the allotment so that the rent and bills could be paid with money left over.

'Hurry up, Cat!' Anne's voice broke into her thoughts.

'Nearly finished.'

'I've coaxed Jacko into carrying our cases and he's waiting.'

She snapped the locks shut, then pulled on her beret. 'Ready!'

'Anyone meeting you?' Anne asked, as they struggled along the companionway to the foot of the stairs, where the burly figure of the stoker stood waiting.

'Only my friend.'

She craned her neck as she reached the top of the gangway, trying to peer over the shoulders of the other members of the crew, all of whom were going ashore and were shouting and waving to relatives below. Some brandishing the 'docking bottle' as an indication of the good, old-fashioned 'do' to celebrate their homecoming, parties to which all relations, friends, acquaintances, and usually most of the street as well, were invited. Even the dockers were shouting up to them, knowing there would be the usual bartering and rich pickings if they could get such illicit items past the Paddy Kelly* on the dock gate.

'I can't see her!'

'Oh, don't worry, she'll be there. Somewhere among that crowd of wives and mothers and kids, all waiting to get their hands on the wages before they get spent in the Caradock. See you in two weeks, Cat!' Anne called.

She smiled, then scanned the sea of faces below as she descended, hoping no one had come to welcome her home in case David or someone else should see them. Then she caught sight of Marie, waving madly.

The two girls hugged each other and over Marie's shoulder she saw Joe. As soon as Marie released her she hugged him. 'Oh, it's grand to see you! I've missed you both!'

He clasped her tightly then held her at arm's length. 'You look worn out! Enjoy it, then?'

'Oh, yes! I was sea-sick, homesick, run off my feet, but I loved it!'

An uneasy glance passed between Joe and Marie when she asked how everyone was.

'We'll get a taxi, we can't lug that case on and off

*Dock policeman

the tram!' Marie was already making her way along the side of the cargo shed.

Her heart beat slowed. Something was wrong.

'Joe, what's the matter?' She clutched the bag of gifts tightly.

'It's your Ma, Cat . . .'

'Oh, not pleurisy again?'

He shook his head.

'Then what?' A nameless fear began to loom up.

'Pneumonia. I'm sorry, Cat, I didn't want to be the one—'

'Where is she?' She grabbed his arm and began to shake him, without realising what she was doing.

'They don't think she's strong enough . . . she's in the Royal Infirmary.'

'Oh, Dear God! Why didn't they get the doctor . . . ?'

'Cat, I was away myself and you know what Maisey's like about doctors, if I'd been at home—'

'But she could afford the doctor, she had the allotment!'

'She didn't . . . well, you know how your Ma is with your Pa, she never could refuse him anything.'

All thoughts of houses and gardens, of the hopes of reforming him, the memories of childhood, vanished as though they had never even existed. 'So while I've been working like a dog, thinking it would help her, she's been giving most of it to . . . to—'

'If I'd have known, Cat, I would have had a word with Maisey. I swear to God I would! Only your Ma could have signed for it, but then—'

'She gave it to him! I'd have sooner thrown it overboard than give him a penny!' She was shivering

232

with a mixture of anger, fear and frustration and her heart sank further when they all got into the taxi and Joe instructed the driver to go to the Royal, Brownlow Hill. Her mother must be bad, very bad to have consented to go to hospital. She dreaded even the mention of the word.

The infirmary was a grim, square, soot-blackened old building. Originally it had been a workhouse and as she followed Joe into the green-tiled waiting room, she felt it still retained that atmosphere of despair and sorrow. The air was permeated with the odours of carbolic soap and ether.

They were directed up one flight of stairs and a sister in a starched white apron and cap ushered them into the ward with strict instructions that they could only stay for a short while and must make no noise to disturb the other patients. It was only because of her occupation that they were allowed in at all, she informed them curtly. It was most unusual and quite a concession.

The ward was chilly although a wood-burning stove was set in the centre. The half-tiled walls heightened the illusion of coldness. Narrow beds with black iron bedsteads and uniform white coun-terpanes lined both sides and it was in the bed nearest the far wall that she found her mother. The walk between the rows of beds was the longest walk she had ever undertaken. She was horrified by what she saw. This woman looked so old, so haggard, so shrunken, her eyes closed and dark circled. Her lips tinged with bluish purple. She took one wasted hand.

'Ma! Ma! It's me, Cat,' she whispered.

Her mother's breathing was laboured and a

queer gurgling noise emitted from her throat, but she slowly opened her eyes and tried to smile.

'Oh, Ma! Ma! Why did you do it? Why did you give it to him to drink away? Look where it's got you and all the time I thought you'd be well and warm and comfortable!'

Ellen Cleary tried to speak but the words were difficult to form, the effort it cost great. 'He's . . . my husband, Cat. Right or wrong, I vowed . . . better or worse . . .'

'But, Ma, he took the same vow, but he's never honoured it!'

'Two wrongs . . .'

She pulled the stool close to the bed and buried her head on her mother's shoulder, thinking about the hours of back-breaking work, the agony of sea-sickness, and all for . . . this. She raised her head. 'I'm staying with you, Ma. I won't move until you're better!'

She felt a tap on the shoulder and looked up

'The doctor wants to see you, Cat,' Joe said softly.

She rose. 'I won't be long, Ma.'

The doctor was sympathetic. Her mother's condition had been too advanced when they had brought her in. He couldn't hold out much hope of recovery. She was worn out, her constitution undermined by malnutrition, poor housing, worry and despair. Her chest had been weak ever since the attack of pleurisy. He expressed the opinion that probably it had been weak for years.

She faced him white-faced and dry-eyed, clenching

234

her hands tightly. 'You are telling me she is going to die?'

'I'm sorry, Miss Cleary, but that is the only conclusion I can come to. If she had been brought in sooner. If she had had proper care. If she had looked after herself . . .'

'If! If! If! Doctor, I left money so that she would be well cared for, money that only she could draw upon, but . . . I'll kill him! I'll swing for that swine!' she cried bitterly.

He remained silent. He'd seen it all before and with such dreary monotony that it had almost become commonplace. The days when he had railed against the conditions his patients suffered were long past but he sympathised, for in her he saw a flash of his young self.

She fought down her anguish. 'May I stay with her, I nursed her through the last time?'

'It's not allowed, I'm afraid.'

She was outraged. 'You tell me my mother is dying and then you tell me to go! To leave her here to die among strangers – alone!' Her voice had risen to a scream.

'Miss Cleary, please! Remember where you are!'

'How can I forget! I'm staying right here or we're both going home now! I swear I'll carry her myself and you won't stop me, if she dies in my arms it will be better than dying here! It's no better than the workhouse!'

He began to lose patience. 'Miss Cleary, pull yourself together! You are a young woman of some common sense, those days are over, she will receive the best attention!'

'I'm staying and you'll have to call in the police

and have me dragged away screaming!' Her voice was steady, almost cold, and the hard light that blazed in her eyes drew a grudging admiration from him. She meant what she said.

He had relented and she stayed. She sat on the hard, wooden stool beside her mother's bed, listening to the increasingly laboured breathing, the ugly gurgling of the fluid that was drowning her lungs and she prayed as she had never prayed before. All the pleasant memories of childhood, few though they were, came flooding back and when she thought of the plans she had made for the future – for their future – her heart felt as though it were being torn to shreds. She loved this gentle, self-effacing woman so much. She had tried so desperately to ease all her burdens. The pain of grief, despair and guilt grew as the hours passed.

She was with her at the end, as was Father Maguire and Shelagh. She had flatly refused to allow Eamon in and had confronted her father like a virago, grief turning to blind fury as she dared him to take one step inside the ward. She had smelled the drink on his breath and a red mist danced before her eyes as he had slunk away.

In the end she went peacefully, quietly. So quietly that it was the priest who took her hand from within Cat's own.

'She's gone. She's at peace now, past all pain and suffering. She's with God.'

For the first time in years the two sisters clung to each other, all past enmity forgotten. Cat blamed herself for her ambition and gullibility. Over and over she muttered, 'I should have known! I should have known!'

Joe was waiting with Maisey and Eamon who buried his head in Maisey's skirt when he saw them.

Maisey dabbed her reddened eyes with a handkerchief and crossed herself. 'God 'ave mercy on 'er soul! She never 'ad a bad word ter say about anyone! Cum on, Eamon, lad, I'll take yer 'ome, now.'

Shelagh groped for Maisey's hand and Cat looked up at Joe, dry-eyed. He took her into his arms, holding her close and stroking her hair. 'Oh, Cat! Cat! What a homecoming! I'd give anything to have spared you this!'

CHAPTER FOURTEEN

The Requiem Mass was held at Our Lady's and the whole street attended it. Maisey wore the fur hat Cat had brought from Montreal for her mother, and had gently laid the leather-bound Missal and the maple leaf brooch – which she had treasured – on top of the coffin.

Throughout the service Shelagh had sobbed loudly and continuously, her exhibition of noisy grief grating on Cat's already shredded nerves. She herself had stood the whole expense of the funeral. Shelagh had confessed with loud lamentations that she was 'flat broke' and after telling her father in no uncertain terms what she thought of him, Cat refused to speak to him or allow him to contribute a single penny, which she doubted he had anyway. Joe and Mr O'Dwyer had been her towers of strength, dealing with all the official formalities. She had told Joe that despite custom, there would be no wake. She didn't care what the neighbours would say or think, she wasn't having the usual drunken do which frequently ended in a brawl. Her mother was going to be buried with some dignity.

'But what will the neighbours say, Cat? They'll say she 'asn't been given a proper send-off an' that yer flyin' in the face of tradition!' Maisey had demanded, still swollen-eyed.

Shelagh had started to cry noisily again.

'I don't care what anyone says! My mother is going to be buried with dignity! We've nothing to celebrate and neither have they and I'm not having my money spent on beer for the whole street! It's enough that he drank it all and put her in her grave!' she had yelled furiously, spurred by grief.

So after the interment she went home with Marie, accompanied by Joe. Mrs Gorry had laid out a small meal for them in the dining room and after hugging Cat and patting Joe's arm, left them alone.

'Cat, you must try to eat something,' Marie pleaded, passing her a plate of sandwiches.

Under Joe's gaze she took one and nibbled at it.

'Cat, don't bottle things up inside. "Grief should come out," Mum says. You haven't cried, not one single tear!'

'It's . . . it's not that . . . I can't, Marie. I just can't! But I'm crying inside, in here.' She pressed her clenched hand against her chest.

'Mum says you can stay here, if you want to. Until you sail.'

'I'd be very grateful if I can, Marie, I can't go back there, there's nothing there for me now, not with —'

'When do you sail, Joe?' Marie cut in.

'In two days and it will be a longer voyage this time, I'm afraid. Will you be alright, Cat?'

She nodded, the bread tasted like sawdust and stuck in her throat. She coughed. 'Then I won't see you for months, Joe. We're cruising this time. I'll be away for over four months.' She leaned wearily back in the chair. She was tired, bone tired. She hadn't slept for the last two nights.

Marie looked worriedly at Joe. 'She will be in and out of New York.'

'I'm bound to be in New York at the same time, even if it's only for a day. I'll try and see you then.' He leaned forward in his chair. 'Maybe it's best this way, Cat. It will help you try to forget . . . you won't have time to . . . brood.'

'We don't know what we would have done without you, Joe, and I really mean that,' Marie said quietly.

He managed a smile. He liked Marie. There was no snobbishness about her, despite the fact that they were comfortably off. 'I know at least she's in good hands here, Marie, that helps. Seeing as how I have to leave so soon.'

'It's a pity I can't go with her.'

'How much longer have you got at that college?'

'Oh, ages yet!'

'Have you never thought of applying for a job as a stenographer?'

She looked surprised and he saw the flash of interest in Cat's eyes.

'I could, couldn't I? By the time you get back from cruising, Cat, I should nearly have finished my course. If I can get them to let me take my exams early, then I could apply.'

'I'd feel happier if you were with her. It's no picnic on those ships – even cruising, and if she starts to neglect herself, not eat . . .'

'Will you both stop talking about me as though I wasn't here!' she snapped. Her nerves were raw, her grief so intense, didn't they understand that? How could they go making plans when her world had crumbled?

'Sorry, but you know how we both worry about you, Cat.' Marie ignored the outburst.

She stared into the fire. The feeling of loss was so great that at times it was as though part of her had died too. Suddenly she thought of David, thinking detachedly, that it was the first time she had thought of him. Over the past days it was as though he had never existed.

'Will you come to see me off?' Joe asked.

She nodded but Marie shook her head.

'It would be better if you came here. She's exhausted . . .'

He knew she was right. Parting would be another painful burden for her. It was best done in private. 'I'll come on Monday morning.'

It was a tender farewell in Mrs Gorry's parlour. She had relied on him so much and now they were to be separated for months. She did feel a little better. Sleep, rest and supportive company had helped.

'You look better, Cat.'

'I feel better. They're so good to me, Joe.'

'Cat, you must not feel guilty, you must try not to grieve. She wouldn't want that. She was so proud of you, you know. You gave her hope and dignity. Maisey said she showed all your letters to everyone. She never had much out of life, you did give her something to show for the sacrifices she made. But you've got your whole life ahead of you, Cat.'

'Mrs Travis once said that. She said she envied me.'

'She was right. You've got to look to the future.'

'But it looks so bleak, Joe, there doesn't seem much point . . . now!'

He took her in his arms. 'You'll soon forget all

this misery. You'll never forget her, Cat, but just try to think about the places you'll see, the people you'll meet. It's a world away from all this!'

'Time heals, Mrs Gorry says.'

'She's right, Cat, look to the future.'

'I'll miss you, Joe, I often think of you.'

'I think of you, too, Cat.'

'Oh, Joe! I know I can always rely on you, lean on you, you're always there when I need you most!'

'Isn't that what friends are for, Cat?'

She leaned against his shoulder and so didn't see the flash of pain in his eyes.

It was a week after Joe's departure and she was busy getting her white uniforms, caps and shoes ready for packing when Marie came to tell her that Shelagh was at the door asking for her.

'What does she want?'

'I don't know, she wouldn't say. But she looks upset.'

'She's probably lost her job, is broke or Maisey has thrown her out, or all three.'

Marie sighed. 'Cat, she is your sister and she is very upset.'

Cat nodded. 'I know, perhaps some good has come out of . . .'

'I've put her in the dining room.'

Cat ran down the backstairs, through the kitchen and hall and into the dining room. She hadn't seen her sister since the day of the funeral. Shelagh was sitting in a chair in front of the fire, dressed in a shabby, cheap, red coat. She looked pinched and drawn and utterly dejected. Cat's heart softened.

'What's the matter?' She sat down in the chair opposite.

'I've come to ask you something, Cat.' She was near to tears.

'What is it? How much do you need?'

'It's . . . it's, not that. I don't need money, not really. Can you . . . well, can you get me a job like yours?'

Cat was surprised. So surprised that she didn't answer at once. Then she gave a sad little laugh. 'Shelagh, are you daft in the head? You know how hard I had to work, at evening classes, elocution . . . everything! They'd just never have you and I'm not being unkind. I went once, when I worked for Mrs Travis. They wouldn't even take my name! They looked at me as though I was a piece of rubbish!'

There was nervous desperation in Shelagh's face. She shifted her position in the chair. Pulled a grubby handkerchief from her coat pocket and clenched it in a tight ball in her hands. 'Can you get me something, anything, in the kitchens . . . anything! I'll do anything, Cat, just get me on a ship going anywhere!'

Her words brought back a well-remembered feeling of apprehension. 'I don't have that kind of influence, I don't know anyone! What's the matter, what have you done?'

Shelagh jumped up, stuffing the handkerchief back into her pocket and clutched Cat's arm. 'You've got to help me, Cat! You've got to help me get away!'

'Why? Is it that bad, Shelagh?'

'I'm . . . I'm in the club!'

The fact that she was pregnant did not give Cat

the shock she thought it would, she had expected something far worse. 'Oh, Shelagh, you fool! Who's the father, won't he marry you?'

Shelagh gnawed at an already bitten-down thumb nail.

'Don't you know who the father is?'

'No, and even if I did, it wouldn't matter! Maisey will throw me out! Everyone will laugh and point and call me names! Where will I go? I've got to get away! It would have been alright, in the end I mean, if Ma had lived, but . . . now . . .'

Understanding dawned on Cat, with such clarity that for a few seconds she was bereft of speech. Her eyes narrowed and her hatred of her sister was so great that she had to clasp her hands tightly together for fear of lashing out. 'You selfish bitch! So that's why you were in such a state when Ma died! It wasn't grief at all! You felt nothing for her, it was because you knew you were pregnant! You knew if she had lived you could have stayed with Maisey, once the gossip had died down things wouldn't have been so bad! You never even thought of what your condition would have done to Ma! You heartless bitch! Now, when Maisey finds out, she'll throw you out! That's why you were crying and wailing, not because of Ma, but for yourself!' She gave a caustic laugh. 'And I thought you'd changed, I really did! But you'll never change will you, you're just like Pa! You always were!'

'How did you expect me to feel? I've been a fool, I know that now!' Shelagh cried, still clinging to Cat's arm.

Cat shook off the grip, her disgust and anger blazing in her eyes. Still no word of regret for her mother.

'You've got to help me. Cat! You've got to! Maisey will drag me round to Father Maguire and it will be back to that Home and I'd sooner die on the streets than go back there! Oh, God, you've got to help! I'll be out on the streets, I'll starve!'

Cat's cold, contemptuous gaze swept over the desperate, cringing figure of her sister. If Shelagh had only uttered one word of regret, one word of true sorrow, then maybe . . . 'I can't!' she snapped.

'You won't! That's what you really mean! You've got money, I know you have! I won't need much to go away somewhere, somewhere where no one will know me . . . You won't be bothered with me again . . .' she babbled on, the tears flowing freely. She wiped her running eyes and nose on the sleeve of her coat, despite her handkerchief. Disgust showed clearly on Cat's face.

'No! You'll get nothing from me, Shelagh Cleary! You're right, you've been a fool! A cheap, common whore! And I'm glad Ma's not here to see your shame! I never thought I'd have cause to say it, but . . . but I'm glad she's gone! You never cared about her, not the way I did. You never did anything to make her happy, just kept heaping on more worries, more shame! Even now, not one word of regret . . . I won't help you! I've worked too hard, suffered too much and mainly at your hands! Time and again you've humiliated me! You used to enjoy it, jeering and mocking, do you remember that night in Ma Boyle's? Go back to your friends, you were always boasting how your friends thought you were so wonderful, such a good laugh. Go and see if they'll help you, because I won't! In fact if I never see you again I won't worry about it! Now get out!'

Shelagh's face contorted with rage, fired by despair. Gone was all her pleading, despairing attitude. 'I knew I shouldn't have expected anything from you, except abuse! May the Divil blast you, Cat Cleary! I'll get even one day, wait and see! I'll treat you the way you've treated me, no matter how rich and respectable you become, you'll never find happiness! Never! I'll make sure you don't! I'll make you sorry you turned me away when I needed help!'

Cat flung open the door. 'Get out of this house before I get Mr Gorry to throw you out! You slut! You whore! You've got a nerve coming here! Go on, get out!'

Shelagh stormed past her and up the hall, but Cat darted in front of her and pulled open the front door. Shelagh turned. 'The Divil's curse on you, Cat Cleary! I'll get even one day!'

She slammed the door shut and leaned against it, trembling with the force of conflicting emotions. She didn't fear Shelagh's threats, but the knowledge that her sister's grief had been only for her own predicament filled her with hatred. She never wanted to set eyes on Shelagh ever again.

The *Empress of Britain* sailed on the morning tide, leaving Liverpool in the grip of what promised to be a long, hard winter. Making her way along the coast she headed for Southampton, there to take on passengers bound for New York.

Cat was not sorry to leave Liverpool, the place looked as desolate as she felt. She'd left an allotment of a few shillings for Eamon, to be drawn by Maisey and only Maisey. She hadn't seen David during her leave, but he had telephoned and Marie had told him of the death in the family. A large bouquet had arrived the following day with a card bearing the simple message, 'With my deepest sympathy, David'.

Some of her depression was dispelled when she found she would be working on B Deck and the full opulence of the ship was enfolded before her eyes. The Salle Jacques Cartier dining room occupied the full width of the ship on D Deck and had been designed, as had the two smaller, private dining salons, by Frank Brangwyn, who had also designed the cold buffet which rose in tiers from the floor to the ceiling of the enormous room.

On the lounge deck was the Empress Ballroom with its huge domed ceiling on which was painted a mural of a representation of the sky on the night the ship was launched. The Mayfair Lounge had been designed by Sir Charles Allom and the walls were panelled in polished woods of varying hues, all blending and merging, adding a depth of warmth to the Palladian Lounge. At the forward end was a large tapestry panel that covered the entire wall, depicting the hunting exploits of the Emperor Maximillian. In the Cathay Lounge, which was also the smoking room, Chinese lacquer vases and motifs and rattan furniture lent it an Oriental theme.

At the head of the wide, deeply carpeted, main staircase was an enormous painting by Maurice Griffenhagen, RA of *Champlain Bringing his Wife to Quebec*. The Olympian Pool, the largest swimming pool on any Liner, was at the after end of F deck. Water poured into the pool from a large turtle carved from Portland stone and the pool itself was inlaid with blue mosaic and illuminated from below. Alongside were Turkish baths and massage rooms. On B deck there were squash and tennis courts. There were numerous other bars and lounges, including the Knickerbocker Bar, a cocktail lounge in very modern taste.

The first-class passengers had the choice of six de-luxe suites which included a vestibule, sitting room, double bedroom, bathroom and small dressing room, all furnished in pastels and prints. And there were the spacious two berth cabins or fourteen special state rooms. Such unimagined opulence took Cat's breath away. The lustre of polished woods, the soft plush and velvet upholstery, the crystal chandeliers, the long balconies with their exquisite fretwork, the sweeping staircases, the gilt framed mirrors, the ornately framed pictures. It *was* a floating palace. She also learned the origin of the word 'posh'. It was made up from the first letter of each word of the phrase 'port out, starboard home'.

In one of the state cabins, she smoothed the satin coverlet with gentle reverence. Its delicate shade of turquoise-blue matched the rest of the furnishings and toned with the pale, cream-coloured carpet. The rosewood furniture gleamed. So this was how the fabulously wealthy lived and travelled! Helping themselves from the range of exotic culinary delicacies arranged with cunning artistry on the cold buffet; being served dinner on fine china; wine in crystal glasses, coffee from solid silver services. Fresh flowers on the crisp white tablecloths, seated in velvet upholstered chairs with carved gilt frames. Indeed it was another world. A world she had never, even in her wildest flights of imagination, ever envisaged. She glanced around. Soon the wardrobes would be bursting with expensive gowns from exclusive shops. The dressing table would be covered in bottles of French perfume and cosmetics. Flowers would fill the room. She could almost smell the perfumes, hear the sounds, the tinkling laughter, taste the wines. Oh, one day she would travel like this. In sheer, abandoned luxury. She gave the coverlet a last pat and came back to reality. Not yet. Not for a long time yet. There was still work to be done.

She found Anne's comments on the nature of the rich and famous to be mainly true. There were few sharp rebukes, no constant complaints, no petty requests. The ladies she attended, bringing fresh towels, changing the flowers, laying out their clothes, serving them breakfast and afternoon tea, were pleasant but not patronising and she therefore found her work less physically and nervously demanding.

They made the crossing in record time for the *Empress of Britain* was the biggest and fastest ship of her day. Within a matter of days Anne was dragging her up on deck for her first view of New York. If her first sight of Canada had enthralled her, then her first sight of New York amazed and overawed her. There was no need for Anne to point out the Statue of Liberty or Ellis Island, where so many of her own countrymen had landed, destitute, and had risen to wealth. The grey winter twilight was a backcloth for the myriad of lights on the horizon, reaching into the sky itself as Anne pointed out the Empire State building and the skyscrapers of the Rockefeller Centre, like diamond-studded candles rising into the sky. As they drew closer the panorama widened. The spark of excitement Cat had first felt had turned into a blaze.

'I'm . . . I'm just . . . speechless!' she stammered.

The tooting of the Staten Island Ferry heralded their approach and was taken up by the tugs and other shipping and again the great White Empress gracefully received the salutations of her peers as she entered the Hudson River, to be guided into Pier No. 7 where the longshoremen were waiting for her.

Anne turned away, complaining of the cold for it was a sight she had seen before, but Cat remained, gazing at the spectacle of twinkling lights that stretched before her. She felt as though she were dreaming, that in reality she was two people. One half of her was the wide-eyed waif, the other the confident young woman. 'You've come a long way, Cat Cleary,' she whispered aloud. 'Whoever would have believed that you, a Dublin slummy, could ever have come so far? To see such a sight. To be part of such a welcome. To be part of such a ship.' She smiled to herself as she turned to follow Anne below.

There wasn't much time ashore but David duly escorted her around some of the sights. Times Square and Broadway. Central Park. Fifth Avenue and Madison Avenue where she drooled over the stores. She found New York a bustling, abrasive, exhilarating city and was disappointed when they returned to the ship for the last time.

She had found herself trusting David more and more, for he was fun to be with, he made her laugh and forget the more serious thoughts that troubled her. Yet he was thoughtful, buying her the odd trinket, the single flower, presented with such theatrical flourish that she found she could only laugh and not suspect any ulterior motives. In fact they spent so little time together that there wouldn't have been much time for anything else, she mused.

'We'll have more time to explore when we get back, we'll be lying up for a week before the next onslaught, then we'll really be able to "go on the town".' He had promised.

She tickled his cheek with the bunch of violets he had bought her. 'I'll probably be too exhausted to do little more than sleep.'

'Well then, I'll have to make sure we both put our time ashore in the Caribbean to good use.'

She laughed. 'Can there be anywhere as exciting as New York?'

'A million and one places and we'll see them all, I promise!'

'All at once?'

'No, you sweet, silly fool! Next year we're going on a world cruise and then "the world will be your oyster, M'am!" ' He swept her an exaggerated bow which made her laugh again.

'Oh, be serious, David! I've only just got used to the idea of visiting places like Cuba, Jamaica, Haiti! It's like taking a trip straight out of an Atlas, except that instead of pictures I'll be able to see them, hear the sounds, smell the exotic perfumes . . .'

'Some of the perfumes are far from exotic, I can assure you!'

'Oh, don't be such a killjoy!'

He pulled her close and kissed her. 'I've seen them all before, Cat, but it will be fun exploring them all again with you.'

She didn't pull away from him. 'Do you really mean that?'

'Of course I do! You are a joy! You see everything through eyes that are not jaded or sceptical. Your bubbling enthusiasm is catching, you're . . . You're so sweet!'

'I've never been called that before!' she laughed. 'When I first met you you said I was independent. Did I give you a false impression?'

'You did. I never expected that beneath the cool, elegant and rather superior woman, there was a charming, sweet, bubbly girl!'

'So you think I've changed?'

'No. I think you were always like that. Miss Prim and Proper was just a façade to hide behind, but what you were trying to hide I don't know!'

Her smile faded, remembering her childhood and her desperate and determined obsession to overcome those handicaps. 'Perhaps you're right, David, but I still have my ambitions. I'm still a very determined person!'

'And so am I,' he murmured before he kissed her goodnight.

As they were not sailing far enough south to cross the Equator she was saved the usual horseplay that accompanied 'crossing the line', although Anne warned her that she wouldn't escape forever and after listening to the tales of the drenchings and duckings of the other stewardesses, Cat was greatly relieved.

The weather grew steadily warmer as they sailed south, leaving behind the dismal skies, the rain and the wind, and, whenever time permitted, she went up on deck to savour the warmth of the sun. The night sky had changed, too. It was now of sapphire velvet, studded with stars that seemed bigger and brighter than those further north. The breeze was warm and perfumed, sighing as it rippled through her hair. The sea was changing colour. A vivid aquamarine by day, a deep purple at night. The ripples from the bow wave like the undulations of a satin gown.

She was enjoying her work now and the pace seemed slower. There was no constant ringing of bells in her ears, for the demands made on her by her passengers were small, compared to her first trip. Their first port of call was Havana, Cuba, and when work was finished they were allowed four hours ashore, which, as Anne commented drily, was just enough time to have a drink and buy the traditional cigars for your dad. As Cat had not the slightest intention of buying anything for her father and had a slight headache, it was with some reluctance that she was persuaded to go ashore.

'What's the matter with you? You've got to come, make the most of it, see everything! I thought you were bursting with excitement?'

'I am, but —'

'Oh, I see! You'd sooner Mr Barratt take you ashore?'

Cat shrugged. 'He can't get the time off.' Anne had accurately hit upon her lack of interest. She had been disappointed, then depressed when she had received the message. Their first port and she had wanted to see it with him. These days she seemed to want to share all her new experiences with him. He was so unlike any man she'd known

254

before. He was handsome, intelligent and oh so charming. He made her feel she was someone very special and no one had ever made her feel like that.

'So you're going to sit here and mope? Get your bag, you're coming with us!'

She had enjoyed it more than she had expected. The company of the other girls lifted her spirits and the city was bustling and very Spanish. They had a long, cool drink in a café within a courtyard where the tinkling of water splashing from a stone fountain had a soothing effect, a vivid contrast from the bustling street outside. There were flowers everywhere: bouganvillea, trailing wisteria, begonias, jasmine and Spanish moss hanging in misty shreds from the trees. The breeze rustled the fronds of the palms and palmettos. She accompanied the others on a rather frenetic shopping spree, governed by the time. In the narrow streets and alleys of the older part of the town she had bought a lace evening shawl, so fine it looked and felt like gossamer. It had cost one hundred pesos, but the others assured her that had she bought it in one of the elegant shops the price would have been treble. They catered for the tourists.

'Where am I going to wear it?' she wailed in mock despair.

'Oh, I'm sure our Mr Barratt will find time to take you somewhere very chic!' Anne teased.

She wore it on the first night ashore on Haiti. David was taking her to the Hotel Excelsior for dinner. He had hired a horse-drawn cab, explaining that it was better to see and smell the sights and sounds of Haiti than from an enclosed taxi cab, whose owners were notorious for their erratic driving.

She had glimpsed the white pavilions of the presidential palace as they had sailed past La Gonave Island, but was looking forward to seeing them at close quarters. As they turned from the Rue Roux into Grande Rue, they entered the main stream of traffic. Everything from limousines to donkey-carts passed them but she noticed, too, that there were many beggers and cripples thronging the wide concourse.

They passed the Café Savoy-Vincent and at last pulled up outside the Colonial, two-storeyed, white portals of the Hotel Excelsior. David paid the driver and escorted her along the pathway flanked by a riot of perfumed shrubs and flowers. The reception hall was magnificent, the floor of cool green and white marble, the furniture copies of French Louis XIV. Flowers filled huge marble urns and palms were grouped together in corners, providing secluded niches. The dining room was in true Creole style and David assured her that it was finer than many he had seen in France. A coloured orchestra sat on a raised dais flanked by palms and flowers. A handsome mulatto waiter ushered them to their table.

The meal was unlike anything she had ever tasted: crayfish in wine sauce, turtle eggs, seafood in parcels of light, puff pastry; mangos, breadfruit, papayas, all washed down with a heady wine, followed by a cocktail of white rum and fresh fruit juices. When they had finished and the dishes had been removed and the coffee set before them, Cat's mind went back to the Salle Jacques Cartier dining room on the Empress. Now she felt like her passengers, surrounded by such luxury, cossetted, tempted with exotic meals and wines. She fingered the solid silver coffee spoon. She wanted to stretch like a pampered cat, it was such sheer bliss. She could quickly become accustomed to a life like this. Instead she sipped her coffee from the bone china cup.

The maître d' approached, his handsome features impassive and a little arrogant. His black, frockcoat and high-winged collar adding dignity to his bearing. He placed a silver salver in front of her. On it lay an exquisite orchid.

'With the compliments of the hotel ma'm'selle. The orchid is Haiti's pride, they grow wild in the forests.'

'Put it on!' David instructed as she just gazed in astonishment at the tall, dignified man.

She picked it up, still staring at the man. 'Thank you! It's beautiful!'

He bowed stiffly and walked away.

It was David who pinned it to the lace shawl, then led her out on to the dance floor which, in turn, led on to a terrace. He held her closely as they moved in time to the rhythm of the orchestra. She closed her eyes. This had to be a dream but she was afraid to pinch herself. She didn't want to face reality. He guided her towards the terrace where the indigo sky pressed heavily against the dim shapes of the mountains beyond the city. The perfumes of orleander, jasmine and night-flowering blossoms, all enveloping. She sighed deeply.

'Oh, David, this must be paradise on earth!'

His lips sought hers and she responded with warmth, surrendering to the heady mysticism of the island and the feelings it evoked in her. 'There is a much more beautiful place than this, Cat.'

'Oh, David, what can be more beautiful?'

'Petionville, that is paradise! Let me take you there, Darling?' Each word was accompanied by a kiss.

She drew away from him, not trusting her emotions. 'How do we get there . . . and back?'

He smiled. 'The same way we got here and don't worry, Cat, I'll take care of you. We'll be back on board in good time.'

CHAPTER FIFTEEN

They stood on the verandah of the Ibo Lele Hotel surrounded by delicate wrought-iron fretwork, over which tumbled a profusion of flowers. They held their cocktails in their hands, their bodies close, as they looked down on Port-au-Prince, sparkling like a burnished sheet of glass. The mountain-banded bay focusing the sky's deep velvet blue, like a giant reflector. Gonave Island lay beyond, cloud-capped, misty, mysterious. To the north-east stretched the Cul-de-Sac plain, its carpet of intensest green, gridded with sugarcane. A vast expanse of darkness beyond which lay the great salt lake of Saumatre, that in daylight shimmered with ghostly unreality. A mirage on the distant border of San Dominica.

He took the empty glass from her hand and placed it on a nearby table. Gently he took her in his arms and stared down at her. 'Cat, Oh, Cat!' His lips brushed hers and then she was clinging to him, returning his kisses. He drew his mouth away and then his lips burned the skin of her throat and shoulders. She was trembling but a warning bell sounded in her mind and she forced herself to pull away from him.

'David, I'm sorry . . .'

He lifted her chin. 'Cat, I love you! I've loved you from the day I took you ashore in Montreal!'

She closed her eyes, the waves of joy his words evoked made her cling to him. 'Oh, David, I love you, too! I think I've loved you from the day we first met, even though I didn't realise it!'

'I know you've been hurt and I promise I won't hurt you, I love you too much to do that. Do you believe me, Cat?'

'Yes. Oh, yes!'

His lips sought hers again and her arms slid around his neck. He pressed her close to him, so close that she could feel his heartbeat, or was it her own? So close that she could also feel the stirrings of desire in him. Again the warning bell sounded and again she pulled away from him, but this time it cost her more of an effort.

'No, David! It would be sinful!'

'Is it a sin to love someone so much?'

'No, but . . . but I want you to respect me, David, and you wouldn't, not if . . .' Her Catholic upbringing rose to the fore and with it the memory of Shelagh and her mother. No, no one would point the finger at her. She caught his hands and held them tightly. 'David, I do love you! But please don't ask me . . .'

'Haven't I just promised that I will never hurt you! Do you think I'm such a cad as to go back on my word?'

She smiled at him. She should have known. He was a gentleman in the true sense of the word. 'I don't want anything to spoil tonight. I've never been so happy.' She nestled against his shoulder as he slipped his arm around her.

'And nothing will spoil it. One more drink and then we'll go back.'

She smiled up at him, relaxed and trusting and

happy. She would always remember Petionville and tonight.

There were no other nights like that one but they spent as much time together as their working schedules would allow. From Haiti they sailed to Santa Domingo, the capital of the Spanish colony of San Domenica, the other half of the island. In St Thomas, the Virgin Islands, she bought souvenirs in the shops of Charlotte Amalie and sailed with David in a glass-bottomed boat and marvelled over the gardens of coral beneath the curelean waters. In Spanish San Juan, Puerto Rico, she explored the quaint old town and El Morro, the fortress overlooking the sea.

She, with Anne and a party of girls and stewards, made the trip from St John's in Antigua to English Harbour and Nelson's Dockyard. They spent the rest of the day lazing on the white sands, beneath the waving palms and swimming in the clear, warm water. It was a never-ending fairytale for Cat, each island more beautiful than the last: Bridgetown, Barbados, so very English; Fort-de-France, Martinique, so very French; Grenada, with its wide beaches, lush mountains and pervading essence of spices; Port of Spain, Trinidad; Curacao, a miniature of old Holland. She explored the old wooden houses and narrow streets of Williamsburg and David insisted she try the liqueur named after the island.

The hours she spent with him were the most precious of all and she knew that these islands would be linked forever with the love she had found.

On the night they left Curacao to return to New York, they stood on deck at the foreward end, his arm around her shoulders, watching the sunset. Watching the mighty draperies of scarlet and vermillion deepen to magenta, then black and finally darkness had fallen. The moon rose, a huge silver penny, and the warm wind filled the sails of the few small clouds and sped their shadows over the silvered surface of the sea. In a few hours they would be leaving all this behind, she thought. In a few hours night would be chased by day beyond the sea's end, and they would be heading back to the cold, grey days of winter.

'It's nearly over, David,' she whispered sadly.

'Only for a few weeks, then we'll be back. Back to our paradise.'

'I'll never forget this trip.'

'I'll never let you forget it.'

Their bodies were entwined in a tender embrace until the sound of the bell, recalling them both back to duty, invaded their cocoon.

Those four months had passed almost as quickly as a week, she thought, as they steamed back across the Atlantic to Southampton. It had been a long, beautiful dream. She studied herself in the small mirror above the washbasin in her cabin. Anne had said she was 'starry-eyed' and that meant she was in love. Anne didn't know how right she was! She looked older but felt younger than she had felt for years. Happiness danced in her eyes. She sang to herself as she worked and nothing was too much trouble. In fact she had received some very generous tips from her passengers, one of whom said she had never experienced such delightful, cheerful service. She was in love. Even the thought of going back to Liverpool while the Empress was laid up for a month, couldn't dispel her happiness, for David was going home, too, and they would see much more of each other.

They made the journey from Southampton to Liverpool together, with most of the crew accompanying them, so there was little time for privacy, and at Lime Street Station Marie and Joe were waiting for her. Joe in his uniform.

She hugged them both, chattering ten to the dozen.

'Oh, it's been so long, it's seemed like years and years! Let me look at you!' Marie held her at arm's length. 'You look wonderful! Look at that tan – and the sun has lightened your hair!'

The two men stood quietly eyeing each other until Cat took David's arm. 'David, this is Joe. Joe Calligan. I told you about him, he's a very old friend.'

Joe shook the hand that was extended. He wondered if this was another one like Stephen Hartley. He also noticed the shining light in her eyes when she looked at him, the way she clung to his arm. She'd grown up. She was a woman and a beautiful one at that. The old longing rose and with it jealousy.

'I'll get a cab, I can drop you off,' David offered.

'No one coming to meet you?' Joe enquired.

'My father was supposed to be here, but I can't see him. I expect he's been detained.' He walked away towards the taxi rank.

Joe took Cat's arm. 'Cat, I'm due to sail tomorrow, I have to talk to you and it can't be said in front of him!'

'Why?' She was disappointed that he would be leaving so soon, she had so many things to tell him.

'It's about Eamon,' Marie stated flatly, raising her eyebrows.

'Oh, now what? Every time I come home there is something!'

David returned and the conversation ceased.

'I've got you a cab but I've just spotted Dad, he'll have the car so I'll have to leave you, I'm afraid. But come over and meet him. I want you to meet him and I know he'll be delighted to meet you?'

She caught Joe's warning glance and was torn between the desire to meet David's father and the ominous matter of Eamon. She felt irritated, deflated, but she smiled up at him. 'No, you go, your Dad's a busy man, there will be another time.' She looked meaningfully up at him and smiled.

He looked a little crestfallen and he sensed the animosity of the young engineer.

He bent and kissed her. 'I'll phone you, tomorrow.'

Joe turned away, taking Marie's arm.

'So that's how things stand between those two,' Marie commented.

Joe didn't answer.

Once the luggage was in the boot and Joe had given the driver their destination, Cat turned to them both.

'What's the matter with our Eamon? Each time I come home all the happiness just evaporates!'

'He's been running wild ever since . . . ever since your Ma died. Maisey's done her best, but your Pa hasn't been much help.'

'That's nothing new. What's he done?'

'Been running around with a gang of back-crack boys and generally making a nuisance of himself, until last week.' Joe twisted his uniform cap between his hands.

'So?'

'Last week he got caught pinching sweets and some other things from Woolies, caught red-handed. He went before the Juvenile Board and he's at Rose Hill Police Station. Apparently he's been warned before, this time he's for the birch!'

She gasped. 'Birch! I'll birch the little sod myself!' She rapped on the glass partition and the driver slid it down. 'Never mind the first instructions, Rose Hill Police Station!'

'I'm sorry, Cat, really I am, to spoil your home-coming again. I only found it all out myself this morning. Maisey came to see me.'

'It doesn't matter, Joe. It can't be blue skies all the time, can it, not with a family like mine! Have you seen anything of our Shelagh?'

He looked acutely embarrassed.

'I know about the baby, she came to see me before I left.'

'She's got a place, up round Upper Parliament Street.'

'So she's alright?'

'For now. I hear she's "resting" until after the baby and then . . . then the girls she's with, who've taken her in, will expect her to . . . to, well, pay them back.'

'So she's going to make it her profession instead of giving it away free, is she! I'm glad Ma's not . . .'

Marie flushed.

'Is that how you've learned to speak, mixing with the toffs, Cat?' Joe rebuked her.

'I didn't mean it to sound like that, but you know what I mean, Joe, she was always wild . . .'

'You could have helped her, you could still help her, she is your sister, Cat.'

'I would have helped her! I'd have given her my last shilling but for one thing! When Ma died and she was so upset I thought her grief was genuine, but it wasn't! She knew she was pregnant then and she was crying for herself – not Ma! I'll never forgive her that! Never!'

All three of them lapsed into silence until they reached the police station.

Once inside she went straight to the desk sergeant at the counter.

'Can I help you, luv?' he asked, genially.

'I'm Eamon Cleary's sister. Is he still here, has he had his punishment?'

The geniality vanished. 'He is and he's had five strokes. You're the one who goes away to sea, are you?'

She nodded curtly.

'It would have been better for him had you been home. Looked better when he went before the Beak, if you know what I mean. He's not a bad lad really, just got into bad company. He's sorry and I don't think we'll see him in here again.'

'I'll make damned sure you won't see him in here again! Just wait until I get my hands on him!' she fumed.

'Harry, bring the Cleary lad up! His sister's come for him!' he yelled along the passageway. He turned back to Cat. 'At least he's got one responsible person who cares about him.'

'If his Pa had any guts or go about him, he'd have seen to it that this would never have happened.' Her eyes smouldered as she paced the tiled floor. Oh, what a family! Her sister a budding whore, her

266

father an idle drunkard and now a brother in trouble with the police! There was nothing she could or would do about Shelagh or Pa, but Eamon wasn't going to grow up a common felon!

The lad appeared with the constable. He'd grown but his hair was still unkempt, his clothes too short and dirty. His pale face streaked with grime and tears. The relief in his eyes disappeared as she made a lunge at him.

'I'll box your ears so hard your head will ring for a week, my lad!' she stormed.

Joe held her back. 'Cat, he's had enough! Can't you see he's scared stiff! Leave him!'

'Leave him! I'll leave him for dead!'

Eamon shrank closer to the constable at his side. Even this 'scuffer' who terrified the daylights out of him was better than the raging virago who faced him.

'He took his punishment well, Miss. Let him be, now.' The desk sergeant intervened.

She fumed silently while the sergeant checked with the constable that the boy had been examined by the police surgeon and declared fit to leave.

'Take him home, miss, and we don't want to see you in here ever again, me laddo!'

Eamon nodded, still keeping a safe distance from his sister.

It was Marie who took his grubby hand in hers. 'Come on, let's go. She's upset that's all. Just coming home today and finding this out.'

'Yer won't let 'er belt me, will yer, missus?'

Marie smiled at him. 'No, I won't and don't call me "missus", my name's Marie.'

'What am I going to do with him?' Cat cried, once they were outside.

'First of all we're all going home, that is to our house. Then we'll decide what to do with him.'

Cat blessed Marie's sound common sense. The whole incident had upset her more than she realised. Her four months of paradise had vanished abruptly. It was as though when she had stepped from the train she had stepped out of a dream and the old Cat Cleary, with all her attendant problems, had stepped into her shoes.

Joe hailed a passing taxi and they resumed their journey with Eamon kneeling on the floor, his head in Cat's lap, the beating he had received making it impossible to sit down.

When he was cleaned up and dressed in some of Mr Gorry's cut-down cast-offs and sat, on a pile of cushions, eating a plate of steak and kidney pie, Cat watched him, wondering frantically what she was going to do about him.

'Why did you do it, Eamon?'

'It was a dare, the others said I 'ad ter do it, like.'

'And you were stupid enough to agree and stupid enough to get caught! I notice none of the "others" were in the nick! And I suppose you haven't been to school for months?'

He wouldn't meet her eyes.

She stood up and began to pace the room. 'What am I going to do with you?'

'Can't yer take me with yer, our Cat?'

'No, I can't and talk properly! It's "you" not "yer". I'm not having you grow up like Pa, Eamon! I want you to have a good job, a good life and you can if you try hard enough! If you work hard at school and stay out of trouble, you could get to be an engineer, like Joe.'

He stared at her over the rim of the mug of tea.

He liked Joe Calligan, he often gave him a penny. He liked the idea of growing up like Joe, wearing a uniform, having money in your pocket and going to sea. School wouldn't be so bad if you really could be like Joe at the end of it. He hated school. He was fed up with being cuffed for untidy work and stupid things like that. He didn't mind Maisey or most of the O'Dwyers. Shelagh had gone off; he'd heard dirty whispers about her. Pa never hardly spoke to him, Cat had gone off and gone all 'dead posh' as his mates jeered.

He missed his Mam. She never yelled at him like Maisey did, or belted him like Pa and he'd missed Cat. She was different now, was Cat. All grown up and telling him he could be like Joe, if he worked hard. His backside was sore. The scuffers wouldn't catch him again, not likely. He looked around the kitchen. He liked it here. It was warm and clean and the pie was good, and if he could be like Joe . . . The girl who had told him to call her Marie poked her head around the door. He liked her as well.

'Cat, I want a word with you.' She jerked her head in the direction of the hall and he watched his sister follow her out.

'I've had a talk to Mum and Dad and Dad's willing to take Eamon on as an errand boy, office boy, tea lad, anything to keep him off the streets. He can live here, that way they'll be able to keep an eye on him and give you peace of mind while you're away.'

'Oh, Marie, I couldn't shove the responsibility of him on to you and your parents! He's my brother and my responsibility!'

'What else can you do, Cat? Once your back is

turned he'll be off again, getting up to God knows what! The only alternative is to send him to boarding school and I think he'd hate that and probably run away.'

'I can't afford to send him, anyway!'

'Then it's settled! He'll stay here, you've got no other choice. He will be working for his keep.'

'But there is still the responsibility, he can be a right little sod at times!'

'Look, Dad will keep him so busy during the day and he can do his lessons after tea so he won't have time to get up to anything!'

'Oh, what would I do without you all! You're more family to me than my real family! I'll leave an allotment for him, for your Mam to collect and your Dad has my full permission to box his ears if he thinks he needs it! Oh, Marie! What can I say!' Cat hugged her, tears in her eyes. 'All I hope is that the next time I come home, I won't have to face another trauma!'

'We'll share it, you won't be sailing on your own again, Cat. I'm coming with you!'

Cat gasped in delight.

'Yes, I've left college. I've got a job as a stenographer, I think they call it, on the *Empress of Britain*! Now I'll be able to keep my eye on you, Cat Cleary!'

As Cat hugged her again a small dark cloud appeared on her horizon. What would she tell David? Marie was supposed to be her sister, at least in David's eyes.

CHAPTER SIXTEEN

The domestic situation was explained to David
after she had discussed it for hours with Marie. It
was impossible to keep up the charade of Marie
being her sister, so they decided that they must be
cousins, first cousins, that she had lived with the
Gorry's ever since she had left Ireland, that after
her mother's death, her father and Shelagh had
returned to Dublin and they decided not to mention the existence of Eamon at all.

'There's already enough complications as it is,'
Marie advised.

'How shall I explain living with you and not
them all these years?'

'Just say you didn't get on with your Pa, that's
true enough. That you visited your Ma whenever
you could. Tell him you didn't get on with your
Shelagh either. It does hapen, Cat. Families don't
always stay together. Especially those who are not
forced by circumstances to do so.'

'Should I just cast caution to the wind and tell
him the truth, I hate all these lies?'

'No! Well, not yet, anyway.'

'But he loves me, it won't make any difference!'

'You never know. It might not make any difference to him, it may make a world of difference to
his family and that could influence him in the end!'

271

'No it wouldn't, they didn't want him to go to sea but he did.'

'But in the matter of a wife, well, that's different.'

'Oh, I suppose you're right. You usually are, you know much more about people . . . like them, than I do. Not everyone is like your family, I suppose.'

'Our family!' Marie corrected. 'You love him, don't you, Cat?'

A smile lit up her face as she nodded. She had been disappointed that she had only seen him once since they arrived home. He had gone for a holiday in Scotland with his parents and Miss Sabell and there had been no way he could get out of it, he had explained ruefully as he had kissed her.

'Will you tell them that we're going to get married?'

'Not just yet. I want you with me when I tell them. I want them to get to know you.'

'Oh, David, what if they don't like me? What if they don't think I'm good enough for you?'

'Hush, you mustn't even think like that! They'll love you just as much as I do. My aunt already likes you.'

She smiled as she remembered the conversation.

'I like him. I wonder if I'll meet someone like him?'

'You will. You'll be lucky, you'll have your own cabin on Fluff Alley and mix with the higher ups more than we do. You're bound to meet someone, maybe a millionaire, who knows!'

Marie laughed. 'That would be one up on our Marlene. She's courting a bloke who is "something in Income Tax" as she puts it. She's giving herself all kinds of airs and graces. "He's a civil servant, quite high up, too," she's always saying! But seriously, Cat, I wouldn't tell David everything –

not yet – your Shelagh is going to take some explaining away. Beside her your Pa and Eamon pale into insignificance!'

Cat had to concede to this point and so she continued with the charade, but she was uneasy, feeling the web of lies she was spinning would one day trap her.

Amidst all the preparations of buying new uniforms and shoes, cotton day dresses and a couple of cocktail dresses, Cat made time to go to see Maisey. She had never forgotten Maisey O'Dwyer's kindness to both herself and her mother over the years. For once she found the house deserted, except for Maisey herself.

'The girls is workin' now, the little 'uns are at school. Himself has got steady work at Bibby's an' 'e's out. I told 'im ter clear off from under me feet,' came the explanation.

'I'll be off again soon, but I wanted to see you.'

'Cum 'ere an' let me look at yer! Eh, yer look grown up, Cat. Ellen would 'ave been so proud, I miss 'er yer know, I really do.'

Cat's eyes misted. 'You heard about Eamon?'

Maisey nodded, while putting the kettle on to boil. 'I tried, Cat, luv! I nagged an' nagged at yer Pa, Blast 'im! But yer know 'im an' we never knew where the little sod was, day or night!'

'I know Maisey. You did your best but he wasn't your responsibility, you've got enough worries of your own with your lot. Eamon's with me now, at least he's going to stay with Mr Gorry, he's going to put him to work.'

'They've been good to yer, Cat, that lot, 'aven't they?'

Cat assented. 'Oh, let's forget all that, Maisey.

273

Here, I brought you these!' She placed the carrier bag on the table, amidst the dirty tea cups, the crumbs from breakfast and an assortment of odd buttons that Maisey, in one of her rare moments of patching and mending, had been using. She watched with amusement as, with one sweep, Maisey shoved the whole lot to one end of the table and oh'd and ah'd over the cheap souvenirs she had brought from her cruises. The necklace of coral got the most admiration, along with a hand-embroidered tablecloth bought in Havana.

'I'll keep this fer best, special occasions like.' She fingered the fine lawn with red, work roughened hands. It never occured to her how many hours of work had gone into its making, or just what 'special' occasion she would use it for. She'd never had any linen like this before. 'On second thoughts, it's too good fer any of my lot, they can drape it over me coffin when I've gone!' she joked. 'Eh, but yer work too 'ard to spend yer coppers on me, Cat!'

'Maisey, you were good to us. You took us in when we first arrived, shared everything with us. You looked after Ma, you tried with Eamon and . . . Shelagh. I don't forget things like that!'

'Well, yer should forget all about 'er! I've said it before an' I'll say it again, she'll come to a bad end will that one! I sent 'er packin', I'd 'ad enough. It might not be a palace but it's a respectable 'ouse!'

'She came to me for help and I was all set to help her, until I realised that she'd only ever been thinking of herself. All that hysterical weeping was for herself! I don't regret it, I think she's always hated me.'

'She was jealous of yer, Cat, an' it was eatin' 'er up. But forget about 'er, the tea should 'ave brewed

274

now, we'll 'ave a good jangle! Tell me about all them there foreign places!'

It was on her way back from Maisey's that she met Joe, by accident. She bumped into him as she rounded the corner of Vauxhall Road.

'I thought you were still away!'

'Haven't you got a calendar in that house? It was only a trip to New York and back.'

'I've been so engrossed getting everything ready that I just didn't realise, Joe. Where are you going?'

'Nowhere special. Fancy a walk?'

She slipped her arm through his as they made their way towards the Dock Road.

'You've changed, Cat. You've grown up.'

'I suppose I have. Don't you approve?'

'Of course I do!'

'You don't sound convinced. Did you want me to stay sweet seventeen forever?'

'In one way, I suppose I did.'

'Because then I would always have been dependent on you?'

He stared straight ahead of him and didn't answer. His gaze seemingly fixed on the smoke belching from the 'ugly sisters' of the power station.

'Sorry, I shouldn't have said that.'

'I care about you, Cat, that's all. I don't want to see you hurt again.'

'You mean David Barratt?'

'Yes. I don't know him so I suppose it's not fair to judge him.'

'No, it's not. He's very sincere, Joe, and he cares. Really cares.'

'I'm glad.' There was a note of harshness in his voice.

She looked up at him and realised with surprise that he was a man. He was no longer the boy she had grown up with, joked with, cried with. She recognised in his handsome face and dark eyes the raw feelings of passion, longing and jealousy. 'Joe, you know I wouldn't hurt you for the world.' She paused, choosing her words carefully. 'When you asked me to marry you, after Mrs Travis died, I was still a child. I didn't know what I wanted. I didn't understand, I thought you were asking me out of pity and I was headstrong, stubborn . . .'

'You haven't changed in that respect, Cat.'

'I have, Joe! Oh, I have! I love David, it's not like the infatuation I felt for . . . for Stephen Hartley. Not the deep affection I have for you, an affection that will never change, Joe, truly it won't. But I do love David, and—' she stopped. She couldn't tell him.

Those were the words he had never wanted to hear her utter. He felt cold. She was too attractive not to have collected a string of boyfriends, he'd accepted that, but he had hoped that in the end she would come back to him for good. He couldn't hide his lacerated feelings. 'And what if he turns out to be another Hartley?'

'He isn't married and he's not like that! He's worked too hard to get where he is to have dallied with many women at all!'

'Is that what he's doing with you, Cat – dallying?'

'Joe, please! In a few days I'm leaving on a world cruise, I may not see you again for months and months!'

'Maybe that will be the best thing for both of us!'

'But I don't want us to part like this!'

'You want me to be your friend, I think you said

that the last time! Those days are over, Cat! I'm a man, not a boy! Don't you understand that I can't settle for that kind of friendship? And I won't hang around to pick up the pieces if he uses you and then throws you aside!'

'He won't! I told you he's not like that!'

'Has he asked you to marry him?'

She bit her lip to stop it all blurting out.

'Oh, I see! He expects you to wait around until he's ready, until he decides or rather condescends to marry you?'

She covered her ears with her hands. 'Stop it, Joe! Stop it!'

He caught her roughly by the shoulders and pulled her to him, bruising her lips with his mouth before she fought her way from his embrace.

'You'll never throw my feelings in my face again, Cat Cleary! Don't come to me looking for sympathy if things don't turn out as you want them to! I'll be gone! I was coming up later to tell you, I've been promoted and transferred to the *Aquitania*. I don't think we'll see each other for a long time, if ever again! Goodbye, Cat!'

He turned on his heel and walked away, leaving her staring after him. She felt utterly miserable and bereft. She had always depended on Joe. He had always been there. She took a step forward then stopped. He was a man now and he had his pride. A pride that she had unintentionally hurt time and again. A dull depression settled over her as she watched his disappearing figure. He was going out of her life, maybe forever, and there was nothing she could do about it for she had given her heart to another man.

*   *   *

Three days before they were due to sail, David telephoned her to ask her to come for tea the following day. He would pick her up at 3.30 pm. He apologised for the invitation being at such short notice, but what with the holiday and everything . . . but his parents would love to meet her. She had replaced the receiver but kept her hand on it.

'Not bad news, you've gone as pale as—'

'No, I suppose it's good news, it's just that . . . he's taking me to meet his parents tomorrow!'

'Oh, now that sounds interesting!'

It hadn't sunk in yet, but with Marie's words came the full realisation of the implications. 'Oh, I feel sick just thinking about it!'

'Why? They can't be that bad! His father looked quite nice when we saw him at the station. He waved and smiled, don't you remember?'

'No. I was too preoccupied by what Eamon had done! He's a bank manager, did I tell you? Oh, they must live in a really posh house! What will I say? What will I wear?'

'Just be yourself, he won't expect you to behave any differently.'

'But what if I forget and say something wrong, something about Eamon or Maisey?'

'Just try to think before you speak,' Marie advised, sagely, before dragging her upstairs to sort out a suitable outfit from both their wardrobes.

She wore Marie's new silver-grey linen suit, with its short jacket, narrow lapels and nipped-in waist. The skirt was calf-length, slim but with inverted pleats front and back. Underneath the jacket she wore the white, hand-embroidered blouse she had bought in Port-of-Spain. Her own black court

278

shoes and bag, Marie's pale-grey gloves and a white Bangkok straw hat completed the outfit. She paced the floor, smoothing the fingers of the gloves, checking her bag for a clean handkerchief, her purse, her keys.

'For heaven's sake, keep still, you'll wear the pattern off the carpet! You're working yourself into a right state!' Marie chided.

'I can't! I can't help it! I don't want to go!'

'You'll be fine! You look attractive and smart, but elegant in a quiet way. There's nothing brash or common about you! Stop worrying. Anyone would think you were going to meet the king or the pope!'

'I think it would be easier. At least I wouldn't have to talk much or take tea with them!'

'He's here! Now go on and stop fussing!'

He complimented her on her outfit and kissed her cheek as he helped her into the car, which was large, comfortable and grand.

'David, you'll have to forgive me, I'm a little nervous.'

'Don't worry, Cat, they're dying to meet you. Mother says I never stop talking about you and Aunt Eileen has given a very good account of you.'

Her stomach turned over. She'd forgotten about Miss Sabell! 'Will she be there, too?'

'Of course, she's been on holiday with us, remember?'

She lapsed into silence, trying to keep her fingers from fiddling with the clasp on her bag. She'd always found Miss Sabell to be approachable, even friendly on occasions, but to meet her socially was quite another matter. So preoccupied was she that she hardly heard a word he said during the whole journey.

At last he swung the car through the gates of a very imposing house on the Serpentine and as he opened the door for her, panic engulfed her. Her legs felt unsteady and she clutched his arm for support.

'Are you alright, darling?'

She managed a weak smile. 'Yes. Fine. I just stumbled.'

His father greeted them at the door and he beamed at her. Marie had been right, he was friendly, the warmth of his welcome was genuine. She felt a little better. He ushered her into a large, sunny drawing room. She never could remember the exact details of the furnishings, except that the curtains matched the pastel, flowered chintz-covered suite and the carpet was of an oriental design. Her gaze fell first on the familiar features of Miss Sabell who was dressed in a fine wool crêpe dress of eau-de-nil, which made her appear younger. She had only ever seen her in uniform and it was strange to see her sitting back in the armchair, a cigarette in her hand.

'So, you are the young lady David has never ceased to talk about?'

Her attention was drawn to Mrs Barratt. She looked nothing like her sister. She was older and of more ample proportions. Her hair, set in sculptured finger waves, was darker than her sister's. The light in the hazel eyes more appraising, closely scrutinising, yet with that deft way some people have of not appearing to seem to be scrutinising. Cat felt every item of her clothing had been checked and assessed.

'It's Cat, short for Catherine, I believe? How quaint!'

Cat shook the hand extended. It felt limp.

'Do sit down, dear. Tea won't be long. Eileen, could you ring for Sarah?'

As Cat sat down, clutching her bag tightly on her knee, Miss Sabell extinguished her cigarette and rose to pull the bell sash. A bell tinkled somewhere in the vicinity of the back of the house.

She relaxed a little as both David and his father tried their best to ease her obvious nervousness. Even Miss Sabell smiled encouragingly when she spoke about her work. But she felt Mrs Barratt's gaze on her all the time, yet even when she spoke to her directly, she seldom held Cat's gaze for more than a few seconds. It was a mannerism that unnerved Cat more than the directness of her questions. And there seemed to be an endless succession of those. Had she enjoyed her life in Dublin? How old had she been when she had left Ireland? Were her father and sister still living there? Did she enjoy living with relations? What exactly did her uncle, Mr Gorry — was that his name? — do? Did she enjoy her work? Did she intend to make a career out of it?

Obviously David hadn't yet mentioned their intended marriage, she thought as she endured this inquisition, although she thought she understood why. Obviously in the society to which they belonged, it was not the 'done thing' to bring home a strange girl and immediately announce one's intention of marrying her. Things must be done in a prescribed manner and the first meeting was the first step along that road.

'Oh, come now, Marjory, of course she does! It's an excellent career for a girl, aren't I the proof of that?' Miss Sabell saved her from the last question, but it was followed by another.

'Yes, but Eileen, you know how I feel about girls having careers! I'm afraid I'm rather old-fashioned. Is it a career, Cat?'

Miss Sabell started to protest but her sister silenced her with a wave of a plump, be-ringed hand. 'A good career is essential for a man and we have high hopes for David, don't we dear?' Her gaze rested on her husband. 'Command of his own ship one day! Nothing less will do!'

Miss Sabell lit another cigarette. 'Marjory, I've told you it takes years and he is still very young!'

'That's just the point I'm trying to make!'

Despite her nervousness Cat was no fool. Mrs Barratt was impressing on her the fact that whether she was deemed suitable or not, she must in no way interfere with David's career. She decided she didn't like Marjory Barratt at all and she sensed that the feeling was mutual. This real-isation gave her courage.

'I totally agree with you, Mrs Barratt, in that respect, and I can assure you that my views are very much in line with those of Miss Sabell. In fact, one day, I hope to become a chief stewardess myself!' It came out very crisply, her tone clipped, and she wondered if she had gone too far.

'Then I'll have to watch you very closely, Cat, if it's my job you're after!'

She froze but then relaxed. Miss Sabell was smiling and she had never called her by her Christian name before. She also noted that neither David or his father had very much to say.

When she finally escaped, two hours later, she leaned her head back and closed her eyes. The ordeal was over and she never wanted to have to repeat the experience.

'You mustn't mind Mother, she's always like that, always has been. Dad says she's never happy unless she's organising something or someone. But they liked you, Cat, I could tell that much.'

'Do you really think so?'

He patted her hand. 'Of course!'

'You didn't say very much, David,' she murmured after a while.

'There were two reasons for that. Firstly, I wanted to let you have the limelight, so to speak.'

'You mean you wanted to see if I could speak up for myself?' She was a little surprised at herself. Occasionally this happened. Her thoughts popped out before she could stop them and she hadn't meant it to sound like that at all.

'Oh, Cat, darling, wherever did you get that idea? I just wanted them to see what a lovely, natural girl you are!'

'And the second reason?'

He laughed. 'I should have thought that was pretty obvious! It's difficult to get a word in edgeways with Mother most of the time!'

She laughed with him but she couldn't tell him that she was certain his mother didn't like her. Or that she had the distinct feeling she hadn't come up to expectations. She had never spent a more fraught or exhausting two hours in her life. Well, she didn't care! It was David she was going to marry, not his mother! David was the only person who really mattered to her. But if that was what form the 'opposition' took, she knew she could never, ever tell him the truth about her family.

*   *   *

The *Empress* sailed from Southampton for New York the following week and from Pier No. 7 she set out on her world cruise. On her maiden voyage the then Prince of Wales had sailed on her, and now, as King Edward VIII, with his romance with Mrs Wallace Simpson being common knowledge, the competition for the very state room he had occupied on that voyage was intense. The *Empress* sailed with a full compliment of crew and passengers.

Cat stood with Marie on deck as they left the Manhattan Pier and moved up the Hudson. Marie was still enthralled with her new life and surroundings, but Cat was silent and preoccupied. Ahead of her she could see the *Aquitania* tied up and she thought of Joe, wondering if he was watching the White Empress leave, knowing she was aboard.

Among Cat's passengers were a very wealthy American couple, Mr and Mrs Van Reitenburg, the Earl and Countess of Rossmore and to her intense trepidation, HRH Princess Mary. This addition required a special briefing from Miss Sabell.

'Her Royal Highness has travelled with us before. She wishes to be treated as just an ordinary passenger, but that of course is impossible. It is all our duties, from the captain down to you, to keep the insatiably curious from imposing themselves on her, as some are quite likely to do. She will take her meals in the first-class dining room with her lady-in-waiting. She is a very gracious Lady and although she does not stand on ceremony, that does not mean there can be any familiarity on our part, do you understand?'

'Yes, M'am. How should I address her? Will I be expected to curtsey?'

'No, you will not be expected to curtsey on every occasion. I don't want you bobbing up and down like a cork while in her presence, only when you first enter the room, and before you leave it. You will address her as "your Royal Highness" and you will speak only when spoken to. It goes without saying that anything you see or hear goes no further, no matter what inducements are offered to you. If anyone is persistent, then you must report them to me, that includes everyone!'

'May I ask why I have been given such an honour?'

'Because, in my opinion, you deserve it. It is also a test, I shall be watching your every move!'

Cat thought she saw the glimmer of a smile in the chief stewardess's eyes and she remembered her conversation about careers. She turned to leave.

'Oh, before you go, I want a private word with you, Cat.'

She was taken aback. She hadn't expected Miss Sabell to call her by her Christian name outside the precincts of David's home. 'Yes, M'am?'

'My sister, as you may have gathered, has high hopes for David.'

'I know that, he told me how his parents didn't want him to go to sea at all.'

The older woman nodded. 'Don't expect too much from him, not yet.'

She stiffened. What was his aunt trying to tell her?

'He has a lot of hard work ahead of him. There is a great deal of pressure on him and . . . well, it wouldn't be fair to increase that pressure, would it?'

'No, M'am. I understand.' She didn't understand.

What did she mean by 'pressure'? Pressure from his mother? Was she telling her that David was a little wary of his mother? He wasn't weak. He was strong and determined, he believed in his ideals. Perhaps she was trying to tell her in a roundabout way, that his family did not approve of her? Perhaps it was her way of warning her.

'I knew you would understand, you're a sensible girl. Now get on with your duties . . . Miss Cleary.' She smiled.

Cat was more than a little perturbed as she went back to her cabin.

Marie was speechless, then there was no stemming the flow of words. 'Oh, imagine! Oh, you'll have to tell me what she looks like, what she wears, what she says—'

'That's just it, I can't! She made that absolutely clear! Unobtrusive service and no gossiping! She said she was testing me.'

'You shouldn't have told her you wanted to be a chief one day! But, Cat, what an opportunity! What an experience!'

She found the experience far from nerve-racking. HRH Princess Mary, The King's sister, was a woman of nearly forty. Quietly spoken and plainly dressed, although it was obvious that the Herbie sports suit was expensive. She was neither haughty, patronising or over-familiar and after her first introduction, Cat saw little of her. She was only asked to serve afternoon tea once. The lady-in-waiting attended to most of her needs.

They had the usual time ashore in Havana and Port-au-Prince and this time it was Cat who ushered Marie around the sights and had to restrain her friend who seemed intent on buying everything that took her fancy.

'We have seventy-one ports in which to buy things and at this rate you'll be broke before we even reach the Far East!'

'Are you going ashore with David tonight? Brian Rothwell, the second electrical officer, has asked me out. We can make up a foursome?'

Cat sighed, gazing along the Champs de Mars. 'No, he's on duty. I wish he wasn't. Haiti is special for me, it was here that, well . . . it's just special. Get Brian to take you up to Petionville, the view is fabulous and the twisting, winding road is flanked with such pretty, quaint houses and hundreds of flowers!'

Marie stared at her hard, a note of deep tenderness had crept into Cat's voice. 'I will, if it's that beautiful, or maybe it was viewed through rose-tinted spectacles?'

'I suppose you could say that. But go, just the same, it's worth it.'

They sailed through the Panama Canal with only seven and a half inches to spare either side in the locks. The *Empress* was the biggest ship ever to sail through and, looking down from the promenade deck, it seemed to Cat that any minute they would become stuck. It was to everyone's relief, not least the captain, that they slid out into the waters of the Pacific Ocean, heading for Hong Kong, Bali, Singapore, Malaya, Siam, Japan and Ceylon and India. And when Cat first saw Bali, in a spectacular sunrise, she knew that this was even closer to paradise that Petionville.

Through markets and temples, pagodas, gardens and parks they wandered, both feeling as though they were on a different planet entirely. They dined in floating restaurants amidst lotus blossoms, sampling delicacies inexpertly with chopsticks, while laughing at their clumsiness. Sometimes Cat and David went ashore alone to find privacy amidst the palms on beaches of pure white sand and sea so clear and blue that it was like a tinted mirror. Beneath the whispering palms and in private little pagodas their love blossomed. She felt for David as she had never felt for any other man and all thoughts of Joe had been obliterated from her mind.

Marie, too, had found romance with Brian, for they had many things in common and so they placed no restrictions on each other and there was no division of loyalty, no straining of the bonds of friendship they had built up over the years. They were each content to be with the man they loved.

When they docked in Colombo they were allowed longer time ashore, having completed half the cruise. The harbour was filled with craft from the small junks, to freighters and smaller liners. They found it a town of indigenous cultures and a mixture of influences. There were Portuguese names and words, Dutch buildings, fortresses strung along the coast. English was the predominant language but the two main religions were Hindu and Buddhist, and everywhere there were magnificent, gilded temples of both religions.

After wandering the streets for a few hours they went their separate ways. Marie and Brian to find a restaurant that had been recommended, David and Cat to one of the beaches just beyond the city.

'I would have brought my swimming things, if I'd known. The ocean looks so inviting,' Cat sighed as she sat down, her back resting against the trunk of a gently swaying palm. She closed her eyes, letting the warmth of the sun and the sound of the surf wash over her. The sun was already sinking. When she was with him the hours just seemed to fly.

'I wanted some time alone with you, Cat.'

She opened her eyes to find him leaning towards her. She smiled, her heart in her eyes.

'There is something I want to tell you. I was going to leave it until the end of the Cruise, but . . .'

She sat up, puzzled by his serious expression. 'What?'

'I've been offered promotion. Second officer. It's not often someone as young as me is given such a chance, but it won't be on the *Britain* it will be on the *Empress of Japan*.'

The breeze was suddenly cold. The sound of the surf beat against her ears and her heart plummeted. The tears started in her eyes.

He took both her hands. 'It's a chance I can't pass up, darling! You do understand that, don't you?'

She nodded miserably. It was all she could do.

He took her in his arms. 'Cat, I love you! You mean everything to me, but you do understand how hard I've worked for this? I do have to justify the promises I made my parents, the pride they have in me. It's difficult being an only child. The pressures, usually absorbed by brothers and sisters, are concentrated on me. I love you and I don't want to be away from you!'

'Oh, David!' she choked. She was losing him. She

knew it. She felt it and the thought terrified her. They would seldom see each other and ... An even more terrifying thought took hold of her. What if he found someone else? There were other girls – stewardesses – much prettier, better educated! He would see them every day! What if he forgot about her? What if he really wasn't serious about her?

'Darling, Cat! Don't cry! I hate to see you upset, it won't be forever! And in the long run it will be for us.' He wiped her eyes with his handkerchief but she continued to stare at him pathetically. He traced the shape of her lips with his finger and then kissed her, gently at first, but then with more passion. She responded with every fibre, driven now by fear. His lips burned the skin of her throat, his fingers were gently caressing her neck, then her breasts.

Despite her longing she instinctively drew away from him. 'No! No, David! It's wrong, especially now!'

'Cat, don't you understand? I love you and I want to marry you! I want you to be my wife, I want to love and cherish you forever! Will you marry me, Cat?'

The fear evaporated as she uttered a strangled cry of joy. How could she have doubted him? Then she was in his arms and he was covering her face with kisses.

'Say yes, Cat? Say you'll marry me?'

'Oh, David! David! Of course I will! Oh, I will and you'll never regret it!'

'Neither will you, my love, I'll make you the happiest girl on earth! Anything you want will be yours, that's what I meant by my promotion being for us in the long run.'

A little dart of fear niggled as she thought about their separation. She was being a fool! He wanted to marry her. He wasn't interested in anyone else. She clung to his lips, her heart racing.

'But let's keep it a secret for a little while, at least until I've told my parents. You know how the crew gossip and I won't have you talked about, not like that.'

Oh, she loved him for that too. It was so characteristic of him. He wanted things done 'properly', he wasn't going to make her a target for idle speculation. She couldn't fight her longing and now was there really any need to? Her head was swimming as she felt his body close to hers, his hands moving over her shoulders, the thin cotton blouse falling, just as she was falling, sinking into the warm darkness of the tropical night as she gave herself willingly to him.

She lay in his arms, her eyes closed, her senses saturated. 'I'll always remember this night, David.'

'So will I, Cat. This feeling of love is like a blossom and as I was the first to gather that blossom, I will protect it! Trust me, darling!'

She stroked his hair. She did trust him. He was so strong and honourable. Passionate, yet gentle and sensitive.

'We'd better be getting back,' he sighed, ruefully.

She sat up and adjusted her clothes. At his words some of the euphoria disappeared and down over the years, unbidden, came a whispered warning. *Never marry a sailor, Catherine*. 'Oh, David, I wish we could just stay together as we are now!'

291

'Darling, so do I but things change. Sooner or later promotion would have come and with it separation. But it's for us, don't you see that?'

She stared out over the now darkened beach and inky ocean. She was seeing months and months of loneliness.

He drew her to her feet and held her closely, trying to lift the sadness he had glimpsed in her eyes. 'What about your ambitions? How often have we talked about them? Chief stewardess, have you forgotten that?'

'No. Oh, I know I'm being stupid, David! But I love you so much and I can't bear to think of being away from you. My ambitions don't matter any more!'

'But they should, Cat. I persuaded Aunt Eileen to give you the Princess. I'm trying to help you.' He didn't understand this facet of her character. When he had first met her that had been the one thing that had impressed him. Her ambition and her determination, both of which he had watched grow with a certain amount of pride. He had thought the fire of ambition that consumed him, burned in her also.

'Your aunt has many years with the company still, what chance is there for me? I'm far too young, I've only just been promoted to first-class.' The words came out slowly, with an edge of coolness that she didn't feel inside.

'You don't have to wait for her to retire, there are other Empresses, other ships!'

She shook her head. There would never be another ship like the *Empress of Britain*, not for her. Just as there would never be another man like him, and he wanted to marry her. That was her only ambition now. To be his wife. She smiled up at him.

'That's better. I don't want to see the future Mrs Barratt looking so sad. We have years ahead of us, Cat, we don't have to settle for second best, either of us!'

Part Two

1939

CHAPTER SEVENTEEN

For three long years she had lived with those words and the hopes and dreams they both shared. Oh, she had missed him when he had left to join the *Empress of Japan*, but they had written, they had managed to meet – snatched hours – in Liverpool and Southampton. She had lived only for those hours. Absence did make the heart grow fonder, she told him. In return he assured her all the waiting would be worthwhile, that the separations were the true test of their love. To her consternation he revealed that he had made a promise to his parents the day he had embarked on his career. A promise that he would never marry until he had command of his own ship.

'You never told me that when you asked me to marry you, David!'

'Cat, does it matter so much? We're young, our love is strong, so strong it's survived all the heartache of separation!'

'But why didn't you tell me?'

'Because it's not important – not to us! We have something so very special that it will survive anything! But I do owe it to them, just as I owe you the life I've promised you and it's a promise I won't break. I don't break promises, Cat, not to the people I love. Cat, I love you so much, you do believe me, don't you?'

She loved him far too much not to believe him and he was looking at her with the light in his blue eyes that she thought of as 'special', reserved only for her and she couldn't resist that look. But she still wished he had told her about it earlier.

She had been to tea twice since that first time, and knowing his mother, she realised that she would never allow him to forget that promise. She had begun to realise, too, that his mother tended to dominate him, as she did his father. And this was a side of him that surprised her, that she had never seen before. He had always been so self-assured and assertive, but on those occasions, apart from 'Yes, Mother' and 'No, Mother' and 'Of course, Mother', he had hardly spoken at all. Only Miss Sabell appeared to be totally unperturbed or in awe of her sister. Cat had realised early that the redoubtable Marjory Barratt was going to be a force to be reckoned with and she remembered and understood now the conversation she had had with Miss Sabell, about 'pressure'.

There had been a wonderful Christmas in Sydney, the day the two Empresses sailed into the harbour, side by side, accompanied by a flotilla of small craft, and fire ships, their hoses spraying jets of sparkling water. The noise of the small craft blared out their welcome, the Empresses answered with full-throated blasts. It seemed like the whole of Sydney had turned out to greet them.

The White Empress had become her home; she knew every inch of her from bow to stern and she loved that ship. There had been parties on board both ships, parties on the beach, barbeques and dances, and they had made love with a passion never before experienced, knowing how precious their time together was. It had been that Christmas, too, that Marie had announced her engagement to Brian Rothwell.

Brian had been Marie's first boyfriend, but she didn't regret the fact that she had never had a succession of them, as her sisters had. At first she had been a little shy with him, but no one could stay shy with Brian for long. His natural sense of humour saw to that. He came from Aintree and his father had a small but thriving factory beside the railway line and shunting yards, manufacturing containers, mostly of tin. Their interests were similar, their backgrounds were similar and neither had wanted to stay home and work in the family business. Close friendship had deepened to love and, with the approval of both families, they had become engaged.

She had been overjoyed but she couldn't help envying Marie as she showed off the the emerald and diamond ring. She wondered why David had never mentioned becoming engaged. After all, people did have long engagements and it would make their relationship more – she searched for the right word – solid? No, it would show everyone that they were deeply committed to each other. In particular his mother. She had come to realise that the one flaw in his nature – and it had taken her a time to admit that he had any flaws at all – was his subservience to his mother. At first she had told herself it was because he loved and respected his mother that he acquiesced to her demanding nature, but she was no fool. In time, even her love for him could no longer hide this trait in his nature and it disturbed her.

'But, Cat, we *are* deeply committed!' he argued when she broached the subject.

'I know, but if we were engaged it would be seen to be more – official!'

'I don't know what's the matter with you, Cat. You still love me don't you?'

'Oh, of course I love you!'

'You've always been so content, until now.'

She had lost her temper with him then, knowing it was fear of announcing this step to his mother that made him so reticent. But in the end she had her own way.

They bought the ring, a diamond cluster, in Sydney and the announcement was the excuse for yet another party.

'Happy now?' he asked her as they danced on the promenade deck of the *Empress of Britain*, surrounded by revellers from the crews of both ships.

'Yes.' She nuzzled his ear. 'But for one thing.'

He held her away from him. 'What?'

She smiled. 'The fact that tomorrow we will be parted again. You sail tomorrow night or have you forgotten?'

He held her tightly as they danced away the hours.

She had always saved most of her money, but Marie was a born spendthrift. When they sailed she vowed to Cat she was a reformed character. From now on she would save hard and the only way she knew how to would be to increase the allotment to her mother.

'I'll send her two-thirds of my pay. That way if I can't get my hands on it, I won't spend it, will I?'

'That's sound enough reasoning, for you.'

'You will be my bridesmaid, won't you?'

'What about Doreen and Marlene?'

'Oh, they'll have to be matrons of honour, seeing as how they are both married. I'd thought of sweet pea colours. Pale blue crêpe de Chine over lilac satin for those two, a delicate shade of pale pink over azalea satin for you. And white satin and Guipure lace for me!'

'You're going to bankrupt your dad at this rate!'

'But you will be my bridesmaid?'

'Of course I will, even if I have to wear my uniform!'

'God forbid!'

After that Marie had started to save her money, buying only useful household items and talking of little else than setting up home with Brian next Christmas, but the ache in Cat's heart grew. Her letters to David became more heartrending.

She had visited more countries than she had ever hoped or dreamed she would. From the Far East to the shores of the Mediterranean. From South America to South Africa and a million and one islands in between.

Then there had been their meeting in Southampton last June, when he had told her that there was a chance of him being transferred back to the *Empress of Britain*. She had been ecstatic. The separation would be over, at last they could think of the future. Even the ominous rumblings in Europe, that stemmed from the rise of Adolf Hitler, could not spoil her hopes.

She had lain next to him on the bed in the flat he had 'borrowed' from a friend, sated, and dreaming of all the nights they would spend like this. After that she had taken more interest in all Marie's wedding plans, thinking soon it would be her turn, despite Miss Sabell's veiled warnings. She didn't wear her engagement ring during working hours and the chief stewardess had mentioned the fact.

'Very wise of you. It did cost rather a lot of money and could be damaged while working. I think it would also be wise not to wear it on your next visit to my sister, either. She takes David's career very seriously, if you follow my meaning.'

She had nodded, feeling rebellious.

'Everything comes to those who wait, so the saying goes, I believe. He's very highly thought of in the higher echelons of the company. I think you'll find he is worth waiting for, he will probably be the youngest captain in the company – in any company.'

When she had first suspected she was pregnant she was shocked, then frightened, but after confiding in Marie – whom she swore to secrecy – she felt a new thrill, for as Marie had said 'You'll be married before me now and I'll have to have three maids of honour!' She had lain awake picturing his face, his expression, when she told him. He would be surprised, then he would smile and take her in his arms and kiss her and tell her that she was infinitely more dear to him. And that even though his mother would be extremely upset, she would have to come to terms with it.

Shelagh Cleary leaned against the wall, just out of sight of the policeman on the dock gate. Her once rounded figure was becoming overblown, but she still considered herself attractive. Men seemed to like a woman with some flesh on her bones, as opposed to the skinny young girls who often came to the Barracks. Her hair had been peroxided and was painstakingly curled and waved. The use of heavy make-up and rouge disguised the lines that had begun to appear, at least from a distance, and most of her clients, as she preferred to call them, didn't look too closely at her face. They were more interested in her other attributes.

She was used to her lifestyle now. It was easy money and just as easily spent. It was a damned sight easier than slaving in a factory for a few bob a week and the lad was no problem, there was always someone to keep an eye on him. From time to time she had heard of her sister – she numbered among her clients men from the crews of the Empresses. At first she had tried to block Cat's very existence from her mind, but that had proved impossible. Then as she realised that her sister was quickly rising in her chosen career, her hatred and jealousy had taken hold of her. She wouldn't admit it, but she would have swopped places with Cat without any hesitation, for at heart she wanted the one thing she would never have and that Cat appeared to have in abundance. Respect.

When she had heard of her sister's attachment to the young second officer, who had been described to her as 'the rising star in the company', a black hatred had consumed her, but it was one of her regular clients who had given her the information that she was about to use to gain her revenge.

She ignored the suggestive remarks of a couple of deck hands, she wasn't in the mood for that type of business today. Then she saw him. She had seen him before, but he had never noticed her. She stepped forward, smiling like a cat about to savour a saucer of cream.

'You're David Barratt, aren't you?'

She ignored his icy glare.

'Just got yourself engaged, I hear?'

'Clear off before I call the police and have you arrested for soliciting!'

She threw back her head and laughed. 'I'm not trying to pick you up, luv! Now would I do that to my own sister's fiancé?'

He stared at her hard.

'You heard me, it is Cat Cleary you're engaged to, isn't it? I always said our little Cat would do well for herself!'

'Who the hell are you?' he snapped.

'Hasn't she told you? I'm her sister. Shelagh. Shelagh Cleary, but these days I call myself O'Mara. Mrs O'Mara. It's for the boy's sake you see.'

'When . . . when did you come back from Dublin?' he stammered, feeling as though this common tart was an apparition.

'Back from Dublin? God 'elp us, it's years since I left Dublin! Since we all left Dublin! What's she been tellin' you, she was always a sneaking little cat, that's the name I gave her when we was kids. Did she tell you that?' She caught hold of his arm, he had gone very pale. ' 'Ere, you look as though you could do with a drink, luv!'

In a daze he let her steer him across the road and into the lounge bar of the Caradock and it was she who ordered and paid for the drinks. Two large whiskies.

' 'Ere, get this down you, you look terrible!'

She watched him toss down the drink, then drained her own glass. Oh, revenge was sweet. She could almost taste it. It was Cat who had turned her into a whore, so she only had herself to blame.

'Oh, yes, she was always a quiet one, was our Cat. Proper little Miss Prim and Proper, butter wouldn't melt in 'er mouth! Like 'ell it wouldn't! After the old woman she worked for – in service she was – died, she got all kinds of ideas, especially after she took up with that Gorry girl! We weren't good enough for her then, and after all Maisey and me did for her!'

'Maisey?' He repeated, dully.

'Maisey O'Dwyer. We lived with her in Eldon Street. All of us, Ma and Pa, me, Cat and our Eamon. God, but there were some fine bust-ups in them days, I can tell you! Then she took up with that Stephen Hartley.' She waited for his reaction. This had been her trump card. It was from him she had first learned of how Cat had met David Barratt. What Cat saw in this man she didn't know. He looked like a stunned cod fish. 'I think we'll 'ave another! Got a ten bob note on you, I'm a bit short right now?'

Without a word he took the money from his wallet and just stared into space as she went to the bar.

She put the change in her purse and put the drinks down on the table. He left his untouched.

'Carryin' on with a married man! It would 'ave broke my Ma's heart if she'd 'ave known. That's how she got her job, she threatened to tell 'is poor wife about it all unless he got you to help her. Joe Calligan wasn't 'alf mad about it!' She sipped the drink. She was enjoying every minute of this. It had been Stephen Hartley who had recounted to her these details, cursing Cat viciously, when by pure coincidence she had mentioned her sister to him on one of his weekly visits.

The whisky burned his dry throat. 'Joe. Joe's just . . . just a friend,' he muttered, inanely.

She laughed raucously. 'Is that what she told you? Oh, Joe's a friend alright, a very old friend! That carry on 'as been goin' on ever since she was sixteen!'

He felt ill and his throat was so dry he couldn't utter a word.

'I've seen 'er a couple of times, leavin' the ship. Done up to the nines 'an laughin' an' jokin' with that Marie Gorry. Mind you, they was good to take her in after Ma died. Pa never knows what day of the week it is, always half-cut, he is. But give credit where it's due, she was never a fool, was Cat. She's done alright for herself, especially landin' a catch like you! I've 'eard them say you'll be the youngest captain in Liverpool soon. God, but there'll be no holdin' our Cat then! Bloody Lady Muck, she'll be then! Probably 'ave to make an appointment to see 'er, we will! Probably won't even ask us to the weddin'.' She seethed with mock indignation. 'another drink, luv? Can't do any 'arm, havin' a few drinks with me prospective brother-in-law, can it?'

He didn't know how he had got out of the pub and back on to the ship. He remembered nothing, except that once back in his cabin he had taken his 'docking bottle' and poured himself another whisky. It hadn't helped. He couldn't get Shelagh Cleary's revelations out of his mind. Everything fitted, like pieces in a jigsaw puzzle. He would have dismissed the whole thing as a pack of vicious lies, except for one thing. Stephen Hartley. Cat had never mentioned him in all the years he had known her, except on that first occasion in the Imperial Hotel. And she had admitted that she had a sister called Shelagh. He flung the empty glass against the bulkhead where it shattered into a million pieces on the floor. It summed up his life, he thought bitterly. Shattered into a million pieces by a lying, cheating, conniving . . .

There was a knock on the door. 'Come in,' he barked.

'I'm sorry, David, am I interrupting you?' Cat said.

'No. There's no one I'd sooner see, come in!'

She had never heard him sound so angry. Then she noticed the whisky bottle on top of the locker and the fragments of glass on the floor. 'What's the matter?'

'I've just had a long talk with someone you know very well!'

The anger in his eyes and the fury in his voice drained all the happiness from her. She had come to tell him about the baby. There was only a skeleton crew abroad and Miss Sabell had already left the ship, so there was no one to tell tales or spy and she had judged this to be the right moment. Obviously it was not. 'Who . . . What?' she stammered.

'Your sister!' Shelagh Cleary, or Mrs O'Mara as she now calls herself! The Mrs O'Mara of some repute among the lower elements of the crew and not only of this ship – any ship! A whore!'

The room began to revolve slowly and every-thing she had intended to say was forgotten.

'And it was not a pretty tale she told me, either!'

'She's always hated me, David!' she cried.

307

'I can believe that! But why all the lies, Cat, and for so long? Lies about your family, about Marie and her family?'

She was too stunned to think clearly. 'Because . . . because . . . I love you! I didn't want you to think . . .'

'I could have forgiven you that, except for Stephen Hartley!'

She clung to the edge of the locker for support. How had Shelagh found out about him? She started to protest but he cut her short.

'You never did tell me how you met him, in fact you would never even speak of him, but your sister told me! She told me just what you got up to and how you blackmailed him!'

'No! No! It wasn't like that! I didn't know he was married . . . he used me!'

'And what about Joe Calligan? That affair has been going on since you were sixteen, hasn't it? I'll bet you've both been laughing yourselves silly behind my back!'

'It's all lies, David! Filthy lies! She swore she'd get even with me, one day, because I wouldn't help her! Don't you see, it's all lies!'

'I don't think they are! What had she to gain? What had she to lose? Nothing! While you . . . you stand to gain everything and lose everything. Everything you planned and schemed for! Someone of my background with my future! You used me, latched on to me and to my aunt, to claw your way up from the gutter and then, when you realised I was vulnerable . . . you could sit back and be a lady for the rest of your life! Live in luxury! But of course you could have the best of both worlds, couldn't you? A lovely home, comfortably off and with a loving husband conveniently out of the way for months on end, so you could carry on your little liaisons – providing you were discreet! And me, bloody fool that I am, would never have known! You're beneath contempt!'

'David! David!' she cried imploringly.

'God, you've made a fool of me! I even bought you a ring! Half the crew of at least two ships in this port must be rocking with laughter!'

She reeled back before this verbal onslaught, her back pressed against the cabin door, and dimly she realised she was losing everything and that she must try to fight back. She had never lacked courage.

'So I told you a pack of lies, but not about Joe or Stephen Hartley and you can ask Marie for verification! Ask her! Go on, Ask her!' she screamed. 'I've never slept with anyone but you and you know that! You were the first. You knew and I don't care if you believe me or not! I love you, David! I've loved you for years and I've waited for you, despite the fact that I know just how domineering your mother is! Many a girl would have given up years ago!'

'But you didn't give up, did you?' His sarcasm was scathing. 'You knew you had too much to lose! Don't try to lie your way out of this now, Cat! It's over, finished, and I never want to see you again!'

'I'm having your child!' she screamed at him. She was past caring now, she didn't care if the whole ship heard her.

The expression on his face didn't change. In fact he hardly moved a muscle, but his eyes were so cold and hard that she cringed. She had never seen such cold contempt as that now portrayed in his glacial stare. And when he spoke his voice was cold, too. It was the voice of a stranger.

'Don't add to the lies! Do you think I'm fool enough to fall for that one? Don't you think I've enough intelligence not to see you're grasping at straws? You can't fool me any longer! Get out! Get out before I forget I'm a gentleman!'

Her breathing was shallow, her hands were placed palms flat against the door, as though she were using the pressure to keep her upright. Something inside her head snapped and she turned on him. Her mocking laughter echoed round the cabin.

'Gentleman! Gentleman! Is that what you think you are? There are galley-boys who are more of a gentleman than you'll ever be! And they've got more guts too! They aren't tied to their mother's apron strings, afraid to open their mouths and express an opinion! Promising 'Mother' they will be good little boys and not get married! Not until she lets them! I'm going and I never want to see you again! I hope you rot in Hell! You'll never see your child and I'll make sure it grows up hating you, you spineless, gutless toad!'

When she reached her own cabin she was violently sick. She leaned over the basin, her head swimming. Shelagh! Shelagh had caused all this! She hoped venomously that her sister would one day be found in some alley with her throat cut!

Hours later Marie found her lying curled up on her bunk, staring at the wall. She tried to console her. She wanted to go and try to talk some sense into him but she vehemently refused to let her do that.

'I have my pride! There's not much of it left

right now, but I still have enough left to stop you from crawling to him! I could have stood his anger at the lies about my background, I deserved that, but he believed the lies she told him about Joe and Stephen Hartley! How did she find out about Stephen Hartley?'

'I don't know, Cat, maybe she didn't know, maybe she was only guessing. Maybe she met Stephen some time!'

She didn't care. She felt as though she would never, ever care about anything again.

CHAPTER EIGHTEEN

She had finally plucked up enough courage to tell
Mr and Mrs Gorry on the Sunday evening. She
had been so withdrawn, so weighed down by
shock, that she knew nothing of the events of that
fateful Sunday. She walked into the parlour that
evening, ready to tell them that she was bearing a
bastard. She found them grouped around the
radio set. She heard the voice on the radio. A quiet,
serious voice. A voice she remembered having
heard before, a few weeks ago aboard the *Empress*
as they had sailed home from Canada. It was the
King's voice. She wondered vaguely why King
George was making a radio broadcast. As the
serious tones continued she realised why. Britain
was at war with Germany.

She hadn't told them that night, they were too
shocked by the news. But she told them the following morning after everyone had spent a restless
night, wondering what the next months would
bring. Only Mr Gorry, who had served in the Royal
Navy in the first Great Conflict, had any concep-
tion of what faced them. Mrs Gorry had not wept
or raged or shown her the door. Sadly she had
shaken her head, patted her shoulder and then, as
always, looked to her husband for advice.

'He won't marry you, Cat?' Mr Gorry asked.

It was Marie who had related David's betrayal,

313

prompted by Shelagh's vindictiveness. When she had finished Mrs Gorry had tears in her eyes.

'Then it's well rid of him, I say! A fine husband he would have turned out to be. I never could understand why he kept you dangling about for so long. He could have married you years ago and still carried on with his career!'

'Mum, there's no use talking like that now, it won't help.' Marie chided gently.

'I can't stay here. I won't bring this shame on you, not after all you've done for me and for Eamon. It was partly my own fault, I shouldn't have lied to him about my family. I shouldn't have embroiled you in my lies, it was wrong! I can't bring more shame on you. There must be a home for . . . for girls like me, but I don't think I could bear it in Liverpool!'

'We'll have no more talk like that, Cat! You're not going into a "Home", you're not a bad girl! Foolish, maybe, but not bad!' Mr Gorry retorted.

'I can't stay here, you have your reputation . . . the business and then there's Marie and Doreen and Marlene!'

'They are both married, it's nothing to do with them.'

'But what about Marie? What about Brian?'

'Oh, to hell with me! And Brian's not like that . . . that swine!' She squeezed Cat's hand. 'Have you still got the address of the parents of that Welsh girl you met on your first trip? Didn't you say you'd get out to see them some time?'

Hope flickered. 'That was years ago! They won't remember me, probably Megan expected me to go years ago!' But it was a tiny ray of hope in all the darkness. 'I've still got the address somewhere.'

'Then that's the answer! Go and stay with them!'

'I couldn't do that! They're total strangers and what will I tell them about . . . the baby?'

'Marie's right. I'll write to them today. There are lots of mothers-to-be being evacuated now. God alone knows what we have to face with the country at war! It's the best for you.'

'At least you won't have to resign from the company, not with us all being laid off because of the war.'

Cat smiled wryly. That was true enough. She could leave with an unblemished record. This terrible war was, in that way, a blessing in disguise. No, there was nothing about the months that faced them all that could remotely be described as a 'blessing'.

'You'll have to call yourself Mrs,' Marie interrupted her thoughts.

'Mrs what?'

'Well, you haven't seen Joe for years and he is away at sea.'

'Marie, I can't tell more lies! It's because of all the lies that I —'

'Not entirely. I was partly to blame, I encouraged you, but your Shelagh's got a lot to answer for!'

'I can't Marie, I can't lie anymore!'

'Cat, you've got to try to build a new life and not just for yourself, for the baby. You can't tell them the truth, wasn't that why Megan went to Canada? No one will ever know except us and you haven't heard from Joe in years and you're not likely to! You'll have to tell them you're Mrs. Calligan. Do you want your baby born in a home for fallen women? The place and address will be on the birth certificate! How will you explain that away in later years? You've got no choice, not if you really think about it!'

So with reluctance and foreboding she agreed.

The reply came back quickly. Yes, Mr and Mrs Roberts remembered Cat, Megan still asked about her, if they had seen her. Yes, they would be delighted to have her stay. Megan was doing very nicely in Canada now, she had a husband and two children. She would never forget how kind Cat had been to her, and it definitely wasn't safe for her, in her condition, to stay in such a vulnerable city.

With a cheap wedding ring on her finger and her case, she and Marie had been driven through the Mersey Tunnel and the quiet lanes of North Wales to the little market town of Denbigh, with its ruined castle on the hill and its cobbled market square and stone market hall. In Lenten Pool at the bottom of the steep hill, they had asked the directions for the tiny village of Henllan with its church and chapel, its schoolhouse, a few rows of cottages, one shop and Mr Thomas Roberts' new house and building yard; set admist the rolling green pastureland of the Clewyd Valley.

Mr and Mrs Roberts came out to greet them and Mr Roberts took the luggage from Mr Gorry, handing it to his son, Thomas, of the new house and building yard. Hands were shaken all round and they were ushered into the farm kitchen where tea and Bara Brith were waiting. Mrs Roberts was a small, rotund woman with a fresh complexion and dark eyes. She asked Cat when the baby was due and said she must stay with them until it was born. The country was the place for babies, not smoke-filled, noisy towns that were likely to be bombed. She asked when Mr. Calligan would be home and Cat answered, truthfully, that she didn't know. Mrs Roberts had tutted sympathetically.

She had thought about Joe during those early months, when she went for solitary walks, out past the little thatched pub. He had said he wouldn't be around to pick up the pieces and he wasn't. She hadn't seen him since that day. She'd heard of the movements of the *Aquitania* of course, but her heart was heavy and she felt so alone and lost without him to turn to.

Her baby was born on 30 March and she called her Hilary Josephine. One of the ships of the Booth Line had been called Hilary and she had always liked the name; she added Josephine after Joe. Her labour had been short and the birth easy but her recovery was slow, plagued by a sense of loss and uncertainty and depression. For days she lay prostrate, incoherent and half-delirious. She wasn't recovering as most women in Mrs Roberts's experience had and she wondered if she should send her to the hospital in Denbigh.

For Cat the hours before dawn were the worst. She would lie in the narrow bed, the crib beside her, and watch the cold, April light creep into the room. She felt that life held out no hope, that she was just waiting for the beginning of another empty day whose hours stretched before her like purgatory. She stared at the wall with eyes that saw nothing but cold emptiness. A heart that was like a piece of stone, a mind that would not let her rest. But gradually she pulled round. She was healthy and the post-natal depression lifted. The day came at last when she had taken Hilary into her arms and felt for the first time a surge of tenderness and a fierce protectiveness for this tiny scrap of humanity that had been born into such a world of sorrow.

She thanked Mrs Davies and closed the door of the tiny shop behind her. The bell tinkled. She bent and placed the few groceries in their brown paper bags, on top of the pram, then adjusted the sun canopy. The June day held the promise of being hot but it was early yet. She'd walk the long way around. Down the hill, up past the church and along the shaded lane. That way she wouldn't meet many people or pass the school or Thomas's fine house, Bryn Arwel, with the building yard at the back. He was also the local undertaker and passing that yard always depressed her, although he was pleasant and his wife, Margaret, always had a cheerful word for her.

Further up the road she sat down on the little wooden bench in the shadow of a huge elm tree. The baby was asleep. The long shadow of the square, stone tower of the church fell across the pram. Her head was beginning to ache. She closed her eyes and sat for a while, listening to the droning of the bees in the hedgerow. Then she glanced up at the church clock. She'd better get back, she'd promised to help with the baking. She looked around at the green fields, peaceful under the clear blue sky, the meadows lush with grass, the black and white cows grazing beneath the trees. The overhanging trees shut out most of the sunlight and

318

it was pleasantly cool, their shadows dappling the narrow lane.

You could see the farm once you rounded the next bend. The house was old and stone-built, its small windows gleaming in the sunlight. Behind it and beside it were the stone barn and byre. She remembered the day she had first seen it. On a bright October morning when the leaves were turning orange, vermilion and gold. When the air smelled damp but pungent with the earthy odours of autumn. When the stubble fields had turned their cropped faces to the pale sun. The house was in sight now. The door open, the chickens scratching in the yard and Peg, the old Border collie, lying with her head on her paws, just outside the door, waiting for her master.

When she had closed the wicket gate behind her she bent and patted the dog's head before lifting the groceries from the pram.

'On guard, Peg!' she said softly, for the baby was still asleep. The dog instantly pricked up its ears and moved closer to the pram. Not even the Angel Gabriel himself would get past that dog now, she thought. She could hear voices in the kitchen. It must be later than she had realised. Mr Roberts was in for lunch. She lifted the latch of the low, wooden door and stepped inside.

'Hello, Cat!'

She gave a shriek of delight and flung herself into Joe's arms. 'Oh, Joe! Why didn't you let me know you were coming! How did you —' she stopped herself, remembering her hosts.

'Isn't that a nice surprise, now? Came in on the early bus he did,' Mrs Roberts beamed. 'Wanted to go and meet you, he did, but I said to wait. Better to have some privacy here than have half the village looking on.'

She'd never expected to see him again. Waves of joy and relief swept over her. She just stood staring up at him. Oh, how she'd missed him. Then she noticed the uniform. It was that of the Royal Navy. A puzzled look came into her eyes.

'Now why don't you both go into the parlour, you must have such a lot of news to catch up on and you'll want time on your own and I have this lot to feed, see. I'll bring you in a tray,' Mrs Roberts urged.

She thanked her profusely and led the way into the parlour. For the first time she felt uneasy in his presence. 'How . . . how did you find me?' she asked after she had closed the door.

He eased himself down into a chair. 'Marie. I went looking for you when I got home, to tell you I was . . . sorry. It wasn't time for harbouring old anger.' He looked down at his hands, as if embarrassed. 'I heard that the *Empress of Britain* is now on war service and I knew you'd have been laid off.'

She began to pluck at the hem of her skirt, a lump rising in her throat. She felt despicable, somehow dirty and soiled. She found it hard to think, to speak. 'Did she . . . did she tell you — ?'

'She told me everything,' he replied quietly but one glance at the dark eyes told her he was betraying nothing. Not anger, not contempt, not hurt – nothing.

'It was Shelagh.'

'She did you a favour, Cat.'

'Favour?'

'I never liked him.'

'You never liked anyone that —'

320

'If he'd have loved you he wouldn't have kept you hanging about so long.'

'It was what we both wanted – at the time.'

He rose and faced her. 'I've known you too long to know when you're lying, Cat. You never were much good at it. Not with me, anyway.'

She couldn't meet his eyes and her words came slowly, painfully, bringing back memories she wanted to forget. 'It served me right, living all those lies for so many years. You . . . you can't build a life on lies, not a secure one.'

He said nothing and she stood, head bowed, eyes filled with incipient tears.

'I'm still doing it,' she choked. 'Sometimes I get so tired of it all, I just want to tell everyone the truth! They are so kind, so generous! Oh, Joe, where will it all end?'

He took her cold hands in his and she wanted to cling to him as she had done in the old days. But there was too much hurt between them now. She bit her lip. She didn't want to cry. She didn't want his pity.

'We could end it all right now, Cat.'

She looked up at him through eyes misted with tears and confusion. 'You mean tell them?'

'I mean marry me? You already call yourself Mrs. Calligan and the baby has my surname.' The words were spoken calmly, measuredly.

She dropped her head and tears splashed unheeded on to their hands. Never in all her life had she been so touched. She felt humble, so very humble. He was worth a hundred David Barratts. She knew she would never respect any man the way she respected Joe. Dear, kind, loving Joe. It would be so easy. So easy just to open her mouth and let the word slip out. It formed in her mind, it rose in her throat, her heavy heart urged it to the tip of her tongue. She raised her head. She couldn't see him clearly through the tears.

'No. No, I couldn't do that to you, Joe. I couldn't let you take on another man's child. Another man's . . . cast-offs! You're too good, too honest for me. I'm not worth it!' The words wrung her heart and hung suspended in the air.

He didn't speak and she looked away, afraid of what she would see in his eyes.

'Oh, Joe! Why do I always hurt the people I care most about? I'm unlucky, Joe! Everything I touch turns sour. Banjaxed, Ma would have said. I . . . I can't do that to you, not to you, Joe!'

He still held her hands tightly. 'Cat, you've always known how I feel about you. I swore to myself I'd put you out of my heart forever. And I did, for a while. I won't lie, I've had other girls. But it doesn't work like that, Cat, I couldn't forget you! I can try to forget the past if you can? Marry me, Cat, for I'll not ask again? I have my pride. Marry me, let's have some time together before, well . . . I've joined the Royal Navy.'

Into the quiet, peaceful parlour where dust motes danced in the rays of light filtering through the curtains, the war with all its implications thrust itself.

'Joe, isn't that even more reason why you shouldn't saddle yourself with a wife and child? More reason to worry? You know how I feel about you, Joe, and God knows I've missed you! I've missed your strength, your comfort, your understanding. I've never needed to lie to you, Joe. You know where I come from, what I've come from.

322

But I can't do this to you, you're too good a man to waste your life on me!' She felt calmer. She had stopped trembling, her eyes were dry. She withdrew her hands and placed them lightly on his shoulders and looked up into the dark, handsome face. 'Thank you, Joe, for offering me your life and your love. The most precious gifts of all. Wealth and ambition are nothing beside them. I'll never forget it. I'll never marry. I've been hurt and I couldn't hurt you – ever again.'

He took her hand and raised it to his lips. She had never looked as beautiful as she did now and he had never loved her quite so much, not least for her honesty. She understood him. She knew that because of the child, the shadow of David Barratt would always lie between them. That there was a chance, a very slight one, that one day David Barratt might try to claim the child and he knew that if that day ever came, he would kill him.

It was Mrs Roberts's intervention that separated them and diffused the emotionally charged atmosphere. She set down the tray, told them to help themselves and left. The tea and scones lay untouched as they sat together in silence. A silence of resignation and understanding on both their parts. At last he spoke.

'What will you do?'

'I don't know. I have some savings, I'll manage for a while. What about you?'

'I've been assigned to a frigate as engine room artificer. That's why I came today. I've to be back late this afternoon. The convoy sails tonight.'

Dear God, was this what war meant? she thought. He faced two enemies. The Nazis and the sea. She looked at him with real concern. 'Is the danger from the U-boats very great?'

'I'll be honest, Cat, they scare the daylights out of me. It's one thing being able to see the enemy, to shoot back, but it's the uncertainty, the silent enemy that strikes before there is chance to hit back, that really scares me. And even if you manage to survive there is always the sea.'

She remembered Miss Sabell's words. She remembered the storms, the tail-ends of the hurricanes they had caught and how a ship as big as the White Empress had been tossed about like a child's toy boat on a park lake. She knew how he felt. There was no greater enemy than the sea if it turned against you.

CHAPTER NINETEEN

On Sunday, 8 September she told Mrs Roberts that she was returning to Liverpool.

'I can't stay here forever, my savings are nearly all gone. I have to work, not only to keep us but for the war effort. Marie has written that everyone is working, that women are desperately needed in the munitions factories and the voluntary services. The port is working flat out!'

'But you can't take the baby back to that, Cariad! Who'll look after her while you're at work?'

'Mrs Gorry.'

'But she's got enough to do and they've already started dropping bombs! No one will be safe! Leave her with us, please, Cariad? A city at war is no place for a baby, especially one as important as Liverpool. Come and see her whenever you can, she'll be safe with us here!'

'But you have enough to do already!'

'Margaret will help me, give her some practice, see.' She smiled. Her daughter-in-law was pregnant and she was delighted with the thought of being a grandmother again. But this time her grandchild would not be thousands of miles away in Canada as the others were.

So she had left Hilary behind although it had nearly broken her heart to board the bus alone.

But she could not refute sound common sense. A city in wartime was no place for a baby.

'Joe's home.' Marie informed her as she met her off the ferry at the pierhead. She had got the bus as far as its terminus at Birkenhead.

She looked around her. Little seemed to have changed except that the trams had been painted grey and there was wire mesh over their windows, hoods over their headlights and the front bumpers painted white. But there were uniforms everywhere. Even Marie's tailored suit looked like a uniform and there was a gold WVS badge on the lapel. During the day she worked in one of the offices of the Ministry of Defence.

'When did he get back?'

'Last night. They limped back into the river about midnight.'

'How many?'

'Six out of eighteen and four of them are badly damaged. Holed, rigging mangled and twisted.'

A shudder ran through her. The wind seemed suddenly colder.

'They have to keep the port open. It's the lifeline of the country. You remember our last trip, when the King and Queen came home from Canada, when the little princesses came aboard to meet them? That's why they went, to strengthen our ties with Canada and America. Everyone knew this war was coming.'

Everyone, except me, she thought. She had been too engrossed with her own affairs to think much about politics. 'When do I start work?'

'I've arranged it all, everyone's needed. Dad will take you out to Kirkby on Wednesday, but tomorrow you can come with me to the Angel Club. We provide meals for servicemen. An evening meal for 1s 6d, a clean tablecloth and decent dishes, too. Then they often go next door to the State because it has a dance.'

Cat was greeted with a warm welcome from Mrs Gorry and both Doreen and Marlene who made it a practice to 'look in' on their parents frequently. She hardly recognised Eamon. He had grown up and it was with a shock that she realised that he was now eighteen. It was even more of a shock to see that he was proudly wearing the tight-fitting jumper and bell-bottomed trousers of an able seaman in the Royal Navy. This couldn't be the scruffy, back-crack boy with the shock of unruly hair? Not this tall, smart young man who was grinning at her with the shadow of his impudent smile.

'Eamon! Eamon Cleary! You're so . . . so grown up! When did you join up?'

'Nearly a month ago. Everyone's needed, isn't that why you've come back? How's my niece, I've not even seen her? I can't get used to being an uncle!'

She laughed and hugged him. 'Oh, she's fine and next time you're on leave I'll take you to see her!' She'd missed them all so much but she hadn't realised just how much until now.

On Wednesday morning Mr Gorry drove her out to the village of Kirkby, some miles outside the city boundaries. There was a church with a square tower, some pretty cottages, a few shops, the Railway pub, beside the station, and then beyond, the long, low buildings of the munitions factories. She reported at the gate and was sent on to an office, given her official papers to sign, her identity pass, a list of rules and regulations and her hours of work. She was also given a medical and declared fit. It was a very perfunctory affair. The doctor asked her if she had any of the following, which he read rapidly from a printed list, to all of which she answered 'No'. He sounded her chest, looked in her eyes and ears and that was it. She would start work on the 7 a.m. shift the following morning.

She had tried to see Joe that day but he had not been at home and so she tried again after finishing her shift at the factory on Thursday, before going to help the ladies of the WVS in the dining room of the Angel. He was sitting at the table reading the *Liverpool Daily Post*.

'I'm back, Joe. I started work in the munitions this morning.'

There was no uneasiness, no tension between them. They had parted friends and besides, war left no time for festering emnity. He looked tired and his skin seemed drawn tightly over his cheekbones.

'How was it?' she asked.

'The same as usual. Stinking hot, smelly, dirty, all engine rooms are the same, only the sizes differ.'

'Oh, I hate to think of you down there, if anything were to happen, you know what the chances are.'

'Don't say it, Cat! Don't say it! I'm superstitious enough to believe that to name a fear is to experience it. It must be the Irish in me.'

'Where is everyone?'

'Mam's gone to the shops. The rest of them are away. Dad on convoy. Jimmy's in a sub somewhere in the Mediterranean and Kevin's on the *City of Benares*.

'Your poor Mam. All of you at sea.' She sat down at the table.

'Did you bring the baby with you?'

'No. Mrs Roberts persuaded me to leave her, it will be safer for her. I'm going to try to visit her at weekends, but it all depends on the work, its shifts, but I'll go as often as I can.'

'I don't suppose we'll see much of each other, with you on shifts?'

'I'll see you each time you get home. Even if it's only for half an hour. When do you leave again, or is that "classified"?'

'It's supposed to be, but tomorrow night.'

'So soon?' Mentally she calculated the date. Friday, 13th September. Dear God what an omen, he wasn't alone in his superstitions.

'We have to get the supplies in as quickly as possible. They've already realised that if they can completely blockade the ports, they've got us! We'll be under seige, the whole bloody country! The supply lines have to be kept open, no matter what the cost, or we'll all go down the plughole, as Dad says!'

She wished she had stayed in Wales. There the war had seemed so distant, it hadn't touched her. Here, everyone was preparing for a seige and she was afraid. The skin on the back of her neck prickled.

He folded the paper. 'Can I take you out dancing tonight?'

'It will have to be after I've finished at the Angel. I help out there.'

'Fine, we'll go to the State. What time?'

'I might be able to get away about 8.30.'

'I'll meet you outside.'

She rose, then bent and kissed the top of his head.

She had been late leaving the Angel for the crews of all the ships in the convoy were enjoying their last night's shore leave. The State was packed to capacity and so they decided to sit in St. John's Gardens at the back of St. George's Hall. It was a fine evening, one of those mellow, golden autumn evenings and as the fulvous light gave way to dusk, she leaned her head against his shoulder.

'It's so strange to see a city without lights. I got used to it in the country, but here . . .'

'Will you take care of yourself, Cat, munitions work can be dangerous?'

'I will, will you? You won't . . . you won't go risking your life with heroic deeds?'

'We're all cowards at heart, Cat, at least those of us who know and respect the sea are. Do you want me to keep my eye on me laddo? I see he's with us. I never thought I'd see the day Eamon Cleary would be an ABS. That scruffy kid!'

She smiled. 'Neither did I, but I won't ask that of you. He's old enough now to look after himself.'

'Have you been to see your Pa?'

'No, and I don't intend to!'

'Things change, must change.'

'Not between him and me and it wasn't just over Ma, it was Eamon as well.'

They fell silent watching a flight of pigeons head

into the darkness above the bulk of the *Echo* offices.

'What about Shelagh?'

She drew away from him.

'Well, if not for her then for her lad, Sean, he's nearly five and he's your nephew and your Ma's grandson, would she want him to be living like he is?'

'He's also Pa's grandson!' she snapped. She didn't want to know anything about Shelagh or her son. She had enough worries and he was spoiling these few hours of peace by mentioning them. 'He's not my responsibility!'

'He should be someone's! He's left on his own most of the time, so I hear from Maisey. Don't you remember Eamon's childhood, Cat?'

'Eamon is my brother, at least we knew who his father was!' As soon as she'd said the words she regretted them. A sense of family was very strong in both of them. Poor little Sean Cleary was a bastard, like her own child, but worse off – at least Hilary wouldn't be left alone to run the streets. At least she had known and loved Hilary's father, however painful the memories. 'I'll see what I can do,' she muttered.

He squeezed her arm.

He had given her a good bye peck when he left Marie's and she had hugged him tightly, before releasing him.

'Joe, take care and God go with you – with you all!'

'I will.' His voice was husky.

She knew it was uncertainty he was fighting for he was no coward, but everyone feared the unknown – even herself.

'I'll keep my eye on Eamon, Cat!' he called.

She stood at the gate listening to his footsteps and in the darkness of the quiet street she thought she heard him whistling. The tune was familiar. 'It's not the leaving of Liverpool that grieves me, but my darling when I think of you.'

Three days later as she was coming home from work she heard the newsvendor's cry and, thrusting the penny into his hand, she virtually snatched the copy of the paper from him. Her stomach began to churn and her hands trembled as she read. She felt suddenly faint and leaned against a wall for support. The old man peered at her.

'You alright, luv?'

She nodded.

'Shape of things ter come, luv! God 'elp us all!'

She finished the long column then closed her eyes, tears seeping beneath her lashes. So soon! Oh, dear God, so soon! Convoy CB 213 had sailed on Friday, 13 September, nineteen ships had passed the Bar Light heading for the Atlantic and Canada. She remembered the *City of Benares*, a fine modern liner. Joe's brother's ship. She had been carrying ninety children amongst her passengers and cargo. In a gale and in heavy seas she had been torpedoed and sunk. Most of the crew were lost and so were seventy-seven of those children!

She bent her head and wept unashamedly, thinking of her own child and Joe. Joe, who must have watched the death throes of the *City of Benares* knowing . . . knowing . . . yet unable to help. She thought of his words about Sean Cleary. She thought of those children. Something would have to be done for the child. She straightened up and wiped her face with her handkerchief. The old newsvendor was right. God help us all, she prayed.

It took her a week working in munitions to begin to hate it. The work was dirty, monotonous and dangerous. The buildings were set out with two rows of small rooms running down each side, with a wide, blast-proof corridor between them. Four girls worked in a room and were grouped in numbers 1 to 10. Group 1 was the most dangerous for the women there fitted detonators. She had been allotted to Group 8 where she filled anti-tank mines with TNT which had a strong, obnoxious smell and needed stirring to stop it clouding. The nose and mouth were protected by a mask, the hands with gloves. She also filled 3.8 shells which then went on to Group 1. There were frequent accidents in all groups, but mainly in Group 1 and every week women were maimed and injured.

There was a set procedure which she soon found tedious. When you arrived you were conducted, like sheep, into what was known as the Dirty Room where shoes, clothes, hair clips, jewellery were removed and placed in lockers. Wedding rings were taped over. You were then moved into the Clean Room where one was issued with navy-blue cotton overalls, white turban and flat shoes, rather like plimsoles. From there you went to your work room. She worked with two older women both of whom had husbands in the Army, and a girl of her own age who lived in Fazakerley, the nearest city suburb to the factories. Nancy was engaged to a soldier. The hours dragged by. At first she had to concentrate on her tasks while the others chatted, until she, too, became so proficient that she could hold a conversation. She had little in common with Lucy and Ivy, but with Nancy she discussed the arrangements for Marie's wedding which had been brought forward to October.

It was to be a much smaller, quieter wedding than had originally been planned. The service at the Church of the Blessed Sacrament. A meal afterwards at home, then a few days in Southport with Brian. He had stayed with the *Empress of Britain* and so, she had heard, had David Barratt.

Despite all her earlier plans for white satin and Guipure lace and sweet pea colours of crêpe de Chine, Marie refused to have the traditional wedding because of the growing shortages.

'Everything has to be brought in by ship and as my Brian is part of the convoys, I won't waste his time or anyone else's. If everyone gave up fripperies and concentrated on more important things, I'd feel a lot happier!' She had replied to her mother's pleading that she should at least have a proper wedding dress, as the other two had. 'What would I do afterwards with yards of white satin, Mum? Make it into lampshades?'

Mrs Gorry had thrown up her hands in despair, muttering that there was no romance left these days.

She had gone with Marie to Hendersons and helped choose the two-piece suit of lavender wool, the collar of which was trimmed with white fur.

She had bought a hat of lilac velour with a small veil and matching gloves and shoes.

'They will all be more serviceable and I'll wear my white silk blouse the one I bought in Bangkok.'

'It really does look very smart, you will look every inch a bride, especially with your bouquet,' she had concurred. She herself, as the only bridesmaid, had bought a sage-green, two-piece in Owen Owens and a beige hat, gloves and bag. She couldn't waste money now. Mrs Gorry had insisted on flowers and a cake. Mr Gorry had insisted on an Anderson shelter, for the first bombs had fallen on 9 and 10 August on the other side of the Mersey.

Early on the morning of 26 October, David Barratt was on the bridge of the *Empress of Britain*. He felt edgy but then he had felt this way ever since their arrival on 8 September last year in Quebec when the white hull had been painted grey and they had been laid up awaiting orders. The *Empress* had been requisitioned as a troop ship and had sailed for the Clyde on 10 December, on her first convoy. It had been then that this edginess had first manifested itself. It hadn't been so bad when they had left Wellington in May, in the *Million Dollar Convoy*, in the company of the *Empress of Japan*, the *Mauretania* and the two Cunard *Queens*. He had felt fairly safe then.

He scanned the grey horizon with the binoculars but saw nothing but the vastness of the cold ocean. He had thought about her on that trip for the first time in years. And for the first time he had wondered about Shelagh Cleary and the truth of

335

her allegations. He had been so furious, so hurt by Cat's lies that he had never bothered to check them out, yet there were so many things about her he couldn't forget. His friendship with Brian Rothwell had come to an abrupt end for Brian had waylaid him and called him a 'coward, a cad, a bastard'. He had liked Brian and Marie and Marie's obvious closeness to Cat had sown the seeds of doubt in his mind. But he had never pursued any enquiries. He still smarted from the accusations she had flung at him. Tied to his mother's apron strings! Afraid to even express an opinion! Deep down he knew she was right, but that only made him more determined to try to forget her.

He pushed his hands deep into the pockets of his duffle coat. He was cold and tired and his eyes burned. By now he knew Cat's baby would have been born. She hadn't lied about that, Brian had told him. His baby. His child. Or was it? He thought he heard Shelagh Cleary's mocking, raucous laughter, or was it just the wind? Was it a boy or a girl? What had she said, she would make sure it grew up hating its father? What did it matter now? He looked at his watch. Nine fifteen. Three-quarters of an hour and he would be relieved.

He scanned the horizon again. Nothing. The edginess returned but he shook himself. It was only because they were sailing alone, he thought. Because of the *Empress's* size and high speed of knots, it had been judged safe and RAF Coastal Command would meet her off the north-west coast of Ireland and they had come this far safely, via the Suez Canal and well clear of the Azores. They were carrying military personnel and their families back to Britain, 224 of them, outnumbered by a crew of 419, including himself.

He asked for their position and the voice on the intercom informed him 'Sixty miles off the north-west coast of Ireland.' Then he heard the drone of an engine and trained the binoculars skywards on the port side. Coastal Command at last. 'Not before bloody time, either!' he muttered. He followed the flight pattern then his blood froze. It was not Coastal Command! He slammed his fist down hard on the alarm button and immediately the klaxon blared out, 'Action stations! Action stations!' But the sound was drowned out as the first bomb exploded on the top deck, near the tennis courts. The mighty liner shuddered and he was flung to the deck. He clawed his way to his feet and looked back in horror. The whole of the midship section was ablaze. Black smoke belched up through the gaping hole that reached as far as D Deck. Frantically he tried the communication system. It was dead. He turned back in time to see the plane coming directly for them, its machine guns spitting. He threw himself to the deck as bullets raked the bridge, sending showers of glass and splinters of wood flying everywhere. He felt a searing pain stab his chest and darkness began to claim him. He heard the signal faintly. 'Abandon Ship! Abandon ship!' but he couldn't move. Then he was thrown violently against the superstructure amidst broken glass and instruments as another bomb found its target.

Somehow he managed to drag himself upright.

Tiny, grotesque figures were running through the black, billowing smoke and wicked, leaping flames. He fought for his breath. The plane was coming back again. He could hear the vicious staccato of machine guns. They were the last sounds he heard as he slumped back onto the deck. A trickle of blood oozed from the corner of his mouth, his sightless eyes staring upwards to where the enemy plane turned for home, well out of range of the stricken ship's high-angle three-inch gun and four Lewis guns whose fire continued until it was a mere speck in the sky.

Most of the lifeboats were ablaze but Brian Rothwell helped lower one of those that was still intact. He would have expected pandemonium to have surrounded him, but there was only a queer silence. A forced calmness, broken occasionally by the sob of a terrified child. The heat was intense, the smoke choking. He looked down. God, but it had never looked so steep before! The boat was slung off its davits and plunged downward, hitting the sea, knocking him into the water. He looked up and there were tears in his eyes. The ship was doomed! She was ablaze from bow to stern! One plane! One bloody plane! Where the hell was Coastal Command?

There were people around him in the water, jumping from portholes on the lower decks, clinging to liferafts. The lifeboat was already over-crowded but there were women in the water. He shouted to four other members of the crew and without a word they all slipped overboard, joining him in the freezing water, pulling, pushing the survivors towards the boat. If he could just keep a hold on the boat, but already his fingers were becoming numbed. There was something wrong with his legs, they wouldn't move, no matter how he tried.

They were drifting away from the stricken *Empress*, he was losing sight of her. He was losing all feeling in his body, the sea was claiming it. The colour of the sea and sky merged until all he could see were the tongues of flame. So near to home. So big a target. So small a plane. She was dying, dying before his eyes. The thoughts spun in his head. Everything was getting darker. 'Must be the smoke,' he muttered.

They pulled him aboard and tried with what little resources they could muster, to revive him. A woman, her life-jacket over her dressing gown, her hair dripping, looked at the others. She had been a nurse before her marriage. She shook her head. 'It's no use. He's dead.' The faces around her registered only blank shock. 'I didn't even have time to thank him,' she murmured.

At four o'clock HMS *Echo*, accompanied by some trawlers picked up the survivors. The *Empress* was stricken but in no danger of sinking. Her mighty bulk still maintained some dignity emphasised now by the gaping holes in her decks, her shattered rigging, the absence of her three funnels. She was taken in tow by the naval tugs *Marauder* and *Thames* who pulled her slowly towards home, towards the protection of the destroyers *Highlander* and *Harvester*. She was shattered but not destroyed.

In the early afternoon two days later, with *High lander* and *Harvester* steaming protectively at her bow and stern, she was within thirty miles of home. No one saw the evil black snake of the periscope. No one saw the torpedoes streaking like black arrows beneath the surface of the dark waters, but they found their mark. The Great White Empress suddenly heeled over to port and disappeared beneath the sea.

Two days later the U-boat, U32 was attacked and sunk by *HMS Harvester*. The White Empress was avenged.

CHAPTER TWENTY

They heard about it first from Brian's father who telephoned. His call had been followed by a very brief one from Miss Sabell. A call Cat had taken.

In the first traumatic seconds of shock Marie didn't cry. But then Cat fled to her room, threw herself on the bed and covered her head with the pillow, as Marie's first hysterical screams pierced the silent house. But she couldn't shut out the sound. She wanted to run to Marie, to try to alleviate the grief and shock. To try to answer the tortured questions Marie screamed aloud.

'Why him! Oh, why him? Oh, Mum, why my Brian?'

But she couldn't move. Shock had caused temporary paralysis and she didn't cry either. Not at first.

The screams had subsided to muffled sobs and at last she found she could move. She pushed the suffocating pillow away. Her room was in darkness. The winter dusk was falling rapidly and there were no street lights to brighten it. The blackout had begun. She muttered a prayer. 'Oh, not tonight, dear God! Please, not tonight.!' The wail of the air-raid siren was something she knew she couldn't bear. Not tonight.

Her thoughts were confused. Her mind would focus clearly on one image for a few seconds, then it faded. Then would come a void in which there was no thought pattern at all. This was replaced by disjointed phrases, half-formed thoughts and blurred images. In these moments she heard David's voice, felt his presence. Hollow laughter, faint music, the elusive smell of forgotten perfumes. Words and places, Petionville, Williamsburg, Colombo – all drifted in and out of her mind and she was cold. Deathly cold.

She reached out to pull the eiderdown quilt over her and her hand knocked against the chest of drawers beside the bed. Her fingers closed over an object. She peered at it, trying to recognise it. It was a little sailor doll. Its uniform of blue velvet, its white cotton hat, replicas of the uniform Eamon wore. It was a souvenir she had bought for Hilary. Even though it was dark and she couldn't see it clearly she didn't need light to read the gold lettering on the black hat-band. She knew it from memory. *Empress of Britain.* And then she cried.

The pain started deep within her, crushing her chest, burning her throat until the scalding tears dropped down on the head of the doll pressed against her cheek. She was crying for David, for Brian and Marie, for all the others – all her friends – and she was crying for the White Empress. The tears soaked into the velvet suit and smudged the painted face. She was alone. There was no one to comfort her in her grief; not even her baby for whom she had bought the ship's little mascot. Hilary was the only tangible thing left now of the life that had ended when the great White Empress had turned her keel skywards and had died. And for once the dreaded siren was silent, all through

342

the long hours of the night and into the cold, grey dawn.

They tried to regain some semblance of normality, despite the fact that the air-raids, which had become heavier in September and October, were adding to the increasing strain of daily life. Everyone felt as though they were walking on a razor's edge. It was a situation that was totally alien, the underlying fear and tension sharpened by grief. Many buildings now lay in ruins or were badly damaged – The Customs House, Wallasey Town Hall, the Anglican Cathedral, Central Station – and the banshee wail of the siren was becoming increasingly familiar.

Cat found a reserve of strength hitherto unsuspected and Mrs Gorry proved to be a stronger character than she had ever imagined. Two days after the news of the loss of the *Empress*, she returned to work. The following week Marie went back.

'It's the best thing for her. It will take her mind off . . . and there are others who have lost loved ones, she won't be alone in her loss!' Mrs Gorry stated, firmly. 'And there is a war on!' It was a saying that was on everyone's lips these days.

In the evenings, those dreaded evenings, when they would all sit waiting for the doleful wail that would send them all down the garden and into the shelter, it was obvious that Marie had lost her zest for life. She was like a martinet, her movements mechanical, her conversation stilted. Desperation filled Cat when she looked at her old friend. The happy-go-lucky girl had gone and she was afraid she would never return.

At the end of November Joe's convoy limped back into the Mersey. Each time they returned, breathing a heartfelt prayer that they were in safe waters, he scanned the waterfront. Each time his heart was heavier. Each time there was more evidence of devastation. He wasn't suffering the nightmare alone. He shared it with the citizens of Liverpool as they sat huddled in Anderson shelters or in the crowded, public shelters, waiting, waiting . . .

They had heard of the loss of the *Empress*. Half the world had by now and most of it grieved for her. After ascertaining that his own family were safe, he took the tram to Walton.

She hugged him with relief. 'You heard?'

He nodded. 'Brian was a decent bloke. How is she?'

'I can't explain it, she's changed. I don't think she'll ever get over it. Something's gone from her.'

'And you?'

'It's changed us all, Joe. It's impossible not to change. I . . . I was sorry about . . . David. Sorry about all the others, too. Sometimes I have dreams. I can see her . . . twisted, broken, burning . . . and people running.'

He shook her. 'Stop it! Stop it!'

She steadied herself. Her finger traced the outline of the brass buttons on his uniform jacket. 'I'm sorry. I was sorry about the *City of Benares* and . . .'

He looked past her. That was his own private hell. His brother and all those children!

'Joe! Come on in! Fancy keeping him in the hall,

Cat!' Mrs Gorry's rebuke was accompanied by a smile of genuine relief.

'Is Eamon alright?' she asked as they went into the kitchen.

Marie looked up and smiled. The ghost of a once-bright, animated smile.

'I don't suppose you've had anything to eat? I'll make you something while you sit and talk to Cat,' Mrs Gorry disappeared into the scullery.

Joe sat down.

'How long ago did you leave Eamon?' she asked.

'Oh, about an hour. I went home first to see Mam. Dad is home, too. But Eamon won't be long now, it's nearly twenty past seven. He's probably got a girl he wants to see.'

Mrs Gorry continued the conversation from the scullery. 'How is your mother managing, Joe? Is she short of anything? If there's anything I can do, you know . . .' The rest of her words were drowned out.

Marie jumped nervously then clenched her hands tightly, the knuckles showing white. The wail rose to a crescendo and both Cat and Joe jumped to their feet.

'Oh, blast them to hell! Here, Cat, take the kettle! Be careful it has boiled! Bernard, get those blankets! Come on, luv!' Mrs Gorry seemed more annoyed than afraid as she caught her daughter's hands and pulled her to her feet.

They crowded into the shelter and Mr Gorry lit the candles. At first they had tried using a Tilley stove, fired with paraffin, for heat and oil lamps for light, but the fumes from the stove had nearly choked them and the lamps had smoked, adding to the discomfort.

'This place is always cold and damp! Here, Cat, give me the kettle!' Mrs Gorry grumbled. Cat just stood staring at her. 'What's the matter?'

'Eamon!' She started to shrug on her coat.

'You're not going anywhere! He'll be alright! If he's still at Mrs O'Dwyer's they'll all be in the nearest shelter now and if he was already on his way, they'll stop the tram and get them all somewhere safe!'

'But what if he's walking? What if—'

'You're not going out, Cat!' Joe added his voice to the argument.

Marie had started to cry softly and she allowed Joe to pull off her coat. Then she sat beside Marie, holding her hands, while Mrs Gorry made a cup of tea.

For three hours they sat and listened to the drone of the enemy planes and the shrill whistling that preceded the explosions, while Mr and Mrs Gorry and Joe tried to keep up a lively conversation. She was too worried about Eamon and too nervous either to listen or sit still for very long. She refused to join in the game of Ludo that Mrs Gorry suggested when conversation had been exhausted.

At ten o'clock the all-clear sounded. She fastened up her coat and put on her hat.

'I'm going to look for him!'

'Don't be a fool, he'll be on his way now and you'll miss him!' Joe argued.

'I don't care! It's bad enough while he's at sea, but now . . . if you won't come with me I'll go on my own!' She was very near to tears.

'Oh, alright!' he conceded.

*   *   *

346

They got a tram as far as the Rotunda Music Hall, then they had to walk and she began to realise that Joe's logic had made sense. Fires were blazing all over the city, the glowing red patches lighting up the dark sky. Fire engines and ambulances hurtled past them and the nearer to Vauxhall Road they walked the worse it got. Broken water mains flooded the roads. The stench from damaged sewers was nauseating. They had to skirt huge craters in the road, clamber over piles of bricks that a few hours ago had been houses. Streets were cordoned off because of the dangers of fractured gas pipes and partly demolished buildings. The nearer they got the more appalling were the scenes and she wished she hadn't come at all.

'It's never been as bad as this!'

'Look, Cat, you'll have to go on by yourself! I've got to help, I can't stand by while people are trapped!'

'But what if—'

'Go on, Cat! You'll be alright!' He turned and ran back, clambering over a heavy wooden beam to where the police and wardens were starting their grim task of searching for people trapped in the rubble.

She could see the flames ahead and smell the smoke. The docks had been hit again. Then she gave a cry of relief and began to run. Eldon Street had escaped.

She hammered with her fist on the door of number 8.

Maisey opened it. 'Cat! Gerrin 'ere! What the 'ell are yer doin', cumin' out?'

'Oh, Maisey! Is everyone alright? Is Eamon here?'

'Course 'e is an' we're all fine!'

She leaned against the wall and closed her eyes.

'Cum in, I was just makin' some tea.'

She was smothered in her brother's embrace but when the first surge of relief passed she turned on him. 'Why didn't you come straight home? You had me worried half to death? You should have been in the shelter with us, this . . . this is the worst raid we've had!'

'Leave 'im alone, Cat, 'e was safe enough with us, we was all under the stairs!'

She was incredulous. 'Under the stairs! Why didn't you go to the shelter? If the house, or next door, had gone, you would all have been buried!'

'Stairs 'as been good enough in the past! 'Ow was I ter know they would blast 'ell out of us fer bloody hours? Is it bad?'

She nodded. 'Joe's gone to help. It looks as though half the city has been hit, there's fires everywhere!'

'Bloody incendiaries,' Eamon muttered.

'Is Joe cumin' on?'

'I don't know.'

'I'll go and see what I can do. I'll get back home as soon as I can, Cat, and you'd better get back, too.

They'll be worried about you.' Eamon had gone before she could stop him.

Maisey placed the mugs down on the table. 'Cat, we've all gorra pull tergether, these days. I'm not lettin' no bloody Jerries get me down! Mind you, I'm goin' ter burn that dress of our Dora's!'

'What dress?' She wondered tiredly what a dress had to do with the present situation.

Maisey sipped her tea then continued. 'She

bought the dress in C & A. Red-white-an'-blue-striped taffetta it is, an' every time she wears the damned thing ter go out, she an' Bessie get ter the end of the street an' the siren goes! An' then I'm yellin' me 'ead off at the door fer them ter cum back, an' the pair of them leggin' it round the corner fer a tram! I don't care 'ow much she kicks up, that blasted dress is going'! It's like red rag to a bull!'

She smiled. 'It's just coincidence, Maisey!'

'Well tharran' all, but it's goin' on the back of the fire, just the same!'

She sipped the tea and watched the young O'Dwyers' noses pressed to the windows, peering out. Trying to outdo each other in counting the fires. It was all a game to them, she thought. She had been considerably shaken by the events of the night and watching the children made her think of Sean Cleary.

'Have you heard anything of . . . Shelagh and Sean?'

'No! I'm norra bad-minded woman, but I've enough worries an' so 'ave you.'

'She's still my sister.'

'An' she ruined yer life! What she did was downright evil, Cat, don't forget that! She set out ter hurt you as much as she could!'

She finished the tea. There hadn't been any sugar in it but she hadn't noticed the fact until now. 'If I hadn't lied so much, she wouldn't have been able to hurt me.'

'She always 'ated you.'

'But she's still my flesh and blood.'

Maisey started to interrupt but she stopped her.

'Everything has changed Maisey. The world's gone mad. No one knows if tomorrow will even come, if we'll survive another night! It's no time for harbouring grudges, for hating . . . the old life has gone. Everything about it has gone, except Hilary and Joe and it was Joe that set me thinking of Sean.'

'So, what do yer intend ter do?'

'Go and see her.'

'Yer not goin' up there, ter that place?'

'I am! I want her to let me take Sean to Wales, he'll be safer there.'

'She'll laugh in yer face, Cat!'

'Maybe, maybe not, but she must care something for him! She can't be that bad!'

'Well she doesn't from what I've 'eard! 'Er that runs the place – face like a ruptured custard she's got, I've seen 'er 'round the town – sees to 'im most of the time.'

'Then I'll talk to her . . .'

Maisey crossed herself. 'Yer poor Ma would turn in 'er grave at the thought of you talkin' ter that . . . that . . . one!'

'Where's Pa?' The reference to her mother had automatically brought him to mind.

'Finally cum to 'is senses. 'E's out with our Hughie, 'elpin the wardens. 'E 'elps repair damage in the daytime, too. Just my luck ain't it? I gets the two of 'em with steady work and fer once in me life I'm not short of a shillin' or two an' there's 'ardly anythin' in the bloody shops ter buy!'

After her shift next day she went to see Maisey

again, this time for directions where to find The Barracks. She was tired. No one slept well these days. It had been nearly dawn when she heard Eamon's key in the door. She had gone down. She was on the early shift anyway. He had been grey with fatigue. His eyes red-rimmed from dust, lack of sleep and the horrors he had seen. He was filthy dirty and his hands were cut and bleeding. He informed her that Joe had gone home but that he'd be down to see her that night, providing there wasn't an early raid. She'd made some breakfast, then sent him to get a wash and some sleep.

In the miserable, damp November daylight, the full extent of the damage was even more hideous. Gangs of workmen struggled to clear the roads and restore the water, electricity and gas supplies. Others continued to search for survivors amongst the still smouldering piles of rubble that had been homes, shops and offices. In Rooney's, the small corner shop Maisey frequented, the windows had been blown in. But the glass had been swept up, the rubble piled in one corner and all the stock that was salvageable was set out on a makeshift counter. Tacked to a piece of splintered window frame was a piece of paper, announcing 'BUSINESS AS USUAL'. Underneath was the caption 'And a bit of Liverpool muck never hurt anyone!' A reference to the sorry state of some of the provisions. She smiled. It was typical. There were battered but unbowed. The shop was crowded.

As she entered the kitchen Maisey slammed down the old iron stew pot on the range, then clipped her youngest around the ear for wiping his nose on the sleeve of his jumper. 'Use yer 'ankie!'

she snapped, poking the fire vigorously. Cat saw the charred remains of the striped taffetta dress. Obviously there had been a row.

'I thought you'd 'ave changed yer mind?'

'No.'

Maisey grunted. 'Then go straight up Upper Parlie Street, turn left, then right an' it's a big square 'ouse, looks like an army barracks, but fallin' ter bits! An' don't say I didn't warn yer!'

Maisey was obviously in a far from convivial mood, so she thanked her, placed some rashers of bacon wrapped in greaseproof paper on the table, and turned to leave.

''Ang on a minute, yer not goin' up there by yerself! I'd not rest in me bed, I'm cumin' with you!'

'No. You've got enough to do. She's my sister.'

'Aye, God 'elp yer, she is, an I know 'er, so I'm cumin' too! So yer can just wait 'til I get me coat an' 'at!'

CHAPTER TWENTY-ONE

It did look like an army barracks. It was a big, square, austere house and, had it been in pristine condition, would have been the most dominant house in the street. Eight square windows with small, dirty panes in each were set into the upper storey and the same number on the ground floor. The front door was battered and scarred and totally devoid of paint. The front gate was missing and weeds were waist-high in the overgrown garden.

The woman who opened the door, in response to Maisey's hammering, was not dissimilar to the house. She was big and square. She seemed to have no soft curves, even her face was angular, somewhat different to Maisey's description of a face 'like a ruptured custard'.

'Is Shelagh Cleary, or O'Mara, in?' she asked.

Maisey was peering intently into the hallway behind the woman.

'Who wants 'er?'

'Her sister. I'm Cat, Catherine Cleary.'

The hard, suspicious eyes softened. 'Why didn't yer say so? Cum in, luv!' She stepped back a pace.

'Cum in! Cum in! Yer 'ardfaced trollop! I'd sooner set foot in an Orangeman's Church than in this . . . this . . . whorehouse! Go an' ger 'er!' Maisey fumed.

'Who the 'ell are you?'

'None of yer business, now go an' ger 'er or I'll call the scuffers!'

'I'll put yer bleedin' eye in a sling if yer do!'

'Oh, for heaven's sake, stop it!' said Cat. 'We haven't come here to start an argument! Could you please ask Shelagh to come out?'

The woman glared at Maisey, retreated a few paces and then bawled out to Shelagh that there were two women to see her. One of them said she was her sister, but she sounded so posh she thought she must have the wrong house and the wrong name. The other one looked like 'Yer owld gerl!'

At this insult Maisey took one step forward and yelled, 'I'll purra lip on yer!'

Cat dragged her back. 'Ignore her, Maisey!'

Maisey folded her arms over her ample bosom, the light of battle in her eyes.

Shelagh at last appeared. A stained mauve, satin dressing gown clutched to her, a cigarette in her hand. Cat was shocked by her appearance. Even though it had been years since she had last seen her, Shelagh had changed so much she hardly recognised her. She was grossly overweight, the dressing gown clinging to the sagging breasts and outlining the distended belly. Her hair was a brittle, peroxide blonde, but the roots were dark. Her face was bloated, the eyes seemed to have grown smaller. Smudges of mascara, rouge and lipstick were left from the night before. The stale smell of cheap perfume mingled with body odour and stale tobacco.

'Me dream's out! I never thought I'd see you again!' Shelagh laughed, leaning against the door and appraising Cat from head to toe, the bemused grin lingering on her face.

'An' if I'd 'ad me way she wouldn't be 'ere now!'

'Maisey, please!' she begged. It was going to be difficult enough and she didn't want to antagonise her sister from the outset.

'Well, what do you want? I heard your ship got sunk and that he was dead.'

She felt anger begin to rise but she fought it down. She refused to be provoked. 'Yes, but I haven't come to talk about that . . . any of it.'

'Need 'orse whippin', the whole lot of 'em!' Maisey muttered.

'Found another rich feller, then, or are you still hanging on to Joe Calligan? At least he's better than nothing!' Shelagh sneered.

This was too much for Maisey. She drew herself up to her full height, bosom heaving. 'Tharrell do you! 'Ardfaced little bitch! Any more of that an yer'll feel the back of me 'and!'

Shelagh turned on her. 'You sod off, Maisey O'Dwyer! You chucked me out, so don't come here with your Holy Mary attitude!'

Maisey crossed herself and stormed down the path. 'If I stay 'ere I'll swing for 'er, so 'elp me I will! I'll wait at the corner, Cat!'

'You haven't changed, have you?' Cat said quietly.

The smirk left Shelagh's face. 'Yes, I have! Just look at me! Go on, take a good look!'

She couldn't meet her eyes. There was nothing in this overblown, brassy tart that reminded her of the old Shelagh.

'An' its all your fault! You could have helped me, so don't you start preaching at me! But I got even, didn't I? I swore I would—'

'And I've just told you I've not come here to talk

about that!' she interrupted. 'Shelagh, listen to me! Things have changed . . .'

'Not here they haven't!'

She ignored the interruption. 'Last night's raid was the worst we've had, so far. It might get worse. It's no time for hatred, bitterness, old scores.'

Shelagh finished her cigarette, threw the stump on the floor and folded her arms. 'So?'

'So don't you think it's time—'

'Oh, God! Don't tell me you've come up here expecting a show of sisterly love? Let's forget the past and all that shit! You got what you deserved, Cat —'

'Stop it! Stop it, Shelagh! We're even now!'

'Are we?'

She faced her squarely. 'Yes, we are! There was never much love lost between us, was there, and obviously we will never even be . . . friends.'

'So what have you come for?'

'To talk to you about Sean.'

'What about him?'

She took a deep breath. She'd promised herself she would be honest, no matter what the cost. 'I have a child myself. A little girl.' She waited for the ridicule, the jeers, the burst of malicious laughter. None came. Shelagh pulled out a crumpled cigarette packet and offered her one. She shook her head as her sister lit hers, then waited for her to speak.

'He didn't marry you?'

'No. It doesn't matter, I've already told you that!'

'Where is she?'

'In Wales, with friends.'

'You always had friends, Cat, didn't you?'

'Let me take Sean to stay with them and Hilary?

You must care for his safety and it's not safe here, not any more! Please, Shelagh, let me take him?'

Shelagh pulled herself upright. 'No! You got what you wanted out of life! You always had more than me, even Ma loved you more than she loved me! You've still got more than me. A good life, good friends, people to look after you and your baby. Well, you're not having Sean as well! He's mine!'

'I don't want him, not in the way you mean! I'm only thinking of his safety!'

'No, you're not! You want to take over, you want to bring him up to look down his nose at me! To be ashamed of his mother! Well, he's staying here! I've got friends, too. Oh, they may be whores but they're better than the likes of Maisey O'Dwyer and the other hypocrites!'

She tried again. 'Shelagh, please, do you want him to be hurt or even—?'

'We've got shelters, too! He's staying with me!'

'You won't change your mind? I'll bring him back to see you as often as I can?'

'No!'

She knew it was useless. 'Then I'll just have to pray that he will be alright . . . and you, too.'

'Pray all you like, it won't do any good! If there was anyone up there do you think he'd let all this go on? Live for today, enjoy yourself, that's my motto!' She smiled, but without malice. 'He's all I've got, can't you understand that?'

Reluctantly she nodded.

'Go home, Cat! Clear off, you'll give the place a bad reputation!'

She saw a fleeting glimpse of the sister she had known in the wry smile and she smiled back, sadly.

If only . . . but it was no use to dwell on the past. At least there had been a reconciliation, of sorts, between them. 'Pa's working and helping out in the raids as well,' she ventured.

'That's a bloody miracle! Don't expect it to last too long though, nothing ever does!'

She turned away. 'Bye, Shelagh, take care.'

That night the raiders came again and tons of incendiaries and high-explosive bombs rained down on the city. There was nothing anyone could do except sit and wait – nerves stretched to breaking point – listening to the continuous droning and the whistling that preceded death and destruction, the explosions that shook the whole of the city and the sound of the anti-aircraft guns.

'Don't worry, they say you don't hear the one that's got your number on it, that must be a blessing. It's only the near-misses you hear!' Mrs Gorry tried to sound light-hearted but failed.

She thanked God that at least Eamon was with her but she prayed for Joe and the O'Dwyers, Shelagh and little Sean Cleary and her father. 'Please Holy Mother, keep them all safe! Let them come through this night!' But even if her prayers were answered – this time – she knew it would go on and on, for the convoy was to sail again tomorrow. Unless every ship had been blown out of the water.

After those two nights in November the raids eased up, on Liverpool at least. The Luftwaffe turned its attentions to other cities. It would be a depressing Christmas, she thought as she travelled home on the train from her shift. In fact it would be miserable. Everything was getting shorter, the strain of waiting and worrying grew worse. Over thirty destroyers had been lost so far and thousands of tons of merchant shipping. But the port stayed open, the dockers working flat out, despite the difficulties. Joe and Eamon were due home on 19 December but she didn't know if they would both still be home for Christmas.

Marie was slowly getting over her loss. Occasionally she would smile and laugh. Some days she was almost like her old self, almost but not quite. Other days she would be silent and withdrawn.

The battered, depleted convoy arrived. Joe never said much about his experiences and she didn't ask.

'I've got a treat for you. I've managed to get tickets for a show at the Empire on the 21st,' he announced when he met her from work. She told him of her attempts to make Shelagh see reason.

'Do you want me to go and see her?'

'No! I'm not having you going to a place like that!'

'She might listen to me?'

'No!'

It was getting dark and bitterly cold. She pulled her scarf up around her ears. The traffic on Walton Road was heavy and noisy. She pushed the thoughts of her sister to the back of her mind and brightened up at the forthcoming treat. There wasn't much fun in anyone's life these days, it would be good to relax for a few hours, knowing he was safely beside her and that Eamon was home, too.

As they reached the corner of the road the siren sounded.

'Oh, no! Not this early! It's only half past six!' she cried.

Joe grabbed her hand and they began to run. Fortunately it wasn't far but they were both out of breath as they hammered on the front door.

Eamon opened it. 'Quick, get out the back! We've got all the stuff!'

They ran through the darkened house, down the garden and into the shelter. Mrs Gorry was standing with the frying pan still in her hand. Marie was sitting on one of the narrow metal bunks, the tea plates on her lap.

'Well, that's the liver and bacon ruined! And I had to queue for hours, too! You'd think they could have waited until we'd got the tea over!'

Joe laughed. 'Mrs Gorry, you're a treasure! We'll eat it raw if it will make you happy!'

She smiled at him. 'You might have to, I forgot to get more paraffin for the primus stove!'

It was the longest and most terrifying night she had ever known. It was fairly quiet at first and as they ate the half-cooked, half-cold meal, Mrs Gorry debated aloud whether it wouldn't have been wiser to have waited for supper. Half-cooked liver was not good for the digestive system and obviously it wasn't going to be a long raid.

Then at eight o'clock it got worse. Far worse than anything they had experienced before. It was impossible to talk. The shelter shook, the dishes clattered, the candles flickered and only the quick actions of Eamon stopped two of them from falling

360

on the bunks and setting the blankets alight. She clung to Joe while Mrs Gorry hugged Marie to her, her hands over her daughter's ears in an ineffectual attempt to blot out the noise. Eamon smoked continually and his hands shook. Mr Gorry sat as though in a daze. Each explosion dragging up memories twenty five years old, of men and ships blown to pieces before his eyes. And still it went on. They sat huddled in blankets on the narrow beds, wondering if it would ever end, if this was the night they all dreaded, the last night of their lives. It was 4.00 am the following morning when the all-clear sounded.

They straggled back into the house, exhausted, cold, hungry.

'We'd better see what we can do to help,' Mr Gorry said, dully.

'Not before you've all had something to eat! Fine Christmas this is going to be!' came the acid remark from the scullery where his wife was already busy.

'I'll come with you,' she offered.

'No. You'd better go and see if the O'Dwyers are alright and . . . and my Mam, if you will?' Joe asked.

She nodded. 'If everyone's alright, I'll go straight to work, that's if there's any work left to go to!'

It was ten times worse than the November bombings. Services had had to be brought in for miles around. Food warehouses in Dublin Street were still burning, as was the Waterloo Grain House. A huge pall of black smoke hung over the docks. The Cunard Buildings had been hit as had the dock board offices, but the devastation of houses was the worst.

Maisey and her family were shaken but she was worried about Mr O'Dwyer who had been out all night through the height of the raid. He hadn't returned home yet, but upon hearing from Cat the extent of the bombing, she said firmly. 'Well, I don't reckon as 'ow we'll be seein' 'im until dinner time!' She had always been of an optimistic nature.

Mrs Calligan's home was in ruins, but she had spent the night in the shelter. Cat found her sifting through the rubble, sorting out the pitifully small hoard of belongings that were not totally ruined. She hugged her before telling her to tell Joe that thing's weren't too bad. After all, what were bricks and mortar compared to safety of life and limb? She'd be moving in with her sister.

Loss of home and belongings was infinitely better than the loss of a loved one, Cat thought as she retraced her steps.

She was making her way to the station: they needed all the munitions they could get now, she thought bitterly. But then she realised that she was walking away from Central Station and not towards it. She was walking through a maze of streets that were no longer streets. They had no uniformity, no familiar landmarks and then she realised where she was going.

A few weeks ago it had been a large, square house, neglected in appearance. All that remained of it now was a pile of smouldering rubble. Glass cruched under her feet. She bent down and picked up a piece of mauve satin. Men were still working, clearing the rubble. Not one house was left undamaged in the whole street. She climbed over the debris and caught the sleeve of one of the rescue team. He turned. His face was blackened with dust and sweat. Anger, hatred, frustration and pity were in his eyes.

'Did . . . was anyone—?' she gulped.

'Only a few, luv. There's a girl over there with the WVS. He pointed to a makeshift lean-to where ladies of the WVS were trying to serve hot soup and tea.

She felt nothing as she picked her way across to it. People huddled in blankets, were talking in stilted whispers. Shock and horror on all their faces. A girl sat on the edge of the kerb. A blanket wrapped around her, a mug of soup held in her shaking hands. Under the blanket she could see a coat and a gaudy dress. She gently touched her on the shoulder.

'Were you in there? Were you in the Barracks?'

The girl shook her head.

'I'm looking for my sister. Shelagh Cleary . . . or O'Mara, was she in there?' The words were sticking in her throat.

The girl nodded slowly. 'Party . . . something about a party . . .'

She closed her eyes. Oh, Shelagh! Poor, stupid, selfish Shelagh! 'What about the boy?'

One of the WVS ladies took her arm. 'She's in shock, she won't be much help. Is there anything I can do?'

'My sister was . . . was in . . . that.' She pointed over her shoulder.

'I'm sorry. They haven't got everyone out yet.'

'She had a little boy. He's five, does anyone know . . .?' She couldn't go on. Guilt overwhelmed her. She should have *made* Shelagh see reason, she should have taken Sean by force!

'I'll have a word with the warden, he's been here all night, poor man.'

He made his way towards her. He'd been on his feet for nearly twelve hours, the worst twelve hours of his entire life.

'Was there a young child in . . .?'

'There were a couple of kids, we've put them all over there. We're waiting for an ambulance or a lorry.'

'My sister—'

'Can you identify them?'

She nodded slowly.

They were covered by a tarpaulin sheet. He lifted it and her stunned gaze swept across the row of mutilated bodies. She nodded as she felt the vomit rise in her throat. Even in such hideous death, she recognised her sister.

'And the child?'

She fought to control herself. She had never seen him, but both Maisey and Joe had given her a good description. He wasn't there. The pathetic, broken little bodies were those of little girls. Anger broke over her. 'Why didn't they send them away somewhere safe? Why?'

'God knows, luv, I don't! Is it one of them?'

'No. He's not there.'

'He. You should have said it was a little lad, you could have been spared some of it. He'll be at the school, they've taken all the children there.'

She thanked him and then turned away. Shelagh had gone. She could never hurt her again. She forgot the enmity between them. She remembered how they had played together in the dirty back streets of Dublin. Sean Cleary was her responsibility now.

*　　*　　*

The priest in charge at the school was greatly relieved that at least one of his charges had been claimed. Like the others he had been on his feet for over twelve hours and his church was in ruins.

'Poor, helpless, innocent little souls! They'll have to go into orphanages or be evacuated now, most of them.'

'He'll be safe now, Father. I'm taking him to Wales after Christmas. He'll be well cared for.'

'God bless you and keep you both safe! Off you go now with your aunty, young Sean!'

He looked up at her with his mother's eyes and her heart went out to him. She took his hand. 'We're going home, Sean.'

At the news of Shelagh's death they all expressed regret, but death was becoming no stranger to them now.

'We're still going out, Cat!' Joe said firmly.

She had arrived home to find him waiting for her. The little boy had said nothing at all throughout the journey and stood staring around him in bewilderment. Mrs Gorry fussed over him. Gave him a bath, then wrapping him in an eiderdown quilt, sat with him on her knee in front of the fire.

'I don't feel as though I can cope, Joe! I'm so tired and what with Shelagh . . . it doesn't seem right.'

'We're going! For a few hours you can put all this out of your mind! I'll go and see Mam, then I'll come back for you.'

'She's at your auntie's.'

'I know, you've told me three times already. Poor Mam, she loved her little house and all her stuff.'

'She said it didn't matter. It was only bricks and mortar.'

'She was always one to put a brave face on things. Be ready, I'll have to try and brush up my uniform. It's all I've got now, everything else was in the house.'

She was glad she had come. A lighthearted atmosphere pervaded the theatre and her spirits lifted. The place was packed. She settled into her seat and Joe produced a bag containing half a dozen barley-sugar sticks. 'Everything you need for a good night out!'

She smiled. 'Where did you get them?'

'Never mind! Just eat them!'

'Shouldn't I share them out?'

'No, I saved them for you!' he rebuked her. He didn't mention the fact that they were part of his survival rations.

Just as the curtain rose to the slightly discordant fanfare from the orchestra pit, the sirens sounded. She froze.

'Oh, sod off, Fritz! Gizza break, it's bloody Christmas!' someone yelled from behind her. Everyone cheered. Joe squeezed her hand and she managed a weak smile.

The show went on, despite the fact that often the music couldn't be heard at all and the spotlights flickered on and off, the chandeliers suspended from the ceiling swayed dangerously, but the audience was in a defiantly cheerful mood and everyone cheered and clapped loudly. She couldn't concentrate, she could feel the underlying fear. She was tense and nervous and half rose from her seat with each explosion, but Joe's arm around her shoulders restrained her.

At about ten o'clock a massive explosion rocked the building. Plaster flaked from the ceiling, the stage lights dimmed and a silence descended. Then the rumour buzzed around that St George's Hall had been hit and was on fire. There was no panic. People rose unhurriedly and made their way out into the foyer, spilling on to the pavement under the canopy.

She clung tightly to Joe's arm and his arm around her waist pressed her closer to him. They gazed upwards. The beams of the searchlights that swept the sky picked out the sinister outlines of the enemy bombers, still overhead. It was as bright as day, for the whole of Lime Street as far as William Brown Street was illuminated by the flames, and the heat was intense. Flames were rushing and roaring from the long roof of the beautiful, colonnaded building opposite. The huge, bronze lions that guarded the plateau where the Punch and Judy show took place every Sunday appeared to be glaring their defiance. An ineffectual gesture not convincing enough to maintain the morale of the stunned spectators, many of whom wept openly. Liverpool's greatest architectural treasure was being destroyed before their eyes. The Assize Courts were burning fiercely out of control, thousands of legal records adding fuel to the conflagration. She buried her face against his shoulder, unable to bear the sight, oblivious of the bombers still overhead and the sound of the anti-aircraft guns that valiantly fought to repel the raiders.

'I've paid me money an' 'itler an' his bloody

firework display ain't goin' ter ruin me night!' came a voice from the crowd. Someone else shouted. 'Good on yer, lad!'

People started to move, not away from the theatre but back inside. She looked up at Joe. A grim, determined smile twisted his lips.

'We're going to stay until the end like everyone else!' he said as he led her back into the theatre.

St George's Hall survived but Mill Road Infirmary, the Gaiety Theatre, St Anthony's School, Crescent Church and St Alphonsus's Church did not. They were among the hundreds of buildings destroyed that night.

It was after 4 a.m. when they got back. The All Clear hadn't sounded until 3.30 a.m. The house was in darkness and even though it was late, she insisted Joe come in for a hot drink before starting the long trek back to his aunt's house in Anfield.

Eamon was sitting in the darkened kitchen. Cigarette butts littered the hearth where the embers of the fire still glowed.

'Why are you sitting in the dark? It's over. Why aren't you in bed?'

He rose as she switched on the light, thankful the electricity supply hadn't been affected. He looked worn out and so old, she thought.

'Pa's dead, Cat!'

She swayed, catching hold of the table for support.

'Cat . . .?' Joe's hand closed over hers.

'I'm . . . alright.'

'When? Where?' It was Joe who voiced her questions.

'Tonight. He was with Mr O'Dwyer when St Alphonsus's got it! Mr O'Dwyer's gone, too.'

She groaned. 'Poor Maisey!' Her head was swimming. First Shelagh and now . . . Oh, she'd never had much time for either of them but she'd never foreseen anything like this!

'At least he died better than he lived!' Eamon's voice cracked with grief and bitterness.

'That's enough!' Joe said quietly. 'You've had a rotten day, Cat, go and try to get some sleep, we'll sort everything out tomorrow. Eamon and I.'

'Maisey—' she said tiredly.

'We'll see Maisey, too. Get to bed now!'

As she climbed the stairs, clinging to the bannister rail for support, she wondered about tomorrow and all the tomorrows to come. Would it never end? It would be a bleak and bitter Christmas.

CHAPTER TWENTY-TWO

The late April sunlight streamed in through the windows of the bus. The trees were just about to burst into bud and bright splashes of yellow daffodils could be glimpsed in cottage gardens. She had longed to stay in Henllan. The tiny village was so tranquil beneath spring skies; so restful after the mayhem created by the dreaded Luftwaffe. She had wanted to linger there, to nurse her baby, to play with her. To push Hilary in her pram along the narrow lanes where the hedgerows were bursting with new life and only birdsong filled the air. To smile as she watched Sean, his cheeks glowing with health, run ahead to 'explore' and bring back his 'treasures' to show her, then to be presented with measured care and grubby hands to his small cousin, who would immediately try to cram them into her mouth. For three whole days she had found an oasis of happiness, devoid of fear and anxiety.

Sean had settled down far better than she had anticipated. After those first two days of dejected bewilderment, he had erupted into a tiny whirlwind that had totally disrupted the household. He threw screaming tantrums when he would bite and kick anyone who tried to go near him. He hurled anything that was within reach and destroyed the books and toys bought for him for Christmas. The tantrums were followed by bouts of sobbing when he had pleaded to 'go home to me Mam'. He was totally unconvinced by their explanations about his mother having gone to live with God and the Angels. He had stamped his feet, his small, pale face contorted and had yelled that he 'hated that God an' them Angels!'. He took to bedwetting and sleepwalking, which caused further anxiety and disruption.

Strangely it had been to Marie that he had gradually turned, placing in her the trust he denied to everyone else. She, in turn, had shown infinite patience; a quality her mother remarked that had never been one of her stronger characteristics. A bond had developed between them and she had wondered if they both sensed each other's loss and loneliness. It had been Marie who had persuaded him to go to Wales and it had been Marie who took him the first time and stayed with him for over a week.

Her stay had been prolonged, providentially, by the severe weather, for it had been one of the worst winters for years. Heavy frost had covered the countryside. The rivers and streams were frozen into ribbons of silver that laced the niveous meadows. In the city the water in the pipes had frozen. Then a blanket of thick snow disguised the ugly scars of the Christmas raids. It also made transportation of any kind dangerous. Over Christmas and in the early months of the New Year of 1941 the raids had been sporadic and never as heavy as those two dreadful nights in December.

She closed her eyes and let the sun, through the glass, warm her cheeks. Oh, she had missed her baby so much. Hilary was thirteen months old now. She had David's blue eyes but the whispy curls were the same colour as her own. When she lay asleep in her cot, her chubby arms flung wide, Cat would bend and kiss her and then it hurt so much, knowing she would have to leave her. Knowing she was missing all the little things that meant so much and could never be recaptured. The first tooth, the first step, the first recognisable word. But Hilary's safety was paramount.

The bus jerked and juddered and she opened her eyes. The fields were giving way to suburbs and the pace of the vehicle slowed as the driver negotiated the hastily repaired roads. She sighed. So short a distance – so few miles – and yet it was as if she had been transported into another world. 'Cheer up, Cat Cleary, tomorrow is the first of May and Joe and Eamon will be home on the third, God willing!' The O'Dwyers were managing, as were the Gorrys and Marie had started to go out socially again. Richard Hocking was older than both of them, but he worked in the same building as Marie and she had accepted his invitation to a concert at the Philharmonic Hall. All in all, she had a lot to be thankful for, she thought, as the bus slowly moved through the fissured roads to its terminus.

She had quickly slipped back into the routine of work when she returned to Kirkby the following day. She was the last one home.

'Oh, am I the last one in? Sorry, I dawdled.' She grimaced. 'I hate that place! It's not until you get away for a few days that you realise just how dreary it is! And if Nancy goes on any more about how she is altering her entire wardrobe, as explained in her

373

mother's magazines, I'll scream! She's so empty-headed!' She sat down at the table. 'You look nice, are you going out?' she questioned Marie.

Marie nodded.

'Another concert?'

'No, the cinema.'

Cat and Mrs Gorry exchanged glances.

'And when are we going to get the pleasure of meeting . . . Oh, No! Here we go again!'

The sound of the air-raid siren was common-place now. There was no panic. No hasty grabbing of kettles and dishes and blankets and bumping into each other in the process. Mrs Gorry now kept blankets, matches, candles, two biscuit tins packed with whatever was available, and a thermos flask of tea, all in a pile near the scullery door.

'Oh, well, it will have to be the cinema tomorrow night!' Marie sighed.

The raid was comparatively light but on the following night Marie had to cancel her date again and it was becoming obvious that their respite was over. As the hours passed the old fears returned. She threw down the dress she was stitching by hand for Hilary, made from one of her cotton petticoats. She couldn't concentrate and had jabbed her finger with the needle. She sucked it then cursed herself, seeing a tiny bloodspot on the dress. Mrs Gorry stoically continued sewing the first pair of mittens cut from the piece of sheepskin that Cat had begged from Mrs Roberts on her trip.

'What time is it?' she asked irritably.

Marie glanced at her watch. 'Nearly nine o'clock.'

She picked up her sewing. 'I suppose I'd better get on with it. At this rate she'll have grown out of it before it's even finished! And we could all be here for hours!' She reached over to place the candle closer and it began to shake in her hand although she knew her hands were steady. The shrill whistling increased until its piercing stridency forced them to press their hands over their ears. Naked fear was in all their eyes.

The whole shelter vibrated. The ground under their feet moved and cracks appeared in the concrete base. The blast threw Marie to the floor and knocked her sprawling across the bunk, the candle falling against her arm. It flickered for a second then went out. She didn't even feel the pain of the molten wax.

Mrs Gorry was the first to recover, scrabbling in the pitch darkness for the matches. She struck one, located a candle, then struck another to rekindle the flame. 'Oh, my God! That was close!'

Marie crawled to her mother's side. 'Where's Dad tonight, Mum?' her voice shook.

Mrs Gorry didn't answer, she just got up stiffly.

Marie clung to her. 'Mum, you can't go out! You can't!'

'I . . . I wasn't going to.'

Marie sat down and covered her face with her hands.

Her mother patted her shoulder. 'Come on, luv, we can't let it get us down! Dad's going to be just fine, I know he is! There's nothing we can do but sit it out!'

Marie didn't look up. Cat had seen Mrs Gorry's self-control crumble, just for a few seconds, and it frightened her far more than anything else. She drew her own strength from the older woman, as Marie did, and she knew that if Mrs Gorry broke under the strain then they would all degenerate into babbling lunacy.

Just after midnight Mr Gorry appeared like an apparition – literally – for he was covered from head to toe in plaster dust.

'Can't stay, but I just wanted to check that you were all—'

Both Marie and her mother launched themselves at him and clung to him.

'Come on, Cat!' he laughed. 'Give us a kiss, everyone else has!'

She laughed, too, out of sheer relief. 'Was it Walton Hospital?'

'No, thank God! It was further down, towards Walton Vale, but I think we've lost most of the roof!'

'Our roof?' His wife was incredulous.

'There were two or three direct hits, almost simultaneously.'

'It just sounded like one big one, didn't it girls? Do you have to go back, can't you stay? Surely, it can't last much longer?'

He shook his head. 'Sorry, I've got to get back.' He kissed them all before he left.

An hour later the all-clear sounded and Mrs Gorry, now outwardly composed, was first out of the shelter. She stood, hands on hips, and surveyed the damage to her home. It wasn't possible to see too clearly as it was still dark, but the chimney had gone and broken slates littered the yard and the garden.

'Well, it's no use going in until it's light enough to see what kind of a mess we're in, we might as well try and get some sleep,' she stated firmly, ushering the two girls back inside the shelter.

They heard later that the Church of the Blessed Sacrament in Walton Vale – the church they all attended – had been hit and badly damaged, as had many houses in the vicinity. Their own house had come off lightly. In daylight it was clear enough to see the gaping hole in the roof, the worst damage being at the front of the house. Ignoring the layer of plaster dust, the glass and shattered crockery in the kitchen and scullery, Mrs Gorry went straight into the parlour. There was a large hole in the ceiling and a bed was swaying dangerously in the gap, weighed down by the plaster and broken lathes from the bedroom ceiling that had collapsed on to it. Glass and debris littered the room. Mr Gorry went upstairs to try to move the bed to a more stable position.

'Oh, Mum, what a mess!' Marie cried.

'Just be thankful we've got a mess to clean up at all! Well, would you just look at that!' Her mother reached out to touch the Waterford crystal vase that still stood in pride of place on the mantlepiece. By some miracle it had held together. It was a family heirloom, brought by her mother-in-law from Ireland and was a bone of contention between herself and her sister-in-law, Nellie. But as her fingers touched it, it crumbled into a thousand slivers. She stood staring at them. 'Well, now there's nothing to argue over, is there?'

'At least the pianola's not damaged, it's only scratched a bit.' Marie interrupted, running her fingers over keys which were a uniform grey colour.

Her mother turned and her eyes alighted on the

rolls of music. 'Right! Sort through those rolls and anything that's composed by anyone remotely German, put on one side. We're going to have a bonfire!'

'Oh, but Mum, they'll be irreplaceable!'

'Irreplaceable or not, they can burn and if I could get my hands on Adolf Hitler I'd put him on the top and he could bloody well burn as well!' And with that she resolutely kicked the fragments of the vase into the empty fireplace. 'Cat, see if you can find some shovels and brushes, then we'll all set to and clean up! I'm not having our Nellie up here from Aintree in her fox furs to see if we're alright and the place in this state! And if she so much as mentions that vase, she can take the bloody pieces home with her in a paper bag!'

They had done the best they could and Mr Gorry, with the help of some neighbours, had covered the hole in the roof with tarpaulins and, to his wife's relief, her sister-in-law did not appear. Out of the four lorries and three horse-drawn carts he had owned, Mr Gorry informed them grimly that only one lorry had been salvaged. He did not tell them that there had been tears in his eyes as he had surveyed his wrecked yard and stables, from which the charred bodies of four cart-horses had been dragged.

'Perhaps we can all get a decent night's sleep tonight. They never strike so heavily for more than two nights on the run, blast them!' came the vituperative remark from his wife when beds had been brought down and made up in the dining room. Such was the devastation that no one had gone to work.

'I'll go down and see if Maisey's alright. The convoy is due in today, so I'll go and meet Joe and Eamon.'

'You come back as soon as you can, especially if it's late and it's bound to be. They may even have been diverted after last night!' Mrs Gorry warned.

She hoped and prayed that it had not.

The sights and sounds were familiar now, heart-renderingly familiar. But even so she wasn't pre-pared for the sight of Eldon Street. Half of it was little more than a mountain of smouldering rubble and number 8 was part of it, but her heart leaped as she heard the familiar voice calling her name from a house that was still standing. Maisey and all the O'Dwyers spilled out on to the street with cries of delight.

'Maisey! Oh, Maisey!' she cried, wiping her eyes.

Maisey dabbed her eyes on the corner of her pinafore. 'We 'eard you gorrit bad your end, too?'

'Not nearly as bad as this!'

'God knows what we're goin' ter do now! I 'aven't even gorra clean pair of drawers! An' yer should 'ear 'er! You'd think she'd lost the Crown Jewels instead of all that tatty stuff she used ter drape 'erself in! Gorrup like a Christmas tree sometimes she was! I told 'er it was dead common ter wear all that jewellery at the same time!'

'That cost me milluns, our Mam, an it weren't tatty!' Dora flung back with some exaggeration. She had obviously not forgotten the striped taf-fetta dress.

Despite herself, Cat burst out laughing. It would

379

take more than a heavy air-raid, the loss of her home and all her possessions to defeat the likes of Maisey O'Dwyer!

The convoy hadn't been diverted and late that afternoon she stood on the landing stage and watched them come slowly up the river. Sections of the docks still smouldered and an increasingly bigger swathe of destruction had been cut through the heart of the city, but the port was still working. They looked like tired, battered, old warhorses, she thought, their hulls as grey and dirty as the murky water that buoyed them up. Her eyes misted as, behind the convoy and sailing alone, she recognised the *Empress of Japan*. There was nothing about her now of that majestic ship that she had stood and gazed at, on this very spot, years ago. Her hull was a dirty, mottled grey. Patches of rust were visible, her rigging was damaged and only her three funnels, partly camouflaged, identified her as the former flagship. The muscles in her throat constricted as she thought of that other Empress that lay on the ocean bed, and of all the Canadian Pacific ships that had gone down. The *Beaverbrea*, the *Montrose*, the *Beaverburn*, the *Niagara*, the *Beaverdale* and *Beaverford*. Seven from a fleet of twenty-two, in one short year.

It was nearly an hour later when she hugged them both, after fighting her way through the crowd of wives, mothers and dockworkers.

'Holy Mother of God! When did all this happen? How is everyone?' Joe asked, shocked.

'Last night. We've got a hole in the roof, Maisey's been bombed out and the city is devastated, but we've all survived and we're managing! And, as

380

they probably won't be back tonight, I think we've all got something to celebrate!'

'A lot more than most, I should think.'

'I promised I'd come straight back. I've seen Maisey and both of you, so I'd best be off now.'

'I'd better go and see if Mam is alright. How about us all going for a drink tonight? You, me, Eamon and Marie?'

'I don't know about Marie, she's been out a few times with a chap from work. I wrote to you about it.'

'We got no mail, this time.'

'I've promised to meet a few of the lads later.' Eamon interrupted.

'Then it's just you and me, Cat. Shall I pick you up?'

'No, I'll come in on the tram. There's no sense dragging you all the way out to Walton, just in case they do come again.'

She had insisted he only saw her safely on to the tram, he looked so tired, he needed some rest, she urged. She'd be fine, didn't she manage all the time he was away?

'I worry about you, Cat! I worry all the time!'

'Well don't, you've got enough to think about . . . out there.'

He placed his arms on her shoulders and looked down at her. He knew he had changed, there were times when he felt he would never regain that spirit of youth, that optimistic enthusiasm for life. He felt like an old man. A tired, bitter, old man. But looking down at her she looked no different from the girl he had always known, although now she was a woman of nearly twenty-six. But the love he felt for her had not diminished, it had increased.

'Look after yourself, Cat—'

'Oh, Joe! You know I will!'

She placed her arms around his neck and he drew her close.

'Oh, I miss you so much, Joe!'

His lips sought hers and she responded. It was the first time he had held her and kissed her like this since . . . Oh, it was a lifetime ago! But the jealousy had gone now.

She drew away from him and looked calmly up into his eyes, but before he could speak she placed her fingertips on his lips.

'No! Not yet! Not yet!'

'Cat!' There was agony in his voice.

'I know, my own dearest Joe, but what kind of future . . . how much time—?'

'It's better than nothing at all, Cat!'

She knew he was too proud to plead, even in such uncertain circumstances. She reached up and kissed him tenderly. 'I couldn't bear it, Joe! I couldn't stand to lose you! I'm not strong, it's just an act we all put on, otherwise we'd all go out of our minds! But if . . . when . . .'

He drew her close to him and kissed her forehead. 'I'll hold you to that, Cat Cleary! It will end one day and I'll be here! I've let you slip through my fingers for the last time!'

A feeling of infinite peace surged through her. 'I've been such a fool, Joe, forgive me? I was always my own worst enemy.'

'There's nothing to forgive, Cat.'

She pressed her cheek close to his. 'I love you, Joe Calligan. I think I've always loved you but I've been too blind, too stubborn, too proud to admit it, until now.'

He stroked her hair. Once her words would have filled him with a fierce passion, now he felt contentment and an all-consuming tenderness for her. 'You've always known I loved you, Cat, I can't deny it, and I suffered a hell of jealously and rage when . . . well all that's over. I may never get to be second officer but—'

'Oh, Joe, living like this has made me realise that wealth and status are empty, useless things. This war has swept away everything I once thought was so important. It's people who matter, and love and kindness and loyalty and those are the greatest gifts you have to offer and I love you for sharing them with me!'

They stood in silence, clinging to each other, praying that the bond of love that had been forged ten years ago would not be broken by tragedy.

His weariness had left him as he watched the tram trundle away. He'd waited so long, suffered so much, but it had been worth it. When all this was over, she would be waiting for him.

He made his way back towards the docks. His aunt's home was dreadfully overcrowded, as yet another group of relations had moved in. Families were doubling and trebling up as more and more homes were destroyed. He wanted some peace and quiet to think, to reflect, and there would be more chance of that back on board as most of the crew of HMS *Firefly* were ashore.

He had reached the Dock Road when the sirens sounded. It was 11.10. His first thoughts were for Cat, but he realised she would be well on her way home and would be hastily sent off to the nearest shelter, as the tram was evacuated. The droning of the first wave of raiders followed almost immediately. There hadn't been much of a warning. He began to run as the first incendiaries found their target, sending a shower of sparks into the air, he increased his pace, oblivious to the explosions around him. He kept on running. He hadn't sweated and toiled, prayed and wept, watched the deaths of so many, many ships and men to run for cover now. Not now when they had come to destroy the precious cargoes they had nursed all the way home. He reached No. 2 Husskison Dock barely able to speak, he was so breathless. Already there were fires raging and engines hurtling in from all directions. The bastards! The bastards! He cursed to himself. He stopped and leaned against the wall of a shed to regain his breath. Ahead of him, outlined by the glare, was the *Malakand*. Men were working frantically at the pumps and were successfully dousing the flames over the No. 1 hatch. He jerked into action. They would need more help. The *Malakand* was loaded with 1,000 tons of high-explosive bombs!

He reached the dockside and raced up the gangway, as a shower of incendiaries burst around them. Explosions rocked the entire dock and soon the cargo sheds were alight. The fire engines continued to arrive, the men playing their hoses on the sheds on the east and south sides. Dim figures that became lost in the dense smoke, only to reappear as men bent double over the hoses as they fought to contain the fires. As he raced along the deck he could feel the heat through the soles of his boots. Sweat poured down his face from the searing heat, but he set to work with the crew.

The blaze had reached the contents of the cargo shed on the south side and the building errupted into a solid wall of flames.

'It's no use! It's spreading!' someone yelled.

He turned. The flames had reached the *Malakand*.

'She'll go up! Get the hell out of it!' The officer-in-charge swore roundly. The fire was a blazing beacon and the raiders homed in on it. The heat and smoke were suffocating as more incendiaries fell and the bombers flew lower, so low at times that their black shapes seemed only a few feet above them.

He began to cough and his eyes were smarting, the deck was red-hot. He turned again. Above the cacophany he heard Captain Kinley give the order to 'Abandon ship'. He followed the others down the gangway and to a point where the shed was least affected by the fire. The *Malakand* was ablaze from stem to stern.

The fire officer in charge, Mr Lappin, shouted for them to help his own men, and grappling with a hose, beside two other men, he fought to quell the inferno. His arms and shoulders ached. The enemy aircraft droned overhead unheeded. It was useless, the blazing wall of cargo sheds made it impossible to get near enough to try to train the hoses on the ship.

Across his path of vision he saw a blurred figure running along the side of the shed. He rubbed his eyes with the back of his hand. In this hell of heat, smoke and flames it was impossible to recognise any individual. But as the figure ran towards them a face flashed into his mind. Eamon! He heard the others curse him as he began to run. The roaring and rushing of the flames drowned out his warning cries. He looked up and launched himself bodily across the few feet that separated them. They collided, falling on the wet cobbles, rolling over and over with the momentum of the impact. There was a groaning, splintering sound as the roof of the shed collapsed. They were both soaking wet, the cold water drenching them, as a fire hose was played on them, extinguishing their burning uniforms.

He dragged himself to his knees. Eamon lay sprawled on the floor. Shaking his head to try to clear his vision, he tried to pull him upright. His strength seemed to have drained from him. His arms felt like lumps of lead, his legs were unsteady. Somehow he half-pulled, half-dragged the unconscious lad backwards until he felt hands reach out for them both and he was borne bodily away. The last thing he remembered was a blinding flash of white light and a roaring in his ears so loud he thought his brain was bursting through his skull. The *Malakand* had exploded.

CHAPTER TWENTY-THREE

Compared with the flood of casualties around them, their injuries were superficial and they both became voluntary stretcher-bearers. A heavy bomb had fallen in the back courtyard of Mill Road Infirmary, demolishing three hospital buildings, damaging the rest and many surrounding houses. The resulting carnage was appalling and patients were transferred to hospitals that were already overcrowded.

When the flood had diminished to a trickle and they were both exhausted, they stepped out into the street, surprised to find it was daylight. The sun and a blue sky lay somewhere beyond the pall of smoke that hung over the city. They were shocked at the sights that met their eyes but too exhausted even to feel anger and hatred. The burns to their hands and faces began to smart now that there was time to reflect on them.

They found Mrs Gorry alone in the house. Cat and Marie had left for work and Mr Gorry, despite being out all night, had gone to try to maintain his business.

'Thank God! We've been out of our minds with worry, where've you been?'

'First we were at the docks; the *Malakand* blew up, and then at the hospital – you heard about Mill Road?' Joe answered.

She nodded grimly.

'Apart from a few scratches and minor burns we're alright.'

She stopped chopping the carrots, potatoes and the small onions she had managed to get from the greengrocer's. It would be 'blind scouse' tonight, she hadn't been able to get any meat. Not even a bit of scrag end. She went into the scullery and returned with a stone jar which contained the precious dripping.

'Hold out your hands, both of you!'

They complied like small boys and she smeared the grease over the raw patches. 'Didn't they put anything on them? Didn't they give you something to put on them?'

'They needed everything for the more serious cases.' Eamon winced as he eased off his jersey while she gently rubbed the grease across his back.

'What state are the docks in?'

'Pretty bad, but not out of action.'

'Then you won't be off again too soon?'

'No. We'll be here for a few days, I should think. We'll have to report back though. I'll wait and see Cat then I'll get off and see Mam.'

'Not before you've had some sleep, my lad! Dear God! It's enough to make the angels weep! Still, they must be running out of bombs by now, surely?'

Mrs Gorry's ever-optimistic hopes were dashed. Far from running out of bombs they came again that night and attacked with equal ferocity. Cat and Marie had returned from work and Joe was about t0 leave when the raid started.

They tried all the usual diversions. Improvised

games, family reminiscences going back generations, general chit-chat, until everything was exhausted. Then they tried to sleep but everyone was too restless and on edge.

Just before midnight and with no sign of let up, Cat broke down. Joe took her in his arms as both Marie and her mother fought to control themselves.

'Oh, why? Why? Why don't they leave us alone?' she sobbed.

'Because of the port, Cat! They've got to try to stop the port from working and the convoys.'

She raised a tear-streaked face. 'Isn't it enough that they've already sunk so many ships? It's people now! Innocent children, women and old folk!'

'Stop it, Cat! This is just what they want, to terrify and demoralise us so that we'll give up!'

'But we can't take much more! Three nights in a row now! There won't be anyone or anything left to give up!'

He held her away from him and shook her. 'What's happened to you, Cat Cleary? Is this the same girl who swore she'd be chief stewardess of an Empress, no matter what? What's happened to all the fight, all the pig-headed stubbornness?' he shouted at her, mainly to emphasise his words but also because the noise of the bombardment had grown louder.

The other three sat watching tensely, aware that the outcome of this challenge would affect their own attitudes. In their eyes Cat had fought and triumphed over every obstacle that malign fate had thrown in her path. But she was weakening and that fact eroded their own confidence.

Joe could feel her trembling.

'It's all gone, Joe! At the end of this there won't be any Empresses! There won't be any ships . . . they'll have gone . . . like the *Empress of Britain!'*

He caught her right hand and jerked it upwards so that her fingers were immediately in her line of vision, the back of her hand facing her. 'Do you remember what I said when I gave you that ring? The tiger's eye? You can be a right little cat at times, isn't that what I said? You've fought everything and everyone for years, you can't stop now! I won't let you stop! You've got to fight on, we've all got to fight on!'

Her gaze left his face and flickered across the faces of the others, before resting on the ring he had bought her all those years ago and which she had always worn. She felt calmer. Common sense always had that effect on her. In some ways they all looked to her for strength, even Mrs Gorry, indomitable though she appeared. They all needed each other, depended on each other for support. He was right. She couldn't give up. They couldn't give up.

Next morning when Joe and Eamon had gone – Joe to see his mother before reporting back to his ship – she went to see Maisey, dreading what she would find. She found her and her brood sitting huddled dejectedly on the edge of the broken kerb, their possessions in bundles, around them. And although Maisey greeted her with her usual cry of delight, she realised that Maisey was badly shaken.

'So the rest of it's gone now,' she sighed, gazing down the street.

'There won't be a bloody 'ouse left in the whole

city at this rate! I've 'ad enough! Even the rest centres aren't safe an' they're so crowded I can't keep my eye on this lot!'

She sat down on a mound of rubble beside them. 'What are you going to do? Mrs Gorry will gladly take you in, you know that. She's always telling me to tell you that you're all welcome. Mind you we'd be like sardines in a tin in the shelter, but that wouldn't matter.'

'No, luv, we'll manage. We're goin' out ter Huyton Woods to sleep. Everyone's goin'.' She indicated the small groups of her remaining neighbours, all sitting patiently in the roadway. Cat waved to the Abbotts.

'There's an American canteen lorry what comes 'round, from some place over there, the name's plastered all over it.'

'Charlotteville,' Dora interrupted.

'Aye, you'd know well enough wouldn't yer! Yer do enough chattin' up the driver! Al or Abe or wharrever 'e calls 'imself! As if I 'aven't gorrenough on me plate without 'er flashin' 'er eyes at them Yanks! A few pair of stockin's an' she's anyone's! If yer Da was 'ere, me girl—'

'You mean you're going out to Huyton to sleep?' Cat interrupted. Huyton was a small, rural village on the vast estates of the Earl of Derby.

'It's a damned sight safer than the city or what's left of it! They pick us up about five an' drive us out there in a lorry. Then we gets a 'ot meal an' a cuppa. It's not that bad. It's not cold an' we've all got blankets. An' it's 'ealthier bein' in the open. Them shelters breed consumption and lice. Yer can't get nothin' now ter shift the nits, they just shave all yer 'air off.' She pointed to a glum, embarrassed Lizzie who was wearing a knitted pixie hood, even though it was warm.

'They can keep their 'ands off my 'air!' Dora stated emphatically.

'Then yer mind who yer stick yer 'ead next to! Tharrall stop yer sneakin' off when yer think I'm asleep!'

It was as though they were back in the kitchen of number 8 instead of sitting in the road where the house used to be, she thought. Nothing really seemed to stop the bickering.

'But what about during the day?'

'Oh, we'll manage. The kids still 'ave lessons, in the church now. The school is a rest centre or at least it was yesterday. Them two can go ter work, termorro.' She nodded in the direction of Dora and Ethel. 'As fer me, well I'll just try ter keep our few bits clean an' decent, like everyone else does. Anyway, it'll only be for a while, until Jerry gets fed up an' goes an' blasts the daylights out of some other poor sods!'

Maisey's optimism cheered her up. It was contagious, and she sat with them, occasionally joining other groups to 'catch up on the news' until late in the afternoon. She hugged them all as one by one they boarded the lorries that would take them to the comparative safety of Huyton Woods for the night.

'I'll come up and see you tomorrow!' she shouted, waving as the lorries started up.

'Don't yer go worryin' about us, Cat. Jerry's not cum up against us scousers before, we're a 'ard lot ter shift!' She yelled back.

She stood and waved until they were all out of sight.

*   *   *

By the end of that first week in May, 50,000 people were sleeping like the O'Dwyers, as night after night the relentless bombardment went on. From Seaforth to the Husskison Dock the flames raged, in ships, warehouses, dockside sheds and in all the narrow streets that were left. On the night of 8 May the New Brighton ferry the *Royal Daffodil II* was sunk at her moorings. The head post office, the Central and Bank Exchange, the Mersey dock buildings, Oceanic buildings, India buildings, Georges dock buildings and the Central Library had been destroyed. St Luke's Church, at the top of Bold Street and the Parish Church of St Nicholas at the Pierhead were only two of dozens of churches that lay in ruins.

At the end of that horrendous week the lone statue of Queen Victoria, seated in her dome monument at the top of Lord Street, looked down on a radius of three-quarters of a mile of wasteland where not one single building remained standing.

Ships had been damaged, sunk and diverted, sheds, warehouses and their contents destroyed; dock communications interrupted; gates, basins and quaysides struck; cranes left as mangled, twisted lumps of metal. But the port struggled on and at the end of the month, when the enemy had seemingly exhausted itself, the first convoy sailed.

They all went to see Joe and Eamon leave and it seemed that most of the city went, too. There was an atmosphere of grim defiance and on the faces of the crowd there was pride. Despite everything the Port of Liverpool remained operational.

'Eh, up, girl! Purrim down, yer don't know where 'e's been!' A grinning docker called to her as she hugged Eamon.

'I bloody well should do, he's my brother!' she laughed.

'Oh, that's alright then, I thought it was yer 'usband!'

In such a crowd there wasn't much chance of a private goodbye she thought as Joe took her in his arms, but she clung to his lips just the same. After the horrors of the past weeks she had drawn a little comfort from the fact that they had endured it together. He had been safe, if anything could be considered safe. Now he was leaving her again. Leaving to face the silent, unseen enemy and the merciless sea.

'Promise me there won't be any repetition of that night in the shelter?'

'I'll try! Oh, come back safe!'

He kissed her again. 'Don't worry I will! I've got you to come back to.'

She pulled off the tiger's eye ring. 'Take this! Take this to remind you.'

He kissed her again and she never wanted him to stop, locking her hands tightly behind his head, until at the warning blast of the *Firefly*'s siren, he pulled them gently away. He pushed the ring on the only finger it would fit. His little finger.

'I'll buy you another one in Canada. A proper engagement ring!' And with a final hug he turned and shouldered his way through the crowd.

She clasped Marie's hand tightly, her vision blurred by tears. 'I don't want an engagement ring! He can buy me a wedding ring when he gets back!'

'And I'll be your bridesmaid,' Marie answered with a trace of sadness as she returned the squeeze.

* * *

It wasn't often that Joe and Eamon had time for conversation. At sea they seldom saw each other and when they did it was usually just a hurried exchange. They had different messes, different watches and different jobs which kept them apart. Joe's domain was the hot, smelly, noisy engine room, in the bowels of the frigate. Eamon was a gunner, having shown an early aptitude and a rare accuracy which he put down to his deadly aim with a catapult as a lad in the back-streets of Liverpool. He could always hit a tin can, or more usually a 'jigger rabbit' from a fair distance, he had told his mates when he had been elevated to his present position.

He didn't envy Joe now, though he still looked up to him, as he had always done. Joe Calligan had been his boyhood hero. But as they steamed through the cold, dark waters of the Atlantic, eyes always searching, ears always straining, he knew Joe's chances in the engine room were slim should they be hit. He'd seen it happen all too often. No, it was better to be on deck, despite the cold, the rain, the wind and often mountainous seas. The only time he felt uneasy was when he went below to sleep and he never slept deeply. Exhausted though he often was, some sixth sense made him wake instantly, immediately alert, at any unusual sound. Joe, on the other hand, could only hear the noise of the turbines, see only the boilers, pipes and gauges in the steamy gloom of the engine room. No, better to be up top, even if it was huddled, cramped and often bitterly cold, in the gun turret.

He studied Joe's tall form, outlined in the dim lights of the bridge. Tonight for the first time their watches had coincided. Chief Petty Officer Drummond stood at the wheel, a silent and morose man, lost in his own world. He would go for hours without speaking.

'What's the matter, missing your boilers and the warmth?' he joked, sensing Joe's tension.

'I've got used to it now and all this,' he threw out his arm in a wide sweep indicating the ocean, 'makes me uneasy at times. Especially at night.'

Few men voiced their fears. It was defeatist and bad for morale. Drummond said nothing. Eamon respected Joe for his frankness, though, remembering he had been at sea for years when the sight of the ocean at night had held no hidden terrors.

'What were you shouting to Cat when we left? Are you going to make an honest woman of her at last?'

'Yes. I promised to buy her an engagement ring in the first port we reach.'

'Don't count your chickens, Calligan,' Drummond muttered.

'When I was a kid, she used to say work hard at school and you can grow up to be just like Joe. I thought you'd have married her years ago.'

'It's a wonder you didn't grow up hating my guts, having me held up as such a paragon!'

'I never looked at it like that. I only ever saw you as grown up and usually in a fancy uniform and able to hand out a few coppers for sweets.'

'So that's why you joined the bloody Navy?' Drummond questioned flatly.

They exchanged glances. He was talkative tonight.

'She's got a lot to answer for has Cat.' Joe's voice was amused.

'God, I used to hate her when she dragged me round to Our Lady's school and Father Maguire used to put the terrors on me! Funny how things like that stick in your mind. Funny how your outlook changes too, I look at him now and he's just an old man and a nice enough bloke, too.'

Joe shifted his position. The weather was foul. It was not a typical May night, but then the North Atlantic was never typical, always unpredictable. A cold drizzle was falling. The sea was heavy, breaking over the bows, and the wind from the south-south west was threatening to develop into a full gale. They were well into the danger zone, some sixty miles north of the coast of Ireland. Ahead of them, strung out, was the convoy. A shiver ran through his body. Someone walking over his grave, he thought.

'Must have been somewhere near here that the *Britain* went down. I hate the North Western approaches, I'll feel better when we're further away from land – any land!' Eamon muttered.

Or someone passing over the grave of others, entombed in another ship fathoms below, Joe thought, before pushing superstition away.

'How did she take it? I mean really take it, when they got news of the *Britain*?'

Eamon didn't reply for a while. He had talked for hours with Mr Gorry about that terrible day. He had been away at the time.

'She was upset for Marie, Brian and the others. She was upset about the ship itself. Everyone thought she was too big, too fast, and Cat loved that ship.'

'Everyone thought the same thing . . . then,' Drummond interrupted.

Eamon lowered his voice. 'But she wasn't heartbroken about him, if that's what you mean. I asked

Mr Gorry. He said she had cried, but it was more for . . . for everyone, collectively. She'd got over him. I wasn't sorry about him, God forgive me. I should have been – poor sod, we all know what he faced. But he'd hurt her and at the time I could have killed him for that.' He paused again, sweeping the murky darkness with his binoculars. 'He would have made her life hell. He was weak, basically. You know the type, domineering mother, he had to try to prove he was strong when he was away from his mother's influence. Dinny Lacey was like that. Terrified of his Mam. She was always belting him and bawling him out. But away from her he acted big, bullying everyone who wouldn't stand up to him. Now I hear he belts the daylights out of his wife, whenever he's home. Barratt was like that, I don't think he'd have physically harmed her, but . . . why the hell did you let her get involved with him?'

'There wasn't much I could do about it. You know what she's like.' He smiled grimly. 'But she won't get away from me this time.'

'We're in for a wild night,' Drummond interrupted, as the sea broke over *Firefly*'s forecastle.

'What's our position?' Joe yelled over the increasing howl of the wind.

'About Latitude 59°, North. Speed about thirteen knots.' Drummond yelled back. The ship was plunging and straining.

'I can't see the convoy!' Eamon was peering through the binoculars.

'No bloody wonder in this weather! We'll be lucky if they're not scattered by daylight.' Drummond clung tenaciously to the wheel.

A huge wave broke over the plunging bows and

there was a dull thud. The ship shuddered, then a huge column of water erupted high into the air. The ship listed to port, sending them all sprawling on the deck.

Joe clung to the wheel against which he had been thrown. 'Jesus Christ! Torpedo! We've been hit!' he yelled. Every light had been extinguished and from the angle of the deck he knew they were beginning to settle by the stern. For a split second he thought of his mates in the engine room. Poor bastards! He fished in his pocket for the electric torch. Other small flickers of light could now be seen in the darkness. He knew the drill. They were sinking fast. Two more lights flickered close to him.

'Calligan! Cleary! Get to your boat station, we're going down!' Drummond's voice held no note of panic.

Four boats had been lowered, the others had been smashed by the column of water. In pitch darkness they had somehow managed to unhook the huge blocks. He heard someone yell 'Mind the blocks!' and then they were plunging downwards, the dark shape of the sinking frigate frighteningly close. They hit the head of a breaker, then plunged down into the trough, taking in water. They all knew the danger they faced and strained to pull away, otherwise they would be dragged into the maelstrom as the *Firefly* went down.

He saw glimpses of the other three boats, but the great combers roaring down from windward were too steep to enable them to stay together. And there was only one thought in all their minds. Their own survival.

The only officer in the boat was Drummond and

as the wind rose to gale force and the spray flew over them in sheets, he decided the only thing they could do was ride to a sea anchor and hope for a break in the weather. The heaving seas filled the boat to the thwarts and they had to bale continuously. Everyone was cold and saturated, many of them were seasick. There was no time to feel terror at the sight of the mountainous walls of water that bore down on them. Unless they continued to bail they would be swamped.

The boat tossed wildly. 'Mr Drummond, sir, the sea anchor's gone! Been carried away!'

Joe recognised Eamon's voice. Relief flashed through him before he turned his attention once more to keeping the boat free of water before the next wave broke over them.

'Lash three oars together, lad! They'll have to do!' The chief petty officer yelled back.

There were hours and hours of baling. His movements were mechanical, his brain sending one message only to his leaden limbs. Bail! Bail! Bail! And it was with a feeling of detached wonderment that he realised that the light he thought he had seen in the distance was the breaking of a wan dawn, struggling through the tattered clouds.

The wind and the sea had abated a little and he slumped back against the side of the boat. They were up to their knees in water. The faces around him were grey and haggard. Eyes either dull and staring or darting wildly around as they estimated their chances of survival. Four of the crew were dead of their injuries and exposure and CPO Drummond recited what he could remember of the Burial Service, then committed their bodies to the sea. Eamon crawled over to Joe.

'We've no chance, we'd better start praying!'

'What the hell do you think I've been doing all night!' He'd sailed these waters many times before and knew that daylight, even at this time of the year, was a subfusc twilight that lasted only a few hours. In these conditions, in an open boat . . .

'No use trying to sail, we'll ride to the sea anchor and hope! Better start praying, it's the only thing left!' Drummond instructed.

Conversation ceased. Apathy and exhaustion claimed them all. In the dim light that passed for early afternoon CPO Drummond was again forced to recite the Burial Service. Morale had hit rock bottom.

It was Eamon who saw it first and at his startled cry the others roused themselves from their semi-comatose state.

'You're havin' hallucinations, lad! It's a piece of wreckage!' Drummond scanned the still heaving, grey surface.

'No, sir, it's not! The lads didn't call me "Hawk-eye" for nothing! Look!'

A few hundred yards to their port the grey conning tower broke through the waves. It had been a periscope Eamon had seen. With the last reserves of energy they all began to shout, arms flailing, then one by one they fell silent, seeing the black swastika on the side of the U-boat.

'God 'ave mercy on us now!' Eamon muttered.

'So that's what they look like, I've always wondered! Murdering bastards!' Joe spat out a mouthful of salt spray.

Figures were already appearing on the conning tower. CPO Drummond stood up, his hands raised above his head. 'On your feet, all of you! There's nothing else we can do now!'

Epilogue

1950

CHAPTER TWENTY-FOUR

Cat replaced the receiver and smiled to herself. She wondered how Joe would take the news. She drew out a writing pad and envelopes from the drawer of the sideboard and searched for a pen. Then she took everything to the table that faced the French windows that overlooked the fields beyond the house. She started to write.

Dear Miss Sabell,
    I was delighted to . . .

She stopped and chewed the end of the pen. She would write but she wouldn't post it, not today. Tomorrow morning, when she took Hilary to school, would do. After she had seen Joe. It was fortunate he was home, she mused, otherwise she would have had to turn it down flat.

The sun bathed the neat little garden and the fields beyond in a fresh, clean light. May. A month she could never recall without thinking of the May of 1941. Was it really nine long years ago? Was it already three years since Joe had come home and they had finally been married? Idly she twisted the gold band on the third finger of her left hand.

She had thought her world had ended that May nine years ago when they heard of the loss of the

Firefly. The world had been such a black place then. No hope. No end in sight. No Joe. She hadn't cried much. Although now, looking back, she realised that she couldn't remember very much about that awful summer. Then word had come that they were both alive and prisoners of war somewhere in Germany. But after the first rush of relief, there had followed the desperate hopelessness.

She wrote hundreds of letters, not knowing if any would reach him and she had heard nothing from him or Eamon and her fear and desperation had risen again. Looking back she didn't know just what had kept her going, kept hope alive in the five years that had followed. And then it had all been over.

She had joined the ecstatic crowds that had spilled out into the streets. Singing, dancing, hugging and kissing each other on VE Day. She had been able to bring Hilary and Sean back to live with her and they had both hated it, at first. They were used to the wide, open countryside, knowing everyone in the village by name. The devastated city, full of strangers, had terrified them but gradually, they had adjusted, as children do.

And then he had come home. Older, thinner and with streaks of premature grey in his dark hair, but still her Joe. They had been married in the Church of the Blessed Sacrament which was still in some disrepair, due to the May Blitz, and they had spent a whole blissful week in Southport.

He hadn't wasted those years spent in captivity. CPO Drummond had taught him a great deal and with the dire shortage of experienced manpower, he had gone back to sea, sailing as chief engineer on the *Aorangi*. One of the six Canadian Pacific ships left from a fleet of twenty-two.

She ran the end of the pen along her lower lip, her eyes not seeing the thrush perched on the branch of the sapling elm they had just planted. It had been then that they had decided to find a home of their own. It hadn't been easy for houses were in very short supply. But they had at last found this house in Moorhey Road, Maghull, beyond the city limits, and she had fallen in love with it at first sight. It was a struggle, as they were buying it. But the shortages of the war years had meant she had been able to save and with Joe's greatly increased salary they were just managing.

She wrote a few more words and then paused. She would have to ask Marie to come and look after the children. She laughed aloud. Children! Sean was fifteen and an apprentice in an engineering factory. Her gaze wandered to the photograph of her daughter on top of the sideboard. The small oval face with the serious blue eyes and neatly plaited, chestnut hair made her smile. She looked so demure, but she could be a handful at times. She reminded her of herself at eleven. But Marie had a way with them both. She had always been very close to Sean. Marie had married Richard Hocking and was desperately hoping for a child of her own. They lived quietly with Mr and Mrs Gorry in Yew Tree Road.

Maisey had a 'prefab' as they were called, on the East Lancashire Road – a single-storeyed house of prefabricated blocks which were being used to ease the desperate housing situation. Gradually the bombsites were being cleared and new houses built. Maisey was ecstatic with her hot and cold running water, bathroom and inside toilet. She kept it like a palace and no speck of dust was allowed to linger on any surface of her utility furniture for more than a few hours. The O'Dwyers had dwindled somewhat in number, for Dora had married the driver of the Charlotteville canteen lorry and gone off as a GI bride to live in Charlotteville. Ethel had married a Norwegian sailor she had met and had gone to live in 'that Godforsaken country with names yer can't pronounce,' as Maisey called it.

Her gaze rested on the photo of a young man in naval uniform. Eamon hadn't wasted his time either. He had also been a pupil of Drummond's. He had stayed in the Royal Navy and was carving out a career for himself, having reached petty officer. Her thoughts returned to the letter and Joe. She still hated the time he was away at sea and only lived for his arrival home, so why on earth had she told Miss Sabell she would accept, pending his approval? She had almost forgotten what it felt like to have the deck beneath her feet. Almost, but not quite.

'Salt water in your veins, nostalgia or maybe latent ambition?' she said aloud to the black and white cat, lying on the floor by the windows, luxuriating in the sun's warmth but with one eye fixed on the thrush still perched on the tree outside. She pushed the letter aside and went to the sideboard cupboard and drew out a large, brown envelope and emptied the contents on the table. She spread the photographs out, then picked one up. It was of the *Empress of Britain*.

She sighed to herself. 'You're part of the past now.' There had been six Empresses in 1939 but only two had survived. One of them had been the *Empress of Japan*, renamed *Empress of Scotland* in 1942 when the Japanese had entered the war. It was this Empress that now filled her thoughts. On 9 May the *Empress of Scotland* was due to sail on her first voyage after being refitted on the Clyde. Miss Sabell, now retired, wanted her to consider taking charge of the stewardesses for this first peacetime voyage.

Joe waited outside the school gates. Any minute now the doors would open and they would burst out, laughing, pushing and shoving, but he could always pick her out by her red-brown hair and vivid blue eyes. For years those blue eyes had caused him a great deal of soul-searching. When he had come home she was nearly seven and at first she had resented him and he had resented her, for whenever she looked at him he was reminded of David Barratt. Gradually all thoughts of her natural father had diminished, until they had become irrelevant. She didn't know about him and she never would. The name on her birth certificate was Hilary Josephine Calligan and that was who she was: his child, for he had legally adopted her. She was his daughter and he loved her.

'Dad! Dad, can I go to Lucy's for tea?' She was tugging at his sleeve. She was tall for her age and, as usual, her hair had escaped from its braids. He noticed the ribbons stuffed into her blazer pocket.

'Well, that's fine thanks I get for coming to meet you. How was your day, Pudding?' he laughed. The nickname was one he had conferred on her, for it was the exact opposite of her stature. She was as slender as a rail. Cat worried about her, saying she was too thin, that if she got any thinner they could use her for a clothes prop! 'Alright, except for Miss Concannon! Can I go to Lucy's, Dad? Her mum said I can?'

He laughed at the earnest, upturned face. 'Oh, go on, then! But you mind your manners and I'll be round to collect you at seven!'

The two of them giggled.

'What's so funny?'

'Send Sean round for me. Lucy's sister likes Sean.' They collapsed into giggles again.

'Ah, so that's it! Well, I'll spare him the suffering, I'll come myself! Off you go, Miss, and behave yourself!'

When he arrived home Cat was sitting at the table scribbling away at a letter. He smiled. She'd obviously forgotten the time. He tousled her short, curly hair.

'Oh, Joe! Oh, Lord, is that the time and there's no meal even started!'

He laughed. 'A nice reception, I must say. My daughter can't wait to rush off with her friend and my wife is so engrossed writing letters . . .'

She ran her fingers through her hair. It was a gesture he loved.

He took her in his arms. She was more beautiful in his eyes now, as a woman of thirty-five, than she

410

had been as a scrawny sixteen year old. 'What is so important, Mrs Calligan, that you have used up nearly a whole writing pad? You never take so much trouble when you write to me – or do you?'

She looked up at him and for an instant he saw the little Irish slummy peering at him.

'What are you up to, Cat? I know that look of old?'

'I had a telephone call from Miss Sabell. The *Empress of Scotland* is sailing on the ninth and she wants me to sail with her, as chief stewardess.' It all came out in a rush, but she surmised it was better to tell him like this than beat about the bush.

'Go back to sea?'

'For one trip only. Until they appoint a new, permanent chief. Marie will look after the children, I know she will!'

He threw back his head and laughed. 'Oh, Cat, you never cease to delight me! Here I was thinking you were the epitome of the domesticated wife and mother, and you still hanker after the sea! The great White Empress sails again! And I thought you'd finally got over it!'

'It's all your fault, Joe! It was you who dragged me off the cattle boat to see her!'

'And how I've regretted it!'

'Do you remember when I once said, "Wouldn't it be wonderful if you got to be second officer and me chief stewardess?" And you said it would be a bloody miracle? Well, you can eat your words!'

'Not quite! I'm only chief engineer and I've not said anything—'

She cut off his words with a kiss. 'But you won't say no, will you? Do you realise that this is the same ship, the very first White Empress I ever saw and I can still remember the way I felt. It was like a St Patrick's Day Parade in Dublin. The crowds, the band, the cheering, the streamers! We nearly made the miracle come true, Joe!'

He kissed the top of her head. 'I think we have made it come true. "Mrs Calligan. Chief Steward-ess". It has a certain ring to it, don't you think?'

She stood on tiptoe and kissed him. 'I made it, Joe! I finally made it, even if it's only for one trip!'

THE END

ELLAN VANNIN
BY LYN ANDREWS

Life was not easy for George Vannin and his young daughter. Ellan's mother had died when the child was four but somehow George had managed to rear the child alone. Ellan adored her father.

She was ten when the shaft at Foxdale Mine collapsed, and her father never came up. From then on she lived – and drudged – with Aunt Maud, a dour, stark woman with a quick temper and a harsh tongue. Maud's husband had died in the mine disaster too, and she never forgave the family at the Big House for their part in the tragedy. When Ellan was offered a chance to better herself – tweenie at the Big House – Aunt Maud savagely forbade it.

But Ellan's chance was to come when Jamie Corlett asked her to marry him. Everything changed, the future looked bright and a new life beckoned in a new world. But it was to be many years, and Ellan was to travel to many places, before happiness was finally within her grasp.

0 552 13855 X

LIVERPOOL LOU

BY LYN ANDREWS

Aunt Babsey considered herself a cut above her neighbours on Everton Ridge. For one thing she was 'trade' – she ran a greengrocery shop in public, and a money-lending business in private. She taught her children to be respectable, keep up appearances, and not to mix with people like the Crowleys who were both Catholic and Irish. She ruled her family with a rod of iron.

Fourteen-year-old Louisa was the only one who didn't quite fit into the family scheme of things. Louisa, with her mother dead and her father away at sea, was becoming increasingly conscious that while Aunt Babsey's family was comfortable enough, all around them was hardship and the grinding poverty of the thirties. As she grew up into a graceful and gentle young woman, so the tough conditions of Liverpool began to impinge on her life – love, war, betrayal, death – all made her determined to seek her own path, both in the man she loved, and the work she wanted to do – work which would eventually make her famous throughout her city – as *Liverpool Lou*.

0 552 13718 9

THE SISTERS O'DONNELL

BY LYN ANDREWS

They were called The Sisters O'Donnell in County Tipperary. They resembled each other a lot – both in temper and looks. They all had the flaming red hair of the O'Donnell clan and tempers to match.

When they came to seek their fortunes in the Liverpool of the '20s, they were full of ambition, hope, and a lust for life. Gina planned to be a star of the theatre, Mary Kate wanted to find a husband. And Bridget – gentle, timid Bridget – just wanted to get away from the fighting all round her and have a calm, peaceful life.

But Liverpool wasn't what they thought it would be, and neither was their Aunt Maura, who was supposed to set them on their paths to fortune. Maura turned out to be a miserable slattern, living in the poorest part of Liverpool, and uncle Bart was a scrounging and lascivious old man. Work was impossible to find and their money was running out.

The O'Donnell girls had a long way to go before they could realise some of their dreams.

0 552 13600 X

A SELECTION OF FINE TITLES
AVAILABLE FROM CORGI BOOKS

THE PRICES SHOWN BELOW WERE CORRECT AT THE TIME OF
GOING TO PRESS. HOWEVER TRANSWORLD PUBLISHERS RESERVE
THE RIGHT TO SHOW NEW RETAIL PRICES ON COVERS WHICH MAY
DIFFER FROM THOSE PREVIOUSLY ADVERTISED IN THE TEXT OR
ELSEWHERE.

☐	13600 X	THE SISTERS O'DONNELL	*Lyn Andrews*	£3.99
☐	13718 9	LIVERPOOL LOU	*Lyn Andrews*	£3.99
☐	13855 X	ELLAN VANNIN	*Lyn Andrews*	£3.99
☐	12887 2	SHAKE DOWN THE STARS	*Frances Donnelly*	£3.99
☐	12387 0	COPPER KINGDOM	*Iris Gower*	£3.99
☐	12637 3	PROUD MARY	*Iris Gower*	£3.99
☐	12638 1	SPINNERS WHARF	*Iris Gower*	£3.99
☐	13138 5	MORGAN'S WOMAN	*Iris Gower*	£3.99
☐	13315 9	FIDDLER'S FERRY	*Iris Gower*	£3.99
☐	13316 7	BLACK GOLD	*Iris Gower*	£3.99
☐	13631 X	THE LOVES OF CATRIN	*Iris Gower*	£3.99
☐	13521 6	THE MOSES CHILD	*Audrey Reimann*	£3.99
☐	13670 0	PRAISE FOR THE MORNING	*Audrey Reimann*	£3.99
☐	12607 1	DOCTOR ROSE	*Elvi Rhodes*	£3.50
☐	13185 7	THE GOLDEN GIRLS	*Elvi Rhodes*	£4.99
☐	13481 3	THE HOUSE OF BONNEAU	*Elvi Rhodes*	£3.99
☐	13309 4	MADELEINE	*Elvi Rhodes*	£4.99
☐	12367 6	OPAL	*Elvi Rhodes*	£3.99
☐	12803 1	RUTH APPLEBY	*Elvi Rhodes*	£4.99
☐	13732 3	SUMMER PROMISE AND OTHER STORIES	*Elvi Rhodes*	£3.99
☐	13413 9	THE QUIET WAR OF REBECCA SHELDON	*Kathleen Rowntree*	£3.99
☐	13557 7	BRIEF SHINING	*Kathleen Rowntree*	£3.99
☐	12375 7	A SCATTERING OF DAISIES	*Susan Sallis*	£3.99
☐	12579 2	THE DAFFODILS OF NEWENT	*Susan Sallis*	£3.99
☐	12880 5	BLUEBELL WINDOWS	*Susan Sallis*	£3.99
☐	13613 1	RICHMOND HERITAGE/FOUR WEEKS IN VENICE	*Susan Sallis*	£3.99
☐	13136 9	ROSEMARY FOR REMEMBRANCE	*Susan Sallis*	£3.99
☐	13346 9	SUMMER VISITORS	*Susan Sallis*	£3.99
☐	13545 3	BY SUN AND CANDLELIGHT	*Susan Sallis*	£3.99
☐	13756 1	AN ORDINARY WOMAN	*Susan Sallis*	£4.99
☐	13845 2	RISING SUMMER	*Mary Jane Staples*	£3.99
☐	13856 8	THE PEARLY QUEEN	*Mary Jane Staples*	£3.99
☐	13299 3	DOWN LAMBETH WAY	*Mary Jane Staples*	£3.99
☐	13573 9	KING OF CAMBERWELL	*Mary Jane Staples*	£3.99
☐	13444 9	OUR EMILY	*Mary Jane Staples*	£3.99
☐	13635 2	TWO FOR THREE FARTHINGS	*Mary Jane Staples*	£3.99
☐	13730 8	THE LODGER	*Mary Jane Staples*	£3.99

All Corgi/Bantam Books are available at your bookshop or newsagent, or can be
ordered from the following address:
Corgi/Bantam Books,
Cash Sales Department,
P.O. Box 11, Falmouth, Cornwall TR10 9EN

UK and B.F.P.O. customers please send a cheque or postal order (no currency) and
allow £1.00 for postage and packing for the first book plus 50p for the second book
and 30p for each additional book to a maximum charge of £3.00 (7 books plus).

Overseas customers, including Eire, please allow £2.00 for postage and packing for
the first book plus £1.00 for the second book and 50p for each subsequent title
ordered.

NAME (Block Letters) ....

ADDRESS ....

....